PIRATE CODE

PIRATE CODE

BEING THE SECOND VOYAGE OF
CAPT. JESAMIAH ACORNE & HIS SHIP,

Sea Witch

BY

HELEN HOLLICK

www.penmorepress.com

ISBN-13: 978-1-950586-17-2(Paperback)
ISBN :-978-1-950586-18-9(e-book)

BISAC Subject Headings:
FIC002000 **FICTION** / Action & Adventure
FIC047000 **FICTION** / Sea Stories
FIC031070 **FICTION** / Thrillers / Supernatural

Illustrations © Avalon Graphics 2011

Address all correspondence to:

Penmore Press LLC
920 N Javelina Pl
Tucson AZ 85748

Formerly published:
2011 by SilverWood Books of Bristol
www.silverwoodbooks.co.uk
ISBN 978-1-906236-60-1

PART ONE

NASSAU—SEPTEMBER 1718

Thunder grumbled beyond the horizon and a squall of rain scythed across the ocean, sending it boiling and foaming like an unwatched cooking pot.

The surface heaved, irritated by the disturbance as Tethys, the spirit—the soul—of the ocean, awoke. She tolerated the sailors who roamed her jurisdiction, but treated them with disdainful contempt. After all, she had the choice of those she wanted; at her whim she could claim their bones, their very souls and take them down into the darkness of her vast, water-world realm. But she resented the wind and the rain for they challenged her superiority, undermined her wishes and often made their own choices to destroy those who were human and mortal. She was jealous and lonely; she needed things of beauty to call her own and did not want to share. Among her many desires she wanted to possess the human sea captain called Jesamiah Acorne, for he was, indeed, beautiful.

~ I want Acorne. ~

~ You cannot always have what you want, Mother. ~

Annoyed by her daughter's insolent answer, Tethys sent a tidal wave hurtling towards the shore.

Her daughter laughed, mocking her.

~ Your power is waning, Mother. There are those, now, with more strength than you. You are becoming weak, you will soon be as forgotten as all the others of our kind. ~

But despite her scorn, the daughter was curious. What manner of human was it who had so stirred her mother? And was he, truly, beautiful?

~ I will visit this man, Acorne, and see him for myself. Then perhaps, should I choose to do so, I will help you, Mother. ~

She did not add, as she swirled away over the white-capped grey of the seas, racing before the wind and those brewing clouds of a thunderstorm, that if she liked him she may well decide to keep him for herself.

CHAPTER ONE

SUNDAY NIGHT

Jesamiah, Captain Acorne, lay awake unable to sleep. He watched the intermittent flicker of lightning and listened to the distant thunder as it trundled away out to sea. Out in the main part of the great cabin, rain was beating against the skylight and the five stern windows, was drumming on the wooden deck above. From the far side of the harbour, the cracked bell in Nassau's dilapidated church rang the hour of ten several minutes slow, the sound tinny and distorted. Tucked safe within the curve of his arm, his woman, Tiola, slept soundly. Her breathing was light and even, her dark lashes feathered against her cheeks and a slight smile tipped one corner of her mouth upward. He needed to kiss her but did not want to wake her. Did not want this night to end or tomorrow to begin.

Uneasy after the storm, his ship, *Sea Witch*, shuffled restlessly at her anchor cables. Jesamiah knew her every sound; the mithering creak of her timbers, the chattering of her rigging. The trickle of rainwater draining out through the scuppers. He listened for a while ensuring all was as it should be, identifying each individual murmur as if eavesdropping on a one-sided conversation. He knew his ship as intimately as he knew Tiola's body. Every curve, every joint, every mark. He was consort and lover to them both.

Closing his eyes he groaned silently beneath his breath, sighed again, puffing the air silently from his lips. Anxious thoughts were tumbling in his head as if they were drunken acrobats refusing to receive their applause and make a final bow. What was he to do? What in the name of all the gods could he do?

Tugging at her bower anchor *Sea Witch* rocked as the wind huffed against her side, the ripple of the tide gurgling against her keel as it scurried past. She had been moored on two anchors set in different directions, but Jesamiah had pulled on his breeches and shirt and gone on deck to supervise setting the kedge as well. Only a fool risked allowing his ship to pull free and drift.

Tiola had squealed at his icy touch as he slid, cold and damp, back into bed; had then suggested a way he could get warm again. Responding with lust and eager enthusiasm he had approved her idea, and his lovemaking had been more tender, less fierce and longer lasting than the earlier tumble of passion spurred by the delivery of that wretched letter.

His anger on reading it had erupted as explosive as the storm. Furious, he had crumpled the neatly written document between his callused hands and hurled it across his cabin where it had bounced off the light-oak panelling, fallen onto the faded square of carpet and malevolently unfolded itself again.

"I am not having it!" he had shouted as he paced the few yards from one side of the cabin to the other, automatically stepping around the bulk of the starboard-side cannon, which Tiola had belligerently draped with a lace-edged cloth to disguise its hideous presence. His enraged shout had been as loud as the cannon's roar. "Van Overstratten's a bastard! He has no right to do this!"

Brushing aside a strand of Tiola's black hair that was tickling his chin, Jesamiah sighed. Unfortunately, the Dutchman had every right to summon her before a court of law on a charge of adultery. He was her husband. Jesamiah Acorne, her lover, ex-pirate, owner and captain of the *Sea Witch*, had no rights at all. The fact that Tiola had walked away from the marriage meant nothing to Stefan, and he did not tolerate being so publicly cuckolded.

Tiola stirred, drowsing in the languid pleasure of being abed and in that warm, delicious place half way between asleep and awake. She snuggled closer to her man lying naked next to her, wondered if he had remembered to shut the centre one of the stern windows. She might get up in a minute, close it.

"Jesamiah?" She nudged him with her elbow.

"Mm?"

"Did you close the window?"

"Mm."

She felt his arm tighten around her, his hand covering her breast, loving and possessive. The headache that had been nagging all day had moved above her right eye; a dull, annoying nudge of pain. She would have to do something about it if it was still with her come daylight.

Jesamiah had been so angry as he had stamped about the cabin, the blue ribbons he wore tied into his chaos of shoulder-length black hair fluttering like banners behind him, his arms waving. So very angry because he did not know what to do about the situation. There was not much he could do. As a pirate he had no regard for the law, but as an ex-pirate, bound under the code of a recent government-granted amnesty, he was obliged to take note of it.

She had sat, legs curled under her, on the velvet cushions piled along the lockers curving beneath the line of the stern windows; had suppressed a smile as he had surreptitiously kicked at the cloth draped over the cannon as he had walked past. She knew he resented its prim femininity here in his masculine domain. From habit, he had ducked beneath the overhead beams. Only under the rectangle of the skylight

3

could he stand upright to his full five feet ten inches. She so loved him. Had only married Stefan as a means to save Jesamiah's life. Looking back, it had been a stupid thing to do, but she had not had much choice at the time.

"Any other whoreson would have cleared off back to where he bloody came from bloody weeks ago," Jesamiah said into the darkness as he shifted his arm clutched around her waist.

"Would you have done so?" Tiola asked implacably, moving her head to nestle more comfortably on his shoulder. "Were the boot on the other foot, would you allow another man to so publicly make a fool of you?"

Itching at his jaw-line beard, Jesamiah tugged at the gold acorn earring dangling from his right lobe. He shrugged, muttered something uncomplimentary about merchant Dutchmen then admitted, "No, I suppose not." As an immediate afterthought protested, "But I would not have acted like this! I would call the bastard out and shoot him. Put a bullet in his privy package where it mattered."

Tiola laughed. "No Jesamiah, you would weigh anchor and turn your back on the law; you would return to piracy and run away, not stand and face what has to be."

Jesamiah stretched his leg, easing a slight strain of cramp. She was right about him weighing anchor. It had been the first thing he had wanted to do when he had read that summons.

"It is no use running," she added. "Once you start running you will not be able to stop. If you break the law, even in this comparatively trivial matter, you will forfeit your right to amnesty. And that will mean every man who sails with you will as well. And anyway, I would not come with you for I will not sail on an active pirate vessel. I will not wait for you to be captured and watch you hang."

4

treasure ships. Not exactly salvaging. Eleven galleons had gone down in a hurricane off the Florida coast and pirates had flocked like sharks to blood for the spoils; only Jesamiah had come up with the idea to go one better. Teaming up with Jennings the pair of them had cockily raided the warehouse where the Spanish had been storing the re-claimed treasure. Had come away as wealthy men. Jennings had retired, buying himself a modest estate here near Nassau, Jesamiah had sailed on to Africa, to Cape Town. Where he had met Tiola Oldstagh and fallen belly-deep in love.

The brandy was good quality—probably smuggled contraband. Jesamiah sipped at it, declined a cheroot offered by Jennings and a fill of pipe tobacco from Hornigold.

"My thanks gentlemen, I do not smoke. I had enough of tobacco as a child. When you've grown up in misery on a tobacco plantation you tend to want nothing more to do with the foul weed."

"Unless it is to steal it and line your pockets with another man's hard-earned profit." Van Overstratten lifted the brandy decanter, poured himself a large refill. Pointedly, neither he nor Jesamiah had greeted each other.

"There are those who steal more of the profits than a pirate could ever accomplish," Jesamiah commented. "Governments, of all nations, have powder burns on their fingers when it comes to reckoning taxation levies and trade tithes."

Hornigold, a man nearing his sixties, and like Woodes Rogers, wearing a shoulder length, heavily curled grey wig, took his pipe from his mouth and guffawed. "Aye, you have it right there lad! I'd wager there are more dishonest men in Parliament than in London's Newgate Gaol!

"And wiser men in Bedlam, eh?" Rogers added.

"Except," van Overstratten countered ignoring the joviality, "men in prison do not have the opportunity to unbutton their breeches and make free use of other men's wives."

"Nothin's free in gaol," Jesamiah retorted taking excessive care to set his glass down, not slam it as he was itching to do. "Wardens charge a high price for a quick, fumbled poke at a woman." His gaze lifted, stared direct at van Overstratten. A lean man in his twenties, with high cheekbones, aristocratic brow and slender hands. His dress and appearance were immaculate; a man who flaunted his wealth and everything he had. Tiola, he had wanted for her beauty and for the begetting of a son. And for getting the better of Jesamiah Acorne.

"Of course," the Dutchman countered disdainfully, "you would be knowing of the debauchery that occurs inside a prison, having extensive personal experience of such places."

Prudently Jesamiah held his tongue, accepting the proffered cheeses Governor Rogers pushed in his direction.

"Try the goat's cheese, lad, it has just the right blend of herbs. M'cook makes it himself, fine man. As black as tar, indentured into m'service. Not a slave. I don't hold with keeping slaves as cooks, couldn't trust the buggers not to put something nasty in the soup, eh? Ha, ha!" Rogers had not changed in the few years since Jesamiah had first met him. A paunch-bellied, opinionated man who relished the sound of his own voice. But he was well meaning, and there were those—especially back in England—who muttered that he proffered too much of a soft touch where the taste of the lash would serve better purpose.

He was right about the cheese.

Before Jesamiah's arrival, Hornigold had been recounting a sea adventure of his youth and the conversation returned to his rambling anecdote. Jesamiah sat quiet, apparently politely listening, his mind dwelling on how easy it would be to draw a pistol, cock the hammer and shoot van Overstratten right between the eyes. Except, out of courtesy, he had handed the weapon to the servant at the front door, along with his cutlass. It did not do to sit at the Governor of Nassau's table with a primed pistol tucked through your waist belt or a cutlass nestled at your left hip. Pity.

The conversation faltered. Taking a breath to steady the anger churning with the sickness in his stomach, Jesamiah wiped his fingers on a napkin. It would not serve any purpose to lose his temper. Not here.

"I have come to plead clemency," he said. "To offer payment for any wrong I have committed against this Dutchman, Master Stefan van Overstratten."

"You could not afford the bill, Acorne," van Overstratten snapped as reply. "You are personally responsible for the loss of at least three of my ships and several thousand pounds in value of cargo. Not to mention the innocent men you killed in the process of your plundering."

"For all of which I have received the king's pardon of amnesty."

"Your king's pardon. I am Dutch. George is not my king. Nor have I granted you pardon."

Swallowing bile and his temper, Jesamiah again stared direct at the man opposite him. He could afford a large payment in compensation. Were he to bother tallying the gold he had stored in various banks he would probably find himself richer than this Dutchman. In the recent-formed Bank of England alone he had a hoard of more than £15,000. With the comparison of a naval captain's wage of £1 per day, Jesamiah was a rich man. He had almost two-thirds as much again stowed in Dutch and Portuguese bank vaults—and that without the value of gems and mercantile goods, barrels of expensive indigo and nutmeg; the fine wines, silks, china, and spices stashed in warehouses in various scattered ports. That all his wealth had been made from stealing other people's property, some of it, aye, from van Overstratten's merchant fleet, was immaterial to Jesamiah.

Quietly he offered; "I will return the *Sea Witch* to you in exchange for Tiola's freedom."

It was not an easy offer.

Jennings, Hornigold, and even Rogers, all three of them captains and seamen, sat staring at him, dumbfounded. A captain to give up his ship voluntarily for a woman? Had such a thing been heard of before?

Van Overstratten was no sailor, he did not see the significance of the proposal, nor the effort it had taken to make it. He threw back his head and laughed outright.

"Of what use is a worm-riddled, rotten-keeled hulk to me? Before you stole her she was a pristine, new-launched ship. You have ravished her, turned her into a stinking, rat-infested pirate menace." He swiped his hand sideways, dismissive. "She is naught but a violated whore. Utterly valueless to me. Worthless."

Feeling his hand inching towards where his cutlass would have been, Jesamiah swallowed a curt retort. The *Sea Witch* was as much a part of him as an arm or a leg—more, she was his life and livelihood. He could survive without a limb but not without a ship. As a counterbalance, though, he could not survive without Tiola. The pain would be unbearable were he to lose the *Sea Witch* but he could, somehow, replace her. He could never replace Tiola.

Van Overstratten failed to mark Jesamiah's bitter silence. With sneered contempt added, "As, of course, you have also prostituted and poxed my wife."

The insult went one fathom too far. Jesamiah half-rose, his face a curled mask of fury. "Then you are no judge of ships, you bastard, nor women!"

Alarmed, Rogers patted the air with his palms calling with authority for the younger man to stay seated. "Gentlemen, gentlemen! I will not have insults traded at my table. Calm yourselves." As a diversion he sent the brandy around again. "If you cannot control your emotions Captain Acorne, I will be obliged to ask ye to leave m'hospitality."

Ignoring him, his hands flat on the table Jesamiah tossed another challenge at the Dutchman. "If Tiola is of no worth to you why will you not accept my offer? I have made it in good faith before eminent men as witnesses; you will lose no honour by accepting."

Van Overstratten poured himself a refill of brandy, leant back in his chair, his arm draped over the curve of the mahogany back, his leg crossed over the other at the knee. He inhaled his cheroot, sent a waft of aromatic smoke billowing from his lips; said, tapping ash from its tip: "Because, pirate, it is you offering it. I do not make a habit of dealing with poxed cockroaches. I prefer to step on them and crush them beneath my boot, without a second glance."

Twice now the Dutchman had called him poxed. Jesamiah stared at the white linen of the tablecloth beneath his palms, a stain of wine to the left had spread into the shape of a sea turtle. His head tilting downward he raised his eyes, menace flaring within the darkness of his dilated pupils, spoke very softly as his right hand went almost imperceptibly to one of the ribbons tied into his hair.

"But I am fully prepared to deal with a snivelling coward, van Overstratten. A coward who would strip a defenceless woman naked to the waist for the degenerate men of this island to ogle, rather than fight the man he really wants to punish."

The ribbon was between his fingers, a knot tied, fast, efficient, at its centre. An innocent-looking strand of blue, silk ribbon. In the right hands—Jesamiah's—a weapon that was strong enough to choke and strangle; to crush a windpipe.

"Jesamiah!" Henry Jennings shouted coming to his feet also and laying his hand on the younger man's arm. "This will serve no purpose. You have signed the pardon and like it or no you must now obey the law. Do not be a fool. Sit down, boy."

Jesamiah shook him off, leant further over the table. "Come outside you worm, settle this in the way a man would. Or are you too shit-scared to face a better man? A pirate?"

Rogers slammed the table with his fist. "Acorne! I will not have you insulting my guests. Apologise or get you gone!"

Coiling the length of ribbon around one hand, Jesamiah turned to Rogers, his stare unblinking and formidable. "I apologise to you, sir," he stated, giving a small, polite bow, "but not to this bastard who would see a woman flogged."

"I have no necessity to soil my hands on scum such as you, Acorne," van Overstratten interjected with a bark of scorn. He had not moved, although his face had drained ash pale. "I believe in justice and law, not in the seditious, empty threats of a thief and a murderer. My wife has broken the marriage vows she made to me in the sight of God and has publicly insulted my honour, for that I will see her punished."

A hideous smile spread over the Dutchman's mouth. "Be thankful I have not also invoked my right to insist it be you, Acorne, who delivers her punishment." The smile broadened into the gloat of a leer at the responding look of sickened disgust coming over Jesamiah's face. "Provoke me and I may well change my mind."

Losing the final restraint of control over his barely held temper, Jesamiah leapt across the table scattering chairs, china, silverware and glass. The candelabra toppled over; the crystal brandy decanter fell with a shattering crash to the floor, releasing the pungent smell of its contents. The ribbon was between his fingers, pulled taut around van Overstratten's neck, Jesamiah, standing behind him, legs braced, arms crossing, locked at the crook of his elbows, pulling backwards, the previously innocuous ribbon as effective as a wire garrotte.

"You can't even pronounce her name correctly, you bastard," he hissed into the Dutchman's ear. "Its Te-ola short, quick, not your lah-di-dah Te-oh-la." He pulled the ribbon tighter. "Yield to me you bastard or I'll strangle you here and now. One way or another I'll bloody see her free of you!"

The Dutchman was clawing at the rigid length of blue silk crushing against his carotid artery, stifling his air supply and the pulse of blood to his brain.

Henry Jennings and Benjamin Hornigold rushed to grasp at Jesamiah's arms, Rogers hurrying to the door to fling it wide and bellow for his militia guard.

Faced with a volley of primed muskets, Jesamiah swore and released the choking van Overstratten. The Dutchman's lips were blue, face suffused red, he fell forwards hands clasping his throat, wheezing and coughing, gasping to suck in lungfuls of air.

Dropping the knotted ribbon to the floor Jesamiah held his hands in surrender. Getting himself shot would not help Tiola.

Nor would it help to spend the rest of the night in gaol, but that was where, at Rogers' explicit orders, he found himself.

CHAPTER FOUR

The silence awoke Tiola, her half-asleep state registering that the rain had momentarily stopped. Sleepily, she turned over feeling the scratch of rough-spun linen sheets on her skin, expected to find Jesamiah asleep on his back, snoring, beside her. He was not there; his portion of the narrow bed quite cold. Far away lightning flickered; then a distant, predatory growl of thunder.

Shivering, all the warmth and comfort of the earlier part of the night gone, Tiola swore a sailor's explicit curse, and winding the sheet around herself padded from the small side cabin into the main room. The headache was above both eyes now, stabbing into her brain and her body felt languid and heavy as if she were carrying a solid weight on her shoulders. The distant flash of lightning through the curve of the stern windows and the skylight provided enough light, although she swore again as she bumped into the truck of the larboard cannon. She hated the things being in here, but Jesamiah insisted they stay. In case. In case of what she never asked, knowing she would not appreciate or approve the answer. Ugly, gape-mouthed death bringers, even when they were cold and silent, squatting there with brooding menace.

She made her way to the door, yelling for someone to bring a lantern, expecting Finch, the ship's galley cook and Jesamiah's self-appointed steward to appear. Or young Jasper who had claimed for himself the duty of cabin boy.

Instead, Rue was there, his hand raised, about to knock and seek admittance. Aside from being quartermaster and second in command, he was Jesamiah's closest friend beyond Tiola. He ducked beneath the lintel, without saying a word hung the lantern he carried on a ceiling hook where it cast an eerie blur of mildly rocking shadows. Thunder, the flash of lightning quick on its tail, the storm was rolling nearer.

"Where is Jesamiah?" Tiola asked, concern making her voice curt and angry, one hand, with fist bunched, on her hip. "Do not tell me he has gone ashore, Rue. Do not dare tell me he is that stupid!"

The Frenchman responded with a loose shrug, his tone gruff. "I was coming to ask you the same question, *ma chère*. You know Jesamiah. When 'e decides to be stupid 'e does it in grand style. The jollyboat is gone and 'e is the only one missing." He glanced into the cabin as if hoping his statement was wrong, hoping to see Jesamiah come from his bed, yawning and scratching at his backside.

Tiola hitched the slipping sheet higher. "If they gave prizes for stupidity, on occasion Jesamiah would be the outright winner." She swore a third time, one of his often used, more colourful phrases. "Hell's balls, I suppose he has gone after Stefan?"

Rue nodded. He supposed the same.

A large man, Rue was burly, with muscled shoulders, a bull neck and stamina to match. In his mid-forties, his dark beard was beginning to show the badgered grizzle-grey of his age, but his eyes missed nothing and his courage was never wanting. He thought of Jesamiah as the son he never had, Tiola the daughter-in-law. Was as annoyed as her at Jesamiah's idiocy. As damned angry at the threat hanging over Tiola.

"Did you not try and stop him?" Tiola admonished as she searched for her clothes, gathering them to her, partially

23

regretting now her abandon with Jesamiah when they had so desperately made love here in his great cabin.

"You ever tried stopping *le capitaine* from doing something 'e is determined to be about?" Rue answered pragmatically. He peered dismally into the rain now falling as if it were being emptied straight from a bucket. Sighed. "You are going to tell me we must go ashore and stop 'im from getting 'imself arrested, *non?*" He paused, wistfully hoping she was going to disagree. She did not. He puffed resigned air through his cheeks. "I will stir the boat crew. They will not be pleased."

"*Ais*, do so. Tell them to complain to their captain. It is his fault we will be getting wet this night."

Five minutes later Tiola was descending the hull cleats and stepping into the gig, a larger craft than the jollyboat, the men grumbling at the oars, Rue, equally as irritated, at the tiller. The rain was falling almost vertical.

The jetty was no more than two hundred yards away but the offshore wind and the swell of the tide made the distance seem twice as far; the effort to pull twice as hard. Tiola screwed up her eyes to peer through the murk, the curtain of rain obscuring the beach to the left with its haphazard sprawl of tents made from sails and oars, and the scatter of the more robust wooden bothies and lean-to shacks. From the upper walls of the fort and some of the grander houses further around the harbour, a few lights were haloed in the shrouding and watery darkness. Otherwise, the town was unlit. There were no bonfires on the stretch of sand this night; no flaring pitch torches. No laughter or carousal, not in this downpour.

Lightning cracked open the sky illuminating everything and reflecting on the restless sea. Tiola glanced at the swirl of water, at the depth of blackness beneath her and shuddered. Something was coldly observing her, she could feel the glare of its all-seeing eyes, the seething hatred. Tethys was awake and watching.

The air suddenly smelt of rotting seaweed and dead fish. Through the rain and the growl of thunder, Tiola heard the voice of the sea, sounding in her head like the wash of a wave lurching upon the shingles of a storm-wracked shore.

~ *I want him. He is mine Witch-Woman. Give him to me. Jesssh..a..miah!* ~

~ *He is not yours to have, Tethys.* ~

For answer, a wave hurled against the side of the gig drenching the occupants further and rocking the boat wildly. No ordinary wave; the claws of the Queen of the Deep.

~ *He is not yours,* ~ Tiola repeated with adamant finality, the words spoken in her mind as she raised a shield of protection around herself and the crew. She should have done that immediately she had felt the ominous presence of Tethys. This damned headache was slowing her reactions, muddling her concentration and judgement!

~ *He is mine, Tethys. Accept it.* ~

~ *I ssh...shall not. I ssh...shall not.* ~

~ *Then you must fight me for him. But remember, those with the greed or death-wanting of the Dark Power cannot win easily over those of the White Craft.* ~

Another wave rolled beneath the boat tilting it to starboard, the oarsmen, glancing uneasily over their shoulders, cursing as they fought to keep it steady.

"*Merde!* What a night!" Rue called to Tiola as he struggled with the tiller. "Damn the fool; 'e will make your situation worse."

"Tell him that," Tiola answered, brushing aside a sodden lock of hair from her face, wishing she could as easily brush aside the foreboding coursing through her like a drowning tidal wave.

"*Oui*, I will be telling 'im," Rue promised, not realising beyond her annoyance with Jesamiah there was anything wrong. "Do not doubt it *ma chère*, I will be telling 'im!"

Tiola shrugged aside the oppressive illusion of fear. There was little Tethys could do to permanently harm one of the White Craft, but Jesamiah was human, he could die. Although, if she was honest, at this precise moment Tiola felt inclined to kill him herself.

~ *Where are you Jesamiah? Do not dare tell me you have played the part of an idiot!* ~ She sent the thought to the harbour towards the taverns and accompanying brothels lining the narrow alleys, and to the ramshackle scatter of huts that made up the pirate slums of Nassau.

Received nothing back.

He either had not heard or had closed his mind to her. He had the knowing of how to do it now, how to erect a shield against the words she sent into his mind, and how to silence his own thoughts against her probing.

Gazing towards the fort, a suspicious feeling that Jesamiah was in trouble nibbled at Tiola's mind. She turned to look back at the rain-blurred form of the *Sea Witch* shifting moodily uncomfortable. The ship wanted the soothing presence of her consort, of Jesamiah. A ship was a thing made from oak trees that had once grown in a forest and had spread their branches upwards to embrace the sky; had thrust their roots downwards to grapple the rich, dark, earth. *Sea Witch* remembered the echoes of once being alive, and possessed a soul, of sorts. In her own way, lived for her beloved captain, and pined for him when he was not aboard.

The gig pulled past the lichen-covered walls of the fort; much of the place was dilapidated, the outer, northward side more a cracked and disintegrating ruin than solid brick; the inner tower crumbling. Only this part overlooking the harbour was intact, the six huge cannons, poking their vicious snouts through the upper battlements, in prime condition.

As were the cells, the dungeons below ground. They were dirty, damp, full of filth, vermin, insects, rats and rot, but they were secure. The inch-thick outer doors were of solid oak, the locks new and oiled. A succession of corrupt governors had stored their portion of looted treasure in those dungeons. Only Rogers used the place as it ought to be used; for drunks beyond ability of keeping the peace, and for miscreants. And idiots.

~ *Where are you Jesamiah?* ~

She received a sheepish, apologetic answer.

~ *In gaol, sweetheart.* ~

Her audible oath startled Rue's eyebrows into raised surprise. An expletive even he, a sailor from the age of ten years old, had not heard before.

"Up oars," he called, and the gig bumped gently against the jetty, Tiola already standing, her skirt hitched in one hand to above her knees, the other reaching for the iron rails of a weed-covered ladder. The jollyboat was warped to a bollard alongside.

As she stepped ashore, a surge of power tingled through her; she frowned. She had been feeling most odd this day. Perhaps it was the heavy oppression of the thunder, or the rain?

"Mistress van Overstratten?" A man, a soldier, dressed in the red tunic of the king's militia stepped from the shadows, his musket resting on his shoulder. Another man, a double as far as the uniform went, with only his leaner build and squarer face different, treading purposefully behind. The fort might be dilapidated but not the men who manned it.

"You are Mistress van Overstratten?" the first repeated.

"You know perfectly well who I am Gabriel Hornsea." Tiola hauled herself to the jetty. "I birthed your wife's fifth child last week. How is the boy? Suckling well I trust?"

Hornsea coughed, embarrassed. "He's doing fine, ma'am, I thank you, but I am on duty now and it ain't fitting fer me t'be talking about me missus an' the bairns."

"No, I can see that." Tiola dipped a formal curtsey in honour of his rank of corporal. "How may I help you?"

His embarrassment deepening, chubby face reddening as cherry bright as his uniform, Hornsea lowered his musket and pointed it at her midriff.

"I have orders to arrest you ma'am. To escort you to a place of confinement where you shall await the constable, and then trial by judge and jury."

Rue, padding up behind Tiola, swore, his hand going to the cutlass at his side, the sound of steel being drawn catching on the lip of the weapon's hanger. "Like 'ell she..."

Tiola set her hand on his arm. "*Non*, I thank you for your concern Rue, but one fool aboard the *Sea Witch* is already one fool too many. I am safe with Corporal Hornsea." She looked at the two soldiers, Hornsea and his friend, Barnabus Bradford. As different—as similar—as salt and sugar. "I may have assurance of that, I assume?"

Lowering his musket the corporal was genuinely shocked at the suggestion. "Ma'am! You will come to no harm on my watch!"

If it were not for Tiola, his wife, and the bairn too, would not be tucked safe in the creaking wooden bed in the loft of their house half a mile along the shore. House was a grand and fancy name for a cobbled-together wooden-built hut, but it was clean, dry and it was home. Vegetables and fruit grew in the garden, chickens scratched in the dirt and a sow grew fat in her sty. The children were fed and clothed and Hornsea loved his wife, even though her face was not as pretty as once it had been and her breasts sagged from suckling the bairns. All the women of Nassau had benefited from the coming of Mistress Tiola. The men too, for a healthy woman was a happy woman.

"I apologise for having to arrest you ma'am, but I have orders."

Tiola offered him a genial smile. "I understand. You must do your duty Gabriel, as maybe," she added as an inspired guess, "it was duty to also arrest Captain Acorne?"

Grim, Hornsea nodded. That episode had not been pleasant either. No one in Nassau agreed with this Dutchman's maliciousness. Most men would have called an offender out and dealt with the matter quickly and quietly. Unless, as the whispers said, van Overstratten was a coward who dare not face a man, a pirate, like Jesamiah Acorne.

Rue's lips thinned at the news, wondering how Tiola knew but he said nothing, accepting she was often aware of things without being told. He knew nothing of her Craft, but equally, realised she was no ordinary woman.

She trusted him implicitly, as did Jesamiah, but they could not risk him knowing what she was. Those who knew nothing could tell nothing. Only Jesamiah knew. Only Jesamiah, and he would go to his grave, torn into bloody pieces, not telling.

Tiola gave Rue a gentle push in the direction of the gig. "Return aboard my friend. I have found our captain; it seems I am to join him for what is left of the night. In a cell he cannot get into further trouble, *n'est-ce pas?*"

The situation was not ideal, but at least her headache had completely gone.

~ *Did you find him, Daughter? Did you see him?* ~

Tethys was eager, excited, with the high, quick laughter of a young girl, although she was as old as Time.

Her daughter remained silent, oblivious of her sodden state. Yes, she had seen him, but she would not, yet, be telling her mother of it. A handsome man, gentle but strong. Lean but muscled. Black hair that curled to his shoulders, a moustache and a jaw line beard. Large, dark, expressive eyes. A gold acorn dangling from his ear. Blue ribbons were laced into that black hair. A handsome man? No. He was beautiful.

She watched the pretty woman from the little boat talk to the two men wearing the cherry-red coats. Watched as she walked away with them.

Mother had said nothing about her!

Melting from sight as the witch came nearer, she faded into the curtain of rain, masking her presence from the exploring feel of questioning thoughts that had briefly touched her existence.

No, her mother had said nothing of the Wising Woman, the witch.

CHAPTER FIVE

Jesamiah was seated on a hard, wooden bench at the far corner of his cell, one knee bent, the other leg straight, arms loosely folded, back wedged into the corner. His three-cornered hat was tipped well down over his eyes. He was asleep. A gentle snore the only sound, apart from the squeak of rats and rustle of cockroaches. Three walls of solid brick and a fourth of iron bars. Gaol. At least on this occasion he was not expecting the prospect of a noose tightening around his neck in a few days' time. Mind, the absence of a tot or two of rum was almost as hard to face.

The outer door opened, a shaft of light bobbed in adding to the one feeble lamp giving a faint apology of illumination. Voices, footsteps; the crunch of snail shells beneath treading boots. It was always cold and damp and stank of rat pee, mildew and human waste in these dungeons. There were two cells, both eyeing each other across a narrow corridor. The other one was full of mouldering straw—straw that very possibly hid things of a lot more value than dried, musty, wheat stalks. Kegs of fine French brandy or hogsheads of tobacco? Caskets of Spanish gold? An ideal secret cache, a prison cell. No one bothered searching where the dregs of life spent their last hours.

Opening one eye, Jesamiah peeped at the door to his cell as it spine-chillingly grated along the stone floor. Hornsea. No one more important. Closed his eye, was instantly asleep again, his mind partially registering the one they were putting in here with him must be dead drunk unconscious, for he was very quiet. The door clanged shut, the key turned with a click of finality, the stronger lamplight receded with the crunch of footsteps. The outer door opened; closed. Jesamiah lapsed into a rasping snore.

"You stupid, stupid idiot! Can you never think before you act?" Someone was swiping at his head, knocking his hat off, tugging his leg away from the bench. He half-fell, half-rolled.

"What the fokken sod d'ye think ye'r...?" pulled up short. Grinned meekly. "Ah. Tiola. Sweetheart."

"Do not 'sweetheart' me, you cock-shrivelled, scabrous barnacle!"

Jesamiah took a step away from her flailing arms, held his hands up, palm outermost in pliant surrender. "What you doin' 'ere darlin'? I ain't in trouble, don't you go makin' a harvest out of a pinch o' corn. The guvnor thought I ought to cool me temper off a bit, that's..."

Tiola slapped his cheek, her strength enough to send him reeling backwards. He sat down, hard, on the bench. Winced as the repercussion shot up his spine. Put his hand to his stinging face.

"Not in trouble? Oh yes you are, Jesamiah Acorne. You are in big trouble! With me!" She slapped him again, harder, the blow taking his breath away. She looked nothing standing no more than about three fingers taller than five feet in her stockings, and as skinny as a maid's broomstick; a deceptive appearance.

She raised her hand to slap again but he moved quicker, caught her wrist. "I said I am sorry. I thought I..."

"You thought? Jesamiah, when do you ever think?"

"I was trying to buy your husband off!" he shouted, losing his temper, his expression like God's wrath against murder. His hand grasped her other arm, his long, tar-grimed and callused fingers encircling her wrist as if they were a bracelet. "I was trying to swallow my bloody pride and do things legal and not kill the bastard! It didn't bloody work, all right?" He shook her, once, pushed her away from him as he let her go.

He strode to the bars of the cell door, clutched his hands around two of them, his knuckles as white as his face.

"It didn't soddin' bloody work! 'E was 'avin' none of it. I was as useful as fetchin' a dead ferret to 'unt rabbits!" Agitated, his speech degenerated into the clipped slang of a seaman. He slammed his palms on the bars, rested his forehead against them and closed his eyes. Took several steadying breaths. Said calmer, "I failed. I'm sorry."

Coming behind him, Tiola slid her arms beneath his rain-damp coat that had once been blue but was now a faded grey, entwined them around his waist, her head resting on his back. Squeezed.

~ *You will never fail me, luvver. You tried. Thank you.* ~ Meeting no solid barrier now, she spoke into his mind, a more intimate, more loving and personal contact.

He turned, hooked his arms around her, bringing her inside his coat close against his body, his chin resting on her head. "No, I've failed you twice over, sweetheart. I've antagonised that ditch-wader of a Dutchman beyond sensibility, and now you're arrested too. Messed it right up, ain't I?"

She shook her head, raised her face for him to kiss her. "You are hopeless, you know that don't you?"

"Aye, but you love me because I'm also handsome and irresistible."

"I do not love you at all. You are a prize imbecile and a degenerate sea crab."

"Oh aye, that an' all."

They stood quiet, each enjoying the comfort of the other's embrace, then Jesamiah sighed, moved her aside. "Sorry sweetheart, I've a need to pump ship." He kissed her again, his lips warm and firm on hers, went to the bucket set in the corner and relieved himself with a satisfied grunt. Finished, re-adjusting his breeches, he settled himself onto the bench again, opened his coat for her to snuggle inside; as it often did, her closeness raised a throb of desire that twisted in his stomach.

"So why are you in bad bread, eh? Pinched the governor's pocket watch, 'ave you, lass?" He tried to make a jest of the situation. She laughed.

"Don't suppose you fancy a quick tumble?" he asked after a moment's thought. "Contrary to popular belief, I've never done it in a cell."

She fixed a stern expression, said imperiously, "Do not push your luck too far, Acorne. I have not yet forgiven you."

He ran his fingers down his moustache. Grinned at her. "I take it that means no?"

Feigning annoyance she slapped away his hand inching into her bodice, said in a serious tone, "Corporal Hornsea informs me I am to stand trial tomorrow morning."

Jesamiah's chuckle faded along with his lust. "Like bugger you will!"

"I will plead guilty to the charge. There is no sense in denying what everyone knows."

"No!"

"Jesamiah." Tiola put her hand to his cheek, caressed where she had slapped him, regretting her anger. "Jesamiah, I am grateful for your concern but it will do no good. It would be best to let the tide take us and get the thing done. I do not mind. A public punishment will be a small price to pay to be rid of Stefan and have you for my own."

"No, I will not leave it!" Fierce, his arm wound tighter about her waist, his stern gaze boring into hers. "You do not know what this punishment is do you? A woman convicted of adultery is paraded through the streets to the market square. There they strip her naked to the waist, tie her to the whipping post and flog her. And, believe me, it ain't the women who come to watch. Half the men of this island will be there for their own vulgar pleasure, the whole thing has nothing whatsoever to do with justice!"

She put her finger to his lips attempting to silence him; knew perfectly well what was to happen. Throughout existence women had paid the price for the perverse sexual needs of men.

Irritably, he pushed her hand away, clutched it within his own. "I hold my hand up to having gawped in the past—the sight of a woman's breasts will get many men up and ready for business. Nor have I ever denied I use whores for the benefit of satisfying my own need, but any man who pursues even a token nod towards fair justice should be able to see this particular law stinks."

Jesamiah kissed the tip of each one of her fingers, added, "Anyone with half a brain can see it is only the young women who are so punished. Never those who have lost their looks and have sagging tits and wrinkled skins."

He folded her hands within his own, determined and possessive. Declared, "I swear, Tiola, you are not going to be humiliated before a pack of scratching dogs."

Quite how he was going to stop it, he did not know.

CHAPTER SIX

MONDAY MORNING

There was nothing Jesamiah could do when they came to take her away except rattle and kick the bars of the cell, and scream his protest.

"You bloody leave her alone, you whoresons!" His knuckles were white, tears of frustration and impotent anger swamping his eyes. "Don't you dare harm her! Hear me? Do you not dare!" He clutched at the bars, shaking the door, willing the hinge to give or the metal to break. Savagely, he kicked at the unyielding barrier between him and freedom.

At the outer door, Tiola called over her shoulder to him, "I will be all right Jesamiah. I promise you."

How could she convince him her ancestors had suffered far worse violations and horrifying deaths in the name of justice? Her great-grandmother had burnt at the stake as a witch because she knew the uses of herbs; others in her past had also died by the punishment of fire. Her grandmother had been tortured to gain a confession of fornication with the devil before being hanged. Far better to receive a few lashes on the back than face a death fuelled by superstition and ignorance.

The door shut. She was gone, marched away between two guards.

"Tiola! No!" Again Jesamiah screamed, heaved at the bars; defeated, sank to his knees.

~ *They cannot hurt me, luvver. Please believe me.* ~

~ *I can't bear it sweetheart. I cannot let them do this. Not to you.* ~

All she could answer was a repetition of before. ~ *I will be all right.* ~

He knew enough of courtrooms and legal procedures to know what would happen next. The crowd in the gallery, all men, pushing and elbowing each other to see better; Governor Rogers in his fine-dressed pomposity presiding. The selected jury making a pretence at honouring unbiased justice—the hypocritical bastards. He doubted there would be one among the twelve who had not slept with another man's wife. And Dunwoody would be there, smirking and discreetly rubbing himself beneath his desk as he recorded in his official book everything that was said.

Someone was coming. Jesamiah shot to his feet. "Jennings? Thank God man. Open this door—get me out of here!"

Captain Henry Jennings, leaning heavily on a cherry-wood walking cane, limped slowly to where Jesamiah stood, offered the prisoner a cheroot. Remembering he had an aversion to tobacco, he put it between his own lips and lifting the lantern down from its hook, lit the cheroot and exhaled a cloud of strong, aromatic smoke.

"I am sorry Jesamiah, I have no authority to release you."

"What do you mean, no authority? Of course you have the authority! You are Rogers' vice governor."

Henry Jennings shook his head. "Governor's orders, you are to stay here until it is over."

"Like fokken hell I will!" Jesamiah roared his fury, hurled away from the bars and swept a pitcher of brackish drinking water from its shelf; for good measure, kicked the

37

piss bucket, sending urine flooding over the dank earth and musty straw scattered on the floor. He swung back to Jennings, his fist raised. "Fokken get me out!"

"I like this no more than you do, lad."

"Save me the platitudes. Bloody *do* something!"

Patient, Jennings replied, "Will you calm down?"

"No, I will not! My woman is going to be flogged, I'll not sodding calm down!"

"There is one way I can be of influence, only one. If you stop shouting at me I might be able to discuss it with you."

Kicking at the bars Jesamiah scowled, remained silent except to ask after a long pause in a gruff, terse voice; "Well?"

Looking around for a stool or something to sit on, Jennings perched his backside on one of the barrels set against the end wall near the outer door; considered the proposition he had been sent to put before Jesamiah. He liked it no less than flogging a pretty girl, but as the governor had said this morning, Acorne is available, why not use him?

"Spit it out man," Jesamiah snapped. "I can see by your face the medicine will taste foul."

"The landowners on Hispaniola are on the brink of rebellion."

"That'll please the smugglers," Jesamiah retorted wryly. Disruption always pushed up the profit when running contraband; both he and Jennings had benefited in the past as free traders when chaos overruled discipline. Brandy, tobacco, tea; indigo, expensive lace and quality cloth— smuggling carried the penalty of being hanged on the spot if caught, but the quick-come, easy-made gain was worth the risk, especially if the militia and excisemen were otherwise occupied. Rebellion on Spanish-held Hispaniola would have the smugglers out in droves for Spain was no different to any other country; imports and exports of luxury goods were taxed to the hilt. Taxes accrued essential revenue, revenue that kings, of whatever nationality, had a penchant to spend without consideration for how it was raised. But unlike the English king, George of Hanover, Felipe V of Spain was in the process of bleeding his Caribbean colonies dry. The long-suffering citizens of Hispaniola, both Spanish and native Creole, had been creeping nearer the edge of tolerance for several years. It did not surprise Jesamiah that they were now on the edge, and in order to survive were ready to take that last step.

"The governor of Hispaniola is anxious to prove his loyalty to his king," Jennings continued—he was a respectable man now, smuggling, piracy and privateering were in his past. He could not afford, personally or politically, to stand to the wrong side of the mast. Aside, he was getting too old for high-sea adventure, and his gout was most terribly painful. Best leave it to younger men like Jesamiah Acorne. He added with a chuckle, "Hispaniola is on the verge of bankruptcy and the additional possibility of rebellion is making the poor fellow feel quite insecure. I have no sympathy for him. He's been a thorn in our backsides for too long. We would do anything to be rid of him."

"Your backside," Jesamiah corrected, "Don Damián del Gardo ain't nothin' t'do with me."

Jennings ignored him. "We have been surreptitiously encouraging this rebellion. Whispering the right words into the right ears, providing arms and ammunition—you know the sort of thing. Everything, as we understand it, is ready. All we need is for the spring to be released from the cable and Hispaniola will fall into British hands."

"I sense a but."

"You are correct, there is a but. Did you hear of Wickham?"

"James Wickham of the *Fortitude*? Aye. She went down in the first of these bloody storms. All hands lost."

Jennings sighed, gave a rueful nod. "Wickham was our man. Like you, his mother was Spanish—from Hispaniola. Her husband was an Irish Catholic hanged by del Gardo for outstanding debts. Del Gardo forced her to become his mistress to repay the money her husband owed. Oh, it was a long time ago now, Wickham was a lad, five, six years old when all that happened. He once told me all he remembered of his childhood was his mother coming home and scrubbing at herself in the washtub." He paused. "As I understand, she left the boy in the care of her mother and threw herself off a cliff. Don't know if it is true." Jennings pursed his lips, shook his head. "We do some god-awful vile things to women y'know."

"Like flogging them for adultery?"

Almost imperceptibly Jennings nodded, then said, "We are in difficulty Jes lad."

Jesamiah folded his arms. Had a nasty feeling he was not going to like this.

"We need someone to replace Wickham. Someone who can speak fluent Spanish to go in on the quiet and finish what he started. You, of course, learnt the language from your mother. You would be an ideal substitute."

"And you'll require someone like Wickham who is clever and quick enough to sneak past the patrol boat of the *guardacostas*." Jesamiah snorted mockingly. "Despite what my woman says, I am not a fool Henry! The last time I went within cannon range of *La Española* I was threatened with a very nasty end." He held one finger up to silence Jennings' attempt at interruption, continued; "If I'm caught I've been promised the entertainment of being drawn and quartered, after a few rather unpleasant preliminaries." Cynically he added, "If you are asking me to bail you out it's because no one else has the balls to help. And if I volunteer I'm likely to lose mine. Literally."

"If we British held Hispaniola, we would have free trade here in these waters."

Jesamiah laughed. "You mean Parliament will increase its tax revenue three-fold. Hardly free trade, Henry!"

"Felipe of Spain permits only one British merchant vessel a year to trade with Hispaniola. One! The rebels will welcome trade—it is the lack of trade that is crippling them, that and the fact that del Gardo is a monster."

"I know who and what del Gardo is, as well as he knows me. I call myself Acorne but by birth I'm a Mereno. I'm not privy to the reason, but he and my father were enemies and his hatred has spilled over on to me. As I've a fancy to hang on to m'personal bits I avoid Hispaniola, and if it's all the same to you, I intend to continue with me hanging on and avoiding."

Patient, knowing he would have his work cut out on this, Jennings smiled. "Would you not find it rewarding to be rid of del Gardo then?"

With a grunt of effort, he stood, clasped the bars from his outer side of the cell. "All we need is someone with a wide smile and a firm handshake, Jes; someone to replace Wickham and take one last message to the rebels."

"You keep saying *we*. You want *me* to go in there. I am not putting my neck into a noose for you, for Rogers, nor for no bloody parliament or king. No. Do your own dirty work." Jesamiah shoved his hands deep into his pockets.

Sucking in his cheeks, Jennings said wistfully, "Were it not for this gout d'ye think I would not be doing it, lad? And besides," he paused not daring to meet Jesamiah's expression, "you would not be doing this for me or Rogers, or king or country. You would be doing it for Mistress van Overstratten."

For a long, long moment Jesamiah stared at him, his eyes sparking intense hatred. Finally, quietly, said, "You bastard."

"We consider you are the best man for the job, possibly the only man. We cannot waste all the months this has taken to set and plan. There are few Englishmen in these parts who speak fluent Spanish, and none who can talk his way in and out of a dragon's lair, possesses a fast ship and also happens to be a damn fine seaman." For emphasis he ticked the attributes off on his fingers.

Cynically Jesamiah answered, "And even if there was another, unlike myself, he would not be in a position to be blackmailed into doing it. Which means there is one bugger of a lot of detail you're leaving out."

In apologetic agreement Jennings cleared his throat, admitted, "You always were astute."

Stamping over to the bench Jesamiah threw himself down, folded his arms and scowled. "Don't bother telling me any more. I don't want to know. I am not getting involved." He pulled his hat down over his eyes, feigned settling into sleep.

"Very well. There is something more important. Wickham had a contact on Hispaniola—a spy."

From beneath the hat, Jesamiah mumbled, "So let him get on with all this."

"Ah, but you see," Jennings scratched at his scalp under the itch of his wig. "All we know is his English code name. Francis Chesham." Jennings spread his hands; "We have no idea of his real name, whether he is Spanish, Creole, English or half-Irish like Wickham was."

"There you go with that *we* business again. I ain't interested."

"Nor do we know where or how to contact him. Wickham never told us, he said we had no need to know."

"How very short-sighted of you not to insist."

"The last we heard from Wickham, he said he thought Chesham was in danger. We are worried that he could be imprisoned or dead."

"How unfortunate."

"Jesamiah you are not being helpful here. I want you to find him. Find out if he is alive, let him know you are taking Wickham's place. It is imperative we contact this fellow as soon as possible."

Jesamiah stood, threw his hat to the bench in annoyance and stared up at the small, barred window. Outside, after last night's rain, it was a beautiful day; the sun bright, birds singing, white puffballs of cloud idling over a blue, blue sky. "No. *Vete a la mierda*," he added coarsely. "Get someone else to piss into the bucket for you."

Annoyed, slapping his palm against the bars, Jennings cursed. "You ought to know; Tiola pleaded guilty, gave no defence of herself. She said nothing except to confirm she is your mistress. They are assembling to witness punishment right now. It is to be the standard twelve lashes."

Jesamiah closed his eyes. *Dear God...*He turned back to face Jennings. Had no choice, the bastards knew he had no choice! "All right, you bloody win. I need to be there. I need to show my support for her in front of this poxed island. Get me out, damn you, and I'll go to Hispaniola, find out what I can about this Chesham. But there is one condition."

"Which is?"

"Rogers stops this injustice, now, and grants Tiola an annulment."

"That's two things. Unless your name is Henry Tudor, Jes, only Parliament can pass a ruling of divorce. It can be a long, costly business."

Jesamiah growled. He knew that. "In Nassau Rogers is the government. If you want me to do this for you, give your word that he'll find a way to circumnavigate the law of divorce."

Dropping the butt of the smoked cheroot to the floor and carefully flattening it with the tip of his cane, Jennings shook his head. "I cannot give that sort of word."

Ambling to the cell door, Jesamiah pressed his face close to the bars, malice puckering his mouth and nose. "What will be in this rebellion for you, Henry? For Rogers? Will you be taking over del Gardo's considerable share of the trade profits once he's gone? Those poor bastards on Hispaniola will rebel, make a fight of it and give their lives—for what? For greedy Spanish masters to be replaced by greedy British ones?"

Jennings was walking towards the door, his cane slowly tap-tapping. He said nothing. What point in denying the truth?

"If you want me to help you Henry, I suggest you get someone in here who can give his word about divorce."

CHAPTER SEVEN

An hour. A long hour in which the sun trundled its slanting rays over the stinking mess of the cell floor, and then another even longer hour. The church bell struck midday, Jesamiah was frantic. No one listened to his shouts and curses; no one even came to yell at him to be quiet. If it were not for his private contact with Tiola he was certain he would have gone mad. She assured him, over and over that she was all right, but Jesamiah had seen women flogged, knew exactly what to expect.

"Soddin' open this door!" It was futile, but he kicked the cell bars again anyway.

"Shouting will give you naught but a sore throat." The outer door opened. Governor Rogers himself stepped through.

Jesamiah opened his mouth to shrill abuse, was immediately silenced by the governor's raised hand, palm held outermost. "If you bawl at me Captain Acorne, I will turn right around and leave you in here for another two days at least." He approached the cell, fumbled in his coat pocket for a lace-edged kerchief which he held fastidiously to his nose to inhale the cologne sprinkled onto the linen. The place stank abominably.

"Captain Jennings has informed me of your conditions of agreement to serve the Crown, although I put it to you, boy, you are not in a position to bargain."

"And I put it to you, sir, that you want my help, therefore, you also ain't in a position to bargain. There is a limit to those who can be coerced upon this island; a limit of one. And you are looking at him."

Rogers tucked the kerchief away, linked his hands behind his back. He was a tall man, stout, the buttons of his elegant embroidered waistcoat straining over the bulge of his belly. He had once, in his youth, been slender and handsome but years at sea had left their sorry toll. One side of his face had been half shot away, the scars left behind, ragged and ugly.

"You over-estimate your importance, Acorne. I have several men I am considering to approach for assistance."

Fixing him with a condescending stare Jesamiah drawled, "Oh aye? Then why is it you are standing here in this shite-hole talking to me, not to one of those other clodpolls?"

Woodes Rogers shifted his wig more comfortable. The day was hot, and although the dungeons were cold and damp, sweat was trickling down his brow. His wife insisted he dress correctly in woollen coats and horsehair wigs, items of attire wholly unsuited to the climate of the Caribbean.

"I have spoken to van Overstratten. He will not agree to an annulment. He is a man of God, and obeys God's laws..."

Jesamiah interrupted, furious, "God's laws? Where in the Bible does it say God permits a husband to flog his wife in public?"

"I warn you Acorne, I will not be shouted at. I do not have to be here."

Choking down his anger and frustration, Jesamiah shut his mouth.

"I was about to add; however, as there are no children nor any form of dowry to be returned I am willing to intervene on your behalf, plead your case, as it were. I cannot guarantee an outcome, but as long as you do not expect anything towards her keep from him, and realise he will not take her back when you find the barrel is empty for breeding."

A scathing retort hovered on Jesamiah's lips but the fight went out of him. He rested his forehead on the cold iron of the bars. Closed his eyes. "Risking my neck to find a lost spy? It stinks and I'm the fool, but if you will stop this punishment of my woman I'll do it."

Nearing the door Rogers shook his head. "Regrettably, I cannot stop it; sentence has been announced and recorded."

Jesamiah's anger flooded back with the force of a hurricane wind. "Well then, you can go to hell on a handcart to look for your soddin' spy! And fuck your bleedin' rebellion!"

"I do not know why you are so concerning y'self over this, Acorne. A few lashes soon heal and women are used to pain, they are child-bearers after all. I'll see what I can do about the matter of divorce, however." He tapped the silver knob of his walking cane on the outer door, seeking an exit.

For a moment of panic Jesamiah thought he was going to leave without freeing him. "Sir!" he shouted, forcing himself to sound contrite, "Sir, please! I need to be with her!"

"What? Oh yes, yes." Pointing his cane at the guard who had opened the door, then at Jesamiah, Rogers barked, "Release this fellow." To Jesamiah added, "I'll be holding y'weapons though. I'll not be permitting ye those until after this business is completed."

The key grated in the lock and Jesamiah was out, pushing past Rogers who, despite being a portly man, grabbed hold of his arm with surprising swiftness. "And I will be having those ribbons from your hair, Captain. I know they are not mere fripperies to give as keepsakes to the numerous whores you romp with in bed."

Growling, Jesamiah yanked them from his hair, threw them to the floor and ran, leaping up the flight of steps and out into the sunlight.

Rogers picked up one of the ribbons and coiled the ends around his fingers, pulled them taut, gave an experimental tug and then tossed the strands around the tied neck of a sack, using it as a stand-in victim. He crossed his arms, pulled, and the sack tumbled from its pile, spilling mouldy corn everywhere.

The sentry guard looked straight ahead, said nothing as Rogers coughed, embarrassed, and left. The sentry did, however, retrieve the ribbons for himself and shoved them into his uniform pocket.

Following more sedately in Jesamiah's wake, Woodes Rogers was pleased with himself. Jennings had said the plan would work. Jennings was right. Mind, the cannon was only loaded and aimed, was not yet fired. Acorne was a pirate and Rogers knew not one pirate who kept his side of a bargain.

There was cheering and an audible rise of noise from the direction of the town. Rogers strode a little faster, best get this wretched business done first, then concentrate on persuading Acorne to do their bidding. It was essential for him to find Chesham. Most essential.

CHAPTER EIGHT

The whores were screaming abuse at the men, a few rotten eggs being thrown along with mouldering fruit and projected spittle, and their common shout of protest. There was not a woman in Nassau who wished Tiola ill, for reliable midwives were treasured. Enough women, even in the short time she had been here, had benefited because of her calm wisdom and dextrous skill. Every woman feared childbirth for too many did not survive its endurance; to be aware there was one among them who knew what she was doing, in itself, was a godsend, but to have a woman who could advise how to prevent a child being formed, or be rid of one? Among those who survived by selling their bodies to pleasure men, such a woman was welcomed indeed. And Tiola knew more; how to stop the milk-fever, ease the cramps of a monthly flux—how to prevent the pox of syphilis and cures for a variety of ailments and illnesses. She was a healer, confidante and friend, and the women of Nassau voiced their objection to this disgraceful treatment of her in vehement disgust.

The militia held them back, bayonets fixed into their muskets, more than one of the soldiers cursing as they tried to concentrate on the shuffling push of angry women, while glancing over their shoulders at one in particular. Tiola was a beauty. There were several men who were eager to see what tantalising secrets were concealed beneath her shift; many who were envious of Jesamiah Acorne. The only ones who stood silent, frowning disapproval or muttering abuse along with the whores, were the loyal crew of the *Sea Witch*.

Jesamiah swore repeatedly as he shoved his way through the crowd. Was all of Nassau here to gawp?

Rue appeared behind him, caught his arm. "It will be over in a few moments, *capitaine*. Grit your teeth and bear it as she will be doing."

"Like fokken hell I will!" Jesamiah thrust the grip aside and peeled off his hat and coat, dropping them into his quartermaster's arms. His waistcoat followed, and he pushed his way through the last of the mob. This was not justice. This was repugnant, public entertainment.

The shouting eased as Rogers appeared and stepped onto a raised platform as if he were a king mounting his royal dais. Already awaiting him there, van Overstratten, dressed in expensive, colourful silks, together with several other town dignitaries, including Henry Jennings.

"Out my way!" Jesamiah barked, forcefully hurling someone aside, his bile rising as he realised it was that sneering weasel, Dunwoody. They had met on only a few occasions and had taken an instant dislike to each other, a dislike that had rapidly expanded into solid hatred.

The governor might have temporarily confiscated Jesamiah's weapons but he had other things just as effective. He bunched his fist, rammed it, hard, into a personal and painful part of Dunwoody's anatomy. Was satisfied to see the turd collapse to his knees, groaning and clutching at himself.

Elbowing aside someone else he recognised, although he could not recall his name, Jesamiah found himself at the front, hemmed in by several hundred men. Beyond them, the women were still calling and hissing their disgust and objections, but they could not push past the militia to be of any service other than voicing their outrage. If something was to be done, Jesamiah would have to be doing it himself.

Dressed only in under-shift and skirt, Tiola's wrists were already secured to the whipping post, her arms out-spread along the cross-rail. They had tied her lovely black hair into a crude knot at the nape of her neck. The beadle, the law officer beneath the constable in command of enforcing punishment, stepped forward, his fingers curling around the neck band of Tiola's shift ready to tear it from her back.

"Hold!" Jesamiah thundered as he stepped into the open space in the middle of the crowd to stand behind Tiola, roughly shoving the beadle out of the way with his elbow. "I admit my guilt of adultery and claim the punishment." He pulled his shirt off, tossed it to the ground.

"You cannot!" van Overstratten spluttered as he jumped from the dais, his hand outstretched to swat Jesamiah aside.

"I bloody can mate!" Jesamiah yelled back, blocking the move with his raised forearm, restraining the urge to punch with the other. "I freely admit my guilt." He glowered at the crowd, silencing the mutters, shifted his challenging gaze to stare at Governor Rogers. "Or is it that this punishment is more about seeing a woman's breasts exposed for all to gawp at? Has nothing to do with the law and justice?"

Jesamiah paused, lifted his head as he added, "Tell this Dutchman I have the right. Aboard ship any man claiming guilt takes the punishment from the one convicted. That is our law, Captain Rogers. The code of the sea. Navy code. Pirate honour. Pirate code."

Rogers looked at the gathered crowd, at the shabby men jostling forward in the hope of gaining a better view—and felt shame and self-disgust gorge in his gullet. He believed implacably in honour and loyalty, believed in what was right, what was wrong. It was wrong to bed another's wife, but it took two to do the deed, and what man among these here present had not committed this self-same sin of adultery? He certainly had. And on more than the one occasion.

Acorne had spoken true: any self-respecting husband would have demanded satisfaction in private, would have met in the quiet of a dawn mist and shot the offender, or run him through. Or lost the argument.

Except, Rogers massaged his chin, rubbed at the constantly aching scar where his jaw had been shot away. Except, he did owe much gratitude to master van Overstratten. It was he who financed the guardship that protected these waters from the rogues who refused to give up piracy, and the Dutchman was busting a gut to assist in improving the situation of dismal trade profits here in the Caribbean. Commerce owed much to him. Parliament—the Commons—almost entirely rich merchants, many of whom owned plantations in these colonies, rated Stefan van Overstratten very highly indeed. They would not be pleased to see him bested, especially by a pirate. If siding with Acorne meant losing van Overstratten's financial patronage, ah, that would be a blow for the Caribbean, for Nassau, and for Rogers personally.

"The lash is for able-bodied men and convicts, Captain Acorne. Not for sea officers," he said with a dismissive gesture. "You will be demeaning your rank."

"Able-bodied men, convicts and women, Governor. I find the thought of flogging a woman also demeans my rank."

Rogers cleared his throat, uncertain whether Acorne was strictly correct in this claim of rights. He searched quickly through the faces to locate Dunwoody; he would know. The man was here somewhere...saw to his disgust how many in the crowd had their hands hovering over the front of or inside their breeches. He pursed his lips, disliking the lewd overtones so clearly displayed in front of him. Damn protocol! He was Governor, he could do as he pleased.

"It is as he says, master van Overstratten. It is his right."

Alarmed, Tiola squirmed her head around. "Jesamiah, you cannot do this. It is not necessary."

"You will not be telling me what I can or cannot do, woman!" He spoke fiercely, adamant, partially through anger, partially through his own doubt. He had never been on the receiving end of a flogging. Had witnessed several, had seen how the lash could cut to the bone; had seen with his own eyes the result of scars carried for life. He swallowed his rising apprehension. It was only twelve lashes. If Tiola said she could endure twelve lashes to the bare skin, then so could he. He settled his body close against her, his legs spread wide to balance himself, arms resting along hers, fingers curling into her hands. His back exposed, not hers.

Tiola closed her eyes, an initial relief flooding her, distress rapidly over-taking it.

~ *My lover. The lash cannot harm me, it will hurt and harm you.* ~

Jesamiah ignored her, glanced up at Woodes Rogers. "Tell 'em to get on with it."

Rogers nodded in a signal to proceed, to get this day's distasteful work done.

"Wait." Van Overstratten's mouth was taut with impotent fury—he might have guessed Acorne would damned interfere somehow. He gestured at the lash held in the beadle's hand. "This whip is a single strand intended for a woman's finer flesh, not a man's. How can that be justice? I demand a cat be used."

Jesamiah swallowed; Tiola felt his body go rigid. He had not bargained on the cat-of-nine tails. Nine strands of knotted cordage, not one. Nine lashes for each delivered blow. One hundred and eight lashes, not twelve.

"You do not have to do this Jesamiah," she whispered again. "I cannot be harmed."

"Shut up," he snapped. "I do have to do this." His anger was a play-act to hide the quiver of fear and the nausea worming into his belly.

From somewhere, almost instantly, a cat was passed forward; someone must have been holding it, for usually a cat was made by the victim, as part of his punishment a few hours before it was needed.

The cat. Every sailor's nightmare, particularly in the Royal Navy where discipline was harsh and adhered to by the book; a wicked punishment used sparingly by a fair captain or frequently by the many devils who were not. Not on a pirate ship; there was rarely a flogging aboard one of the Sweet Trade. When pirates delivered punishment it was judged by the entire crew through democratic discussion. Fines for lesser crimes, or the drudgery of the unpalatable night watch, or scrubbing out the ordure from the heads. For the more serious, marooning—being abandoned on a lonely shore with one keg of water, one pistol and one, solitary, shot.

The cat.

"Twelve lashes!" van Overstratten called, the satisfaction of what was now proposed unravelling to boast the promise of pleasant revenge. He leaned close to Jesamiah, his breath smelling of spiced wine and rich, Virginian tobacco smoke, his body odour of mild sweat masked by the subtle touch of cologne. "Are you sure you still want to play the hero Acorne? It is not too late to change your poxed mind."

"Go piss yourself, you bastard."

Stefan laughed, stepped back a pace. Gestured to the beadle. "Do your duty. And make sure you do it well."

Jesamiah braced, every muscle clenched, waiting, his breath sucking in through his mouth as the first blow fell, stinging across his bare shoulders; the whistle of the nine strands, the crack and snap as nine thongs straked his flesh. His body pressed against Tiola's. His, clenched, rigid and hard, hers soft and yielding, willing him to allow her to absorb his pain.

He gasped, murmured, "Sweet Mother of God!" Was it already a trickle of blood he felt, or sweat?

Some of the crowd, the tavern keepers, shop owners; the craftsmen, marines and sailors of the navy, those who had come to leer, reckoned the count. "One!"

The shout fell uneasily silent as a growl, like the low snarl of a panther, hummed from the watching pirates. The rat-tat, rat-tat-tat of their pistol butts drummed against leather baldrics, the stonework of a wall or wooden bollards. The tap-tap, of a musket stock or cutlass tip striking on the cobbles. An ugly murmur of disapproval joining with and rising above the condemnation of the whores' rowdy catcalls. Pirates, degenerates, whoremongers and slovenly drunkards they may be, but they were also men who were bound together as brethren loyal to their own. And this deed being done to a respected captain was disgracefully unacceptable to them, their running temper held in check merely by the recent-agreed amnesty.

Jesamiah released his held breath, inhaled, gathered himself for the second blow. Two. Eighteen stripes on his back. For a moment, as with the first blow, the raised lines showed white, then the skin split and blood oozed.

Three. No one counted now, save the beadle's assistant. Jesamiah knew for certain it was not sweat but the stream of blood. His hands grasped Tiola's tight, desperate to hold on to his pride through her.

She closed her eyes, concentrated on entering his mind, met nothing except a shout of pain. Tried again. ~ *Jesamiah! Yield to me, let me help you. I have been trying to tell you, I will not feel it.* ~

Four. He moaned.

Thirty-six open wounds seeping over his shoulders and obliterating the yellowed bruising and scarring set there from his brother's previous abuse. He shut his eyes, nuzzled his contorted face into her neck, hiding the burning endurance from the judgmental, silent, stare of the watching pirates. If he cried out he would lose their respect. And his own.

The beadle dipped the whip in a bucket of water to wash away the blood and snags of torn flesh. Brought it up, back, down. Five. Jesamiah groaned. He could not disgrace Tiola by passing out. Could not disgrace himself.

~ *Let me do this for you, as you are doing this for me.* ~

~ *I...can...not...* ~ Six. ~ *Fokken hell...* ~

~ *Please Jesamiah. Please!* ~

And he surrendered, let her whole being flood through and into his mind and body. Allowed her to completely unite with and possess his soul.

Everything fell into the distance as if a sea fog had suddenly swamped the entire island. Sound diminished, awareness faded, only this was not the cold and clammy discomfort of bleakness, this held the pleasantness of a midsummer morning mist. From Tiola he could smell the aroma of new-mown hay, and sweet-scented meadow flowers and herbs, all mixed with the salt tang of the sea; the odour of seaweed and tar, wet canvas and washed decks.

No sound, nothing except the sharp intake of his own breath and her comforting, slower breathing, the rhythm deeper and controlled taking the sobbing ache from his bursting lungs and gradually easing it slower, slower, slower.

Two heartbeats, his, thump-thumping against hers. Her love bringing the racing lurch, the wild thunder crashing in his chest to a steady, calm, pace. *Ta-dmp...ta-dmp.*

The tangible feel of her soft warmth against his bare chest, her buttocks pressing against his loins as he leant into her; his body and mind entwined into hers, hers into his. Two individual beings fused as one, woven together as the warp and weft become the whole, as the solid and the shadow is one. Inseparable, torn only if wrenched apart by force.

Her total possession of him was an odd, yet not unpleasant sensation, similar to the intimacy of the height of passion in sexual intercourse, the closest a man could get to the woman he loved. But this ecstasy was a step beyond the exquisite fulfilment of lovemaking. This, was a consuming, slow-motion explosion of awareness that had the brilliance of the sun and the eternity of the universe about it. He became acutely conscious of how it felt to be a woman; the fine lightness of her bones and the softness of her hair—the absence of itching beard-growth and tender, scraped skin after shaving. The moustache trailing above his upper lip, his body hair on his chest, beneath his armpits, pubic hair, all so much coarser than hers. The swell of her breasts, malleable but firm, the spread of hips designed to support and protect the depth of her womb, a sheltered cradle where one day, he hoped, his child would grow. And the powerful muscles of her vagina that could stretch and push the child into birth; a place he had only known through the intimate pleasures of sex.

This inwardness of a woman intrigued him. Tiola's whole being felt as if she were wrapped in a comforting fur of luxurious sable. Her tender internal secretiveness a peculiar sensation to a man so used to his sexuality being worn and openly displayed on the outside. What surprised him, despite her apparent feminine frailty, he suddenly realised her enormity of strength. The endurance that could sustain her through a lengthy, agonising labour, the monthly acceptance of her flux that tightened internal muscles into cramps and acute discomfort. A quick, assessing mind that could deal with a multitude of emergencies at once. Agile hands, supple, curved body. All of it so beautiful, so gentle, soft and so, so, unbreakably strong.

This, then, was how it was to be Tiola. To be a woman and to be one of the semi-immortal Wise Women of the Old Ones who passed the gift of Craft from grandmother to granddaughter, down and down and down through the aeons of time. From before the first dawn to when the very last sunset would sink as steam into the sea.

From inside her mind he heard the voices of those ancestors, her grandmothers and their grandmothers, the sound whispering and rustling in the distance, as if someone far away was shuffling through piles of autumn-gathered leaves. Only one could he hear clearly enough to understand; her immediate grandmother, also named Tiola; as they all had been, for in reality they were all facets of the one, same, immortal spirit.

~ *You are a good man, Jesamiah Acorne. Into your care I place my granddaughter. Her incarnation carries the accumulation of our wealth of wisdom and knowledge. She must be protected. At all cost, she must be protected, for she is the last of us made mortal. To her falls the responsibility of shielding humankind from the terrible destruction of evil that walks your world.* ~

A question flooded into his head, a question of self-doubt that he suddenly, desperately, needed to ask.

~ *How do I protect her? How?* ~ And then, ~ *What do you mean, the last?* ~

Fear touched him, alarming in its abrupt intensity. What if he failed? Because of his ineptitude, would she die? He could not bear that, could not endure being without her.

But the awareness of being wrapped in the comfort of another's loving soul was shifting balance and the voices and his rise of panic disappeared. The light and perspective was changing.

As if looking through Tiola's eyes, the world glowed a little brighter than perhaps it was, broader, higher. Fleetingly, he touched the wide spread of the oceans scattered with bejewelled islands, and then the sweep of the continents; the New World, Africa. Europe, Asia. The misted, faint edge of the unexplored places that made up the

Australias—no, one place! It was one huge continent, not a scatter of small, unconnected and isolated islands as everyone thought! But the images had swept on, now he was gazing at an expanse of white, blinding ice at the southernmost edge of the world. Upward, travelling upward around the Earth—mountains, jungle, desert, fertile soil and arid plain—then more ice stretching away over the roof of the world. All of it, the entire globe was embraced within the eternal depth of her mind, and passing for this moment only, into his. He would forget most of it when she left him, she would have to ensure he did, for it was not for mortal humans to be knowing of these things before they were ready to be known. But some of it she would allow to remain as a dream, a dream that felt as comfortable as an enveloping shawl made from finest cashmere, a dream part remembered, part forgotten...

Willingly, she showed him the familiar patterns of the eternal tread of the stars; proud Orion, the Plough, Cassiopeia. The Southern Cross—and the ponderous turn of the planets. Venus, Mars, Saturn, Jupiter, and more! Jesamiah caught his breath—those watching assumed it was for the ninth lash—he frowned in puzzlement. Surely there were but six planets? He had no time to ponder the anomaly for Tiola's united, possessive, soul was taking him further out into the hollow of the Universe, beyond the solar system, outward to the very edge of existence.

He felt huge, magnificent and immortal, yet so infinitely small and vulnerable. Smaller than a grain of sand upon the shore, one grain among the many, many thousand, one alone except for his woman. His beautiful, beautiful witch-woman, Tiola.

No pain. Only vaguely, in this exhilaration of being one with her, was he aware of the sting of the lash on his back. Only partially was he aware that it was going to hurt like hell once she left him.

Joy flooded into him as he recognised the presence within Tiola's existence of his second love, his ship, the *Sea Witch*. Tiola and she had once been similarly combined, and after souls had been joined a severing was never made fully complete. Through Tiola, he felt the smoothness of the sun-bleached decks, the soaring height of masts; the neatly furled canvas sails and the taut, tarred, rigging. Was aware of the gentle lift and swell beneath her copper-coated hull, the ripple and tug of the tide nudging at her. She was restless, uneasy at the pain her consort was enduring, was bored with being in a harbour. She wanted to run, spill her sails, feel the wind and the sea hurtle past; wanted, like any woman, to show off her beauty and be admired. Jesamiah smiled.

~ *Soon, my pretty, pretty one,* ~ he murmured in his mind. ~ *Soon shall I be with you, and set you free.* ~

Fleetingly, very distant, very quiet and momentary another presence touched him, unfamiliar and disquieting. An overwhelming sense of drowning, of being pulled down and down into the depths of the ocean, the sun sparkling on the surface far, far, above and the blackness closing in around him. He struggled, fear rising. This was not pleasant.

He heard a voice that sounded like the hush of a white-tipped wave running up onto a sandy beach: ~ *Jessh... a..miah? I want you my Jessh...a..miah. I ssshall have you. You are mine.* ~

It was cold down here; cold, frightening and dark. Jesamiah did not like the dark. His elder brother had often shut him, screaming for mercy, in the loneliness of the dark.

A sudden squall of rain hissed across Nassau harbour, coming from nowhere. And then another voice, not so menacing, quicker, lighter, with a staccato cadence.

~ *Perhaps I want him Mother. Perhaps I shall have him, not you.* ~

Aware of the two intrusive presences slithering into Jesamiah's consciousness, and of his scudding fear of dark,

60

confined, places, Tiola lost her concentration. To keep him safe she had no choice but to step outside of his existence. Quickly she murmured the command to forget, and withdrew, leaving his quivering body vulnerable to the final two strokes of the lash.

As the last one smashed into his torn flesh, the full scream of pain surged through Jesamiah like a storm-wracked tide frothing into the lower decks of a sinking vessel. He began to sag, but Rue was there, his arms going to support his captain, to pull his shirt on over his head, hiding the mess that was now his back from public view.

The *Sea Witch*'s first mate, Isiah Roberts, untied Tiola's wrists. Both men chaperoned their charges through the press of the crowd with angry glares and poking elbows.

Planting himself four-square before them, his arm outstretched towards governor Rogers, van Overstratten raised his voice in protest.

"You are not permitting Acorne to return to his ship? What surety is there that he will not break his amnesty and make sail? He has already made a mockery of me, are you to permit him to do the same to you?"

The governor did not respond, but he was harbouring the same thought. He had made a deal with Acorne, but there was nothing to guarantee this rogue of a captain would keep it, and Rogers did, desperately, require assistance in this thing concerning Hispaniola. He lumbered down the steps and gruffly approached Jesamiah, slumped against Rue.

"I expect you to be in my office tomorrow morning, Acorne. Ten-thirty sharp. If you do not attend I shall declare your pardon invalid. Understand?"

Tiola tossed her rage at him, an overspill of her own fear and apprehension, her anger at pain endured because of her. The savage cruelty of the human animal and the bestial undercurrent of the male craving for sexual pleasure, in all its forms.

"He will be unable to move tomorrow, Governor, as you well know," she snapped, anger swirling into her voice and eyes, sparking and crackling like a charge of lightning.

Rogers coughed, hesitated, unused to this slender, timid-seeming woman stamping her foot at him, her expression openly hostile and glaring. He appreciated the dilemma, but van Overstratten was a man of wealth and influence and his own position as governor was not as sturdy as he liked to publicly pretend. There were those in England who ridiculed his idea of amnesty, who were waiting the first opportunity to pillory him for gross ineptitude. Making contact with the Spanish rebels, for several reasons, most of which had not been divulged to Acorne, was imperative. And Jesamiah had been right; there was no one else.

A little harshly he replied, "Then he ought have thought of that for himself, ma'am, before he acted so rashly to save your discomfort. A noble gesture but misplaced and foolhardy. Government business cannot wait upon the actions of the brash. He will be in my office tomorrow or I shall have him outlawed. Ensure he attends." He paused, conceded, "Later then, three-thirty."

To the crew of the *Sea Witch* gathering closer, their hostility rippling like a rising wind, Rogers announced, "If you sail without my express authority and without your captain carrying a Letter of Marque, I shall deem you to have returned to piracy. There will be no pleas for clemency. You will hang."

Behind him, van Overstratten laughter mocked him. "Do you seriously expect complicity from thieves and murderers? His ship will be hull down over the horizon by sunrise."

Tiola's eyes blazed at him. More than ever before the desire to blast him into eternity swelled within her. Why in all the names of all the gods that were and had ever been had she decided on the fool idea to become his wife? She fought the anger down. She could not entertain hatred, for it was an evil brew that could so easily feed upon itself and grow, consuming all within its path with a rapacious, unassuaged appetite. Why had she wed him? Because at the time, she had not dared risk giving away her ability, because at that time her physical strength had been weak and vulnerable— and because she had desperately needed to get here, to Nassau, to help Jesamiah.

She took several calming breaths, regained her self-control, said. "And do you call me, too, a thief and a murderer, Stefan?"

Van Overstratten regarded her with disappointment. Whatever had initially lured him into wanting this woman? She was pretty, but what use were looks if the belly was empty? She gave no pleasure in bed, was as cold as a fish to his touch.

Tiola guessed what he was thinking. He was not a man to consider that perhaps the fault was his own lack of skill. He would have been surprised had he been given the opportunity to witness the intense passion that burnt between herself and Jesamiah during their lovemaking. But then, Jesamiah was a different man entirely. A man who truly understood what it meant to make love; who knew how and where to touch and caress, who knew when to be easy and gentle or to push, hard, and bring that final thrill of consuming ecstasy to its release. Momentarily lost in thought, Tiola smiled.

Her expression increased the Dutchman's anger. How dare she look at him so! Contemptuously he answered her; "You, madam? *Nean*. I call you a whore."

Jesamiah lifted his head, sight and senses swimming against the carol of pain; glared at the Dutchman. "Then you will not be wishing to keep her as wife, will you?"

He glanced at Rogers who was trying his best to bring law and order to these pirate-riddled Caribbean waters. He would not succeed. He was too indecisive, wanting to please all sides at once, and Rogers assumed all men followed the unwritten code of honour and unswerving loyalty. He was unaware that chivalry had vanished centuries ago. If it had ever truly existed. But Jesamiah also conceded that Rogers had integrity, faith and guts; he held fast to his personal beliefs whatever carnage was happening around him. Even if he failed here in Nassau, Jesamiah admired him for at least caring enough to try.

Pushing himself, with effort, and with a strength of fortitude that came from God-alone knew where, from Rue's supporting arm, Jesamiah stood as straight as he could. If nothing else, Rogers was a man of his word.

"Can you assure me, Governor, that you will see to it that Tiola is set free of her marriage bond? If I come tomorrow, will you give me her divorce?"

For his part, Rogers knew his limitations and his fallibilities. He also admired bravery; what Acorne had done here today was foolish, but undoubtedly brave. To expose your back purposefully for a flogging to save a woman's honour placed this rogue high in his esteem. Knew, full well, that had he been called upon to do such a thing for his own wife she would have been abandoned to a flogging.

Ignoring the Dutchman's snort of contempt Rogers confirmed, "You have my word, Acorne." When van Overstratten began to splutter a protest, Rogers hushed him with a flap of his hand. Repeated, "Ye have m'word."

Suppressing a wince, Jesamiah nodded at him. "Then I will be there."

With a snarl of disapproval Rue shoved Rogers aside and walked Jesamiah away, Isiah at his side, urging Tiola to hurry; others of the crew, young Jasper, old toothless Toby, Finch and Jansy going ahead, shouldering a clear path to the jetty and the waiting longboat. Men already seated there were slipping the oars, the blades feathering the swell of the sea.

In the stern, Tiola carefully took Jesamiah in her arms and as the oarsmen gave way and pulled for the ship, cradled his head into her shoulder to mask the moan of pain that escaped him. His body was shaking, breath hissing through his clenched teeth. The blood ran in streaks down his back soaking through the thin cotton of his shirt.

The rain squall that had come in so fleetingly hushed away towards the sea, the raindrops shimmering in the brilliant sunshine creating a series of rainbows across *Sea Witch*'s deck. The ship bobbed, dipping her bowsprit as if in homage.

Tiola kissed Jesamiah's rain-damp hair. "You are a silly, stupid man who never listens to what I try to tell you," she whispered. "All the same, thank you."

She kissed him again as his arms tightened in an acknowledging squeeze around her waist. She added, "And I love you."

CHAPTER NINE

Taking extreme care not to hurt him, Tiola helped Jesamiah to the great cabin and to the smaller side alcove where, with a sigh of relief, he lay face down on their bed. Chippy, the ship's carpenter, had made it for them; a wooden box-bed slung from ropes secured to the underside of the decking above, and just large enough for Tiola and Jesamiah to snuggle intimately together. She turned away hurriedly as his hands gripped the pillow and he buried his face into its sanctuary of privacy. All the same, she saw the agony ripple through his rigid body.

"Fetch me a bowl of hot water with a handful of salt in it please," she said to Finch who had followed, trotting at their heels.

Expecting the request he answered, "Which is ready. I left the kettle singin', ma'am." Did not comment that he had assumed its need would be for her, not their captain. He did add, "Will ye be wantin' the vinegar and paper?"

Tiola shook her head. The traditional sailor's treatment for a flogging; swill the lacerated back with seawater then liberally apply vinegar-soaked brown paper. A cure that sounded as brutal as the punishment itself, but in a world where few understood infection, and medical practices were governed by superstition and false ideas, a cure that was at least effective. Tiola had better healing methods, ones she used with guarded care as they ran against the orthodox ways of thinking. Her healing came with the ability of Craft; inherited knowledge handed down from the ancient and long-gone civilisations of India, the Far East, and Arabia. A sophisticated knowledge which in the present bigoted world, despite the supposed new age of science and enlightenment, would have had Tiola marked as a witch faster than a spider traps a fly.

As far as the crew of the *Sea Witch* were concerned, they never questioned her methods. All they cared about were the results. They were healthy, their wounds healed fast, broken bones knitted straight and only a few of them carried the cock-pox. And those few were the ones who did not have the courage to seek Tiola's assistance in matters relating to the frequent visiting of whorehouses, or who would not use the lamb's intestine cundums she issued to them all.

From a small, rowan-wood chest she produced rolls of clean linen, cleansing herbs and salves. She was a White Witch of Craft with the gift of healing, but even she did not know where to start with the mess that was now Jesamiah's lacerated back. A small portion of his shoulder blade showed white where the skin had been flayed to the bone; the rest was mangled, bloodied, bruised and swollen. He sucked in his breath as she bathed the congealing wounds, tending and inspecting the damage as gently as she could.

"You are an idiot to have done this," she said tersely, as he flinched and gasped aloud as her touch probed a little too insensitively.

"What was I supposed to do then?" he objected into the pillow. "How could I have stood where you are now, looking at you lying here?" He shifted position, eased onto his side and partially raised himself to face her, suppressing the groan. "How could I have lived with myself if I had let you suffer?"

As she had to watch him suffer. Tiola said nothing, instead she showed him her answer by bending forward and kissing his mouth. An intimate, lingering kiss expressing her love, understanding and appreciation. A more pertinent answer than any spoken words could have conveyed.

Indicating he was to lie down again, she smeared the wounds with a sweet-smelling salve, lightly placed a linen pad over it all and then mixed laudanum with the generous tot of rum that Rue, waiting in the outer cabin to offer help where he could, had measured into a tankard.

"This will help you sleep, luvver," she said, handing it to Jesamiah who sat up awkwardly. "Sleep and time are the best healers of all manner of ills."

"And the pleasure of a good poke," he said, smiling at her, attempting to lift the tension from her face, the tremble from her hands. He well realised she was holding in her tears, that once he was asleep she would go up on deck to the bow where it was private, and weep. "Though I must confess, I don't feel up for it at this precise moment, darlin'."

As he hoped, she laughed outright. "By the height of the mainmast, that, then, must be a first!"

He grinned back at her, settled himself more comfortable. The rum was already taking effect, the laudanum following rapidly in its wake.

"Do not let me sleep on the morrow, sweetheart. I have to meet with Rogers."

From the day cabin, Rue, pouring himself a rum and Tiola a glass of wine, swore in his native French. He was still seething fury at his impotency to do anything to help either of the two people he admired and loved. "*Merde*, like 'ell you will! Rogers can shove 'imself up 'is own *derrière*!"

He caught Tiola's expression as she accepted the proffered wine and nodded an apology for his crudity, "*Pardon ma chère.*"

She waved her hand, dismissive. "Be as coarse as you like, Rue. I could not have put it better myself."

Jesamiah lifted his head, the need to sleep growing stronger, on the brink of overwhelming him. He scowled at his friend and his woman. "I gave my word I would be there. Be there I will."

CHAPTER TEN

TUESDAY MORNING

Dawn had sauntered over the eastern horizon, and a feeble sun was attempting to vie with the lingering rain clouds. On foretopsail only, a Royal Navy frigate inched her way over the sandbar and manoeuvred into a position to restrict the exit from Nassau harbour. Most of the pirate vessels anchored, higgle-piggle with no order or symmetry, were nothing more than leaking buckets with sprung timbers and riddled by teredo worm. Their keels and rudders were mouldering beneath the cling of barnacles and rotting weed; spars were draped with patched sails that looked more like a careless array of last week's unwashed and abandoned laundry.

A mere handful of ships appeared neat and cared for; Governor Rogers' small fleet, or so Commodore Edward Vernon assumed from where he stood on the quarterdeck of HMS *Challenger*. Through his telescope he inspected a blue-hulled, square-rig resting, immaculate, at anchor; read her name painted in gold lettering across her stern. *Sea Witch.* Ah. He knew her, many a newssheet had reported the numerous exploits of the degenerate rogue who captained her. *Sea Witch* was a prime example of the idiocy of Rogers' experiment of offering an amnesty to these cut-throats and thieves. In Commodore Vernon's frequently expressed opinion, pirates should hang without trial and without question. String them up and make them dance. Acorne, being a prime candidate.

Vernon nodded at his first lieutenant and the boom of two cannons belched a salute shattering the quiet of the harbour. Roosting birds screeched into flight and everyone who had been curled asleep and snoring leapt into a frenzy of startled panic.

The fortress should have responded. His lips thinned further into tight disapproval. Did this godforsaken backwater not know the tradition of the salute? Rogers' lackadaisical attitude again he supposed. By truth, unless he achieved something glorious this cruise was going to be most obnoxious. He had beaten the Spanish at Barcelona back in '05 and no Don, nor powder-wigged blustering old British governor was going to ruin his reputation. He had plans for furthering his naval career; bumbling around in the Spanish Main was not ranked among them.

"Drop anchor, if you please, Mr Tyler," he said to his first lieutenant who relayed the order at a sharp bellow. "And have my gig swayed out, I am going ashore immediately. I assume Governor Rogers is aware of his position of authority, and not a man to laze abed of a morning."

Rogers was not abed. Vernon found him partaking of a hearty breakfast.

"Come in, come in! Do not stand on ceremony, sit, sit. Eat. Hi there, bring fresh tea for the commodore, ha, ha!" Rogers was all bonhomie as he ushered the new arrival to join him at the table. "May I introduce Master van Overstratten and m'wife?" Seating himself again he began to tuck into the black pudding he had temporarily abandoned.

Returning the courteous greetings, Vernon bowed politely but obstinately remained standing. He cleared his throat and began to unwrap the canvas package he held beneath his arm. "I am on my way to take up temporary command at Port Royal, Governor, from where I will conduct our strategy in these waters against the Spanish. I bring the mail and news from England." With a flourish he produced a pile of official letters which he placed on the table. A smaller bundle he passed to the Dutchman.

"Your presence here, van Overstratten, is most fortuitous, these are addressed to you. And this," he removed the last sealed document, "I must present direct into your hands, Governor. It contains your orders." With reverent care he placed the package on the table, its royal seal uppermost.

"Is the news sensitive or secret?"

"No sir, by now I would assume it to be common knowledge in England."

Rogers spoke through a mouthful of buttered toast, "Then you can tell me just as precisely what this damn thing contains while being sociable and drinking a cup of tea, can ye not? Standing as if ye have a broom handle shoved up yer backside is puttin' me off m'food."

Normally an affable man, Rogers had taken instant dislike to this officious rule-stickler, and thanked God it sounded like he was only passing through. Let Port Royal have the tedious bore, they were welcome to him!

Four and thirty years of age, Vernon was a tall, ample man, with a long, straight nose, a fleshy face and an inclination towards a double chin. He walked with a slight stoop to his shoulders, and his legs had no muscle to the thighs and calves beneath immaculate white breeches and silk stockings. Equally disliking Rogers, he seated himself but refused the tea. He detested the stuff, thought it a drink for women and over-indulgent popinjays.

With a grave expression he slid the package along the white linen of the tablecloth nearer to Rogers' hand. "I believe it would be more appropriate for you to read it for yourself."

Rogers sniffed, glowered, and continued eating. Mrs Rogers began questioning her husband on some trivial domestic matter, while van Overstratten broke open the seal to one of his four letters and began to read, a frown deepening on his face. Rogers may prevaricate over his correspondence, but van Overstratten did not, especially when he had been somewhat anxiously awaiting the arrival of this particular communication from his London lawyer. Now he had received it, his anxiety had increased twofold. He read it through again, then stared out of the window, oblivious to what anyone else was saying.

Sitting motionless and quiet for a full two minutes while Mrs Rogers prattled about new curtains for the drawing room, Vernon finally could not contain his growing exasperation. Interrupting her he stamped to his feet. "With respect, Governor, I made full sail most the way here. I believe I have clipped four days off the fastest passage; London to Nassau in four and fifty days." He did not mention how he had driven the men, or the number of floggings he had issued. Nor did he mention the three deaths by accident and misadventure. Tersely he added, "I was ordered to make haste, to reach you as soon as humanly possible with this pressing news."

Setting his knife and fork down with a clatter, Rogers came to a wrong conclusion and surged to his feet, exclaiming, "Good grief man, is King George dead?"

His wife hurried her hand to her mouth, suppressing a squeak of distress. Van Overstratten momentarily glanced up at them.

Bewildered, Vernon shook his head. "Whatever made you think that?"

Resuming attention to the last of his breakfast, Rogers expressed a muttered opinion that nothing beyond the welcome demise of that wretchedly useless, non-English speaking fart-arsed king, George of Hanover, warranted such undue haste.

On the verge of losing his temper Vernon spluttered, "War, sir! War is of what I am speaking! We are at war with Spain; the treaty between us has been breached. Hostilities have resumed."

This time, Mrs Rogers did not suppress the slight scream of alarm. Van Overstratten folded his letter and grimly slid it into his coat pocket, Rogers, however, without thinking, slammed his napkin down delighted. He banged the table with the flat of his hand.

"By Gad! How splendid! Ha, ha!"

A few minutes later, when he had read through the admiralty's dispatches he realised the grave error of his enthusiasm. War might bring the Spanish back to Nassau. It would not be the first, nor likely the last time they would attack the British territory. More to the point, though, he realised that war would bring complications to their carefully laid plans regarding Hispaniola.

"Bugger," he muttered to himself. "Bugger."

CHAPTER ELEVEN

Governor Rogers stood at the window gazing down into the harbour, at the array of ships and the navy frigate, *Challenger,* in particular. He dabbed at his florid face with his kerchief. The day was but a few hours old and already hot, sultry and airless. These damned storms were making the climate intolerable. He was a well-intentioned man, but when it came to thinking ahead and being sharp with political matters, he was somewhat naive. Some unkind people even said stupid.

"I do not see what more we can do, Henry. After all, war has been declared and Vernon, as the senior officer at Port Royal, is to take command of all naval shipping here in the Caribbean, so he says. Oh, I'm being friendly and jovial towards him, naturally, as Governor I have no choice, and I admit I have an enthusiasm for war. Never 'ave liked the Spaniards, eh?"

Jennings was sitting at his cluttered desk, one elbow on the top, chin cupped in his hand. Thinking. He had been sitting like that for the past five minutes while Rogers prattled and grumbled.

"You said y'self Henry, everything is ready for the rebels to act, we've done all we can, we're not expected to do any more are we? I mean, it's up to them now ain't it? Ha, ha!" Rogers was trying to convince himself that the situation was not as dire as Jennings thought. "War is just the opportunity they need. That damned man, del Gardo, will be distracted and the islanders will not be too keen to fund a conflict that has nothing to do with them, will they? It is an ideal opportunity for them to rise, don't ye think?"

"But don't you see!" exasperated, Jennings slapped the desktop with his hand. "Vernon has orders to blockade Hispaniola. That will make it difficult for anyone to get in, or out. In a week or so he can dance a jig in Santo Domingo's Cathedral for all I care but for now, both of us are near bankrupt because of our involvement. If the rebels do not rise or if they fail, well, it is a pity, we could have done very satisfactorily out of it, but if Hispaniola is cut off to us—God alone knows if we shall ever see the agreed payment we are due for our efforts!" He slapped the desk yet again. "They have not paid us, and unless we get what we are owed before Vernon sets sail, we will get nothing! Nothing at all!"

Rogers seated himself on the chair on the other side of the desk, legs spread, broad belly climbing over the red cummerbund tied around it. Face glum. The rebel leaders had promised a handsome profit for the English provision of guns and ammunition, for powder and shot. A payment that would have far exceeded the value of what he and Jennings had surreptitiously supplied to James Wickham.

Grimacing, Jennings rubbed at his leg, the pain was getting more intense, travelling upward from his foot. He would have to see the barber-surgeon again soon, ask to be bled and purged; it would have to be in a day or two though, this situation must be sorted first. Curse Wickham! Why did he have to get himself drowned? He was supposed to have collected and delivered the payment before the next full moon. Next week. Next bloody week! Pulling a few charts from the teetering pile, he selected the one for Hispaniola. Stared at it as if he had never seen it before, although he had been studying practically nothing else this last month.

"We will get nothing, Rogers," he repeated, "unless we can find this Chesham fellow. And to do that, we need to slip in before Vernon gets himself organised."

Massaging his chin, Rogers shook his head in frustration. In England he was being ridiculed for his ideas of reform. He had not received a shilling from his share of the prize money owed to him by the companies who had sponsored his circumnavigation of the globe—this despite the fortune he had plundered in their name. He needed money, and he needed it desperately. He did not like this situation one bit; regretted, now, becoming involved in the first place. Wickham, with his glib tongue and persuasive air had made it all sound so easy and straightforward. You supply us with arms and we will pay you handsomely for them. Huh! And now Jennings had suggested getting Acorne involved. One of the wiliest pirates Rogers knew! Were it not for the fact that he was desperate for finances, Rogers would have counselled to forget the whole thing.

He was getting confused by all this, though. Spies, counter spies, passwords, surreptitious trading. Give him a ship to sail and a chart to navigate by, that was all Rogers understood or wanted. Not this secretive bally stuff. "It was this Chesham fellow we've lost touch with who was supposed to bring us payment, was it not?"

Henry Jennings sighed. Occasionally he agreed with those few people who implied that Woodes Rogers had a tendency to be stupid.

"No, we do not know who Chesham is. Wickham told me that if del Gardo ever found out about the fellow helping us, well..." Expressively, Jennings drew a finger across his throat. "Wickham was clever, he never told everyone everything. He trusted nobody."

"Weren't so bloody clever when it came to sailin' a ship that had sprung 'er timbers though, was he?" Rogers jibed.

Jennings ignored the remark. "Wickham ensured that different people knew different things, that way, if one was captured and tortured they'll not endanger the entire plan. From our point of view, Chesham is important because he knows where our payment is hidden and what we are owed. With Wickham dead, he will guess we will be sending a replacement courier to make contact with him. I suggested Acorne because he is the best man for the job." Jennings raised a finger, "But it is important he does not learn too much. Jesamiah may be a friend of mine, but I would not trust him further than a gnat can piss. The slightest inkling of what we are owed and we will never see it, or him, again."

They sat in silence, each man mulling the implications. "I had best send word to the *Sea Witch* that Acorne will not be required this afternoon." Rogers said after a while. "The commodore's invited 'imself to run through his orders; be best for the two of 'em not to meet, do y'think? In case Acorne lets somethin' slip?"

Jennings nodded. Any normal Naval officer could have been supplied with drink and kept out of the way. Not Vernon. The only thing to stop him would be to destroy his ship! Why at this precise moment with all the incompetents the British Navy had on its vast payroll, did they have to send their one able commander?

From what Wickham had last implied, the rebellion was on the verge of reaching its head. In a matter of days del Gardo could be overthrown and everything sorted nicely. Had Wickham not drowned he would have fetched their payment, he and Rogers would have been several thousand pounds the richer and none would have been any the wiser of it.

"I'll send Dunwoody with a message then?" Rogers queried.

Again Jennings nodded. He was thinking; a small idea had sparked in his mind to ensure Vernon stayed in harbour a while. He shook his head, no a stupid plan! Forget it! All he needed was a key, a hook, to get Acorne fully interested. He drummed his fingers on the desk. He would think of something, no doubt. "I'll row over to see Acorne myself later."

He lifted his gaze to meet Rogers'. The governor's eyes were a pale grey, set against a face that was beginning to sag with the onset of old age, although he was only in his late fifties. "That flogging yesterday was a bad business. You ought to have stopped it. Acorne might not go along with us now—he might not even be able to, I don't know the extent of the damage done to his back. Your beadle laid the cat on pretty heavy, you know." He did not add the reason: because too many men standing there watching yesterday, the beadle included, were disappointed at being denied the opportunity to ogle a naked woman.

His confidence returning Rogers heaved himself to his feet. "Offer him something in recompense. Gold, an estate or some such."

"And how will we pay it? Until the rebels settle their debt, I barely have a shilling. Aside, all Acorne wants are the divorce papers from van Overstratten."

Looking around for his hat and cane, Rogers found them a-top a cabinet. "And as I have already said, I cannot grant them. He will have to resolve the issue with the Dutchman, not with me."

"He is our only hope of finding Chesham and getting our money."

"Then promise him the moon, and we'll sort payment for him if—when—we get ours."

Jennings rose in protest, then sank down again as pain shouted at him from his foot. "He's a friend, I'll not betray a friend."

"Then ye'd better think of another way to find this Chesham fellow and get our payment, had ye not?"

CHAPTER TWELVE

Leaving his office an hour later, Henry Jennings almost collided with van Overstratten in the outer hallway. Removing his hat he offered a courteous, if somewhat clumsy, bow. "Good day to you. I see from your cloak it be damned raining again?"

Van Overstratten did not respond and noticing his unusual inattentiveness, Jennings took the liberty of guiding him to a chair. "Are you ill? You look most pale. May I summon a physician? Fetch you a glass of something, perhaps?"

"No, no, I am well, thank you. A momentary set back, I assure you."

All the same, Jennings clicked his fingers at a passing maid and bade her run for a brandy. Pulling up a second chair, Jennings seated himself. "This business with Acorne and y'wife, it must be vexing. I know the man; alas, he can be most stubborn."

"As am I, Captain Jennings, but on this occasion the problem is not Acorne."

The maid returned, Jennings took the glass and handed it to the Dutchman with a conspirator's wink. "It's Rogers' finest; he is most reluctant to share it."

Grateful, van Overstratten sipped, appreciating the restorative palette. "This war," he confided, "it could ruin me."

"As it could ruin us all," Jennings agreed wryly. "I b'lieve many have fingers poked into pies that could become overbaked or remain undercooked. Especially if, God forbid, the Dons manage to win."

Blanching, van Overstratten glanced up, horrified. "You do not think they will do you?" He shook his head, puffed his cheeks. Not that it mattered. He had been sold a midden heap and his creditors in London were breathing down his neck for the settlement of outstanding debts—that was the letter he had received, a curt demand for him to sort his financial affairs. If he did not, he could find himself in a debtor's prison.

He had first voiced plans to expand into the Caribbean a year ago, his brother-in-law, a boorish man of minor Dutch nobility and lazy to the bone, had poured scorn on the idea and mocked Stefan's ability to achieve success in a new market. The bastard had also kicked up a stink about Tiola's lack of breeding and status, for one reason only—he did not want any of Stefan's progeny to take precedence over his own expanding pack of mewling brats—two born, another on the way. Stefan's mouth twisted. These months wed to Tiola and no sign of a child. Another gall to rub a sore in van Overstratten's already injured pride: his brother-in-law and sister bred like rabbits.

He sipped the brandy, it was indeed good, but not good enough to quell the disquiet swilling in his gullet. Maybe Jennings possessed useful information? Outside of the family, van Overstratten rarely talked of himself or his business matters for he was a private person, but desperation often had a tendency to tilt judgement into indiscretion.

"Tell me," he asked, "do you know anything of this indigo plantation I recently purchased from Phillipe Mereno? I hear from its steward the place is run down and of little value." To contain his anger and embarrassment he sipped again at the brandy. "Loathe as I am to admit this, Captain Jennings, I believe I have been cheated. Mereno, when he sold it me, gave entirely the wrong impression."

Jennings was no longer feigning polite interest. He had a quick wit and the ability to seize a useful situation when it presented itself. So, Stefan van Overstratten was in an awkward personal situation was he? How interesting. Another reason why he so resented Jesamiah perhaps? Acorne had never made any secret of his wealth, nor that some of it had been gained at van Overstratten's loss. An idea began to worm its way into Jennings' thoughts. One way or another they had to get someone, preferably Acorne, to Hispaniola as soon as possible. Could this Dutchman's predicament be the key?

"Tell me, Master van Overstratten, why in all sanity do you not just sell Acorne your wife? If you asked the price of the entire Spanish Main he would pay it."

The Dutchman regarded him with a look of utter disdain. "And have the world and his wife know I am in financial difficulties? Have Acorne gloating at me? Has he not already publicly shattered my pride, has he not already humiliated me? I will not let him win so easily. He will have to earn my terms, and earn them damned hard!"

Conceding, Jennings returned to the previous line of conversation, steadfastly keeping the leap of excitement from his expression and voice. Here was the lever they needed, by God! If only he could cast the bait and make the fish bite!

Casually, he said, "It is several years since I have been anywhere near Hispaniola. Must have been," he puffed his cheeks, considering, "oh, before Charles Mereno died, more than ten years ago. From what I remember that plantation never carried a healthy bloom, that's why Charles did not bother with it, although it must have a value of some sort because he never sold up."

He tapped the side of his nose, winked. "Indigo can fetch a high price if placed in the right market, if you know what I mean." He paused, thoughts racing. Said slowly, his voice lowered, "I do know some, small, snippet of information about the place however. Mereno—Phillipe Mereno that is—must have told you he had some dye of exceptional quality held in, how shall I say, private, storage there? He went to some length to avoid the duty on it—some sixteen barrels and ninety-seven kegs of high grade indigo as I recall."

His eyes suddenly brightening, van Overstratten's head lifted. "No, he did not. The deceitful rag!" The Dutchman's face twisted with contempt. He might have known! Mereno was no better than Acorne; all the family were pirates. The whole damned lot of them! He knew nothing of any secreted barrels! That slime-riddled bastard had kept their existence to himself, no doubt to remove them without his gullible purchaser finding out. Had not bargained on his younger half-brother getting the better of him by tossing him overboard. God rot his drowned soul!

Jennings hid a smile. Hooked. Now, play the catch slowly, else the line might break. "Mayhap the indigo is no longer there? Mereno may have disposed of it prior to selling you the land. Do not ask me how, for I cannot answer, but I know it was there two months ago. It might be worth your while asking after those barrels, seeing if they can be, er, quietly removed, if you catch my drift? Sixteen barrels and ninety-seven kegs. That is a lot of indigo."

"All I know of the place is what the steward, a señor..." van Overstratten fumbled in his coat pocket with his tobacco-stained fingers, brought out a well-read letter and glanced at the signature. "...A señor Mendez has written me." He tapped the paper, "This made sorry reading." As did the other letter in his pocket, the debt demand from London, but of that, he said nothing.

Jennings only knew of Mendez through Wickham. He had never met him. "This Mendez? He made no mention of the barrels either?" The incredulity sounded convincing.

When van Overstratten shook his head, Jennings appeared to be baffled. "Perhaps he is being cautious? There is no love lost between the plantations and Don Damián del Gardo. Mayhap your steward does not wish this valuable commodity to fall into the wrong hands? All legal trade from Hispaniola carries a heavy tax burden, and this indigo," Jennings spread his hands apologetically, "again, please do not ask questions that I am not at liberty to answer. All I can say is, I have information that this particular indigo was definitely not intended for legal trade."

Digesting Jennings' implications, the glass of brandy in his hand quite forgotten, van Overstratten remained silent. Sixteen barrels and ninety-seven kegs of purest grade indigo waiting for the right moment to be smuggled out of Hispaniola to avoid export tax? The profit on such a lucrative cargo could see him clear of all financial difficulty and leave him some to spare. Indigo was a prize worth having, no wonder it had been hidden away until it was safe to move it!

Henry Jennings shook his head slowly, lifted one hand, let it drop; now to reel in. He sighed deeply. "If it is still there it will have to remain where it is. We are now at war with Spain, it will be impossible to remove it. Only someone who knows those waters and is, how shall I say, willing to take a risk, could fetch it. You are a wealthy man, though, so I suppose a wait will not matter. Mayhap it will be a short war?" He sighed again, shook his head regretfully. "On the other hand, history tells us of the Hundred Years' War. If memory of my history lessons serves me correct, I recall England lost all of France, except Calais, because of those exchanges."

The hope that had been rising in van Overstratten dwindled; he drained his glass in one gulp. He would not be able to get at that indigo whether they be kegs, barrels, hogsheads or sacks. Whether they be six, sixteen, or sixteen-hundred-and-ninety-seven in number.

"War will have closed the waters around Hispaniola to merchants and traders," Jennings muttered again as he took the empty glass and handed it to the discretely hovering maid. "Only smugglers and the Royal Navy will risk going anywhere near there now." Added, keeping his voice casual, "And pirates, of course."

Van Overstratten stood, began to walk towards the door. He needed more air, needed more time to think what to do. Was already regretting confiding his highly embarrassing predicament to Jennings. "Alas," he said, "I am merely a wine merchant and land owner. I am none of those. There is nothing I can do."

Jennings masked a satisfied smile as the Dutchman walked out into the rain, shoulders hunched, head drooping. Hooked and landed!

No, but you know someone who is, he thought. *You know someone who is!*

Chapter Thirteen

Tuesday Afternoon

Pleading. "You do not have to go."

Terse, Jesamiah snapped out an answer. "Tiola. I do have to go."

"You have already shown your manly strength and courage, Jesamiah, there is nothing more for you to prove."

His fingers pressing into her shoulders, Jesamiah moved Tiola aside so he could reach his hat. His coat he had already awkwardly shrugged on, suppressing any outward show of pain, desperately trying to pretend his back did not hurt like all the tortures of hell.

"I am many things, sweetheart," he said. "If it weren't for this amnesty, in most places where a ship can float I'd be wanted for piracy, pilfering, arson, smuggling and murder. Then there's poaching, thievin', general acts of debauchery, drunkenness and the saints alone know what else. But I ain't got the accusation of dishonour among that lot, darlin' and I don't intend to go adding it now."

Tiola sighed. When Jesamiah was in one of his belligerent moods there was never any moving him. She surrendered, helped him buckle on his cutlass, which had been returned to the ship along with his other weapons last evening as Rogers had promised. "Very well, but do not get yourself into a fight with Stefan. And I meant what I said earlier, Jesamiah, if you offer him money I will leave through that door and never come back. I will not be purchased like a sow."

He kissed her cheek. "I am meeting with Rogers, not van Overstratten. And if he does happen to be around I promise I'll smile sweetly, kiss his devil's arse and be as nice as apple pie to him."

Knowing him well Tiola did not believe a word, but held her tongue except to say, "Get your permission to sail and return to the ship, then let us be gone from here." She shuddered, clutched her arms about herself. That damned headache had returned, and she felt so tired, a little nauseous as well. She swallowed bile, concentrated on Jesamiah. "I have an unease here in Nassau which I cannot fully explain."

These headaches, and the debilitating tiredness, were covering her like a consuming fog. All she wanted to do was creep into her bed, curl up like a hedge-pig in winter and go to sleep. She was beginning to realise that she was not well, that there was something wrong—yet there was no illness about her body, no infection or disease. It was as if a cold, wet blanket had been thrown over her; as if all warmth and light had been removed. Maybe it was just this continuous rain grinding her spirit down? She forced the sluggish depression aside, handed Jesamiah his hat.

He looked so handsome; she was proud of him. Did so love him. Ready, Jesamiah opened his cabin door and walked the few short yards along the enclosed corridor. He paused before stepping out into the open; took a breath and clamped his teeth, knowing his back would cause him agony as he ducked beneath the low beams supporting the quarterdeck. It was not so bad. It hurt, but it was not so bad. Tiola's salves were doing their work.

Out on the deck he stopped short. The entire crew were mustered, wearing their best outfits and lined to either side of the entry port where Rue and Isiah Roberts stood, similarly smart clad. Blinking back the brilliant sunlight dazzling his eyes and the sudden threat of engulfing, stupid, tears he stepped forward, Tiola slipping her arm through his.

"Did you know about this?" he whispered. She shook her head, her own emotion overwhelming her. Bless them, bless them! Each and every one of the whoremongers! What better way to show support and loyalty for their captain than by turning out as perfect and orderly, as smart-dressed, as would any Royal Navy crew?

As Jesamiah stepped forward, his hand entwined in hers, the grip tight with choking emotion, one of the men shouted, "Three cheers for Captain Acorne!" And the still afternoon air rippled with their tossed chorus of voices.

"Huzzah! Huzzah! Huzzah!"

Every man respectfully touched his finger to his forehead as Jesamiah and his woman passed by, those few who had served aboard Royal Navy vessels saluting smarter, with more finesse. At the rail, Isiah lifted a whistle to his lips and piped the shrill announcement that a captain was about to disembark.

The final accolade was almost Jesamiah's undoing—the men down in the gig at the foot of the ladder cleats, waiting for him with oars tossed were all dressed in clean white breeches, dark blue jackets and jaunty sailors' hats. From where they had acquired this symmetry of uniform, Jesamiah could only wonder. Guessed the men of one of Rogers' ships would be searching frantically for their missing best clothing come next Sunday.

Stepping down, Jesamiah acknowledged the salute by raising his own hat, seated himself, dignified, in the stern as Rue took the tiller and gave the order to shove off.

"I suppose this was your doing?" Jesamiah said as they slid smoothly away from *Sea Witch*.

Rue peered steadfastly ahead at the quay. "*Moi? Non*, it is nought to do with me, *mon ami*." He nodded back towards the ship. "This was their own idea."

Jesamiah straightened his back, valiantly attempting to ignore the pull of torn flesh and the burning sear of intense discomfort. If they were honouring him with their devotion and respect, the least he could do was make out there was not a single damn thing wrong.

CHAPTER FOURTEEN

Aware of a prevailing atmosphere of unease, Jesamiah walked into the governor's first floor drawing room, removed his hat and offered a semi-formal bow to Rogers and Jennings. His back hurt too much to do anything else. Van Overstratten, to his relief, was not present, but by the full dress regalia of his rank Jesamiah guessed the third occupant to be Edward Vernon. He had asked about the new arrival on the row across, his men only too eager to supply information about HMS *Challenger*, wide-spread knowledge that had swept through the entire town like a dose of the squits.

The commodore stood, hands clasped behind his back, staring determinedly at the view of the harbour beyond the west window. The sword hanging at his side had an elaborate gold hilt and a dangling tassel. Jesamiah mentally snorted annoyance. This peacock was allowed a weapon, he had been forced to leave his in the entrance hall.

Rogers trundled across the room, booming his laughter and a polite welcome, but sweat beaded his forehead and his handshake was limp and sticky. There was something wrong; Jesamiah could smell it as strong as the pungent body odour Rogers exuded.

"Did ye not get me message lad?" Unthinking, Rogers offered a high backed chair, Jesamiah sat on the edge, his shoulders straight. He could feel blood trickling beneath the padding of linen Tiola had bandaged there.

"And what message might that be?" he enquired, not bothering to mask his irritation. "I received no message."

"Did Dunwoody not inform ye?"

"If he had, Governor, then I would not be sitting here asking, would I?"

Quite probably Dunwoody had passed it to someone else, a ne'er-do-well who had been paid for the errand but had made it no further than the nearest tavern or wench's embrace. Dunwoody himself would not have attempted to come anywhere near *Sea Witch* on his own, not even on official business. Any one of Jesamiah's crew would have shot him without question before he came within fifty yards.

At least Governor Rogers had the courtesy of appearing disconcerted. "I sent him over to yer ship this mornin' to tell ye there would be no need to attend here. I'm afraid," he coughed, chortled a false laugh as if this was an amusing jest, "I'm afraid our discussion of yesterday is no longer viable. I'll not be needin' y'services after all, but I thank 'ee fer the offer of assistance and apologise fer y'wasted trip ashore." Rogers waved his hand at Henry Jennings seated on the far side of the room. "Tell 'im would ye?"

Jennings did not deign to hide his annoyance; if Rogers was not careful he could scupper everything. "Have you not heard? We are at war, Acorne. Commodore Vernon here has been posted to the West Indies to see off the Spanish."

Not missing the tone of heavy irony Jesamiah regarded Vernon, raised one eyebrow and said, imitating Rogers' plum English accent, "What? All on y'lonesome? Good luck to ye, sir." For good measure added the irritating laugh. "Ha, ha!"

Then he narrowed his eyes at Rogers, said formidably, his fingers twisting the new blue ribbons laced into his hair; "So if ye've got Vernon to kick del Gardo's arse you'll not be wanting me will 'ee? Good. Give me Tiola's right of divorce and a signed Letter of Marque and I'll bugger off out of your horse-hair wig to harass the Dons in me own way."

"And turn pirate again?" The scorn in Vernon's voice as he slowly turned to stare disapprovingly at Jesamiah was as sharp as his sword. "As I have already advised, Governor, once you grant these degenerates leave to sail, you will be inviting anarchy and insurrection into these waters. I will not permit it. I will not."

Jesamiah had never held respect for officers, British, Spanish, Dutch or French—all were pompous asses, their knowledge learned from books, not experience. Especially the well-dressed ones who oozed wealth and social connection but little else. Know-it-all know-nothings the lot of them. Few understood the conditions here in the Caribbean, both for men and ships. The currents were strong, the shoals and reefs hidden; the hazards many and dangerous. Yet these upstarts dropped anchor with their fancy written commissions and swaggering contempt, bent on wiping the pirates and the Spanish off the surface of the seas. So far none had managed to achieve either. Last year not one pirate had been captured, let alone tried and hanged. In part that was due to the regular backhanders various blind-eyed officials took as their share of plunder. In Jesamiah's strong opinion, not one of them could catch a roped sea-turtle floating upside down on its shell, let alone a vessel of the Sweet Trade bristling with guns.

Naval officers followed the rules, and rules did not apply out here where God had forgotten life existed. The Admiralty did not permit their captains to take the initiative and act as the pirates did, careening as often as possible; nor did they allow provisioning from any available source, legal or illegal. Naval ships had to re-stock their holds at Port Royal, Antigua or, now that Rogers was *in situ*, Nassau. Damn fools. Was it any wonder pirates such as himself, Edward Teach, Charles

Vane, Jack Rackham and all the other reprobates sailed circles around them?

"Why would I be wanting to turn pirate when I have the Dons to chase?" Jesamiah queried, genuinely astonished. "Spanish holds are usually filled with more profitable gain than any English merchantman would ever carry."

"Why? Because you have no honour." Vernon spoke to Jesamiah with contempt. Like dogs circling for possession of a discovered bone the two men were sizing each other up, hackles raised. "You are an ignorant brute with no concept of duty. You are a drunkard, a murderer and a thief. You will not have the intelligence to disregard your lust for English traders who would fall easy prey to your guns and your swaggering insolence."

Rubbing his hands along his breeches, Jesamiah noticed the left knee was stained; it looked like blood. From yesterday probably. He got to his feet, put his hat on, grinned, confirming the accusation of insolence. "Compliments I can take by the bucket-load Commodore, but you missed out the important ones of liar, smuggler and whoremonger."

Vernon ignored the jibe. "I am here to fight the Spanish; to do so, I have orders to requisition whatever I need." He walked over, stood in front of Jesamiah, one hand resting casually on his sword hilt. "I need to ensure that while I am engaged with the Dons, the scum I leave behind in these waters does not rise to the surface. I do not wish to be chasing renegades while my attention must be on this war. Therefore, Acorne, without my, or Rogers' express permission, no pirate vessel will leave this harbour."

"You'll have a hard job enforcing that, 'specially once you've sailed."

Vernon smiled. "Not if I have ensured there is no scum left to float. I need men, I need ships. The debris of humanity will serve under my command. I shall expect the best of these lazy scoundrels to take the king's shilling and then make my choice of which ships are most suited to expand my fleet."

Jesamiah stared at him, then at Rogers and Henry Jennings; back to Vernon. "And you have the fokken gall to call me a pirate?" He stepped closer to Vernon, jabbed beneath the gold braid on his shoulder with one finger, poking three times. "Pressing men of the colonies is illegal. By British law we are exempt from arse-paddling to George's navy. If you come within a cat's whisker of my crew or my ship, mate, you'll find yourself in need of nothin' more than a winding sheet."

Patting the air with his hands Rogers stepped closer, hastily interjected, "Now, now I'll have no seditious talk here!"

Jesamiah rounded on him, "So give me my woman's freedom, then get out of my way and out of my life."

At a loss of what more to say or do, his eyes pleading to be understood, Rogers shook his head. "You must realise it is out of my hands. We are at war, I cannot be dealing with a trivial matter of divorce."

Furious, disgusted—disappointed—Jesamiah did not wait to hear more excuses. "And I had you for an honest man? Well, to hell with you. All of you!" He spun on his heel and stormed from the room, slamming the door behind him.

Rogers sighed. Pirates? Why had he elected to put himself among a host of bloody-minded, volatile pirates? "Go after him, Henry," he pleaded. "Explain the situation as best y'can, eh?"

"Yes, do," Vernon snapped. "Tell him those who hinder the implementation of my orders shall hang as traitors. Colonial pirates especially."

CHAPTER FIFTEEN

"Captain Acorne? Jesamiah! Heave to there man!" Henry Jennings called as he hurried at a shambling hobble down the stairs. To get attention he banged the stair rail with his walking cane. "Jes lad, please! Listen to me!"

"Bugger off Jennings. I have no intention of having my ear bent to more of your lies and broken promises. I'm weighing anchor. Getting out of here."

Puffing for breath, his gout becoming more inflamed and wracking him with pain, Jennings caught up, grabbed his arm and swung him around. "Without a Letter of Marque and permission you'll have Vernon on your heels, eager to hang you as an example to other rogues. Is that what you want? And what of Tiola? Your crew? If they sail with you they will be subject to the same fate. Think man, think!"

"He will have to bloody catch me first!" Jesamiah snapped, attempting to shake off Jennings' grip and closing his mind to the possibility that Tiola might do as she threatened and refuse to sail with him. "None of his kind has succeeded so far."

"Because none of them know their arse from their elbow. Vernon, however, does." Jennings gave Jesamiah's arm another shake. "He is different. He knows what he is doing and is one of the rare few who do not always play by the rules."

Standing there at the foot of the stairs Jesamiah sighed wearily. He was tired, his back hurt and he did not want to run away. All he wanted was to be able to take Tiola as his legal wife and live in peace somewhere, it was why he had agreed not to run in the first place.

Steering Jesamiah to his cluttered office Jennings ushered him to a seat, from a cabinet produced his own bottle of French brandy and two crystal glasses.

"With this damned gout I ought not be drinking this stuff." Nevertheless, he poured a generous measure for both of them. "Listen Jes. Rogers could not speak openly in front of Vernon, he'd find himself in deep shite if he did. Most of our plans were, well, how shall I say? Unauthorised? You may not be aware, but Rogers financed the idea of this amnesty himself, convinced it was the way to preserve profitable trade in these waters. I happen to agree with him, which is why he has my support. Add to that, he is anxious to recoup a few financial losses and gain the political respect he deserves. Both of which he could have achieved by presenting King and Parliament with the colony of Hispaniola." He shrugged, resigned. "Unfortunately, the usually highly incompetent Royal Navy has arrived in the form of the very competent Commodore Edward Vernon who will now do the honours and claim the kudos." Jennings sipped his brandy as he settled himself deeper into the comfort of a leather chair. This office, although small and untidy was his personal kingdom, a treasured sanctuary where he could do as he pleased and, in his imagination at least, be answerable to no one.

"I too want something, Jesamiah. I am no longer a young man. Aye, the fortune I've amassed should have served me well into my dotage, but a knighthood and a country estate in Suffolk would not go amiss."

"You want the dream, Henry, you chase it."

Setting his glass down Jennings shuffled through his papers, pushed a folded oblong of parchment towards Jesamiah. "Your Letter of Marque."

Jesamiah picked it up, read it and tossed it back on to the table. "It says here I agree to accept a King's Commission. That means I'll be under Vernon's orders. Forget it."

"There is no other way you will be able to leave this harbour." Jennings savoured more of the brandy, fixed his companion with a smile that was part friendship, part pleading. "We still want you to go to Hispaniola, only now there is the extra task of doing so without Vernon knowing about it. Accept a legal commission, sail out of here and slip quietly over to Santo Domingo; find Chesham for us. Please."

Jesamiah thumped the table with his fist. "I weren't born yesterday Henry! You're jumpy because you and Rogers are on the edge of losing all chance of filling your pockets with an easy profit!" He thumped the table again, harder, shouted, "I don't want to fight for the bloody king, don't give a damn about rebellion, lost spies or free trade. All I want is my woman!"

Jennings took a deep breath, calmed himself, knew better than to shout back. "If you help us we'll give you a quarter share of the first year's trade profit."

"I don't want your quarter shares, I already have more money than I know what to do with. Get van Overstratten to grant Tiola a divorce. That is my price. Can you pay it?"

Jennings realised the irony. The only thing Jesamiah wanted was Tiola, the one thing van Overstratten needed was money. He was on the verge of telling Jesamiah of the Dutchman's financial predicament but stopped himself. Van Overstratten would never take Jesamiah's money because he would never admit his problems to him. The stupidity of proud men!

"Then I suggest you get down on your knees and beg for the Dutchman's co-operation, beg him enough, he might agree."

Cramming his hat on his head, Jesamiah walked grim-faced towards the door.

"Won't need to. I've decided to shoot the bastard and have done with it."

CHAPTER SIXTEEN

Taking his time, walking slowly, Jesamiah wandered along George Street, heading downhill towards the harbour. Rogers had already started making his mark on the town, at least in this, the wealthiest area. The streets here were not so rubbish-strewn and the pigs had been removed from inside the church, although their stink lingered. One or two of the buildings were even being repaired and repainted. The church clock struck, cracked and late as usual. Jesamiah half smiled; ah well, perhaps some of the governor's ideas for improving Nassau would take longer than others to complete. The clock apparently sat at the bottom of his list.

He could see *Sea Witch* dozing at her anchor, tugging gently on the fore and aft cables as the lively wind scurried across the water. She was so beautiful. Her dark-blue hull, her three masts, square rigged sails furled, neatly trimmed. Her brass gleaming, rails varnished. She was stern-to; Tiola had the middle window open, was probably sitting sewing on the locker bench; he fancied he could hear her singing. Tiola had a beautiful voice, an exact pitch. Her songs, especially her favourite folk ballads and one or two laments, heart-achingly haunted the mind. Tiola was beautiful also. He did not want to lose her or his ship, ever. But if there was a choice, *Sea Witch* or Tiola? Jesamiah stopped walking, turned his collar up against another squall of rain and thrust his hands deep into the voluminous pockets of his long coat.

If he had to choose? He had once, it seemed years ago, chosen *Sea Witch* over Tiola. He had expected her to join him aboard; it was not his fault she had been prevented from doing so, except, except...he had chosen his ship not his woman, and he had nearly—very nearly—lost Tiola because of it. He did not want to risk doing so again. But without the *Sea Witch* what would, could, he do with his life? There were always other ships; he had the money to buy several, to set up his own merchant business if he wanted, but he was as one with *Sea Witch*, they were partners, wedded and bonded. She was wife, mistress, lover, whore. She was his damn it! Both of them were his!

"Bugger!" he murmured as he realised he had left that Letter of Marque on Jennings' desk, for although he refused it in principle he had intended to pocket it, just in case. He turned around, took a few paces back up the hill, halted, and stood, considering. Why did he need it? If he was to start up as a merchant of some sort he would be free to come and go where and when he pleased. He was not beholden to Rogers and Vernon or the king, none of them. As long as he stuck to what was legal they could not touch him. He kicked at a stone. Could they? For himself he did not care, but he had Tiola and his men to take into account. If there was an embargo on vessels leaving, he would have to get that letter first.

"Sod it, I'll sort it tomorrow, I ain't walking all the way up there again now." Decision made, he ambled on down the hill wondering whether he might call in somewhere for a quick tot of rum. Normally he would pay for a whore too, but his back was agony and he didn't need tavern wenches now he had Tiola. He sniffed, wiped beneath his nose with the back of his hand then scratched briefly at his crotch. Or did he? A quick poke at a whore was hardly betrayal was it? Tiola he loved, whores were...? He chewed his lip, considering. Whores were available, like pots to piss in. A nibble at a pasty did not stop him enjoying his full dinner did it? Dipping his wick was hardly comparable to the pleasure of making love. And what of those days when Tiola was indisposed? Her flux, or when she was away birthing a babe or tending the dying? Was he supposed to sit and whistle, or something?

By the time he had reached the bottom of the hill he had convinced himself that whores were there for the convenience of those who could afford them, and that it would be a shame to waste a provided pleasure. All the same, he decided that perhaps it would be best not to share his conclusion with Tiola.

Stefan van Overstratten sat in the window of the King's Head sipping quality wine, his legs stretched before him, eyes narrowed as he watched Acorne wander down the hill. How unkempt the thieving bastard looked with his shoulder-length hair matted by the wind and rain, his unbuttoned coat, old and faded, boots worn and cracked. Shaking his head dismissively the Dutchman returned to re-reading the letter in his hand. No matter how many times he read it the words did not alter. He sat, pondering, the worrying thoughts revolving around in his mind. If he did not settle those heavy gambling debts he had accrued in London when he was last there he would be charged as a debtor. And now these ill-judged investments he had made. The profit from those was supposed to have paid off the debts.

What had he to sell? The estates, the house, the wine business? None of it was solely his; the business was a family affair with most of the assets entailed. All he owned for himself was the vessel he had sailed here on and this wretched indigo plantation on Hispaniola. He retrieved the second letter from his pocket, the inventory sent to him by the steward of the place. Inventory? It was more like an obituary, and there had been no mention of any indigo. It would be worth a fine price. Since few knew about its existence he could sell it, pay off what he owed to several people and no one in the family would be any the wiser. The idea appealed. He was not, under any circumstances, going to let that pig-arrogant brother-in-law gloat over his misfortune. He was not!

Stefan glanced up the street, glowered at Jesamiah. This voyage to Nassau was meant to have been his honeymoon. Not that the family would object to him returning home wife-less, but oh, the I-told-you-so's he would have to endure! He returned the letters to his pocket. Unless he could get to Santo Domingo he had no way of salvaging his pride. Perhaps he ought to sell Acorne Tiola's divorce? He could ask several thousand pounds sterling—more maybe. But would Acorne then guess how desperately he needed it? He glanced out of the window as another rainsquall clattered against the thick glass, thoughtfully massaged his clean-shaven jaw. I wonder. Sixteen barrels and ninety-seven kegs. No one would be any the wiser about anything if he had that indigo, he mused. Said aloud, "I bloody wonder?" He stood, strolled to the shelter of the entrance porch.

"You look as if you have lost a ship and found a wreck, Acorne."

The Dutchman's voice, coming unexpectedly from the doorway of the tavern startled Jesamiah from his reverie. Automatically his hand bolted for his pistol, pulled the gun from his waist sash, half-cocked it and aimed.

"How fortuitous, you've saved me the bother of searching for you. I told Jennings I was going to solve my dilemma by shooting you. Give me one good reason why I should not."

Emerging from the shadows Stefan stopped four paces ahead of Jesamiah, gestured simply with his hand. "One? That is not difficult. My wife." He smiled, more of a leer than a smile, remembered what Jesamiah had said at the governor's table. "Tee-oh-la," he drawled. His smile broadened into a smirk. A small score, but he could see he had annoyed Acorne. In truth he had been totally unaware that he had not been pronouncing her name correctly, she had never mentioned it. He had always said it that way, right from when he had first met her in Cape Town.

For half a minute Jesamiah, seething hatred, stared at the Dutchman, his thumb clicked the hammer full home, his finger pressed harder on the trigger and at the last moment as the flint fired, he jerked the weapon away and aimed the barrel upwards, the ball spinning harmlessly into the air.

"Sensible," van Overstratten responded. "I suggest you remain so and join me for a drink."

"I have no intention of drinking with you, you bastard."

"Not even to listen to a proposition? You surprise me." The Dutchman retreated inside the tavern, resumed his seat at the window table, called for his wine to be refilled and rum to be brought.

Tempted to snub him, Jesamiah almost walked away but he needed a drink, and if this proposition concerned Tiola, as undoubtedly it did, perhaps he ought to listen? Kicking the tavern door open, he sat down opposite van Overstratten and ostentatiously reloading his pistol he laid it on the table before touching the rum.

"So what pile of steaming bull's shit are you offering me?"

Stefan clicked his fingers, called the pot boy over again. "What form of weevil-riddled food do you serve here, boy?"

"We do stew sir. Good stew, full o' suet dumplin's it is. Gravy's made wiv best ale."

"The dumplings are sawdust and gristle. The gravy is made from ale dregs and ground rats' turds," Jesamiah corrected. "Should be suitable for you, Dutchman. Matches your personality exactly."

Fastidiously, the Dutchman waved the boy away, to Jesamiah said, "The wine, however, is excellent. It is one of my own, of course; most of the taverns in this pigs' byre of a town take it." He sipped, swallowed, added, "In fact, I think all of them do."

"And not by choice, I don't suppose."

Stefan raised his glass in confirming salute, drank, set the empty glass down and brushed fluff from his waistcoat; took a thin silver case from his pocket, removed a cheroot, lit it. "I'll come to the point. You want my wife."

Jesamiah did not deign to answer.

"How much are you prepared to pay?" Stefan blew a perfect smoke ring.

"I told you. You can have *Sea Witch*."

Pedantic, van Overstratten answered, "And I told you, I do not want my ship back, it is pirate soiled."

To hold his temper in check, to stop himself picking up his pistol and firing it, Jesamiah looked out at the drizzling rain. There was that woman again, on the other side of the street standing in the open, her bluish-grey gown sodden, raindrops dripping from the hood pulled low so that he could not see her face. The sun was breaking through the cloud, arcing in a triple rainbow. It glinted on something at the woman's neck, the flash of a single rare diamond cut as a teardrop. Jesamiah's eyes were drawn to her ample cleavage, back to the necklace.

Not a teardrop, a raindrop, he thought.

"What is your price, Dutchman? You obviously have one, else you'd not be buying me rum in one of Nassau's less wholesome taverns," Jesamiah said with a resigned sigh. He could not buy her, nor could he shoot van Overstratten. Tiola would never forgive him an act of cold-blooded murder no more than she would him buying her. "I assume it is something illegal or dangerous. Too dangerous for you to piss your breeches over?" It had to be. Why else this sudden change of attitude? He leered a mocking grin. "Something to do with this war with Spain by any chance?"

When first he had met him, Stefan van Overstratten had dismissed Jesamiah as a fool and a lazy good-for-nothing wastrel, but that was before he had realised the apparently harmless buffoon was wily and sharp-brained. And a pirate. Good-for-nothing and wastrel still applied, but not lazy, and certainly not a fool. Taking his time, one leg neatly crossed over the other at the knee, van Overstratten studied the man sitting before him, noted he was perched stiffly upright on the edge of the chair. Had to admit, grudgingly to himself, that despite the loathing he felt for this sea-wretch, he had courage. Or if it was not courage, the insolence of bravado. And it was bravado, and insolence, that he was in desperate need of.

Van Overstratten did not possess courage, he made use of people to his own advantage. If he wanted something, or someone to do his bidding, he always got his way. Always. It was how he had persuaded Tiola to consent to marriage, by being charming, caring and persuasive; by preying on her vulnerability and wearing down what was left of her spirit. No one said 'no' to Stefan van Overstratten. Rarely, very rarely, did he regret his successes. Winning Tiola Oldstagh was one of those more annoying exceptions. Were it not for his pride, and his determination to not be made a fool of by this upstart knave, he would have been glad to be rid of her.

"I find I am in an awkward position. This war, as you rightly assessed, has disrupted my plans. How would you seafarers put it? Scuppered me."

Finishing his rum, Jesamiah put the tankard on the table. His expression neutral, said; "My heart bleeds for you."

Irritated, van Overstratten clicked his fingers for more wine, another rum. One more sarcastic remark and he would forget this ridiculous idea, get up and walk out. Then what would Acorne do? He certainly would not be getting Tiola! "I deal mainly in wine. As a subsidiary to my vineyards I trade in sugar, and more recently, tobacco. I have also, of late, made an investment into indigo."

Jesamiah stared out through the rain-wet window, reached forward to wipe away the condensation misting the glass. The woman was gone, the rain had ceased and bright sun was dazzling everything as if someone had scattered handfuls of jewels everywhere.

If she's a whore, how come she has such a valuable necklace? he wondered.

He fished a few pieces of silver from his pocket, paid for the drinks, was damned if he would be beholden to this Dutchman. The tobacco deal, he knew, had been made with Phillipe Mereno, his half-brother; a partial deal. The other part had been connected with the kidnap and torture of himself. For their individual reasons both men had wanted Jesamiah dead. Van Overstratten manipulated people, wanted, always, to get his own way, but he was not the sadistic bully Phillipe had been. Although, thinking back... He rubbed his hand along his ribs, some of the vicious kicking had come from this Dutchman's foot. Jesamiah mentally shook his head. No, that had been false bravado, egged on by Phillipe's boundless cruelties. Van Overstratten would never have initiated outright brutality. Mind, he had made no attempt to stop it, either. Jesamiah snorted. Van Overstratten was a man well capable of turning the proverbial blind eye when it suited him. He sipped his rum. "Indigo eh? Expensive."

"Very. And I have sixteen barrels and ninety-seven kegs of it awaiting a suitable sale. The expected profit should double my outlay."

Making an astute guess, Jesamiah grinned nastily. "I take it this indigo is in Hispaniola?" The grin altered to an outright guffaw. "Unless you can get at it, your investment is worthless!"

The Dutchman ignored Jesamiah's cackle of delight, he was playing a delicate game here and he was making each move with careful consideration. "My cargo is awaiting collection in a plantation warehouse a few miles along the coast from Santo Domingo."

Realising where the conversation was leading Jesamiah lost the grin. "You want me to take you there? To risk my ship and my balls to smuggle you in and out again for blue dye indigo? Forget it."

Van Overstratten's expression remained passive. He took another long inhalation of his cheroot, slowly exhaled the aromatic smoke. "On the contrary, I have no intention of going anywhere near the place. However, as I understand matters, you will be in the vicinity, you can, therefore, collect it for me."

Jesamiah leant forward slightly. "Dunwoody's sailin' under the wrong canvas, Master Dutchman. I take it you did get the tattle from that little shite? He is misinformed. I ain't goin' to Hispaniola."

Dropping the butt of his cheroot to the floor Stefan hid his anger. He disliked being gainsaid. More, disliked being misled. Dunwoody would be giving back those gold pieces that had been slipped into his pocket this morning. The Dutchman stood, ground the butt out with his heel. "I thought you were seeking to buy my wife's divorce, Acorne. I have obviously assumed wrong, you do not want her. Will you inform her of this, or shall I? Good day to you." He retrieved his hat from the table, began to leave.

"All right damn you, sit down," Jesamiah cursed. He had no intention of going to Hispaniola for Rogers, Jennings or van Overstratten, but that was no reason to not listen.

Condescending to take his seat again van Overstratten regarded Jesamiah coldly. "Had I not been," he paused, cleared his throat, "hrrmph, distracted, my business deals in London would have been completed by now. From a letter I received this morning, however, I discovered affairs must be concluded no later then the fifth day of November. It will soon be October. It will take a minimum of five weeks for you to sail the Atlantic with those indigo barrels."

"Fifth of November? You sure it's indigo not gunpowder?" Jesamiah drawled facetiously.

Van Overstratten growled his annoyance. "By God, how have you managed to stay alive? Do you take nothing seriously? The ship you have re-named *Sea Witch* is fast. She is a splendid vessel, which is why, of course, you stole her. I begrudge to admit it but you are a good sailor. You know how to quietly retrieve my cargo without people noticing, and you can get it to London and sell it."

Jesamiah tucked his pistol through his belt, wincing as his back suddenly caught him. "I don't want to go to London. And as I told you, I ain't goin' to La Española."

"Oh, but you are, Captain Acorne. I do not care how you manage it, but if you want me to divorce my wife you will have to give me something I want in return. I want that indigo. You will tell the plantation overseer that you have come for those ninety-seven kegs and sixteen barrels of indigo that are in storage." He stood, buttoned his coat, set his hat to his head. "I will draft you a letter to my clerk in London. In it I will write instructions that upon delivery of the indigo he is to provide you with a letter of annulment. The lady in question is barren, that is sufficient grounds. When you have that, you may collect her and do what you wish with her. She will await you in Cape Town. I have no desire to remain here over long."

"That's one heck of a bloody run-around! You're talking eight or nine months at least!"

Van Overstratten walked behind Jesamiah, gripped one of his shoulders and leant in close. "That, Acorne, is the deal.

It is non-negotiable. The quicker you leave, the quicker you will get the woman to yourself."

He straightened, slapped his hand, hard, between the shoulder blades. Jesamiah did not bother suppressing the sharp intake of breath or the grimace of pain. What was the point? Van Overstratten had known it would hurt, that was why he had done it.

"And hope, Acorne, that she don't uncross her legs long enough for me t'get her with child. Eight or nine months eh? She could have a fat belly by the time you next see her, in which case, the deal will be off until the child is born. Unless it is a girl brat. I need sons."

Gritting his teeth, fists clenched, both to fight down the swirl of nausea and the impulse to ram his knuckles into the bastard's mouth, Jesamiah stood. "Give me an excuse to kill you, just one little excuse, van Overstratten, that's all I need. If you think I am going to trade Tiola for a few barrels of stinking indigo, then you'd better think again. With or without a divorce she's mine, so you'd best get used to the fact. You ain't touchin' 'er ever again—get your own bloody indigo."

He stamped outside, letting the door slam behind him, angry. Angry with van Overstratten, with Tiola, with himself. Mostly with himself. He could have got that indigo. Could have walked back up this hill, asked Jennings for that Letter of Marque and slipped out of harbour. He had smuggled enough contraband in the past to know exactly how to do it. But he was buggered if he was going to dance a jig to this butter bag's piped tune! Aside, though he would never admit it, Hispaniola and its governor, del Gardo, frightened him.

The last time he had been there was four years ago. He had been aboard the *Mermaid* serving as crew with Malachias Taylor. A good friend, a good teacher. From him, Jesamiah had learnt all he knew of piracy. The memories flooded back. That had been before they had sailed for

Africa, before they had dropped anchor in Cape Town harbour and he had met with a dark haired girl called Tiola Oldstagh. A few months after that, Taylor had been hanged in Port Royal. They had both, so very nearly, died in Santo Domingo.

Jesamiah swallowed hard, that particular bad memory swarming to the fore and sending a cold shiver down his spine. There would be no lucky escape from a Spanish torture chamber a second time. He stopped walking, leant his hands against the harbour wall and was promptly sick, vomiting up the contents of his stomach into the sea below.

He had seen the inside of that gaol once, the inside of the room next to it. He vomited again. Once had been enough. Even for Tiola's freedom, once had been more than enough.

CHAPTER SEVENTEEN

Van Overstratten reseated himself, finished the wine. It had been a ridiculous idea anyway, asking that murdering thief for help. What had he been thinking? He sighed, ordered more wine. Angrily, he hit the tabletop with his clenched fist. Damn it, damn it! How could he coerce Acorne into getting that indigo for him?

Another twenty minutes. Late afternoon sun was sending the grey clouds scudding into the distance. Tossing a handful of small coins on to the table the Dutchman gathered his things: hat, coat, walking cane, and went out into the street. Everything smelt clean and fresh-washed; damp earth, the saline tang of the sea. The aromatic smell of fruit and coconuts and the heady perfume of exotic flowers.

"Good afternoon to you, van Overstratten, it is pleasant out now the rain has ceased, though this wind has a chill to it."

The Dutchman spun around to find Commodore Vernon approaching. He disliked navy people. Too many of them wanted to pry into his business affairs—not that he was dishonest, but no merchant paid tax when it was avoidable, and the navy was too closely affiliated to the excise men. He smiled politely, touched his hat.

"The wind scurries rather maliciously around the edge of the fort, I have discovered," Vernon added.

111

Van Overstratten made no comment, thought, *What is it with the English and their damned interest in always discussing the weather?*

Commodore Vernon indicated *Sea Witch*. "I did not realise that by right she is your vessel. In your shoes I would be grieved to have lost such a fine ship."

"Grieved I am, Commodore, but Governor Rogers decreed there would be no repercussions for those who accepted his offer of amnesty, the terms were unconditional. Which meant those of us who lost valuables—in whatever form—to these pirate dogs will never have them returned, nor shall we see compensation. All we have is the dubious pleasure of observing a man like Acorne openly committing debauchery with our womenfolk."

A little embarrassed, Vernon cleared his throat. "With your wife in particular, I hear?"

Van Overstratten made no immediate answer, watched with mild curiosity as a man hurried along the jetty from the direction of the shanty huts, unhitched a boat and began rowing as if the devil were after him.

"You hear correct Commodore." Van Overstratten chuckled cynically. "Would it have been Dunwoody who informed you, by chance?"

Vernon inclined his head. "It would. Is his information not reliable then?"

The Dutchman's chuckle became a full laugh. "I believe reliability depends on the value of the coin offered to him as suitable payment."

The man in the boat was heading for *Sea Witch*.

Vernon stared across the harbour at her. She was a fine, fine, ship, better than any he had commanded. Quickly he asked, "Forgive me for prying into your affairs, sir, but why do you allow Acorne to so taunt you? Why do you not merely shoot him?"

Indignantly pulling himself to his full height of five feet nine inches, van Overstratten retorted; "Would you have me a murderer? Would you take me down to his low level of depravity? I am a God-fearing man. I do not condone breaking the Commandments. 'Thou shalt not kill'."

"Then why do you not punish him in a way it would hurt far more than a flogging? A captain, though I doubt the legitimacy of the title for the rogue, would never willingly part with his ship. Take it back, take it off him."

The Dutchman tapped the cobbles fastidiously with his cane. "I do not want it, the thing is fouled. She has the stink of baseness about her." She was actually a company ship and belonged to the business. Selling her would make him no profit at all and would alert the family to his predicament. "Aside, I want something else from Acorne." Thought; *Who will get my indigo if he does not?*

I would have her, Vernon was thinking, his gaze coveting her clean, sleek lines. *I could sail rings around the Spanish with a ship like that.*

The man in the bumboat was holding on to *Sea Witch*'s ladder cleats, shouting up to someone on deck. There was a long pause, then a woman was descending, settling herself in the stern. The man had pushed off before she had barely seated herself. Tiola. The reason was plain. A woman's high-pitched shrieking had been splitting the air this past half-hour, and there had been a lot of coming and going from the third shack along the beach. Women's business was bringing Tiola ashore.

Touching his hat Vernon began to walk away, but halted, watching the approaching boat. "A word to a wise ear. Stay within doors after dark tonight. Nassau may become a little," he cleared his throat with a resounding *hrrmph*, "how do I put this delicately? Restless?" Added, "I am assuming, from what I hear tell, that be y'wife?"

Van Overstratten nodded.

"Should she be delayed," Vernon continued, "I would advise you to keep her out of harm's way." He touched his hat again and strode off, his seaman's gait rolling in his long legged stride.

Watching Tiola hurry to the shack the Dutchman considered matters. An hour, two, until dusk? What had Vernon got up his sleeve? With England at war, navy ships in harbour and insufficient crew to man them he had a shrewd idea. William Dunwoody would know for certain. And that slime-toad of a man owed a favour or two.

CHAPTER EIGHTEEN

TUESDAY EVENING

"Damn fine bit of beef that was," Finch grumbled in his usual curmudgeonly manner as he cleared Jesamiah's barely touched plate from the table. "You moping; Miss Tiola ashore an' not 'ere to eat. Ain't much point you 'avin a personal steward to do the cookin' an' such if you ain't p'ticlar t'take notice of what I does fer 'ee is there?"

Finch always grumbled. The crew maintained he would find something to complain about in Heaven if he managed, against all odds, to end up there.

Jesamiah ignored him. "I'll just have coffee on the quarterdeck."

"As long as yer bleedin' drink it, an' don't leave it t'get stone cold like you usually do."

One shoulder hunched to ease the throb of pain, Jesamiah took the steps of the companionway ladder one at a time. There was more rain in the air. Usually, by mid-September, the rainy season had ceased. Providing the weather did not bring any hurricanes rampaging over the horizon, who cared? He leant his elbows on the taffrail, stood staring at the town. The waterfront was lit by dozens of lanterns and pitch torches, their light spilling from the doors and windows of taverns and brothels. The beach, too, was ablaze with the flare from dozens of bonfires. Those who could afford a roof over their heads and a decent bed, paid for comfort; the rest lived along the shore in tents and shacks fashioned from salvaged canvas and driftwood, held together by hope and a prayer.

He heard a woman's high-pitched laugh; a man's indistinct, drunken shout. The ever-present slap and thud of the sea against *Sea Witch's* hull. Another woman's scream; a long wail of terror that seared louder then stopped abruptly. She had been screaming for two hours now, the sound of a woman in labour and having a hard time of it. Tiola was with her, trying her best to save mother and unborn child. A difficult birth, with one arm caught behind the head, so Tiola had said.

~ *I cannot ease him through the birth canal, I will have to amputate the arm while he is in the womb. He will die, probably the mother also.* ~

Nasty.

Sometimes, Jesamiah wondered why she bothered. Many of the unwanted brats birthed by the whores were dead before they learnt to toddle, and some of the women were probably better off to slip away from the miserable life they endured. Whores were rarely treated well. Used, abused; no whore could ever cry rape even though not all sexual gratification was given by consent. The girls—aye, the boys too—were obliged to please, in whatever way their clients dictated. Several, good at their job, were without front teeth, deliberately removed by their madams and pimps to be the better accommodating when it was by mouth. And most of them, those who were not malnourished, without the pox or internally damaged, were continuously breeding. Birth one child and another would be on the way almost immediately, unless she tried getting rid of it, which usually ended in the same result. The agony of a lingering death.

Jesamiah snorted, mentally shrugged. At least the molly-boys did not have that disadvantage to contend with, although their shared pleasures were illegal and carried the penalty of hanging if they were caught. Personally, he could not see anything wrong with one man preferring another, but he could not understand a man not being interested in the many delights of a woman's body, either.

He occasionally felt guilty about using the street pullets, but then the poor girls had to make a living somehow; and what else was a fellow to do when he had an urge to spend a few shillings on easing a personal need? At least he paid them fairly, and took pride in his prowess in bed. It wasn't just Tiola he treated with respect, he left no whore dissatisfied, either in her purse or her nether regions.

Tiola would be tired and upset when she finally came home. In no mood to discuss her divorce and their predicament, and he was hurting too much, inside and out, to comfort her in the only way he knew; intimately in bed. There again, perhaps a bottle of rum would be a suitable painkiller and he could then rise to the occasion? He smiled to himself at the thought of making love to her as Finch sourly handed him a cup of black, sweet, coffee.

"Bloody 'eads need swillin' out again, Cap'n. They fair stink of piss and shit."

"You know, Finch," Jesamiah responded dryly, his mildly stirring erection instantly collapsing. "You have a wonderful turn of phrase. I ought to suggest you to Tiola, she could make use of you as one of her more efficient contraceptive devices."

Not understanding, Finch shuffled off to his galley where he clipped the ear of his boy helper and wondered what the captain had been on about. Contrary-septic? Sounded nasty. He would perhaps ask Jansy what it meant.

Some of the crew were below, engrossed in the many pastimes that whiled away a sailor's rest hours. Most of them had no money left for women or drinking, having spent the lot already. The London and Boston newssheets occasionally speculated on where Captain William Kidd had buried his looted treasure before he was captured and hanged; Jesamiah always laughed at such nonsense. He'd never yet met a pirate who had bothered to lug a heavy chest of gold to some remote island and bury it. Plunder was distributed fairly in equal shares, and usually fell straight through a pirate's fingers like poured water.

A crow of laughter spiralled up from the open hatchway. Ah, someone had won a few more pennies to spend. Out at sea Jesamiah would not permit gambling for money, it led to too many petty jealousies and major fights. He did not stop the games, but the stakes were wooden buttons or tally sticks. They could sort out who owed what to whom at the end of each voyage. Sensible rules that were followed on most pirate ships; the Pirate Code as written down in the Articles which every man signed as they joined a crew. In harbour, however, as long as nothing compromised the safety of the ship, each man was his own responsibility, could come and go, do, what and as he chose.

Jesamiah's mind wandered to the woman in grey who had stood in the rain watching him. She had been watching him, he was certain. Who was she? He thrust aside the thought that if he did not have Tiola he would have approached her, maybe offered a few gold coins for a night of pleasure. Damn it, what was the matter with him? Had his brains dropped into his breeches or something? Where was Finch with his verbal cold water when it was needed?

Thrusting erotic, guilty, thoughts aside, Jesamiah settled his chin in his hand. What was he to do? What in all hell's bits could he do?

Domingo, the main port and town of Spanish Hispaniola. He groaned, rested his forehead on his arms. He could not go back there, not without a watertight, firm-tied reason. As appointed lick-spit to the British Government he might have got away with it, anything else, he would be dangling from a gibbet without his privy package within ten minutes of stepping ashore. Damn it—why should he be feeling bad about turning van Overstratten down? He could go swing for all Jesamiah cared! Yet... yet, if this was the only way, beyond shooting him, of ensuring Tiola's freedom? He sighed again. It would be so much easier to kill the bastard but Tiola would know and would despise him for it.

Another scream made his head shoot up. That was no woman in labour, that was a man's shout of terror! A line of lanterns and torches were bobbing along the jetty; he crossed the deck, took the telescope from where it always rested beside the compass in the binnacle box. Vernon's men? If they were on the prowl at night it could be for one of two reasons: to arrest pirates—which, considering everyone here in Nassau was under an amnesty of pardon was not likely—or to press men into service.

"Rue!" All melancholy and sexual desire abandoned, Jesamiah leapt down the ladder, ran to the half-closed hatch cover and kicked it open, bellowed again for his second in command. "Rue! How many of our men are down there?"

A few moments later the swarthy Frenchman's head appeared, red-cheeked, smiling, the smell of brandy strong on his breath. "About fifty, *mon ami. Pourquoi?*"

"The press may be out."

Five little words, huge enough to stifle Rue's merriment and to spread unease through the entire below-deck world. Many of Jesamiah's men had served in the British Navy, had jumped ship and deserted to follow the Sweet Trade of a pirate. The life was often shorter but less harsh, was a life of free choice and self-decision. Most of those same men had been pressed in the first place—taken by force, usually while drunk; snatched from families and sweethearts, treated brutally and forced to serve at sea. Those who had escaped and found a better existence serving Captain Acorne knew what it was like to endure the humiliation of a flogging.

Rapid thoughts tore through Jesamiah's mind: *Tiola will be safe, soldiers'll not molest a midwife.* Then: *What if things get out of hand? Close on a thousand men are sprawled along that beach. All of them drunk, as full as goats and spoiling for a fight.* He swore aloud as Rue came to join him at the rail, several of the men with him, all peering uneasily through the darkness towards the shore.

There was more noise now, shouting, the sound of fighting; the *pop, pop* of pistol fire, the sharper, deeper crack of muskets. Shadows were flickering between the huddle of buildings, frightened men running, trying to hide or get away. A few women were screaming; mistresses trying to protect their lovers, whores to keep their customers. Madams and pimps would be throwing men on to the narrow streets, not wanting to be implicated in obstructing the king's men attending their duty. Jesamiah did not need to see to know what was happening over there. He had personally experienced the press closing in; the heart-drub of fear as you hid in the dark, praying, praying they would pass by. For those captured by the press there was little chance of seeing freedom again, not unless the Grim Reaper or Davy Jones came to collect your soul—or peace was declared and there was no further use for many ships and many men.

Nathan, a deserter from the Royal Navy, was peering through Jesamiah's telescope, panning it slowly and carefully along the shoreline. "They are not sailors," he announced with a sniff of disdain. "They are the governor's militia. I can see their white cross-belts."

Frowning, Jesamiah took the glass, held it to his eye. Nat was right, those were armed soldiers spreading through the town.

"The press would choose one or two taverns, maybe blockade a street, take who they wanted then clear out. There could be a bit of resistance, a pistol shot or two, drawn knives, but you don't need an entire regiment of cherry-reds to round up a few drunken sailors. As lieutenant I've supervised the press enough times to know, Captain."

Jesamiah grinned at him, slapped his shoulder. "As a drunken sailor I've avoided the press often enough to understand what you mean, Nat!"

A flotilla of small boats was making way, several heading for *Sea Witch*. Angling the telescope on them Jesamiah was pleased to see the anxious faces of his men come into sharp relief: Jansy, Toby, their carpenter Chippy Harrison. Jimmy, Barnsey; Peter Piper.

Musket fire from the jetty. Jesamiah swore as he saw young Jasper in the stern of the farthest boat slump forward —the press did not shoot men who made a run for it. Did they?

~ *Tiola?* ~ Jesamiah desperately thought her name, cursed his inability to initiate communication. ~ *Tiola? Are you all right?* ~

As he expected, no answer.

The boats were alongside, men climbing aboard, breathing hard, agitated; all hands helping Jasper whose face was crumpled in pain, blood on his shoulder, seeping through his shirt.

Quickly, efficiently, Jesamiah examined the wound; entrance and exit hole, the bullet had gone straight through. No broken bones.

"You're lucky lad, you'll mend." To a couple of the men, "Get him below, make him comfortable. Tiola will see to him as soon as she comes aboard." He turned immediately to Jansy—Mr Janson—"What the hell is happening over there?"

Bent over, almost doubled, his hands spread on his thighs, old Jansy was struggling to get his wheezing breath back. He lifted one arm, patted the air, shook his head.

Toby spoke for him instead, although his breath was as short. "We only just got away, Cap'n, several of the lads haven't made it. The militia's sealing the whole bloody town off. Our amnesty's been revoked."

For a stunned half a minute, Jesamiah stared at him as if he had suddenly grown two heads. "What? They can't do that."

"They can. They have," Jansy interrupted, his hand now on his chest, the breathing easing but his lungs still sounding like a pair of holed bellows. "Able bodied men are to be pressed into the king's service and Vernon is following Admiralty orders to requisition what he needs. Including ships. The best of what's available."

Another silence. The unspoken implication gradually sinking in. *Sea Witch* was the best.

"He can't!" The words escaped through Jesamiah's lips as a low, rushed, hiss of furious disbelief.

"Unfortunately," Nathan said at his side, "the Articles of War state that during declared hostilities, he can."

Rue interrupted the scathing answer forming in Jesamiah's mind by pointing across the harbour. "*Regarde, le bateau.* Soldiers?" He indicated the small gig pulling steadily towards them.

Unable to distinguish clearly who it was, Jesamiah snatched up the telescope, although even with the various lanterns and torches reflecting in the water of the rippling harbour, there was not sufficient light to see well. He could make out two men and eight red-coats with muskets draped over their shoulders. "It's Jennings," he snapped as they came nearer. "I have no wish to see him." Shifting the telescope, he settled on Dunwoody's heavily jowled face. "Nor 'im."

"It may not be what you think." Rue took the bring it close, solemnly stared through it. "Could 'e not, per'aps, be bringing word of Tiola?"

"With armed men?"

"Would you expect 'im to not 'ave a suitable escort?"

Jesamiah shrugged, winced as he remembered his back, grudgingly snapped: "Send most of the men below, I don't want Dunwoody to discover how many we have as crew. Keep a moderate few to hand, though, eh? Just in case." He took the telescope, had another peer through. Stated. "Personally, I'd rather we loaded a cannon and shot them out the water."

Arms folded, Jesamiah made no attempt to help Jennings through the starboard entry port. Ignored the fact that the man's gout was obviously paining him. "Has the code of the sea changed with this war, then? I have always been led to believe it is marked as an act of piracy to board another man's ship without asking permission."

The eight marines and the overweight Dunwoody were following behind Jennings.

"I come in friendship, lad. Believe me."

"With muskets?"

"For my protection, it is a wild night over there."

Jesamiah said nothing, the mere thought of press gangers making him too angry for words. If he voiced his opinion he would say something he would later regret, so he held his tongue on a tight reef. Fortunately, Tiola's voice in his head distracted him.

~ *They died. I lost both of them.* ~

He could hear the tears, her bereft sense of failure.

~ *I'm so sorry sweetheart. You did all you could. Not all battles are won by the good at heart.* ~ Mentally, Jesamiah sent a picture of himself hugging her, arms tight round her, his cheek against her hair. Felt the warm sensation of a returned smile.

~ *Thank you luvver.* ~

~ *Are you all right? There's trouble over there.* ~

~ The men are turning ugly, they resent a promise being revoked, and they are very drunk. Drunken men know not what they are doing and forget common sense. ~

Looking around at the few assembled men, Henry Jennings' attention lingered on Nathan Crocker leaning on the starboard rail. Once a lieutenant, Crocker had forfeited his rank when he had jumped ship some years ago. His gaze then strayed over Mr Janson with his greying hair, Toby Turner, even older. Ageing men, young boys, deserters; the typical mix of crew aboard a pirate vessel. Vernon would hang Crocker without pre-amble and these others were too old, too riddled with the joint ache and too poor-sighted and slow-witted to serve the king. Why Acorne kept them on, Jennings did not know, presumably for their knowledge of the sea and experience? Jesamiah was a man who was very loyal to his friends, and besides, Jennings knew full well the rest of the crew, those who were no doubt hiding below, were healthy young men. If he intended to kick the Spanish from the Caribbean the sort of men Vernon needed were those who could climb a mast, turn a capstan and haul a cannon's truck with agility and ease.

"I assume you are aware of the situation?" he said to Jesamiah, who was staring towards the town, lost in his own thoughts. "Captain Acorne?"

"What? What did you say?"

Jennings repeated himself. Jesamiah only half listened.

~ I'll come and get you. As soon as I've thrown Jennings off my ship. ~

~ No, I am all right. Stefan was waiting. He has escorted me to the governor's house. I will be safe here for the night. ~

"Jesamiah? Are you listening?"

"I heard every word Henry. As I said earlier, Vernon will not be taking my men or this ship."

The Dutchman's words from earlier in the afternoon rang in Jesamiah's ears. *"She could have a fat belly by the time you next see her."* Damn, damn, and double damn.

~ *Stefan? Tiola, what the fok was he doing waiting for you? I don't like this. Don't you let him touch you. You understand? Don't let him touch you!* ~

~ *He can be a thoughtful gentleman, Jes. And I am his wife. But no, I will not let him touch me. Mrs Rogers has made me most welcome.* ~

Dunwoody laughed as he removed his hat, wiped the sweat from his forehead with his coat sleeve. "Oh yes Vernon will, Acorne. He wants this ship badly."

Jesamiah wrinkled his nose in disgust. A gentleman always removed his hat with the inside towards his body so that the greasy sweatband and any crawlers were not revealed. Stefan van Overstratten he would reluctantly agree, could be a gentleman when he so desired. Dunwoody? Not by any stretch of the imagination.

"You should not have boasted how fast she is," Dunwoody clarified. "Vernon intends to get his promotion because of her. Ain't that nice?" He stepped hurriedly behind Jennings as Jesamiah raised his fist, threatening to hit him.

"That's enough Dunwoody. You are here at my sufferance. Governor Rogers ordered me to bring you. I did not appreciate the order." Producing a folded parchment from inside his coat, not noticing his tobacco pouch had come with it and dropped to the deck, Jennings thrust it towards Jesamiah, who ignored it.

"You left this on my desk. Take it. With an official king's commission, Jes lad, Vernon can touch neither you nor your crew. As for *Sea Witch*, well, I'll do what I can, but we may need to find you another ship. I think I can persuade Rogers to let you have the *Delicia*, although she has mysteriously sprung a most unfortunate leak. It will be some several days before she is repaired; then you can legally get yourself gone from here."

"I don't want that tub, I've got me own ship. I'm standing on 'er. And I've told you, I don't want no poxed king's commission neither." With an unhurried sound of grating steel Jesamiah drew his cutlass, shifted it to his left hand and with his right, as slowly, pulled the pistol from his belt. "You are out-staying your welcome, Henry. I suggest you leave."

"You are being a prize fool. Anyone suitable to serve is expected to sign up."

Jesamiah laughed. "So what happened to the amnesty? Our pardons? The promise of our freedom providing we did nothing illegal? It were a bit short bloody lived weren't it?"

"The consequences of war, lad. The sorry consequences of war."

"Your war, your consequences. I ain't giving up my ship or my freedom for a war I don't care about. Please go. I do not want to shoot you." To emphasise his sincerity he half-cocked the hammer with his thumb. "My reluctance is not from cowardice, you understand. Spilt guts do so make a mess of m'deck."

Resigned, sliding the parchment into his pocket, Jennings shook his head. "You leave me no choice, Captain. I regret, I must ask you to accompany me ashore. Governor Rogers cannot risk you slipping away and it will be for your own good, I am sure you do not want a charge of treason around your neck."

Jesamiah was untroubled. "Add it to the tally of misdemeanours. One more accusation will not make much difference. I can only hang once."

"You will not hang. You will be incarcerated and left to rot in London's Marshalsea gaol."

A half-smile creased Jesamiah's face as he stepped forward two paces. "I don't think so. You have to arrest me first—with this lot of landlubberly daffodils? Two of your men have neglected to cock their hammers, three have what looks to be damp powder, so the primer will never fire. Curlylocks on the end has already pissed his breeches, and I doubt the other two have the balls to fire, probably on account of my lads holding blades at their throats." With his pistol he made an elaborate gesture to indicate Jennings was to turn around, see for himself the men with drawn knives and readied pistols who had come silent, on bare feet, from the shadows.

Dunwoody gurgled as Isiah Roberts held a dagger to his Adam's apple, the sharpened blade gleaming in the flicker of the on-deck lamps.

"Whereas my men," Jesamiah smiled indolently, "have dry powder and their weapons are loaded, primed and cocked; as is mine." He clicked the hammer full home. "Of the two of us, Henry, who is more likely to have the order to shoot obeyed?"

"Nay, nay lad!" unafraid, Jennings put one finger on the pistol barrel and turned the gun aside. "I knew it would be futile to attempt to arrest you, but for the sake of formality I had to try." He motioned to his men that they were to put up their weapons and return to the boat. They did not need telling twice.

Dunwoody alone, released from Isiah's grip, complained in his belligerent whine. "You are not going to let him go? The governor's orders were to bring him in. Tied and bound, or even dead if need be!"

With a look of utter disdain Jennings peered into his face. "Then you tie and bind him. Good luck to 'ee."

Blustering, muttering a protest, Dunwoody turned towards the entry port, as he began to descend remembered a secondary mission. He withdrew a small scroll of paper from his pocket, tossed it at Jesamiah's feet. "Van Overstratten said I was to deliver that. Said to tell you the deal is not negotiable. I reckon he's changed his mind about his wife and is going to thrum her hard enough to set 'er breeding."

Furious, Jesamiah leapt at him, rammed his knee into the vile creature's groin and followed with a jab from his cutlass guard to the windpipe. Choking, gasping, Dunwoody doubled over, but Jesamiah caught him, picked him up as if he were a sack of cabbages and tossed him overboard.

Such was the general low opinion of Dunwoody, even the militia settling themselves into the boat, laughed.

Peering down into the dark sea at the spluttering, splashing object, Jennings disdainfully shook his head, "Take no notice of him, Jesamiah. He is a worm with an acid tongue. Unfortunately, I suppose we will have to fish him out." He stepped awkwardly, wincing, down on to the first cleat as his men began to haul an incensed Dunwoody from the water. He paused, said quietly, "Vernon will come Jes lad, later tonight or early tomorrow. He has already informed Rogers that he intends to commission *Sea Witch*. Apart from his own *Challenger* she's the only seaworthy vessel in harbour. If you fight for her he will shoot you. If you try to run, Rogers will declare you a pirate and outlaw you." Jennings nodded towards *Challenger*; "She has twice the men and twice the gun power. Although *Sea Witch* is faster and the better ship to handle, unless you can catch Vernon on the hop you will be blasted to pieces before you get out of the harbour. Do not even consider the idea, even though most of her crew, and Vernon himself, are ashore rounding up suitable men to press into service."

Jesamiah was frowning at the note Dunwoody had delivered. Jennings sighed, had the fool listened to a single word? He had liberally sprinkled hints and information, hoped it had not all fallen on closed ears, he could hardly speak any plainer.

As the oarsmen rowed to the jetty, Jennings peered over his shoulder, looked back at *Sea Witch*; she certainly was beautiful, he could understand why Vernon wanted her. Jesamiah was still standing near the entry port reading that note van Overstratten had sent. Jennings knew what was in it; Dunwoody could never keep a secret near the sound of chinking coins. The first part was instructions to a London clerk about disposing of a secret cargo of indigo, the second, for providing legal papers for an annulment. Jennings smiled. So far, so good but only if Acorne took the bait.

"Good luck, Jes lad," he murmured under his breath. "Use your wits and your skill. Don't let me down boy. Please don't let me down."

Chapter Nineteen

"As I see it we have one of two choices. We stay, lose *Sea Witch* and get ourselves chained to King George, or we say bugger the lot of 'em and fight our way out of here."

Calling the men into the lamp lit gloom of the gun deck, Jesamiah patiently explained the situation. It was not a good one. Deliberately, he made no mention of missing spies, marooned barrels of indigo. Or Tiola.

A moment's thought only and most of his men were nodding for the second option.

"Be aware, lads, Vernon will come after us—if we get out in one piece—or if not him personally any of the several pirate hunters who prowl the sea lanes out there. We'll be marked men. Dead men. Rogers has promised that. Anyone who leaves harbour without a Letter of Marque will hang."

Dramatically he mimed a noose tightening round his neck. A few of the men added gruesome gurgling noises. One shouted, "Don't worry Cap'n, I'll cling on t'yer legs t'send you off quicker!"

"With hangers-on like you, Jenks, who needs Vernon as an enemy?" Jesamiah quipped.

"We expected to hang before we took this offered pardon," Isiah Roberts stated when the laughter had died down a little. "So what has changed? We have had a few weeks' respite, some decent nights in bed with pretty women and more than a few bellyfuls of rum. To be honest, I find myself getting bored with it."

"The strumpets are getting bored with you more like!" someone guffawed.

"Nay! Bored with trying to find his apology for a pizzle in the dark!"

Isiah bore the crude banter well. Laughter, teasing each other, was a part of the loyal brotherhood forged through friendship and respect between comrades. Equally, any one of them would fight alongside the other, watching the next man's back; or when the time came for mourning, would send the fallen to rest in the deep, and grieve for lost friendship.

A group of half a dozen men were at the back. Elijah Perkins stood, fiddling with his cap. "Begging your pardon, Captain, me and Will, along with Carve, Jason and Morrison here, we feel we'd rather take our chance ashore—we don't want to appear disloyal, but Will here's got a sweetheart, and Jason, well, he wants to get back to Devon to see his old mam again; I'd not say no to going with him. It's not that we don't want to be with you, it's just that —"

Jesamiah interrupted with an accepting smile. He knew these men like the pattern of scars on his right arm. "Its just that at the moment you are not outside of the law and you'd rather not deliberately cut your anchor cable. I quite understand lads. I suggest any of you who don't want to make a run for it take one of the boats and pull over to the far side of the harbour, lay low until dawn then go straight to Henry Jennings. He'll sort you out. I'll send a letter explaining you refused to come with us, that'll ensure you keep straight with him. I can't guarantee you'll not end up serving with Vernon or anything, but that's the risk you will have to take."

"Even if we do, Cap'n, 'least it'll be legal."

Letting the rumble of discussion swirl through the men for a while, Jesamiah sat on a barrel, thinking, one arm resting on his thigh, the other leg swinging, outwardly calm, appearing in control. Inwardly, shrieking his rage and despair. Thinking about the note van Overstratten had written, the addendum he had scrawled beneath the instructions to his London clerk:

I have Tiola. No indigo, no Tiola. You will never see her alive again. I'll make sure of that.

And Tiola had said Stefan was a gentleman? Jesamiah wanted to leap up, arm his men and attack the town, wanted to run his own riot through the streets, to burn and plunder and kill; wanted to set loose this congealing tightness of anger that was twisting his guts into knots. But all he did was sit there, thinking.

He was caught between the gallows and the noose. If he went over there to try to take her by force he would be arrested—or shot—and lose *Sea Witch*. If he ran for it, he would lose Tiola. Or would he? If he returned to piracy most certainly, she would not tolerate that. But what if they left harbour and...?

"There is one other alternative," Jesamiah said slowly, the idea growing, mulling it, and weighing the consequences. The excited chatter faded as he waited for complete silence, then outlined his plan in a few, concise words.

"What if we bare our backsides to the English government, to Rogers and his broken promises, aye, and to Commodore Edward bloody Vernon, all in the one go?"

He had their attention. They listened.

When he finished talking the silence brooded as heavy as lead. Then a few whispers and quiet words began to stir; shuffling feet, coughed phlegm was spat on to the deck. More than a few heads were shaking.

Rue, leaning against the starboard bulkhead, massaged his bush of a beard. "That is asking a tall commitment of us, Captain Acorne."

"Have you any alternative ideas then?" Jesamiah snarled back. "I'm asking a lot, but I'll be in this with you, and I will not take anyone with whom this sits ill. If you like not my intention, return ashore with Elijah, I'll not think the worse for any man who does so, even you Rue." It took an effort for him to say that, Rue had been a good friend but if it was necessary he was prepared to sail with a skeleton crew rather than take reluctant hands.

"All I need is enough men to help me get out of this harbour. No more than that." He rubbed his sweating palms along his thighs, anxious. Added, "The gamble, lads, is to hope this war is a damp cartridge, all smoke and no shot. When it's over there'll be another round of amnesties, if things go as I believe they will, we'll be able to negotiate us a new pardon."

"That is a big if though, Cap'n. A mighty big if," Jansy said, sucking on his unlit pipe—even in harbour Jesamiah did not permit smoking below deck.

Jesamiah stood, rested his palms on an overhead beam, leant forward slightly. "Life can be one big if. We are all going to meet our Maker one day, and as I see it, I'd rather be standing hat in hand before Him as a free, happy, man, than a miserable, shackled slave. You die only the once, whether you've led the life of a celibate, sober monk like Finch here," Finch growled and said a crude word, accompanied by a matching gesture. "Or a whore-mongering drunk, like me."

Laughter. The crew were coming round to the idea.

"Me'bbe so," Finch interrupted, "but when me time's up I want t'know I've bloody enjoyed me life, just in case whatever place I end up in turns out not t'be all it's cracked up as."

"You? Enjoy life, you miserable old bugger?" Jesamiah winked at the men, chuckled.

"I suppose you mean in case there's no rum or crumpet down there?" Toby jested.

"No. I mean in case me bleedin' wife's there an' all!"

Amid the roars of laughter, Rue shoved himself off from the wall, unfolded his bare arms as he stepped forward, his French accent strong as often it was when he became emotional. He cleared his throat waited for the humour to subside, gained everyone's attention.

"We roam where we like, taking the easy pickings and enjoying the reward, but none of us, not one of us standing 'ere 'as ever taken it for granted to see another dawn. All we've ever wanted is to enjoy what we 'ave now, not pass our days regretting and thinkin' on the what might 'ave beens. This proposal worries me, I 'ate the Spanish, as I know our *capitaine* 'ates them. But I love this ship. I would do anything to not lose 'er. I am with *mon ami* Jesamiah Acorne, and may God, or the Devil, judge me for my loyalty to comrades and friends. *Et les Anglais*? They can go to 'ell with their broken promises."

"Aye!"

"Well said."

"I'm in!"

"And me."

Voices shouting, more cheers, then Jasper, propped up in a cot to one side of the deck, and masking the pain of his shoulder, hastily patched-up by Mr Janson, queried, "Oughtn't we take a vote on it? Keep the Code? We're entitled to vote ain't we?"

"That you are," Jesamiah agreed, nodding in the youth's direction. "I'll leave you to it. You have a free vote, do as your conscience guides. Not that many of you scallywags would recognise a conscience even if it leapt up and bit yer backsides. I'll be in my cabin. When you're done, there'll be a gold guinea apiece, whether you stay or go."

Not all captains agreed with the idea of the code of conduct. Different ships, different crews, had their own interpretation of the Articles that governed their sea-roving ways. Guiding rules; keep your weapons in good order, no smoking below deck, no fighting or gambling on board. An equal share of the plunder; the right to elect or eject a captain. Jesamiah agreed to most of the common rules, most of them made good sense, but *Sea Witch* was his, he would not be deposed, men were free to serve under him or not as they chose. He never stopped any man who decided he'd had enough from leaving, but most of the crew were content with their captain. Jesamiah was a fair man who gave his word and kept it. He never asked anyone to do what he could not do himself; knew his business, knew his ship. His crew, on the whole, were stubbornly loyal to him; even so, with their captain listening they felt inhibited, their thoughts and opinions hobbled. With him gone the talk heightened, the few growls of discontent were muttered louder, accompanied by expressive gesturing and shaking heads, a few raised voices bordered on argument.

But when it came to loyalty most of the men aboard the *Sea Witch* were united and stubborn. When they voted with a solemn show of hands it was overwhelmingly in Captain Jesamiah Acorne's favour.

CHAPTER TWENTY

TUESDAY NIGHT

Taking a long swig from the rum bottle in his hand, Jesamiah wiped the residue from his moustache and lips on his shirt sleeve. He had every confidence that most of the men would come with him, for they valued their freedom too highly to submit to Rogers or Vernon, or any of those whoreson promise-breakers. It was the lure of freedom that had turned them pirate in the first place. A small thing like he proposed doing would not deter hard-arsed seamen. Would it? Except, of course, it was not so small.

He put the bottle down with a thump on his prized mahogany dining table, sat, went to lean back and with a gasp of pain abruptly changed his mind. Twisting slightly sideways, his elbow on the chair arm to take his weight, he propped one foot on another chair, crossed the other over. Not an entirely comfortable way to sit but it would have to do. His mind returned to what he had proposed; had he the right to be asking this of his crew? They would be sailing into the jaws of death as they tried to clear the sandbar out there. And after that—if there was an after that—they would be going to prod the devil's backside.

Lifting his glass of rum, he held it up to the mildly rocking light of one of the overhead lanterns. Rum was a residue of refining sugar cane. Who was it, he wondered, who first discovered that if you leave the stuff to ferment it turns into the glory that is rum?

The drink in his hand was a dark, rich, reddish brown; when first it became rum, it was a white, clear liquid. The brown colouring came from the kegs it was stored in; the longer the storage, the darker the rum, though some added more molasses or caramel sugar to heighten the darkness and taste. Some, complete madmen like Edward Teach, old Blackbeard himself, even added a pinch of gunpowder to give it a kick. Jesamiah savoured a mouthful of finest Jamaican. It had enough of a kick of its own without spoiling the flavour. Damned stupid of that estate to try and transport a whole shipload to England and not place a single cannon on board. Easy pickings, though the stuff decanted into this bottle was from the last remaining keg of the haul. Perhaps returning to piracy had its attractions?

Tiola! He closed his eyes squeezed back stupid tears at the thought of her. He was intending to abandon her again, leave her for a second time at the mercy of that Dutch butter-ball toad. Jesamiah sighed, put the glass down, unrolled van Overstratten's note again.

I have Tiola. No indigo, no Tiola.

You will never see her alive again. I'll make sure of that.

What did the Dutchman mean? That he intended to kill her? Shut her away in a nunnery or something? Take her back to Cape Town? What?

Furious, frustrated, Jesamiah stood, and swept the rum bottle, glass, china plates, everything on the table to the floor. With it, Jennings' tobacco pouch. Disdainfully he picked it up, unrolled it. The rich smell of tobacco wafted over his face. He wrinkled his nose, he disliked tobacco intensely. The stuff reminded him of Virginia and his childhood that had been one long ache of misery. The first time that Phillipe, several years the elder, had abused him they had been in the tobacco sheds. He thrust aside the feeling of revulsion and toyed with the pouch, opening a leather flap, found very little tobacco, only a fold of parchment tucked into the inside pocket. A keepsake? Half curious he went to pull it out, changed his mind and stuffed it back in again. He flipped the thing shut, tossed it away, not noticing where it fell. Not caring.

What should he do about Tiola? Could he try fetching her? Savagely he kicked at a chair, gasped, clutched at its rim and clenched his teeth against the pain shooting through the torn flesh of his back. There was nothing he could do, absolutely nothing! He would not get two yards along the jetty, let alone anywhere near the governor's house. How could he expect to march up to that front door, demand entrance and the return of his woman? Maybe that was what Vernon was expecting him to do? Maybe the commodore had several longboats full of men waiting in the shadows over there. Waiting for him to go ashore, then they would swoop in, board *Sea Witch* and... He covered his face with his hands, groaned. No! They would not have her! There was only one thing he could do. Go and get that bloody indigo, and work out, later, how he was going to sail back into Nassau harbour once he'd got it.

Rue tapped politely on the door, ducked in, said nothing at the broken, sodden mess scattered everywhere. "We 'ave an accord, *capitaine. Oui*, the men are behind you. Those few who are not are already making their way ashore."

"How many?"

"*Quatorze.* Fourteen."

Jesamiah nodded, pleased, relieved. Fourteen out of more than ninety was not so bad. He had expected Rue to say nearer forty. He walked over to where his hat lay on the floor, picked it up, brushed some drops of rum from it, rammed it on his head, put on his coat. "Let's go then," he said, with conviction. "Tell the men to clear for action."

Rue turned to leave, a loud whoop of rising excitement bursting from his lungs. He too was becoming bored with this idle life of kicking his heels in harbour.

"But Rue."

"*Oui?*"

"Quietly eh? No point in waking this particular devil until his meal be ready to serve. We want to make out, for as long as we can, that we're merely shifting position, savvy? They'll realise soon enough that we ain't."

A moment later a drubbing of feet echoed through the timbers of the ship as men scattered to their stations.

Finch bustled in, grumbling at the mess. "Broken china, glass everywhere? How we bloody goin' t'replace it all then, eh? That's what I'd like t'know."

As always, Jesamiah ignored him, left his cabin to the men who were knocking out the bolts that held the bulkhead screens in place, swinging the stern windows upwards and fixing them to the ceiling. To roll out the cannon. He strode to the quarterdeck, stood back to watch appreciatively as the men worked, marvelling at their utter disregard of the likely possibility of getting blown to pieces within the next twenty minutes or so.

In the dim-lit darkness of the below-deck world, the gun crews were getting ready; the younger lads sluicing buckets of sand for the men to keep a better footing when they ran the trucks in and out for loading and firing. The gun captains ensuring match and powder was to hand, that shot was piled nearby.

The surgeon's workspace was situated directly under the captain's cabin, beneath the water line, safe from the penetration of shot. Mr Janson was tying on Tiola's leather apron, setting out the knives and saws, testing each blade with his thumb. He spat on one, rubbed away some grease. Tiola would have admonished him sharply for that, she insisted on meticulous cleanliness, but she was not here, and they now had no other surgeon, so Jansy would have to manage in his own way. He had acted as loblolly boy for more than half his long life, serving under a variety of ship's surgeons, some good, most of them bad. Not a-one of them a patch on Tiola with her gentle ways and skilled hands.

Out in the waist, men were waiting on the open deck, poised at the braces. Others were gripping the ratlines, their bodies tense, knuckles white. They stood rigid, all eyes towards Jesamiah, hearts thumping, breath quickening; all waiting his signal to hurry aloft, to make sail. To open fire.

Jesamiah's fingers caressed his blue ribbons, then he touched the lucky gold acorn dangling from his ear. If he stayed in harbour he would lose his ship and he was not prepared to do that. No matter what form of hell came to challenge him. To lose *Sea Witch* would be the deepest pit, the deepest layer, the most painful purgatory—no, that was not true, the worst agony would be to lose Tiola. But to keep her he had to keep *Sea Witch*, and do what van Overstratten wanted. But if that was so, he was going to do it his way! He raised his head, heard Tiola, her sweet voice calling him and he slammed his thoughts behind a closed door, did not answer. Stared instead at the run of the tide and assessed the strength of the wind. Rain was coming again. Another drenching.

He gazed over the dark spread of sea at His Majesty's Ship, *Challenger*, so apparently casually anchored close to the exit, her masts tall, black, silhouettes against the night sky, her stern lanterns three flares of yellow light. Henry Jennings had been right, Commodore Vernon knew his business. But then, so did Jesamiah.

At his command, Peter Piper and Toby Turner took their axes to the anchor cable and *Sea Witch* swung free. It meant losing the anchor but they had cut cables before in other emergencies. Replacing it was a simple matter of giving chase to the next ship they saw, boarding and acquiring what they needed. Hopefully, they would meet a Spaniard or a Frenchy. Jesamiah was not particularly bothered if it turned out to be English or Dutch; he would already be condemned once he crossed that sandbar, so what did it matter?

Ignoring the sudden dash of rain battering their faces and making their hands numb with its cold sting, the topmen, strung out along the yards, grappled with the growing area of sail as the canvas begun to flap and bang in the rising wind.

The African, Isiah Roberts, cupped his hands around his mouth; "Man the braces! Come on, you're like toothless old women! Move yourselves, you lubbers!"

Heaving and panting, the men laid their backs into hauling the heavy yards, lewd curses on their breaths as, reluctantly, the spars responded and began to lumber round. Then the wind filled the sails and the canvas billowed out hard and full as *Sea Witch* eagerly gathered way.

Jesamiah took one final glance at the town. Was he being stupid? Was he insane to be doing this? He touched his ribbons again. Stupid, insane, he might be, but *Sea Witch* was under way and he was committed.

He reopened his mind to Tiola. ~ *I'm sorry sweetheart. Please believe I love you.* ~ He groaned. It was no good trying to initiate their communication by thought, he was not able to do so.

Rue took the helm and Jesamiah, standing beside him, also set one hand to rest lightly on a spoke. A lover's caress. He shoved the thought of Tiola aside, looked straight ahead almost as if he did not see *Challenger* looming nearer.

"Starboard a point," Jesamiah said calmly.

"Starboard a point," Rue repeated in French.

A pause as *Sea Witch* slowly responded.

"Bring her round a little more—slowly Rue, we need to come dead straight, then turn as quick as a whore lifts her skirts, and head for the exit. We've a hard task ahead, mate.

We'll be under fire and we can't afford to make a mistake. If we get stuck on that sand bar, Vernon will finish us as if we are a duck sitting on a pond. I want to steer straight through the centre of the western channel where the tide runs deepest."

"That is a narrow gap, and it is close to the fort, right under their guns," Rue said. He nodded towards *Challenger*, finished, "And we will be carrying a fair bit of damage."

"You ever known those clodpolls up in the fort to fire at anything and hit it?" Jesamiah answered. "The best officers will be down in the town with Vernon rounding up all the unfortunate bastards they can. The rest of 'em will be drunk by now. They usually are, why should tonight be any exception? The wind is exactly as we want it, Rue. We duck our heads, loose all sail at the right moment and set her running."

Rue sniffed, said nothing more. Once they were out of the harbour, then *oui*, they would be all right, but that would take precious minutes to achieve. Minutes where they would be under the direct fire of *Challenger*'s guns; two, maybe even three merciless rounds at close quarters? There was no point in making further comment, however; he would not be telling Jesamiah anything he did not already know.

Picking up the speaking trumpet so he may be heard clearly, Jesamiah stepped forward to the rail, set it to his mouth. Men were looking expectantly towards him, everyone waiting. At the open hatch leading down to the main deck, Nathan stood ready to relay orders. In a matter of seconds it would be nothing but smoke and noise and blood and guts down there.

"We will rake *Challenger*'s stern, then come round. We'll be passing close and quick, you will fire as your gun's bear. Gun captains, I want reload as fast as your crews can manage —no, make that faster. I want everything you've got, men, you hear me? We're clewed up for fighting sail, but we need every inch of canvas as soon as we're easing past *Challenger* and we're lined up with the western channel. Wind and tide are in our favour. I said we are going to make a run for it and I mean we are going to run for it."

One last check; all hands were at their stations, *Sea Witch* was gliding forward, the water quietly gurgling past her hull as she increased speed, her bowsprit would soon be level with *Challenger*'s stern. She was ready. They all were. Jesamiah raised his hand, paused, staring ahead.

Shouting, a sudden flurried scramble aboard *Challenger* as the set watch became aware that *Sea Witch* was not just moving from one side of the harbour to the other.

Then Tiola's presence. Distinctly Jesamiah was aware of her nearness, could feel her vibrant being around him, beside him, within him.

~ *Jesamiah?* ~

~ *I'm so sorry sweetheart! Please believe I love you. I have to do this. I've no choice!* ~

Deliberately he shut her out. Concentrated on his men and his ship. He dropped his hand, shouted, "Run out! Number one gun; fire!"

And hell came to Nassau harbour.

CHAPTER TWENTY-ONE

Tiola was seated at Governor Rogers' expansive and well-served dining table. No one seemed to notice the rioting and despair running wild beyond the sheltering wall of the governor's house. Rogers never missed dinner, insisted it was served on time whatever else was happening. The gates were locked, militiamen patrolled the courtyard; no one could get in, they were all quite safe and so no one cared what was happening outside. Except perhaps Henry Jennings, who sat staring into his soup solemnly watching it grow cold. He too had no stomach for the press gang.

At the head of the table Rogers was heartily amusing himself with his own tawdry jests and Stefan, opposite Tiola, ate in stiff silence. Mrs Rogers, as always, twittered away like the empty-head dullard she was. There was fighting out there. Men clawing to keep their freedom, doing it by the only way they knew, with anger and the spilling of blood. Men were dead, dying. Others, many others, were being forcibly subdued and then bound against their will into a form of slavery; forced to serve King George. No matter that they would be fed, clothed and receive medical attention, they were paid a pittance and had to work hard and fight hard against their will. Against their free will. Tiola felt disgusted and sickened. Was more disgusted at herself than these men, for she too was sitting here attending to her soup and not doing anything to help those unfortunates outside.

She sat here because there was nothing she could do. She had not saved the life of the child or its mother, could not save those wretched men, and could do nothing to help Jesamiah.

"I am so glad you have made amends with your husband, my dear," Mrs Rogers repeated, yet again, her hand reaching out to squeeze Tiola's. "It is our duty to serve our husbands, although we receive little thanks for it." She sighed and reached out to straighten her husband's askew wig, smiled conspiratorially at her only female companion. "Mr Rogers does so vex me with his lack of care for his appearance."

Steadfastly, Tiola ignored the woman as she meandered on. It made sense to come here, she could not fault Stefan on that, for the rioting had spread quickly—and was being as quickly stamped out—but angry men with weapons were volatile, and Nassau was like an open powder keg this night. Initially, she had been surprised to find him waiting for her, but in public he was always a man who wanted to be seen doing the right thing; no husband who took pains to portray himself as a gentleman would have abandoned his wife to the mob. And for once it appeared he truly was concerned for her.

Mindful and courteous, he had shielded her from two drunks who barged into them, and taken her arm to guide her away from a brawl ahead. Had raised his pistol twice to threaten potential aggressors. She was capable of taking care of herself but for fear of exposure, she did not like to rely on her ability of Craft, and in truth, she had been grateful for his protection. She had been relieved to find herself brought here, although she strongly suspected Stefan had some ulterior motive for his solicitude. A motive she had not, yet, had opportunity to uncover. Dinner, she realised however, was going to be one of those occasions that she would prefer not to happen. From the outset, Mrs Rogers had assumed the rift, 'Your little upset', as she termed it, between husband and wife had been mended.

"Get yourself with child," she suddenly whispered. "Always the best way to please a husband, they enjoy fussing over and pampering you because they hope for the patter of a little boy's feet." Her whispers, like those of her husband's, were a full-blown trumpet blast.

Woodes Rogers guffawed. "Patter of feet? Good grief woman, that son you presented me with fifteen years past thundered around as if he had nailed boots on!"

"Seventeen, dear. He is seven and ten now."

"Is he by Jove! Well bless me, where does time go, eh? Ha, ha!" He thumped his hand on to Stefan's shoulder. "Get yer poke undone, Stefan, give yer wife something to think about other than that stubbornly unhelpful swab of a pirate. Make sure no bun cooking in the oven is of his dough first though, eh?"

He was not a man who understood the word, or the deed, of tact. Mrs Rogers blushed at his crude humour and hastily changed the subject.

Answering automatically, aye or nay, to a barrage of minor domestic trivialities, Tiola opened her mind to the man she loved.

~ *Jesamiah?* ~ She met the blackness of his shielded mind, as solid as a wall, but she tentatively pushed against it, insistent, and his defence momentarily crumbled. She heard, felt, him respond, a brief snatch of his loving presence, his tenderness and devotion, all of it instantly ripped away in an outburst of distraught anguish.

~ *I'm so sorry sweetheart! Please believe I love you. I have to do this. I've no choice!* ~

And the world beyond the closed windows of Governor Rogers' first floor dining room erupted into a blasting crescendo of sound, the sky was lit as if it were day, the windows rattled, the ground shook. The men were on their feet, hurling their chairs aside, scrambling for the French windows. Rogers hauled them open, hurried out on to the balcony. "Gad! That bloody Fanny Anne Vernon ain't firing cannon at m'town now, is he? I'll have him court-martialled!"

Tiola darted with them, her lace shawl slipping from her shoulders to crumple unnoticed on the sun-faded carpet, her hands pressing hard, covering her mouth to stifle the scream from hurtling outward.

~ *Jesamiah! No!* ~ Was he going? Yet again was he sailing away and leaving her behind? She could not believe this was happening!

~ *I thought you loved me, thought you wanted me! Jesamiah! Oh Jesamiah!* ~

Henry Jennings was shaking his head, one hand going to her shoulder in comforting understanding as the tears began to crawl down her cheeks. Rogers was blustering as loud as the booming echoes that were shuddering through Nassau. Only Stefan van Overstratten remained seated, arms folded, his expression a contortion of intense satisfaction and relief.

CHAPTER TWENTY-TWO

Jesamiah's insistence on discipline during a fight, and the many hours he had spent putting the crew through exhausting gun practice, proved its worth. The guns on the larboard side ripped, one after the other, as their target came in sight. Each one tore through the unprotected *Challenger*'s stern, through the taffrail and across the quarterdeck, smashing her wheel and binnacle box, slamming into the mizzenmast. Shattering through her seven stern windows, the heavy iron balls going on through Vernon's cabin, the bulkheads and straight on along the gun deck, destroying everything in the way, be it wood, iron or human flesh and bone.

Jesamiah roared at Rue to bring *Sea Witch* round, bellowed at the men to shift their arses and meet her. She responded, as always she did to Jesamiah's orders, without griping, moving willingly, fast and efficient. The yards creaked round, her crew swearing and cursing as they hauled on the sheets, the canvas cracking as the wind, full behind, billowed them outward as if they were live things.

Aboard *Challenger*, red-coated militia guards were scurrying aloft in what was left of the lower rigging, but Jesamiah's men at the swivel guns easily picked them off before they even had chance to aim, let alone fire the muskets slung over their shoulders. He did not need to see to know what the carnage would be over there. He felt sorry for

PIRATE CODE

the damage to a proud ship, but it was only a passing regret. Had it been the other way around Vernon would have had no hesitation in blasting *Sea Witch* out of the water—as may well be happening in the next few minutes anyway.

Swept along by the current and the wind, *Sea Witch* was gaining speed, swaying forward parallel now with the naval vessel, less than fifty yards between the two. *Challenger* was firing for all she was worth, her first shots whistling overhead to fall harmlessly into the sea beyond *Sea Witch's* starboard rails.

One...two...three...four...five...swabbed out and reloaded, each of *Sea Witch's* larboard cannon fired one after the other, the noise deafening, the belch of flame from the muzzles; acrid smoke palling in the rain-sodden air. Men wiped their smoke-blackened forearms across their red-rimmed smoke-irritated eyes, desperate to stay alive. The screaming of the wounded and dying was pitiful.

Rain was sculling down as if it were being swept through a drain, so dense it formed a heaving mist. The four guns on the open waist of the *Sea Witch* hissed as steam rose from the hot iron of the heavy barrels; the deck ran with water that poured in a red-tainted torrent out through the scuppers. The smoke writhed and seethed around the masts, clung to the gap between the two ships.

Challenger's guns were finding their mark now, a section of *Sea Witch's* rail shattered in a burst of splinters—a man cried out, fell backwards clutching at his eye where a splinter, several inches long, had penetrated. Blood seeped through his fingers as his body contorted, and then lay still.

Smoke and rain almost obscured *Challenger*, only the flared illumination of blasting flame marking where she was, but Jesamiah reckoned that to them, *Sea Witch* was no different. Neither side needed to see the other to aim and fire. Not now.

149

Jesamiah's only problem: he could see nothing for'ard, nothing beyond the mainmast ahead of him. Momentarily he came close to panic. Was he heading direct for the deeper channel? He glanced at the compass. The needle was swinging in its correct position, but this manoeuvre took more than a compass reading to achieve! It took skill and experience and sharp sight. If they slewed to either starboard or larboard they would run aground on the hard bar of the sandy shallows, or fetch up on the jagged rocks of the shore, would founder and be wrecked, broken to splintered pieces, destroyed, as surely, as easily, by the relentless, uncharitable power of the sea as they may yet be by HMS *Challenger*'s merciless crew firing those maiming, death-bringing, blasting guns.

CHAPTER TWENTY-THREE

Tiola stared, horrified, at the destruction happening on the far side of the harbour. The appalling damage to both ships and to the men aboard them. As she watched, with a creaking groan and whip-lash crack of the separating stays, *Challenger*'s main topmast tilted, lingered a moment, then tumbled slowly downwards as if it were a felled tree. All of it falling as a tangled mass of cordage, canvas and split timbers. Holes gaped like yawning mouths in her side; rudder, stern and railings were nothing but ragged splinters. But Vernon kept strict discipline aboard his ship and his officers and gunners, heedless of the dead, dying and wounded, were retaliating with a savage, almost insane vengeance.

Sea Witch's sails were holed, great chunks of her railing were also jagged and gouged. Her rigging was shredded in places, her fore t'gallant mast tilted at a crooked angle. Jesamiah's men, heedless of the militia aboard *Challenger* aiming their muskets at them, were scampering aloft to make running repairs as best they could. As Tiola watched, one man took a musket ball in the back and fell like a stone. She closed her eyes, squeezed aside more tears, hoped he was dead before he had hit the wooden planking of the deck.

~ Oh Jesamiah! Jesamiah, what have you done? ~

She received no answer. She knew he was alive, she would have known instantly were he to be dead. Early on, when first she had spoken to him in this special, secretive way, he had shielded himself from her presence within his mind by a natural instinct, now, he had learnt how to do it as and when he wanted. He had the right to choose to hear her or not, but sometimes she wished he was not so stubbornly independent. She pushed again, firmer, against the shield he had erected against her, felt its impenetrable solidity. He knew she was trying to contact him, for she sensed a slight, hesitant waver before it strengthened even further. He was leaving her. For a second time he was leaving her behind. And an inner dread that maybe he would not be coming back cut into her as cruelly as any sharpened blade.

The rain was sweeping *Sea Witch*'s bow as she sailed forward past HMS *Challenger*. The density of the downpour partially obliterating her from sight, but rain would not stop the round shot, grape, langrage or the musket balls from hitting her. Rain could not protect *Sea Witch* from being blown to pieces, nor could rain protect Jesamiah from injury —but Tiola could.

She was in pain and anguish from his going, did not know why he was going, but she loved him and trusted him. He had said he had no choice. He often lied, but rarely to her. It hurt, his going like this, but oh, how much more it would hurt were he to be maimed or killed! She was tired, was emotionally and physically drained, but since stepping ashore, at least the headache had gone.

Raising her hand she made a soft "hie...ssh," sound on an exhaled breath and concentrated on the solid shape of the *Sea Witch*. She closed her eyes and freed her spirit, allowed it to spiral upward like a curl of smoke rising solemnly from a chimney. Released from the confinement of her earthbound body, Tiola soared above the imposing governor's residence, and above Nassau. Her inner self, the immortal part of her that held no boundary of form or shape shifted into an ethereal, shadowed mist that writhed itself around *Sea Witch*, safely enclosing her in a protective embrace.

Tiola could have removed *Challenger* with one flick of her finger, could have toppled and sank her as if she were of no more consequence than a holed bucket bobbing on the surface of the sea, but Tiola's powers were governed by restrictions, her abilities limited by the law of her Craft. She was not permitted to do deliberate harm to a mortal unless the necessity was imperative to save herself. Oh, she could, very easily, kill every person in Nassau; she could swipe out their arrogances and their angers, remove all the petty jealousies and the selfish obsessions. One word on her breath, one movement of her hand and all would be gone. Except she would be gone with it, for she existed as the counterbalance to the evils of the world; hope against despair, compassion against indifference. She was the love that drove out hatred, and she could not, ever, permit hatred to consume her.

Her Craft was created to preserve, not destroy. So, instead of harming those aboard *Challenger* she shielded the *Sea Witch*. To human eyes, Jesamiah's included, the ship disappeared into a swirling mist-cloud of fugged smoke and pouring rain.

Thunder ripped across the sky, its roar matching the *whoomph*, of *Challenger*'s cannons and her men ducked their heads against the vicious sting of the rain that pricked spitefully into their skin. They were firing blind at a ship that had become a ghost, a fading shadow. Not a shot hit her, for Tiola's spirit mass absorbed every shuddering blow.

The fort's cannons should also have been in action—there was movement up there on the walls, men were darting about, hurrying to load the guns, a great bustle of confusion, but as Jesamiah had predicted, many of the militia were dealing with the fighting in the town, leaving the fortress undermanned. One cannon roared to life but its shot fell wide, a second had damp powder in the touch hole, and beyond a feeble sputter, did nothing more.

As *Sea Witch* slid past *Challenger*'s bows, Tiola could hear Jesamiah shouting for the men to get ready to let fall all sail. She could see them as they waited alert and tense at their stations, and could feel the great pull of the ebbing tide carrying the ship along. But her energy was fading, it was all she could do to hold the misted shadow-cloak in place. She nearly let it slip! A great cheer arose from the *Challenger* as they saw their target clearly again!

Tiola gasped, closed the gap in her concentration and the cloak of protection. What had caused that? What element had shrivelled in under her awareness and caused mischief? And then she heard the low, hushing laugh, became aware of the waiting, gleeful presence; realised the reason for the headaches and the tiredness. Tethys! The ethereal spirit of the sea, Tethys, was draining her ability!

~ *You are in my realm. I hold power here, not you or your kind.* ~

~ *You cannot harm me, Tethys!* ~

A laugh, the sound of the sea booming against the rocks. ~ *Can I not? As the moon pulls upon me and takes me to where she commands in the form of the ebb and flow of the tides, so I can pull upon you. I can attract the strength which flows within you. And when you have become weak and unable to protect him, I will claim him as mine own.* ~

Sea Witch was surging forwards, captured by the current of the tide, hurrying towards the sandbar beneath the sea, not the deep, safe, channel. Tiola screamed out at Jesamiah but he could not hear. She could do nothing to stop the proud ship from running aground. Could do nothing except watch!

~ *Help him!* ~ she pleaded. ~ *Rain please! Please do not listen to your mother. I beg you, help him!* ~

CHAPTER TWENTY-FOUR

Jesamiah alone saw her, a vague outline of a figure standing on the bowsprit. She was too far away in this downpour to see clearly, but her grey cloak, gown and hair were billowing in the wind, and she was looking out to sea, her right arm raised, finger pointing. Tiola?

~ *Is that you sweetheart?* ~

~ *Right, go hard right, now!* ~

Something was not as it should be! He could hear the drumming of the rain, the roar of the thunder, the crash of the sea and the sound of the waves pounding on to the rocks beneath the fort. Could hear, too, the wide, open, Atlantic Ocean calling to him. That voice, for all it was trying to be, was not Tiola's, but it blended into a roll of thunder and Jesamiah assumed it was the sound of the rain and his own agitation that was distorting her words. It had to be Tiola. Who else would it be?

~ *Starb'd Jessss...amiah! Hard to starb'd, Now! Now!* ~

Without thinking further he grabbed the wheel from Rue and spun it. *Sea Witch* heeled over, paused a moment, and then her bow was lifting, rising and rising to meet the first Atlantic roller that hurried, eager, to meet and caress her.

"Loose all sail!" he bellowed, giving the helm back to Rue and curling his hands around his mouth, while leaping down into the waist. "Drop sail! Now, now, now!"

Sea Witch's mainsail and foresail were tumbling from the yards; she was lifting, her bow rising up and up as she slid over the bar and out into the open ocean. Then her bow dipped downward and her stern swooped up as she fell over the wave. Battered, most of her larboard rail in pieces, holes gaping in her sails, much of her rigging tangled, she plunged out into freedom. Ran, scarred, scratched and scathed, with eight men dead, a further eighteen wounded, but she was afloat and she was free.

Calls, obscene jeers aimed at the *Challenger* falling away astern, and shouts mixing with cheers as sails filled in great, curving billows of thundering canvas that spread grey and elegant against the night sky. Nassau was behind them and *Sea Witch* was through the danger. Broken, battered, but through.

Tiola let her go. Pulling away, she released the ship from the encompassing mist, sent her out into the dark night and the flickering illumination of the storm, which was beginning to abate, the rain easing, the thunder rolling away. She watched as the jib sails began to creep up the forestay. A wash of spray hurled over her bow and *Sea Witch* was gathering way, her beloved captain taking the helm, urging his ship into the exhilaration of a full gallop.

Tears were running down Tiola's face. She could not read the future, could no more tell what may happen the next year, month, day or minute than could any mortal man or woman, but she knew she was losing him, had lost him. The sea would always call louder than could she.

~ *Take care Jesamiah. I can do no more for you.* ~

He did not hear. Did not answer.

~ *His mind is on his ship, Witch Woman. He has forgotten you.* ~

~ *No Rain, he will never forget me. But you are right, his mind, his love, is with his ship, not with me.* ~

Rain pattered down in a steady drizzle, aware that this human male had assumed that she was the witch, had not seen her for what she was, the ethereal spirit of the rain.

~ *My mother wants to keep him for her own. She wants me to help her.* ~

~ *I will prevent you. And her.* ~

~ *Even though he has left you and returned to the sea?* ~

Rain was genuinely puzzled by the Witch Woman's answer: ~ *Even then, for I love him without restraint or condition.* ~

The men had hurried inside with the sudden downpour. From inside the open balcony doors, Henry Jennings called to Tiola. "Come inside my dear, you will catch your death." He had her shawl in his hand, stepped on to the balcony, holding it out to her.

Tiola heard him as her soul passed easily back into the mortal host of her body. She stood, her hands, knuckles white, gripping the balcony rail watching Jesamiah go.

"My dear?"

Tiola turned, a look of anguish crumpling her face. "He has gone," she whispered.

"He will come back, I assure you."

"No. She may not let him."

Jennings looked puzzled. "She?"

Confused, her mind tired and disorientated from the trauma of astral detachment Tiola stepped towards him. "The rain, the sea, they will try to prevent him."

Jennings chuckled, held out her shawl. "He is a competent sailor, my dear. He is in no danger."

Tiola turned around quickly to look at where *Sea Witch* was fading into the darkness of the Atlantic and her shoe, a fancy indoor velvet slipper, slid on the rain-wet tiles of the balcony floor. She fell, tumbling backwards with a small, surprised cry. Her head thumped against the iron railings, and as the world and the stars spun in a dizzying swirl, she heard Tethys laugh triumphantly. Heard nothing more.

Jesamiah glanced forward to the bow intending to thank the spirit-woman, whoever she was, for her help. Tiola must have sent her, but there was nothing there now except the rain-slick decks as the water drained in torrents out of the scuppers. Below, the men were already at the pumps; he could hear the steady *thump, thump, thump* as they siphoned away the water that had sluiced in. He would go down in a minute, inspect the damage—although from what he could see up here, there was surprisingly little. Nothing that Chippy Harrison, the carpenter, could not fix.

He looked astern once, in the general direction of where the governor's grand house squatted up there on the hill. Was she watching? Could Tiola see him sailing away?

~ *I will be back, my darling. I promise you. As soon as I can I will come back for you. Somehow.* ~

He shouted a few more orders, put the helm down and sent *Sea Witch* towards Hispaniola.

CHAPTER TWENTY-FIVE

THURSDAY EVENING

"Ah, Stefan. *Dag*. How be y'wife?"

Closing the governor's sitting room door behind him Stefan van Overstratten walked gravely in, accepted the brandy Henry Jennings offered and sat, one leg elegantly resting over the other, opposite Rogers. He had told him several times already that *dag* meant goodbye not good evening but could not be bothered to continue correcting the annoying error.

"The physician bled her again this morning and your wife has been most kind, *dank u*. I can only apologise for the inconvenience I am causing your household."

"Nonsense, nonsense. Women are fragile creatures, eh?" Rogers did not like to add what he was thinking; that if he were in van Overstratten's shoes he would take the woman aboard ship and clear off back to Cape Town as soon as possible. That would make an end to the matter of Acorne, and if she did not recover, aye well, that was one of those things.

Jennings, seated on the far side of the room away from the blazing fire held his counsel. This whole business was turning sourer by the day. Reneging on an agreed amnesty, Vernon, in a rage after the wanton destruction of *Challenger* was commandeering ships as if there were no oak trees left in the entire world to build another. His temper increasing by the hour as he discovered the leaks, the sprung timbers, split sails and worm-riddled rotten keels. So many pirates never bothered taking care of their ships. Why should they? When one rotted they simply helped themselves to another.

It also galled Jennings that they had not been completely open with Jesamiah, a man he had liked to think of as a friend. He sighed. If Wickham had not drowned, if this fellow Chesham had come forward...oh, the ifs and buts! What a confounded nuisance they were! War was war, but for all that, war stank sometimes.

"Vernon will get the pirate swab," Rogers was saying in between generous puffs at his pipe. He took the poker, stabbed at a log on the fire. The Caribbean was a hot place during the day, but a chill often rolled in from the sea at night, and this persistent rain was making everything so damned damp. "Mark my words, Stefan, the rogue will pay with his life for what he has done."

It was not Acorne's life Stefan wanted, but those barrels of indigo. Vernon would not be going off in outraged pursuit until he had salvaged what he could in the way of arms and supplies from his own ship and had them transferred to the *Delicia*—once he had finished the extensive repairs needed to her hull. It was unlikely he would catch Acorne now. Jennings opted to remain silent on the fact, however. Rogers had been furious at losing his best ship to the Royal Navy. Perhaps it was not a good idea to re-open another torrential spate of swearing and blaspheming. Nor had he mentioned to the governor any of his carefully orchestrated manipulations. Rogers had too large a mouth and too small a sensible discretion to be trusted.

"I told you to not underestimate Acorne," was all Jennings remarked solemnly. "He is not a man to be pushed. Back him into a corner and he will not surrender but fight his way out."

Rogers made a crude noise through his lips. "Acorne will hang for what he has done. Mark me, I say, he will hang from his own yardarm. I made it quite plain those electing to return to piracy will forfeit any rights." He thumped the arm of his chair twice. "I will give no mercy. No quarter."

In an attempt to swallow the scathing retort hovering on his lips, Jennings sipped at his brandy. Failed the attempt. "What did you expect him to do, then? Sit back and watch Vernon steal his ship? I do not hear you being entirely acceptable of losing the *Delicia*! How is it different for him?"

"Different? I tell you the difference! I do not let people down. I do not go back on m'word! And my ship, sir, will not be commandeered into the shame of piracy!"

Avoiding a new conflict, Jennings refrained from reminding Rogers that he had initiated much of Nassau's unrest by withdrawing the agreement of amnesty. Men like Acorne did not take kindly to being buggered about.

Only barely following the exchange, van Overstratten lit one of his cheroots. Today had been a wretched day; the worry was reaching his stomach now, he had developed indigestion and frequently had to visit the seat of ease, where his stools ran from him like water. Last night he had not slept, doubted he would sleep tonight, either. These men assumed his distraction to be caused by concern over his unconscious wife. A proud man, he did not disillusion them.

She lay upstairs in her bed, eyes closed, not moving, not uttering word or sound. The water the maid had managed to spoon into her mouth trickling down her throat as a natural action, nothing more. For the sake of appearance Stefan had sat with Tiola as often as he could. She reminded him of an abandoned house; it appeared to be a home on the outside with its glass windows and painted sills, but inside everything was covered by dust sheets, the clocks were unwound, the cupboards bare. Except for the mice and the spiders no one was at home.

She was a witch! She had to be! How else had he fallen for her beguiling charms? How else had he been lured into asking her to become his wife? God's breath but there was nothing of her, she was a skinny runt with no teats and no seed in her belly. What had he seen in her?

He flicked ash into the hearth then inhaled the comforting taste of his cheroot, rested his head on the high chair-back, closed his eyes. It was the indigo he wanted. The indigo and Acorne! Both Rogers and Vernon claimed he had returned to piracy; they must know, they would not be wrong. To think that he, Stefan van Overstratten, had been so duped by the bastard's daring escape last night! He had been so pleased to see him scuttle away in more or less one piece—had expected him to go, although not in quite so spectacular a fashion. He had assumed Acorne would take the Letter of Marque Jennings had offered him, be gone at first opportunity, fetch the indigo and be back again as soon as may be for his whore.

Dunwoody had put him right. Acorne, he claimed, had refused the letter and had returned to the Sweet Trade. The indigo? Stephan slowly exhaled a stream of aromatic smoke. What madness had possessed him to trust Acorne? Damned, bloody, stupid fool! He tossed the cheroot into the fire, suddenly finding he was not enjoying its taste. Oh, Acorne would be getting the indigo—but he would be keeping it for himself! What? Give up a small fortune for a skinny broomstick like Tiola? Return for her, when he could bed the pick of the whores? Stefan snorted self-contempt. He had actually believed the cockscomb cared for Tiola! How naive could a man be? He sat, brooding, staring into the flames, not hearing the sharp words tossed between Jennings and Rogers, not noticing as a servant came in and discreetly spoke into Rogers' ear.

"What? Yes, yes, send 'im in, I'll see 'im." Impatient, Rogers waved the man away, then leant forward to tap Stefan's knee to gain his attention.

"We have a renegade from Acorne's crew come to share valuable information with us, it seems. I expect his pockets are empty an' he wants a few shillings fer the privilege of tellin' us his captain's returned to a life of piracy, eh?"

Mild curiosity made van Overstratten look up as the man entered, anxiously twirling his woollen cap around and around in his hands. He was grimed, in need of a shave and a wash; his coat stank of damp mould, his body of worse. So, this was the sort of degenerate Acorne commanded?

Jennings was on his feet, beckoning the man forward, thought better than to invite him near the fire for the foetid smell he exuded was bad enough without a toasting. "What be your name, lad?"

"Speak up!" Rogers bellowed, remaining sprawled in his chair. "Spit out what ye've come to say then get ye gone. Ye'll get only a thre'pence fer y'information though, so don't expect anythin' more."

The sailor cleared his throat twice, fiddled again with the red cap then touched his forelock. "I'm Perkins sir, me name be Elijah Perkins. I were on the *Sea Witch* fer nigh on a year. I been 'idin' in one o' those 'alf derelict ware'ouses down by Gallows Rock. Been tryin' t'decide what t'do, like."

"Decidin' which one of us to rob while in our beds? You dog."

"No sir! I swear, no! I came ashore a'fore Cap'n Acorne made sail. Being brought up a Protestant I wanted no truck with what 'e 'ad in mind." He fumbled quickly into a pocket in his coat, brought out a crumpled, dog-eared piece of paper. "The cap'n gave me this t'give t'you, Cap'n Jennings. Said as 'ow it would show I wanted to stay legal."

Jennings took it, read, walked across the room and handed it to Rogers, "He is telling the truth. He left the crew before Acorne cut his anchor cable."

Perkins expression was one of confusion and pleading. Of abject misery and fear. "I didn't know what t'do guvn'r, it's been playing on me conscience badly. I mean m'gran'pap, he fought fer Cromwell, it ain't right what Cap'n Acorne's goin' t'do."

"What be ye babblin' about man?" Rogers snapped as he tossed the letter to van Overstratten. "What the bugger has that old king-murdering Roundhead got to do with it? Acorne's turned pirate not puritan!"

Van Overstratten permitted himself a shallow grimace of distaste as he read the hastily scrawled note. A falling out among thieves? If they did not even trust each other, how had he ever imagined he could trust just one?

"What ain't right Perkins?" Jennings coaxed. He poured the man a brandy, despite Rogers' frown of disapproval gave it to the wretch, who drank it down in one gulp.

"Thank 'ee sir, I be mighty grateful. I meant Cap'n Acorne's idea t'sail t' 'Ispaniola t'ain't right."

A moment of silence. Van Overstratten half rose from his chair, not daring to hope. Had he been wrong? Did Acorne intend to stick to their bargain after all?

Rogers jumped up, excited. "Hispaniola? Is he doin' as we asked him after all? Well huzzah for that! Always said Acorne was a fine fellow, did I not? Ha, ha!"

"Aye," Perkins said, disappointed that these fine gentlemen seemed to know Jesamiah's plans already. He had intended to bargain for a passage home to England. "Aye, he's gone to Santo Domingo. To offer 'is service and 'is ship and fight this war on the side of the Dons."

Roger's delighted laughter ceased abruptly. Silence. Only the crackling of wood in the fire, and along the corridor outside, the somnolent chime of a clock.

Consumed by fury, Rogers swept his hand through his wife's treasured collection of china ornaments arrayed along the mantelshelf. "Spain?" he roared. "He has gone to fight for Spain?" He tipped over a table, then his chair. "Spain? The god-damned, turncoat! The whoreson, bloody traitor! Bugger him! Bugger him! May he rot! I'll geld him for this—so help me, I will geld him then burn him at the stake!"

Jennings pretended to drop his pipe. With his gout it was difficult for him to bend. Reaching down to the floor was the only way he could hide the smile.

By God, he thought, *Acorne's going to bloody help us! He took my laid bait!* He wondered whether to point out to Rogers that this bluff of fighting for Spain would be one of Acorne's more elaborate plans, but decided to keep quiet. Rogers would never be able to fake annoyance, and anyway there was the possibility that Acorne *might* not be bluffing. He had been very angry, and maybe he really had turned his coat and gone over to the Dons?

But was that likely?

Chapter Twenty-Six

Friday Morning

Stefan was a man who usually managed to contain his emotions. He thought in black and white, occasionally shades of grey, but he was not given to flights of fancy or the glorious rainbow colours that painted an imagination. Nor did he usually act on impulse or whim but thought out what was needed rationally and sensibly. Unless he was playing cards. Cards were his weakness, Whist in particular. That and the compulsive need to impress his sister's husband.

The man was a conceited wastrel, but he came from minor Dutch nobility and never let anyone, particularly Stefan, forget his high-status breeding. Stefan's father and grandfather had been merchants lucky enough to buy into the right trade at the right time and had then risen into the new class of self-made wealth. When his brother-in-law discovered he had squandered the family fortune on bad investments—and on losing at cards—there would be one monster of a row. Stefan's only option was to ensure he did not discover it.

Dawn was brightening into a new day, yet still Stefan sat gazing out of his bedchamber window. He had been there all night. He had to settle the gambling debts he owed, and had to restore a healthy balance to the estate's dwindling bank account; to do both it was imperative he obtain that indigo.

He sighed and rubbed at his stiff neck, ran his hand down his face. The same thoughts had been trudging through his mind all night, since he had learnt that Acorne had gone over to the Spanish, and had made everything hopeless.

Until yesterday he had convinced himself that Acorne would come back, but that man, what was his name? Perkins? Perkins had made him see the futility, that it was a useless hope. He stood up abruptly. Who was he fooling? Acorne had never intended to bring him that indigo. What? A pirate pass over the chance of making a fortune? Huh!

Going over to the laver he poured water into the bowl, dipped in his hands and splashed it over his tired, drawn, face. He had one option. One last option. Get the indigo himself. He stood, staring into the mirror at his hollow cheeks, the dark circles under his eyes. Inhaling deeply he washed his face properly, felt better for the cold water on his skin, a plan beginning to form in his mind. He was a merchant he did not require permission to leave harbour, all he needed to do was inform the captain of his sloop that they were to set sail and where they were headed...

I will leave Tiola behind, he thought. *She is of no more use to me. Naturally I will tell Rogers that I will return for her—I can pretend I am going to fetch a physician from Port Royal. This one here is nothing more than a charlatan. What word did he use? Coma? Corma? What nonsense. I will leave and not come back. They can send her to the poorhouse or throw her out to whore on the streets for all I care.*

He began to dress, feeling better now he was doing something positive. Paused as he was buttoning his waistcoat. There were two possibilities he had to take into account. What if there was no indigo? He wandered to the window again. Jennings said there might not be. Or what if Acorne was already there, had already stolen it?

Two solutions.

If Acorne had got there first it might be possible to find him and bargain; the barrels for the bitch. *Ja*, he would take Tiola with him. It made no difference to her whether she lay unconscious in her bed here, or in the one on his sloop. He need not inform the pirate, when he found him, that in the physician's opinion, if she did not wake within a few days she probably never would. If there was indigo, then he could salvage his dignity and return home to Cape Town with no one any the wiser of his predicament. And if, by chance, he still had Tiola with him, assuming she recovered, he would be saying nothing of her indiscretion, and neither would she. He needed a son and he could not face the tittle-tattle, the knowing nods and winks—the sheer boredom—of having to find a replacement wife to give him one. Maybe Tiola would oblige in time?

Stefan put on his coat and hat, picked up his walking cane and left the room. When Tiola awoke she would resume her duties as his wife. He would lay with her every night, if necessary, until he impregnated her. She would bear him a son—she damned would! He shut the door and walked down the stairs, happier now that he had made a decision.

By midday they were under sail. Mrs Rogers had twittered about moving Tiola, but only half-heartedly; Stefan had the impression she was actually relieved to be rid of them.

At sea, heading for Hispaniola, Stefan stood on the deck watching Nassau disappear from view, and made one more decision. If he could not get that indigo he would not return to Cape Town. He was a proud man, he could not stomach the thought of everyone knowing he had made an almighty cock-up of everything from his business to his marriage. He stared down at the rush of foam as it seethed around the bow and curled along the hull. It would be so easy to jump. Quick. Final. And if he jumped, he would be taking Tiola with him.

He smiled, satisfied. *You will be so sorry that you never came back for her Acorne.*

Throwing the stub of his cheroot into the sea Stefan headed below. There would be glowing obituaries and dabbed tears. He would be mourned by his family and remembered by his peers as an honourable, worthy, man. And not for months would they discover the truth that the tragic drowning of Stefan van Overstratten and his wife was likely no accident, given the poor state of affairs that he had left behind.

The eternal void of Nowhere stretched away in all directions, on and on in an expanse of forever. It was pleasant here, tranquil and silent. Tiola's soul was weak and tired, drained of all energy, almost of existence, but here, out here in the emptiness where there was nothing except peace and solitude, she could rest and sleep. And forget.

The white silence washed over and through her as she drifted aimlessly outside of time and place. Drifted, unconcerned and free from mass and weight. Free of care and memory. She did dream, slightly, of being swathed in a blanket and carried—somewhere. Dreamt she felt the rocking motion of the sea, but she was lulled by the timeless winds of the un-being, and paid no heed to things that seemed unimportant.

She had no recollection of anything except the Here and the Now. No recollection of anything. Or anyone.

Not even Jesamiah.

PART TWO

HISPANIOLA

CHAPTER ONE

SATURDAY MORNING

Finding a Chase—a Frenchy—soon after dawn, the crew of the *Sea Witch* had fended off a brief effort at resistance, boarded, and helped themselves to what they needed: replacement sail, timber and three fine anchors with attached cable. The essential repairs had been carried out at sea, and without losing much time, they had raised Hispaniola in the early morning light of this bright and sunny day.

A tropical paradise with magnificent beaches, palm tree groves and luxuriant meadows set beside a hilly landscape where cotton, tobacco and sugar plantations were framed by the high, greenery-covered mountains. Pico Duarte, purple-hazed and visible from several miles out to sea, soared to over ten-thousand feet—the highest point in the entire West Indies. Closer to shore, on the western bank of the Ozama River, the walls of Santo Domingo, the oldest town in the New World, steadily became clearer as *Sea Witch* ploughed joyfully through the surf.

It all looked lovely beneath the clear blue of the sky and the sparkle of the sun. The backdrop of lush, tropical forest tumbling down to white beaches and swaying palm trees.

A pity, Jesamiah thought, *the tranquillity is spoilt by that bloody fortress.*

He watched, transfixed, the dread growing heavier inside him as the sixty-five solid feet of the *Torre del Homenaje*, the Tower of Homage, loomed nearer. The place of despair and death, where tortured, pathetic wretches were incarcerated behind walls seven-foot thick to await their doom. He knew all about the horrors behind those walls. He'd been there.

If it was not for the fact that the tide was taking *Sea Witch* into the estuary that led into the Rio Ozama, Jesamiah may well have changed his mind, ordered the men to wear ship and scuttle away as fast as they could. But it was too late, the tide was making and they were in the river. The day was hot, but as they neared that tower he found he was shivering.

Poke a sleeping guard dog and it comes leaping to life, barking, hackles raised, teeth bared and ready to bite. The only strategy was to offer it a bone and hope it was hungry enough to want it. Jesamiah prayed the bone he held was suitably tasty.

Sea Witch carried twelve powerful cannons on her lower gun deck, four in the waist, two lighter guns for'ard and the two stern chasers in Jesamiah's cabin. With the addition of six swivel guns mounted fore and aft she was a formidable vessel against poorly manned merchant ships, although Jesamiah rarely attacked opponents who appeared to know what they were doing. As with most pirates, when it was more sensible to run, he ran; not an act of cowardice, just one of self-preservation for himself, his crew and his ship. Why start a fight you have every possibility of losing? Especially when the next sail on the horizon may offer better odds. They were sitting ducks out here though. For all her firepower *Sea Witch* could not hope to match the might of those land-based cannons ranged along the ramparts of the fort.

A single warning shot reverberated with a *whoomph* of sound and a puff of smoke from the walls. The ball, whistling through the air as it came, arced over the bowsprit and splashed into the sea a mere two feet away. From where he stood on the quarterdeck Jesamiah could see at least a dozen cannons aimed directly at *Sea Witch*. Their presence up there was no empty threat, nor, when Jesamiah swung the telescope towards the town, did the array of armed militia hurriedly lining up along the jetty show any sign of a warm welcome.

Glancing up at the makeshift white flag of truce—Tiola's white lace-edged cloth flying high from the main topgallant mast—Jesamiah attempted to put a brave face on the situation. "At least we're being taken seriously. Treated with the respect due our position."

At the helm, Rue growled at him, his brows deeply furrowed. "They are ready to blast us out the water. That, *mon ami*, is not respect, nor is it a good position for us to be in."

Digging his quartermaster in the ribs with his elbow, Jesamiah answered, "If they did not respect us, mate, they'd have smashed us already. The only reason they ain't done so, *mi amigo*, is because they're curious about us, and that is a good position for us to be in."

Another shot fell with a fountain of spray three feet from the larboard midships.

Rue glowered doubtfully at his captain, who in return forced a wavering grin and steadfastly assured, "They ain't missing us by accident, Rue." Fervently thought, *I hope.*

A third ball would prove him right or wrong. The previous two were either precisely aimed as a warning or they were ranging shots. In which case the third would...

Squinting against the bright sun Jesamiah refused to follow that line of contemplation. *Sea Witch* was gliding sedately forward as if she had no idea that these could be her last few minutes intact and afloat. But then, she trusted her captain implicitly, had never had a reason to doubt him.

"The line if you please, Isiah," Jesamiah said surprising himself at the calm in his voice. "And fetch the courses in." Five ships were anchored ahead and to larboard, but they were Spaniards, they knew these waters, he did not.

"By the deep nine, Cap'n!" Isiah called a few moments later, reeling in the lead-line and preparing to toss it outward again.

Under topsails, *Sea Witch* crept towards the shore.

"And a half eight," Isiah chanted. Then, "And a quarter eight." The tide was on the flood, at least if they went aground the sea would lift them off again.

"Larboard a point, Rue. Straighten her up. We don't want to look tawdry," Jesamiah said quietly, aware that many critical eyes were watching from the shore. He could not afford to make a poor show of this. He wondered whether he ought to clear for action—no that could give the wrong idea, he needed to show he came in peace, not to fight. "Nat, fire a rolling broadside salute from the larboard battery if you please. Powder only. No shot."

Nathan nodded, turned to run off. "And Nat," Jesamiah added, "I'd be obliged if you make sure it's done 'andsomely in Royal Navy fashion. I'm attempting to make a good impression 'ere, savvy?"

"Aye, aye, Cap'n. Handsomely it is."

Within a few minutes the larboard cannons blasted smoke and noise; one, two, three, four, five ... A salute, to show respect and make it clear that the guns were not loaded for any action of hostility. Jesamiah nodded. Nicely done. If that did not convince those ashore that they were here under friendly terms nothing would.

The whole crew were on deck, standing rigid, watching, waiting—like their captain, waiting for that third firing of the fort's cannon, knowing that if it came it would not fall short.

"Keep that lead going in the chains there!" Jesamiah commanded, his anxiety finally taking its toll in his voice. His stomach was churning; he suppressed the urge to vomit over the side. He could not take his gaze off that tower, that bloody tower.

"By the mark eight," Isiah called.

Well enough still, but this was a river, channels could be fickle, could run shallow at any moment. Again Jesamiah asked Rue to adjust course, the men quietly turning to the braces to tend the yards and meet her.

"And a half seven."

The water was smooth here, *Sea Witch* crept over the glassy surface, gliding above her own reflection, the only sound the ceaseless harping of the rigging, the chuckle of the water under the keel and a slight moan from the wind. The shore was drawing nearer, the spread of the town with its white-walled houses showing up clearer than those built in darker stone. From the great cathedral a flash of sunlight blazed on the gold crucifix atop its roof. The walls of that fort coming nearer. The tower looming higher.

"And a half seven." A pause, a splash, then, "By the mark, a quarter seven."

"Is the anchor clear?"

"Aye, sir."

"By the mark seven."

No point in going further, they were almost up on the nearest of those five ships now.

"Let go the anchor!"

The newly acquired cable roared out through the hawsehole while the men sprang to furl the topsails, and *Sea Witch* swung round to the wind and the tide. For good or ill, they had arrived.

Isiah wiped a hand beneath his nose, indicated the shore. "Seems someone's comin' out to greet us, Cap'n. They must be mighty eager to say hello."

Jesamiah angled the telescope at the longboat. In addition to the oarsmen, a dozen Spaniards, all of them bristling with muskets and pistols.

Assuming there would be some form of reception committee, Jesamiah had already attired himself in the best clothes he could muster; standing in the waist waiting for the boat to come alongside he suddenly wondered if perhaps his old clothes would have been more appropriate. These would be ruined the instant he was thrown into the dungeons of that tower.

His fingers fiddled with the blue ribbons in his hair, sense kept his hand away from cutlass and pistol as a man he recognised stepped aboard. Jesamiah groaned. Captain Augustine de Castilla.

"*Buenos dias*. We meet again *nos enontremos de nuevo, mi amigo*," Jesamiah said in fluent Spanish, knowing de Castilla spoke very little English. He offered a polite bow, then his hand. Both were ignored by narrowed eyes, a glower of intense disapproval and hostile dislike.

"We thought it was you. Your ship, with her blue hull, she is distinctive." There was no trace of hospitality in the man's manner or reply, but then, Jesamiah expected none. He had once, after all, right under de Castilla's nose, emptied an entire warehouse of gold and silver that the Spaniard had been guarding.

De Castilla shoved his face close to Jesamiah's, the sneer lurid. Said, also in Spanish, "If I had my way, Acorne, you would be strung by your balls from your own yardarm here and now, but I have orders to fetch you ashore. I have not been ordered to ensure you remain in one piece, however. I will be delighted to deliver you in little bits, should you attempt any futile resistance."

Moving with slow deliberation, Jesamiah took the pistol from his belt by its barrel, solemnly handed it to de Castilla who passed it to the officer at his side; the cutlass followed, drawn with equally slow measure.

Responding in Spanish, said: "As you see, señor, I come to Santo Domingo in peace. I have no wish to fight against you, in fact I come to offer my services to fight with you."

Captain de Castilla planted his legs wide, set his fists to his hips and tossed his head back in a great belly-deep guffaw of amusement. He then hoiked spittle into his throat and spat disrespectfully at Jesamiah's feet. "Your ship we will accept as a small payment towards the amount you stole from España. For the other part, your flayed hide dangling from the foremast will suffice."

Glancing up at the fortress, Jesamiah absent-mindedly toyed with his ribbons, "*Yo entiendo, señor.*" Then added in the corrupted slang that many in the Caribbean had adopted, and so annoyed the Spanish, "*Yo sabe.*" In English, repeated for the third time, "I savvy, I understand."

He then forced a smile, said, as pleasantly as any sarcastic Spanish comment could be made; "I know for a fact your gunners up on those battlements are accurate, but that is because you have three or four capable gun captains. The rest of the men behind those ramparts are probably drunk out of their tiny skulls and cannot stand upright, let alone shoot straight." Pointedly, he nodded at the blue-coated soldiers arrayed along the jetty. "They look very pretty, most impressive. From a distance. How many have no more than two rounds of ammunition in their pouches? How many of those muskets have rusting barrels and worn flints? I also note their line is only one deep. That is not many men, señor."

He turned slightly, indicated the ships at anchor. "Fine frigates. One is listing to starb'd, she'll be taking on water like a rabid dog if put to sea. That one over there is the *Señorita Doña Medici*. Now, how many times have I already bested her? Three is it, or four? Then those other two, *Dolce* and *Asunción*. Unless you have replaced the dolt who is master of the *Asunción* you may as well not bother with her. He does not know east from west—and that's when he's sober. As for the *Dolce*, well, I admit I have never robbed her. For me she is a prim little virgin."

De Castilla interrupted sharply. "No one can, or will, better her. She is the finest ship in the Spanish Main; she has the speed of a dolphin, has..."

"...The waddle of a flat-footed pelican. I've never beaten her in a fight, señor, because she is rarely at sea! She sits there like a beached whale for God's sake!" Jesamiah threw his hands in the air, exasperated by this rotund, moustached idiot. "And this is the sum of your Spanish Navy here in Hispaniola? Hell's tits, I could sail rings around the lot of you, one handed and with my eyes shut!"

"One handed and blind we can arrange," de Castilla snarled. He too indicated the ships, the fifth one. "You have not mentioned *La Santa Isabella*."

She, Jesamiah had to admit to himself, looked in pretty good shape. "I do not know her. I will have to see her in action to make judgement. Who captains her?"

De Castilla leant forward, spoke directly into Jesamiah's face, his breath stinking of onions and sour wine. "I do, Capitán Acorne. I do."

Tempted to say something along the line of: "Oh, nothing to worry about then," Jesamiah held his tongue. Several of his men who spoke enough Spanish to understand the exchange must have read his thoughts, however, for there was a ripple of sniggered laughter.

De Castilla jerked his arm and angrily gestured towards the waiting longboat.

"What of my crew?" Jesamiah asked as he turned to descend the hull cleats. "I fly a flag of truce. I expect your word of honour for the safety of my men."

"Honour? Among thieves and pirates?" For a second time, de Castilla spat derisively on the deck, reluctantly had to repeat the orders he had been given. "They will remain unharmed provided they sit quiet and remain still. You will order them to be so."

This was a pirate ship, pirates made their own rules, but then, even pirates realised when they did not have a choice. "Do as he says, Rue. Set your backsides and stay quiet. Keep a sharp eye though, savvy?" Stepping down into the boat, Jesamiah settled himself where de Castilla had sat on the outward journey, stared nonchalantly ahead ignoring the Spaniard's glower as the oarsmen pulled for shore. Inside, his stomach was quaking. This could turn out to be a very short, very painful, trip ashore.

Escorted—marched—into the governor's residence he was not surprised to find himself greeted with blatant discourtesy by the two dozen or so men and women occupying the gilded and elaborately decorated room. Gaudy and of no practical use in Jesamiah's opinion, but then, that precisely described both the room and the florid-faced governor of Hispaniola. In his late fifties, he had acquired a bulk of girth and lost the glossy black hair and handsome appearance of his youth. His skin was pockmarked by a residue of smallpox scars, and his teeth were yellowed. A foul man in all respects.

Standing or sitting in small groups, their animated talk wilting into silence, most of the men stared disdainfully at Jesamiah, one or two even turning their backs as he walked past. He recognised several faces; merchants, three of whom he had robbed. The ladies present were more charitable, secretively assessing him from behind the rattle of fluttering fans. He waited patiently while de Castilla spoke into the governor's ear then swept off his hat and bowed low and formally as he was beckoned forward with a single tweak of one fat, raised finger. Ah, so curiosity, as he had bargained, was getting the better of Don Damián del Gardo. There could be no other reason for his agreeing to this interview; del Gardo hated Jesamiah's guts. The feeling was distinctly mutual.

Unhurried, confident, Jesamiah stopped a few yards before the governor and rising from another flourished bow, met the green gaze of a striking redhead seated beside the Spaniard. She met his startled expression passively, her mouth giving a small, amused smile.

"*Señorita*," he said, offering her a nodded bow.

Annoyed, del Gardo took her hand in his own and glowered at Jesamiah.

His mistress? Certainly not his wife, whom Jesamiah knew had not, so rumour maintained, left her bedchamber since contracting smallpox from her husband several years ago. The tongues wagged that the disease had so ruined her face she dared not be seen, even by del Gardo. Returning the redhead's smile Jesamiah wondered at that. More likely she shut herself away because of the whores her husband so openly bedded.

Ostentatiously resting his other hand on his sword hilt, del Gardo said in Spanish, "So, Mereno's younger brat dares to enter my lair? Tell me, bastard boy, why should I not string you up here and now?"

Jesamiah's guts recoiled. Before he was born, even before his elder half-brother, Phillipe, was born, their father and del Gardo had been sworn enemies. He had no idea of the full story behind the bitter animosity, assumed the hatred had arisen during the days when Charles Mereno had sailed as a buccaneer with Henry Morgan. He knew they had attacked Spanish ships and towns, violently looting, murdering and raping. But then, the Spanish had done the same to the English. This particular hatred was personal, went beyond the consequences of a war fought in the name of religion; it was rumoured that Mereno had cuckolded del Gardo's father. But who knew the truth of rumour?

Vaguely, Jesamiah knew his father had left Morgan's service around the time he had made his first fortune and subsequently purchased a tobacco plantation in Virginia. He had also adopted the name Mereno instead of a previous alias—neither that nor his original birth name had Jesamiah discovered.

Charles had married a Spanish lady who presented him with a son in 1686. Beyond those few facts, Jesamiah knew nothing more. She had been a first wife, had died when that son was no more than five years old. As Jesamiah understood it, his father had been so consumed by grief that he had abandoned the plantation and the boy and returned to the life of a privateer, well, to be more honest, to piracy. When he later met and married his second wife, also Spanish, the boy, Phillipe, had bitterly resented his father bringing home a replacement mother and a new baby brother. The bitterness had never wavered, had caused Jesamiah a childhood of such misery that it still haunted him.

Only now, standing before del Gardo, did it occur to him that there were more than a few unexplained gaps in the story. Jesamiah calculated a few figures in his head; he was nearly twenty-five years old, Phillipe had been seven years his senior. Whatever had happened had been more than thirty-two years ago. He knew del Gardo had recently turned fifty, so he had been barely eighteen when he had known Charles Mereno. Jesamiah mentally shrugged. Whatever the reason for the hostility, he doubted he would discover any answers here. Did not particularly want to hear them anyway. He returned his attention to what del Gardo was saying.

"To sail in as if you own the harbour, you are either a very stupid Englishman or have the nerve of the devil," Don Damián sneered. "Which of the two is it?"

Answering, also in Spanish, Jesamiah retorted, "I remind you, señor, my mother was the daughter of a marqués and I have always understood my father to be half-French. I concede I was born in England, but as I spent no more than my first days there I do not consider myself an Englishman. Stupid or otherwise. I am an American Colonist."

Del Gardo snorted disdain. "I heard the slut who spawned you was disowned by her father when she ran off with the pirate scum she claimed was your father. Neither of his wives had a right to any title except that of whore."

Fiddling angrily with one of his ribbons, Jesamiah stared into Don Damián's fleshy eyes, the urge to strangle the fat bastard strong in his mind. He choked it down, let go of his ribbon and smiled congenially. "I pay little attention to rumour, señor." Added in English; "Personally, I have never believed the one about my father bedding your mother. He had better taste in women."

Silence as heavy as stone, everyone aware something unseemly had been spoken. Several whispers, a rustling and uncomfortable fidgeting; questions being murmured behind shielding hands and another, renewed, fluttering of fans. None of the fancy-dressed, arrogant peacocks or their painted ladies spoke more than a little, very poor, English. As Jesamiah well knew.

Don Damián leant towards the redhead. "¿Qué dijo el bastardo?"

"The bastard said he believed his father knew your mother," the redhead answered in Spanish as she smiled at Jesamiah, her eyes gleaming with a sparkle of amused mischief. Added in English, "Is that not a suitable translation Captain Acorne?"

Jesamiah was momentarily taken aback. She was enchanting, her green eyes were pools to drown in and she was, unmistakably, English. He smiled back at her, dipped his head in respectful acknowledgement. "Aye, señorita, I believe you have realised the gist of what I meant."

She laughed, a low, seductive chuckle, as rich as dark, exotic, chocolate. "Unfortunately, I must correct you. I am not a señorita. I am a widow."

Jesamiah gestured an apology. "An understandable mistake, señora."

"*Silencio!*" Extremely annoyed del Gardo beckoned Jesamiah nearer, fastidiously dabbing at his nose with a scented handkerchief as he approached. The handkerchief was quite unnecessary for Jesamiah had made Finch lug out the old tin bath last night and had wallowed sufficiently to ensure he was clean and relatively sweet-smelling, though now he was ashore, in this heat, he did perhaps have a pungent whiff of sweat about him, but no more than everyone else in this airless room.

Don Damián's eyes narrowed as he gazed repugnantly at Jesamiah, the hatred intense. Flicking imaginary dirt from his elaborately embroidered waistcoat he sat forward in his chair. "You take me for a fool, Acorne?" his voice was steel with menace. "It is you who are the fool. Hah! You thought to take me in with this, what you English call a 'cock and balls' story?" He looked around the room with a self-congratulatory smile as his court tittered obediently. Of a sudden his expression changed, his Spanish became a rapid staccato. "Well I will have your cock and balls; I will have them cut off and stuffed down your gullet before you will ever make a fool of Don Damián del Gardo!"

The Spaniard's inept use of an English phrase would have amused Jesamiah had the image not been so foul. He shuddered, swallowed hard, concentrated on staring ahead at del Gardo. Despite himself, his hand made a slight movement towards his groin. He glanced at the redhead, realised she had seen and forced it into his coat pocket instead, willing his nerve to remain calm, his tense muscles to relax.

"I am here because I prefer to help Spain win this petty little war. Whatever your opinion of my mother, señor, she was Spanish and as I said, I have reason to believe my father had French blood, I therefore owe no debt of loyalty to the English; they lie and cheat and go back on their given word. I prefer to fight for integrity and honour."

"¿*Yoro*?" de Castilla commented dryly.

With a nod of his head, Jesamiah congenially agreed, "Aye, and gold. But I am not fussy as to whose gold I can steal. English gold is as good as any. I have no wish to serve King George of Hanover, nor his parliamentarian arse-lickers. I have come to offer the service of my crew and my ship to Spain, and to you, Don Damián del Gardo."

His expression that of insipid disdain, Don Damián waved the offer aside with a flap of his handkerchief. "Do you think me an imbecile? You will sail with my ships then turn your guns on them." He stabbed the air with a pointing finger, his Spanish words rasping out harsh and accusing, "I say you are here as an English spy!"

Be pleasant. Do not even think about slitting this fat bastard's throat. "If what you suggest is the truth then why would I enter your harbour so openly? If I was going to destroy your ships, señor, I could have already done so, or do so as and when I please. I have no need to risk my life by coming into your lair. You need someone who knows what he is doing. You need me, for you have only one decent vessel, the rest are disintegrating ships commanded by useless captains."

De Castilla bristled and spluttered his indignation. "I am a perfectly capable captain! I..."

Jesamiah interrupted him. "You allowed a pirate to walk in to where you were in charge of protecting a warehouse full of salvaged treasure. Subsequently, you got drunk and bedded a whore with him. When you awoke next morning with a headache and your breeches round your ankles, the pirate was long gone and so was the treasure. I'm surprised you are so ready to boast of your capabilities, Capitán. I'm also surprised your masters permit you to keep your manhood after such gross incompetence." Jesamiah leant forward slightly, continued, "Or perhaps they didn't."

Emphasising his point, he made a grab and twist motion with his clenched fist. That robbery had been one of the easiest and most lucrative in his entire career as a pirate. Because of it, he was a wealthy man.

He returned his attention to the governor. "If you are to impress your king you need me, not incompetents like that one." He made an obscene gesture in de Castilla's direction.

Don Damián del Gardo slowly hoisted himself from his chair, came to stand before Jesamiah and regarded him suspiciously, assessing his worth as though he were inspecting a new horse in the market. He circled around, walking with a measured pace occasionally touching his handkerchief to his nose. As much as he did not want to admit it, this pirate cockroach spoke correctly. Those ships at anchorage were in a state of neglect and he had morons for officers. It was the king's fault! How was he to govern an island such as this with virtually no support from Spain? Unrest had spread from shore to shore across the island, nesting among poor freemen scrimping a meagre living, and even among the rich noblemen owning acres of plantation land. According to his spies, an uprising was imminent. These were rebels, native Creoles and settled Spanish alike, on the verge of hammering at his residence door and he had only a dwindling supply of shot and gunpowder with which to defend himself. Barely enough even for that—and the king expected him to fight a damned war as well? In the name of God, with what? He had nothing, not even, as this pirate had so casually observed, a seaworthy fleet.

All he had was his pride and his spies. He flicked his handkerchief irritably; spies who were proving to be as useless as his fleet. Not one of them had discovered precisely when the rebels would rise, who their leader was or how the supplies were getting in. And they were getting in. Somehow, they were getting in!

"Am I to trot a few paces? Show you my teeth and how high I can leap a fence?" Jesamiah asked.

Don Damián circled again, stopped a pace in front of Jesamiah, considering. If this man was genuine in his offer then maybe, just maybe, he could rally some enthusiasm into the militia and sailors; new impetus, a new challenge might stir them up? Ah, but what if this reprobate was lying? It was not wise to invite the wolf into the fold, but then, a wolf near the fire could be the more clearly seen.

He caught his mistress also assessing this English pirate. How useful was she? How far would she go in obeying a direct command? So far she had only told him minor things and for some while he had been considering testing her loyalty. Perhaps this was a God sent opportunity. Decision made, he returned to his seat, crossed one leg over the other, the silk of his pale yellow breeches stretching almost to the limit over his buttocks and thighs. "Some of the things you say make sense, pirate, but I do not trust you. And you are wrong. I require your ship, I do not require you."

Jesamiah masked any reaction. "But you do require a crew, and my men will not sail her without me." He let that sink in, then said, "Give me a chance to prove our worth." One more push, one more lure to gain trust and attention. "When my pirate brethren in Nassau realise I have been welcomed here in Hispaniola, when they hear I am honoured and respected among the Spanish, they will also come. Nigh on every captain who has a ship to sail will flock to your side because of me, and because Governor Rogers has treated us most ill. The Brotherhood does not take treachery kindly." He smiled expansively, spread his hands as wide. He was sincere in what he was saying, had no need to add false bravado or colour the water. They would come, pirates did not take heavy-handed interference lightly. "You could have an entire fleet of experienced seamen at your disposal, Governor. Men who know how to fight. What have you got to lose by hiring me and my services?"

Don Damián was convinced. This was an opportunity not to be missed, but under no circumstances was he going to show his eagerness too soon.

"Very well. But I will require proof that you are not here to spy or play tricks. To show their worth, and your sincerity, your crew will make sail, capture a suitable English prize and bring it here to me. If I believe it to be of satisfactory value, then I will accept your offer."

Jesamiah nodded, that was acceptable. "*Sí, ningún problema.*"

The interview was over. Del Gardo beckoned his mistress to join him and progressed towards the door. His entourage rose and followed as if it were a stately procession, the ladies' wide skirts supported by whalebone hoops swaying as if they too were ships at sea. After several yards del Gardo stopped, turned and said with a sickly-sweet smile; "No Capitán Acorne, you will not be with them. You will be staying here. Your ship will be under Capitán de Castilla's command. If your crew does not return with something worthwhile within ten days then I will assume you are lying and I will hang you." He clicked his fingers at two of the guards standing to attention beside the doorway. "Lock him up."

"You can't do this!" Jesamiah spluttered, backing away, close to panic. "The *Sea Witch* is my ship, no one else captains her! No one!"

"Ah, but I can do this. Your crew will do as I command or they will all hang beside you. And I assure you, Capitán, you will welcome your hanging for that will be the easy part."

He walked away. "I will have you slowly drawn and quartered first."

This had always been the risk, that the animosity del Gardo felt towards Jesamiah would blinker him from any trace of common sense. What Jesamiah had said about the state of his fleet had not been bluff, though, it was true. But to offer to fight for the Spanish? Where did 'common sense' come into such ideas?

Stupidity, more like.

CHAPTER TWO

SATURDAY NIGHT

~ *Do you have him?* ~

~ *He has seen me, heard me, though he does not recognise who I am. But I have him, yes.* ~

~ *Then give him to me! He is mine!* ~

Rain was not going to be so obliging. Why should she give him up? She liked him. She wanted to keep him. ~ *The Witch Woman says he is hers. I might decide that she is right and give him back.* ~

~ *No! No, I forbid it! I forbid you!* ~ *Tethys was furious, how dare her daughter disobey! How dare that sly, pale-faced, black-haired witch interfere! Acorne was hers! Hers!*

She raged, built herself into a torrent of violence that she unleashed against the shore, seething her weight in a frenzy of white-foamed, high-curved, battering waves. But she knew little of the land, and where she spent her temper, among the marshes and sand banks of the Ocracoke, and along the uninhabited North Carolina coast, she did little damage, for she only disturbed the waterfowl and the indigenous boat people. Fisher-folk.

Rain, although she came from the sea, had never cared for her mother. She ran off oblivious to the turmoil she was causing. All she was interested in was him. The one the Witch Woman called Jesamiah.

Dark, small, spaces had terrified Jesamiah since his lonely days of childhood. A legacy of when Phillipe had shut him in cupboards, or the cellar, bolting the doors and leaving him there for hours on end. He would come to let him out, eventually, but always Jesamiah had feared that he would not. On the last occasion when Phillipe had chained him in the dank and stinking below-deck world of a cable tier and subjected him to things that no sane man would have done to another, if it had not been for Tiola and the crew of the *Sea Witch* he would have died. Died with the sound of Phillipe's sadistic laughter ringing in his ears.

He could hear that laughter now, slithering under the locked door with the blade-thin strand of lamplight. He could hear Phillipe coming nearer and nearer, stop at the door, then walk away again. Next time, next time he would come in and...Jesamiah curled his arms around his head, moaned piteously. No matter that this was not a dank cellar but the highest room in the tower, that there was a grilled window giving air and a faint haze of cloud-covered moonlight. No matter that the man outside was a Spanish guard, not Phillipe, he was living in the dread-filled nightmare of his childhood. Summoning the courage to look up, Jesamiah stared at the window. It was cold in here, but he was sweating. Phillipe was dead. Dead! He, Jesamiah, had killed him. Why could he not forget the past, look to the future? He groaned again, closed his eyes. What future was there without Tiola? There had been nothing from her. She had not tried to reach him. There was a huge emptiness inside him, a black pit within his belly as if his guts had been ripped out. She was not with him. Tiola had gone from him.

Inhaling a steadying breath he reached out to touch the man who lay on the floor in a scrunched, untidy heap. Jesamiah had no idea who he was, why he was here or what he had done, all he knew was that the poor sod had been cruelly tortured and was close to death. The reason they had brought the wretch in here, as dusk had fallen, he could guess as well. To show what he faced if *Sea Witch* did not return. Or if del Gardo changed his mind.

Misery permeated the entire tower; its rancid smell was of faeces and fear. Not death. Those chained in this tower welcomed the release of death. He had been imprisoned here before, chained like an animal with the crew of Malachias Taylor's *Mermaid*, in a cell down in the depths of the foundations. For two nights they had suffered there. Two nights that had lasted a lifetime in his memory.

The man was breathing, but very shallowly, the air rasping in his lungs. Jesamiah had already tried to make him comfortable by rolling him on his side, covering him with his coat, but there were too many broken bones and torn sinews. Blood from ruptured organs frothed from his mouth. The rack was a horrible way to die. They had many horrible ways to make a man die in here.

Jesamiah choked down vomit. They had made him watch as they had killed the *Mermaid*'s quartermaster. It was del Gardo's way to make the next victim watch the previous one die. They had fed a long line of knotted linen down the poor bastard's throat, making him swallow it as they poured water down his gullet. Had then poured more pints down to make it curl and snag and twine around within his intestines. Had left him lying there moaning as his belly began to ache. Chained to the wall there was nothing Jesamiah could do except listen. Not watch. When he could he had squeezed his eyes shut. But at the end they had made him look, telling him he was to be next as they pulled the linen out again, bringing everything with it. Disembowelling the quartermaster, pulling his intestines out of his open, screaming, mouth with the linen, inch by slow, agonising, inch. It had taken the poor bastard a while to die. Jesamiah rolled over, spewed his guts into the putrid straw.

They had escaped. Somehow Taylor had bribed the guard and they had escaped. The air, the sea—life—that October dawn, had never seemed as sweet. Malachias had never smuggled cargo into Hispaniola again, and nor had Jesamiah. Until now he had avoided the place, both island and sea lanes. Why had he come back? He must be out of his mind!

It was raining outside. Hard, heavy rain that beat against the brickwork, drummed on the lead roof and spouted from a hole in the gutter beside the window. Some of the rain was coming in and collecting on the floor making the stink of mouldy straw and human waste puddle into a black, sodden and foul mess.

The man groaned again, the sound an agonised wheeze. He stared, bewildered, up at Jesamiah, the faint light from beneath the door reflecting in the pain-wracked whites of his fearful eyes.

"It's all right my friend, I will not harm you. I will stay with you. You are not alone." Were the words of comfort for this creature's benefit or his own? "The pain will go soon. I promise you." Jesamiah would have taken the man's hand, but what was left of the poor bugger's fingers was all torn and bloody.

What was Rue doing? Had he clewed up? Would he think of running on topsails only if the wind increased? Was he taking care of *Sea Witch*? Wiping the taste of vomit from his mouth, telling himself he was being stupid, Jesamiah fought aside threatening tears. It had been hard, so hard, to stand at that window and watch *Sea Witch* sail away without him. She had looked beautiful, her sails spread, her bow lifting as she had met the first roller of the open sea. He was not with her, his hand was not on the helm, his voice was not giving the commands. His feet were not wide-planted on the lift and heave of the quarterdeck. He trusted Rue implicitly, would trust him with his life—his ship—but by God's truth he wanted her back!

Sitting there in the dark, listening to the man's whimpering, he told himself Rue would not permit de Castilla to interfere. It was likely someone had already shut him in the great cabin, bolted the door and left him there. Finch would probably have ensured that the bastard had a keg of brandy, effectively silencing any protest. Rubbing his face, neck and shoulders, massaging the stiffness, Jesamiah stood, eased the ache from his back. The skin was still sore. Nearly all of him was still sore.

The man coughed, attempted to say something. Hurrying to lean close, Jesamiah tried to understand the whispered Spanish, but could make out nothing that made sense.

"What is your name?" he asked, kind, coaxing, gentle. "Who are you?"

"I..."

"I'm listening. Who are you? What is your name?"

The man took a gurgling, shallow breath. "Ches.."

With a gasp Jesamiah suddenly came alert. He bent closer, his ear almost to the man's bruised and bleeding mouth, his hands light on the man's shoulders, restraining himself from giving them a fierce shake. "Chesham? You are Francis Chesham?" *Dear God*, he thought, *I've found their spy.*

"Ches...Must, tell. Ches..."

"No need to tell me anything, my friend. I know of you."

"Must...tell." With a sigh of exhaled breath the man died.

Jesamiah stood, went to the window, clasped his hands around the bars, grateful for the rain that was washing across his face.

Francis Chesham. The man Jennings had asked him to find. He had not said why exactly, but whatever the reason, it was no use now. Poor bastard.

Resting his head on the bars, Jesamiah groaned. No man should die like that. No man should be so torn to pieces and made to say words he did not want to say.

The rain had the smell of the sea in it, or was it the wind that was blowing the aroma in? He could certainly hear it, crashing angrily against the rocks below. A wild sea, frothing and foaming, the spray hurtling and booming into the hollows and cracks as if it was jealous of the rain that was patting his cheeks like a lover's tender caress. A fanciful thought, which brought Tiola's face to his mind, her touch, her love.

Jesamiah turned away, a cry choking his throat, tears trickling. He wanted, missed, his ship but oh, oh how much more he wanted and missed Tiola! Just to hear her voice with its slight lilt of a Cornish accent, to smell her natural perfume that reminded him of summer flowers and sun-drenched hay meadows. And the sea. Tiola also had a smell of the sea about her now. Not seaweed or tar or wet sand, but a subtle, invigorating sea tang. But she had gone, had left him. He had never really noticed her presence within him—does a man notice an arm or a leg or his sight? Nothing is noticed until it is gone. And she had gone. The part of her soul that had united with his, that had taken root within him, had been plucked out, leaving an aching, yawning void of emptiness.

This whole thing had been a stupid, stupid, idea. He had lost his ship and his woman. Without the *Sea Witch* he would never get Tiola back. He would not be able to find that indigo, would not be able to take it to van Overstratten as a trade, and then God alone knew what the Dutchman would do to Tiola. Was he treating her badly? Was he...? It was night. Van Overstratten was her husband and Tiola had turned away from Jesamiah, had shut him out. He moaned as an unbidden image of Tiola and Stefan hit him. He fell to his knees. *Tiola. Oh my love, Tiola!*

Alone, cold and weary Jesamiah wrapped his arms about himself, rocking too and fro in abject misery. Kneeling there in the soiled, musty straw, he sobbed.

CHAPTER THREE

Aboard Stefan van Overstratten's sloop, a maid, one of his chosen servants answerable only to him, irritably pressed the rim of a goblet against Tiola's lips and encouraged her inert form to swallow.

Bitterness mixed with sweet. Honey and lemon, comfrey and other herbs—the dark brew that brought a deep, deep, sleep. By instinct, the human form of Tiola drank. It was easier for the maid to ensure her mistress slept for on the few occasions when she partially awoke she would thrash around and cry out, and the maid was a lazy slattern who preferred to spend her time enjoying herself with the crew below deck. If Tiola awoke there would be more work to do, so she laced the medicine with laudanum, lied to van Overstratten whenever he asked and said the mistress slept on.

None except Jesamiah was aware of Tiola's secret. No one else knew that she was of the Craft; that until her human form roused from the artificial state of a drugged sleep her soul could not return to it. For Tiola, the door to existence was shut. And the key turned in the lock.

She knew she ought to open her eyes; was aware she had been drifting for too long, but it was peaceful here, floating, untroubled, in this calm silence. Tiola half-hearted roused herself, struggling against the tiredness that was weighing her down. She ought to be refreshed by now. Ought to be strong again, and back where she belonged...She frowned in her sleep. Where did she belong? Her soul was a part of the Universe, she was as one with the dance of the stars and the drift of time. She was immortal. Had been there, on this tiny, insignificant planet, when the first spark had struck the first stone, that had evolved and grown into the life of bone, sinew, muscle and flesh.

She should wake, should join with her body. Why was she still here? For a moment she panicked, the spirit that was her being fluttered with alarm and she tumbled and whirled over and over, around and around, confused, disorientated and suddenly very frightened. If she did not return soon her host body, without its protective spirit, would wither and die, and then she would be here forever and fail in her task of protecting those in her care.

It had happened to so many of her kind already; the Immortals of Light, their spirits driven away and their earth-bound forms burnt, buried, starved or dismembered. Her sisters, so many, many of them, condemned and destroyed. And there was a name. A name she should remember... What name? She could see his face, his black hair, his dark eyes. His smile. Could feel his hands on her as he made love... Could not remember his name!

Desperate, she tried to wake but she could not crawl through the tunnel of blackness that separated her from awareness and life, and she was too tired to try again. Too tired to struggle any more. She closed her eyes and drifted on through the quiet of the white, eternal emptiness.

And forgot everything.

CHAPTER FOUR

Grunting his last effort, Don Damián del Gardo thrust again, shuddered and rolled, breathing hard, sweating, from Francesca's inert body. She too shuddered but from disgust, relieved it was over.

For too long she had been forced to endure the degradation of del Gardo's inept attentions in bed. Before that she had sat cloistered at home with her frail father-in-law, grieving over the murder of Ramon, her husband. Oh, it had looked like an accident, but three people knew it was not. Herself, Ramon's father, and del Gardo. She blinked aside tears. Del Gardo had a way of ensuring that no word of his calumny would ever be uttered. Normally he went straight to sleep after fumbling and poking at her, lying there on his fat rump, mouth open, paunch belly heaving upward as if he were nine months with child. She would lie the other way, her back to him, knees drawn up, silently weeping, her mind questioning her faith in her God. It was wrong to kill. Even more wrong to kill herself, but she so wanted to do both, were it not for her child. Her son.

About to turn over, to shuffle as far away from him as she could, she went rigid as he spoke. As if he had read her thoughts he said into the darkness, "Your son. He is how old now?"

Francesca's mouth ran dry, her heart began to beat faster with the pound of fear. "He will be nine come Advent."

"And he is content living here as a brother to my own sons? I believe my wife dotes on the boy."

Don Damián's mouse of a wife detested the boy, but then she detested all her children and refused to see any of them. Señora del Gardo also loathed her husband, which is why she kept herself in her private world of seclusion in her chamber and ignored the endless succession of his mistresses. While they were performing for the evil bastard, she was not having to do so.

He grasped Francesca's breast and pinched the nipple between his fingers. "There is something I want you to do for me, madam."

What? Oh God, not again! What vileness did he want her to repeat now?

"That English dog. I want to know what he is up to."

She stifled the sigh of relief. "Is that not why you have taken him to the Tower? To torture him?"

Del Gardo snorted. "He'll not talk; he'll clack like a market wife as soon as he feels the first brand of pain, but I cannot rely on what he spews up as being the truth. I need to know about the plans for this pathetic rebellion. Do the English think I am such an imbecile that I do not realise he is here to liaise with the rebel leaders? Pah!" Del Gardo heaved his body to the edge of the bed and then to his feet, stumbled over to the piss pot. "I am going to release Acorne on parole." He farted, finished streaming urine and returned to the bed. "That crew of his will not return, pirates are never loyal to a weak captain. What? Come back for a man who gets himself arrested and tortured? Never!"

Francesca was not so sure; she had looked into Jesamiah's eyes and seen strength and courage there. He was not a weak man like del Gardo, relying on brutality and fear to maintain authority. This Captain Jesamiah Acorne was someone worth knowing. A man who might, just might, help her salvage the collapsed ruins of her life.

Hiding her eagerness, she said compliantly, "What do you want me to do?"

"I will release him into your father-in-law's custody. Nursemaiding a pirate is the only thing the old man is useful for now. You will befriend Acorne and discover everything." He moved quickly, reached out and grabbed her hair at the nape of her neck. "Everything Francesca. Do not fail me. I expect you to uncover information about this rebellion. Understand? You have, so far, done well with the information you have brought me; do not go changing sides because you want to spread your legs for a pirate to sniff at your cunny." He twisted her red hair tighter, yanked her head back. "It would be a pity if, like his father, your son was to meet with an unfortunate accident, would it not?"

She mewed with fear. He let her go, turned away.

Her husband, Ramon, had fallen, so they said. Had tumbled, down and down the stone steps that led to the dungeons in the Tower. When he came to rest at the bottom his neck was broken. No one ever mentioned the marks of obvious torture. She lay still, unmoving, hoped del Gardo had fallen asleep.

"Pleasure me again. You were useless last time, I felt nothing. If you do not make an effort to please me I will dismiss you, and then there will be no need for me to hold your son hostage, will there? I may as well dispose of him now... Mouth, woman! Take me in your mouth."

Chapter Five

Sunday Morning

He had been dreaming. A vivid, explicit, dream.

Jesamiah groaned, rolled over. Every bone, muscle, sinew, everything ached abominably. He was also damp; the rain must have come in during the night; his fault for sleeping below the window. It had seemed the cleanest place at the time, perhaps it had not been a good idea after all. Pushing himself to his knees he caught his breath, then slowly and carefully stood up, tugging his coat closer around his body. It was cold in here, this dank, dark place where little sun came in to bring any cheer. Some time during the long night he had retrieved the coat from Chesham—ah he remembered now, it was when the rain had started again. The wind had blown it in, and the wetness on his face had roused him from a dozing sleep. He'd fetched the coat and huddled beneath the window where the layer of ordure was less noisome than everywhere else. Looking at Chesham's stiff corpse, he felt a momentary spasm of guilty disrespect, but shrugged it aside. A dead man had no use for warmth, a living one did.

There was only a dribble of water left in the small pitcher they had left him; he drained it into his mouth, washed it around his teeth, swallowed. No piss pot; nowhere to ease himself. He chose a corner, dug a hollow in the foetid straw with his heel, loosened his breeches and squatted. It was either that or soil himself, and he was not the first to use this corner or any of this stinking cell. Not by any means.

Done, he wandered to the window, forlornly peered out. The rain had stopped, the sky was a washed, pale blue with a few ragged wisps of mares' tail cloud. He wondered how far *Sea Witch* had gone. Where she had gone. If only he had been allowed to speak with Rue first! He would have advised him to head up the Florida coast, aim for Charleston. There were plenty of rich pickings along there, fat merchants with bulging bellies and holds to match. Surely Rue would know that? He had been a pirate as long as—longer—than Jesamiah. Isiah, too, knew his trade and Mr Janson and old Toby. On the other hand, that was Edward Teach's hunting ground and no one deliberately antagonised Blackbeard's regular bouts of devil's insanity.

Jesamiah slammed his fist against one of the window bars, he must stop this self-indulgent wallowing in self pity! Rue would return with *Sea Witch* and have a handsome prize in tow. He would! He would! Closing his eyes, he tried to imagine her sailing proud and beautiful into harbour, sails billowing and straining, her wake foaming behind. But all he saw was Tiola and the dream that had visited him.

He snapped his eyes open, stared out at the blue sky and the white clouds. "Tiola?" he murmured, "Tiola sweetheart, why can I not hear you? Where are you? Talk to me. Forgive me. Please?"

He could not bear this bereft emptiness that echoed, hollow, inside him! Could not bear being without her.

~ *I thought I would be able to tell you everything once I'd set sail.* ~ He spoke the words in his mind, as he always had to Tiola. ~ *I thought I would be able to explain. Please Tiola, listen to me, let me tell you that I have been an almighty idiot and how I have buggered everything up.* ~

Only the wind and the splash of the sea answered him. Gulls were crying and a man's distant voice shouted an impatient command. Nothing else. He could not even feel her presence, that comforting nearness that he had grown so used to. She had been with him from a few months before his fifteenth birthday. He had not know it was her then, had not known it until he had taken her intimately as his own; claimed her as his woman. He had been a boy when first she had come to him; a boy bereft, in pain and drenched in humiliation. Her spirit, her soul, had come to him and laid a hand on his back. ~ *Get up, fight back,* ~ she had said.

Resting his forehead on the mildewed and snail-slimed wall he closed his eyes again. He had no more energy to fight back. Not now, not without her. He saw again the lingering images of that dream. It had been so vivid. So real.

Tiola. With him, with van Overstratten. Making love. He had seen every detail; their bodies, skin glistening, forming the two-backed beast, her legs entwined around his hips as he thrust eagerly into her. She had cried out, her beautiful black hair hanging loose and sweeping the floor as she had tipped her head and arched her body to take him in deeper. As she always had done with him, with Jesamiah. Her scream of ecstasy had awoken him.

He didn't bother stopping the tears; there was no one here to see. He had lost her. He had left her a second time, had chosen the sea over her and she, Tiola, had returned as wife to her husband instead. It was not a random, fanciful dream. It had been Tiola telling—showing—him that she no longer wanted him. He couldn't blame her, look how often he had let her down. Why would a beautiful, intelligent woman like her settle for being hurt over and over again by a useless scumbutt of a pirate?

Lost in the depth of his grieving despair he failed to hear the stamp of boots or recognise the grate of the bolts—spun round, startled, at the creak of the door opening, his fingers hastily wiping at the embarrassing wetness dribbling down his cheeks. Almost vomited as his heart raced and his legs threatened to buckle beneath him. This was it. They had come for him. They were to take him down all those winding stone stairs into the darkness of that chamber below, where they had the equipment to crush your feet or fingers slowly, tools to pry out your eyes, pull out your guts and rip off your balls. The door opened further, he leant against the wall to keep upright; felt the shudder of abject fear ripple through his body and a warm wetness running down his leg. Closed his eyes, muttered a prayer.

A swish of silk, the delicate smell of perfume—the scent of roses. His eyes snapped open, met the green gaze of the redhead. Jesamiah rested his head on the brickwork, released a slow breath of intense relief—followed rapidly by a flush of as intense shame for the tell-tale wet patch on his breeches.

Motioning at the guard to remain at the door the woman stepped inside, fastidiously lifting her skirts high as she attempted to sidestep the worst of the mouldering excrement. "This is not a very pleasant place to be," she said in English, her nose wrinkling at the squalid stench.

"You get used to it," Jesamiah answered, trying to mask his unease, his mind racing. What the fok was she doing here?

Noticing the dead man the woman gave a small, distressed gasp, went to him and squatting on her heels, touched a palm to his chest then the back of her hand to his cheek, confirming what she already knew, her action disturbing the swarm of flies that had settled on the stiffening corpse. "You poor, poor, man. May you rest in peace."

"You knew him?" Jesamiah asked, the suspicion dark behind his question.

"No." She stood, wiped her hand on her skirt. "His face is familiar, but no, I did not know him."

"You! Speak Spanish!" the guard barked in broken English as he lowered the musket in his hand and pointed it at Jesamiah. "Orders I have. You speak Spanish."

The woman looked squarely at Jesamiah, said in Spanish for the benefit of the guard, "You have been released on parole into the care of señor Escudero, my father-in-law. I assume you have no objection to a bath, a shave, clean clothes and a hot meal?"

If this was a new form of interrogation, then it was working. Her mere presence made Jesamiah want to spill everything he knew immediately and pour out his heart, but he had learnt long ago not to trust people he did not know. Especially very pretty redheads. And this one was undeniably very, very pretty.

"That would suit me admirably," he drawled in English, casually crossing his legs at the ankle and folding his arms; squeezing every ounce of courage into appearing relaxed and confident. "But what must I do to earn it? Confess the truth of why I am here? Tell you I am a spy, that I have orders to sabotage the Spanish fleet or to slip poison into Don Damián's wine? Sorry darlin', can't help you out. I recently took vows to always tell the truth."

"I am curious to know why you are here, sí, but I am a woman, would you not expect me to be?"

Jesamiah shrugged, appearing indifferent. Don Damián would not be letting him out of here for no reason—certainly not because of the softness of his heart. This woman was here at the bastard's command to wheedle information out of him.

Fine. He might oblige her, eventually, but on his terms, not hers or del Gardo's. He pushed away from the wall, ambled towards her. "Well, let me satisfy your curiosity. I am here because Governor Woodes Rogers of Nassau has gone back on his word, which has annoyed me. Another man annoyed me, the reason being none of your business. A naval commodore wanted to commandeer my ship, which very much annoyed me. I wanted to do something which would annoy them in return, offering to fight on the side of Spain was the most annoying thing I could think of." And if she thought he was going to tell her any more, she could go whistle.

The woman smiled, a smile that radiated from her sparkling eyes as well as her mouth. "I perceive you to be a very annoyed man."

When he made no further comment she added, still talking in English, "Don Louis Fernandez Escudero is an honourable man, he has sworn to give you hospitality in exchange for your agreement of parole."

"*Español, Español*," the guard growled, tapping the butt of his musket on the floor impatiently. "I musts know of what you speaks!"

They both ignored him.

"He cannot be that honourable if he sends a woman into this stink to fetch me out."

"He is an elderly man and cannot climb stairs. For other reasons also, he is unable to come." She indicated the door. "You may, of course, remain here if you would so prefer."

He did not prefer, but neither did he trust her.

"If you swear to not try and escape, you will come to no harm, Captain Acorne."

"Oh I'm sure I'll be perfectly safe until you've got what you want out of me. After we've made love, perhaps? You'll feign sleep and hope I murmur indiscretions into your ear while I'm sated with pleasure, then scuttle back to your master."

"You think I would want intimacy with the likes of you?"

Very close, Jesamiah leant forward, tucked a loose strand of her hair behind her ear, brushed his lips against hers. "Oh but you do, darlin', you do." Kissed her again, a little firmer, more demanding. The guard shuffled; leered at them.

A squall of rain hurled through the window. Jesamiah pulled away, grinned lasciviously. "You'd best remember one thing, señora. I don't talk in m'sleep; an' even if I did, you'll be far too exhausted to hear. I'll ride you hard, you'll have no energy left to listen." He was deliberately crude. He did not think del Gardo's mistress, here with orders to gain his trust, deserved tender wooing.

He walked across the cell and retrieved his hat from where it lay on the soiled straw; knocked it against his thigh to remove the filth clinging to it before putting it on. He pointed at the dead man. "What happens to him? To Chesham?"

He did not get the reaction he expected. "Chesham?" she answered, genuine puzzlement creasing her face into a frown. "Is—was—that his name?"

"Aye, Francis Chesham. The English spy."

It suddenly occurred to Jesamiah that he could not exactly remember what Jennings had said. Had it been; "He is an English spy," meaning he was an Englishman and a spy, or was it, "he spies for England,"? Which could make him anything; Spanish, French, Creole or English. It was irrelevant now, though.

"Did you and lover-boy discover what he was? Say anything of interest when you had him tortured, did he?"

Stern, she challenged, "I could ask a question of you. How did you know him?"

Jesamiah stepped towards the door. "You ought to be well satisfied señora; del Gardo will be delighted to hear I know of Chesham and what he was, don't y'think?"

CHAPTER SIX

Rain was angry. At herself, at her mother, at everyone. She had been with Jesamiah Acorne all night, playing with his hair, exploring his body. Caressing him, loving him; her delicate touch, to him, feeling like a light pita-pat shower of rain. She had put the dream into his head by whispering into his ear; had made him believe he had seen the witch bedding with that Dutchman.

~ He will turn to me, now. Now he thinks he does not have her, he will want me. ~

She had been wrong. He was totally ignoring her. And now he was with this other woman, the red haired, pretty, human woman.

Rain had screamed and shouted and demanded that he pay attention to her, made love to her. Only he had pretended not to hear or see her. He did not love her at all! No one loved her! She may as well give him to her mother!

But she was curious.

~ Why do you want him, Mother? You have collected the bones and the souls of many who have entered the eternity of your realm. Why do you want this Jesamiah Acorne? ~

~ He is of the sea. I want him because he is of the sea. ~ Tethys crooned as she lay languid, waiting and watching from the bottom of her murked depths.

~ I was there when he was begun, and I was there when he was born. I watched as his human father planted the seed within his mother's womb. I shared the love with which he was made and I wanted him, even then, I wanted him as my own son. ~

Rain did not hear, did not bother to listen. She did not care for her mother. Why should she? Her mother had no care for her! She ran off over the sea, weeping her tears of rain.

~ Maybe I will let you have him, ~ she sobbed. ~ Maybe I will give him back to the Witch Woman. Or maybe I will let that one with the red hair, the green eyes and the lies, have him. ~

Tethys subsided lower into the depths and was silent. In the mud, among the clutter of the debris of wrecked ships, fish and human bones, rotting flesh and shredding skin, she settled, lay still. Unmoving, unfeeling.

She could wait. For a little longer she could wait for the babe who had been born within her embrace. Could wait for the boy who had become a beautiful man. She was immortal; time was meaningless to her. She could wait for him to return to where he had been born, to where he belonged, to the sea.

She could wait.

The carriage ride was short, a mere twenty minutes along the coast to an expensive and tasteful house built on the cliffs overlooking the sea. Jesamiah had yet to meet this señor Louis Escudero. The old gentleman had been upstairs when they arrived, and then Jesamiah had been too busy bathing, shaving, changing into clean clothes that he guessed had belonged to the lady's dead husband, and wolfing down a meal that would have done the King of Spain himself proud.

Finishing the last kidney, Jesamiah leant back in his chair, folded his hands over his belly and belched loudly. Had the decency to grin and apologise. "My pardon ma'am."

Señora Escudero flicked him a mildly reproachful glance and poured coffee. "I take it the food was to your satisfaction?"

Sitting here in this fine house was infinitely more preferable than a prison cell, even if the windows were being rattled by a rainstorm that would rival Noah's flood. By comparison, everything at this moment seemed satisfactory.

Leaving the table, the gold-rimmed china coffee cup in his hand, Jesamiah went to peer out at the tempest. The sea below the sheer drop, not a few yards beyond the walls of the house, was spuming foam over the rocks and up the cliff face. How was *Sea Witch* faring? Was she battling with this wind somewhere?

He sipped at the hot, black, sweet, coffee. Signing those papers before he had been permitted to leave the Tower had galled. They were his promise to make no attempt at an escape. That was a nonsense. Did they seriously think pieces of paper would hold him should he choose to go? An old man and a woman as his jailers—oh he was not disillusioned, he was a prisoner here, a bullet would be put in his back if he tried to leave. Which, he figured, the governor was going to be disappointed about; Jesamiah had every intention of staying put. It was raining outside, there was good food, comfort and a very pretty woman *inside*. He was not stupid. Besides, what else did he have to do?

The señora had witnessed his agreement on behalf of her father-in-law and Jesamiah had read her full Spanish name over her shoulder as she had signed.

"Francesca? Pretty name."

"Only Don Damián calls me that. My friends and my family call me 'Cesca."

Chesca. He had quietly digested the name and the information, had not, yet, found the gall to assume she included him as a friend. Had signed his pledge against the surety of his ship. If he escaped, when *Sea Witch* came back into harbour she would be fired upon and sunk.

"Don Damián," señora Escudero had said at his side, as he had disdainfully read the conditions, "does not expect your ship to return. He believes your men have abandoned you."

"Then there ain't much point in me signing is there?" he had answered. "But since she will return..." and he had put his signature with a flourish:

Jesamiah Acorne. Capt.

*****

His cutlass and pistol had been waiting for him in the carriage, his weapons returned as part of the honourable estate of parole. His ribbons he had kept, del Gardo not realising their usefulness, although he had disposed of them while wallowing in the wooden tub of hot water provided for him in the guest quarters upstairs. They were ragged and soiled; he would have to get some new ones from somewhere. Standing at the window, his fingers automatically went to fiddle with them, was frustrated to find them not there, twirled a strand of hair around his finger instead.

There was more going on here than he was being told, but so what? His belly was full and 'Cesca was one of the prettiest women he had seen in a long while. Add to that, there was a clean-lined two-masted brig moored to a small jetty at the bottom of the cliff.

Kismet. He could read the name painted along her stern. Kismet. Fate. Jesamiah did not believe in fate, he preferred to look after his own destiny.

Watching him, 'Cesca saw how his eyes coveted the vessel; assessed correctly that the call of the ocean would always shout the louder in his ears above any other voice. Yet... yet she had heard that Captain Jesamiah Acorne was a man who enjoyed his women. Any woman who could anchor his affection would be one of exceptional quality. Or who possessed a high talent in seduction. Did Don Damián intend her to sleep with this pirate? She assumed so, although the malicious bastard never usually cared to share his possessions, not unless he had an opportunity to watch. She shuddered. She had been made to endure that humiliation already. Never again. She would kill herself before being passed around like a parcel to his evil friends a second time. Unconsciously she touched her fingers to her lips. The pirate's kiss had been pleasant, erotic.

"You are English?" Jesamiah asked, turning away from the window to smile at her. "Tell me, what is a beautiful English woman doing here in Hispaniola?" He wanted to add, what is a beautiful English woman doing in Don Damián's bed, but thought better of it. He would ask later, when he had worked out the rules of the game that he was unintentionally involved in playing.

"I am a Catholic. Despite the claim that England is now tolerant of us, I found I was more comfortable among those who share my papist belief in the Christ."

"That still does not explain how you come to be here."

She returned his smile, that sparkle in her green eyes so alluring. "It is no great secret." She laughed, the sound trilling, melodic, delightful. "I met a man and fell in love with him. He happened to live here. As his wife, I naturally came with him."

Jesamiah raised one eyebrow, the question plain.

"I was a travelling actress. I met my husband when we were in Cádiz, performing one of Master Shakespeare's romantic plays."

"And now?"

Head high, she matched his look eye to eye. Knew exactly what he was asking. "And now I am a widow and summoned to entertain Don Damián del Gardo whenever he wants me. I am a good actress. I pretend I am honoured by his attention."

Jesamiah sipped his coffee, shifted his glance to the *Kismet*. "You could refuse him."

"No one refuses del Gardo and lives to see another dawn, Capitán Acorne," a voice responded gruffly in passable English.

Both Jesamiah and 'Cesca swung around to see señor Escudero entering the room, walking slowly, relying on the support of his cane and a servant's arm.

Jesamiah swallowed an automatic reaction of revulsion, feeling his guts leap from his stomach into his throat. The man's face was hideous, the skin scarred and puckered on the left side and he had only one eye, the other was a shrivelled, empty socket. His feet were twisted and bent, his hands gnarled, the nails missing from several fingers.

Immediately, 'Cesca hurried to help him into a chair; from her attentiveness she was undeniably fond of him.

"I see my appearance shocks you Capitán Acorne. It shocks many people, save for those who did this to me."

"Forgive me, I did not intend to insult you, señor."

Louis Escudero flapped a misshapen hand in dismissal. "You are probably wondering why del Gardo has seen fit to release you into my care. You are here because he knows for certain neither I nor my beautiful daughter-in-law will go against him." He touched his hand to his face. "Once already he has had me tortured, and discovered I had nothing to tell. And now he abuses 'Cesca and holds her son to ransom. If we betray del Gardo, Capitán, my grandson will be killed in the same manner as was his father. We have had enough pain and misery, we will risk no more. You, therefore, will be adequately supervised while in our care."

Something Jennings had told him tugged vaguely at Jesamiah's mind, but he could not remember it. He said instead, "And if I happen to let some useful information slip, then maybe you can bargain with the bastard to leave your family alone?"

Señor Escudero nodded congenially. "'Cesca said you were an intelligent man. I see she was right."

Rallying a more relaxed atmosphere, the old man asked for coffee, and then said, "So, Capitán, while you are under our jurisdiction, shall we attempt to at least make an appearance at friendship? I had great respect for your father."

"My father?" Jesamiah's head shot up.

"You are the son of Charles St Croix, are you not?"

Relaxing, Jesamiah shook his head, he had been worried there for a moment. "Alas, señor, you are mistaken, I am not. His name was Mereno."

Escudero laughed, not mocking but clearly entertained. "And before he took that name he used the alias of Charles Cross. You surely know the French for Cross?"

Croix.

Jesamiah poked the inside of his cheek with his tongue. Croix. Charles St Croix. So that was it, the name he had not known.

From politeness señor Escudero had remained speaking in English; "You are much like him, although you have your mother's dark eyes."

Jesamiah's attention had wandered to the *Kismet* again but with a gasp leaving his lips he concentrated fully on the señor's words. "You knew my mother?"

He was a grown man, his mother had been dead these many years, so why this absurd lurch of grief dancing a jig in his innards at an unexpected reminder of her? He missed her. Missed her sweet singing voice, her giggling laughter— even missed her scolding tongue that could rattle off a dozen reprimands in the one breath. Missed her as he was missing Tiola. Ah no, he was missing Tiola more. A mother was the one you were born to, you loved her out of respect and duty. A wife? A wife was the woman you chose to be with for the rest of your life. Except Tiola was not his wife, and now, never would be. He swallowed hard, thrust the thought aside.

"Charles brought your mother to this house every year; Don Damián never knew, for he was a master of disguise, your father." Escudero chuckled, then added with regret, "I was sorry to lose them as friends, they were good people. Your father was a good man."

"Not according to del Gardo!" Jesamiah snorted, the pain of bitter memories stabbing at him. Every year when his father had prepared to make sail in one or another of the estate's ships, he had asked where mama and papa were going; had begged to be taken with them, not left behind. And always he had received the same answer; "To somewhere that is not suitable for small boys. Your brother will take care of you."

Oh aye, Phillipe had taken care of him. He still bore the physical and mental scars to show how much care he had taken. Phillipe; his father's firstborn, who had so hated Jesamiah's mother that he had taken his spite out on her child. Jesamiah's lips drew back in a savage snarl, "You must have known his first wife as well, then. Was my half-brother like my father too? Did he also have his mother's eyes?" He saw no reason to mask the hatred.

The old man frowned. "Was? You use the past tense."

"Phillipe is dead. I had occasion to kill him before he killed me."

Nodding slowly, Escudero digested the information; the implications. "The boy never came with them, so I would not know if he was alike his mother or father. You killed him? May I ask why?"

"Aye, I killed him and no, you may not ask why." As an afterthought Jesamiah added, "All you need to know is that he was a bastard."

The old man nodded slowly. "As was his father."

"That's not what I meant," Jesamiah answered quickly. "Phillipe was born in wedlock. As for Papa, I have always guessed he was born illegitimate; why else would he not use his real name? St Croix you say? I have never heard of it until today." He attempted a smile, although he was finding this stirring of emotions difficult. "Phillipe was a bastard in the other sense of the word, however."

'Cesca was standing near him, she heard the pain in his voice. Compassionate, she reached out, laid her hand on his arm.

A renewed burst of rain stuttered at the window; the catch must have been loose for suddenly it flew open. Cold rain and a swirl of wind rushed in, the curtains crazily lifting, items rattled, the tablecloth billowed upward, knocking over a jug of fruit juice and Jesamiah's empty cup. Señor Escudero cried out, 'Cesca ran to help Jesamiah slam the casement shut, his face, hair and front of his shirt and waistcoat were wet. She did not hear the wild cry of frustration, the scream of annoyance as the window slammed; Jesamiah did, but he told himself it was nothing more than the sound of the wind. And the face he had seen at the window, before it had burst open, had been his unease calling up fanciful notions. He failed to notice the puddle in the shape of a woman's footprint on the tiled floor. Had he done so perhaps he would have questioned his sanity.

"Tell me," he asked señor Escudero, "do you know of a Captain James Wickham?" The thing Jennings had said had at last come into his mind. It had been about del Gardo and Wickham's mother; a little boy watching her distress after being used. Abused. Had señora Wickham also gone to del Gardo because, like 'Cesca, he had threatened the life of her child? If so was it any wonder Wickham had wanted to destroy him?

"Diego? Of course. Everyone who appreciates a fine brandy knew him."

Turning to look at the old man, his head cocked on one side, Jesamiah queried, "Then you knew he was a smuggler? Did you know him as anything else?"

'Cesca answered for her father-in-law. "Was he anything else? We assumed he was a privateer. Did he have family? It is a sad thing for a man of the sea to drown."

She had answered too easily and Jesamiah had the sudden distinct impression that she knew more about James Wickham than he did. Very casually he stated; "I believe he knew Chesham."

"Chesham?" Her brows furrowed, then she understood. "Oh, you mean that poor man in your cell? Forgive me, captain, maybe he did, but how would we know if they were acquainted? And since both are dead, what does it matter?"

After a pause, Escudero passed a slight chuckle, "When you have your ship returned, Capitán, maybe you could find me an alternative source for my brandy? I have very little left. Diego's talents will be sorely missed along this coast."

Jesamiah abandoned the idea of asking questions about Chesham. It was of no consequence now, let Jennings do his own bloody digging. His mind went back to the *Kismet*. "I could fetch you plenty of brandy in that brig you have down there."

Louis Escudero smiled expansively. "She is my boat, were you to set foot upon her, you would not be leaving my property. And if 'Cesca were to sail with you, then we would be fulfilling the terms of your parole exactly to the letter, would we not?"

Shaking his head Jesamiah raised his hands and backed away a few paces. "Ah no, no, señor, I could not take a woman on a smuggling run."

"Capitán Acorne, I would appreciate the chance of my daughter-in-law having time away from, how shall I put it? From doing what is expected of her."

I bet you would, Jesamiah thought. You would like nothing more than to find out where I would go and who I would contact. And if she ain't with me she won't be in my bed, wheedling out the secrets I hold, like picking weevils from a lump of hard-tack.

He had no objection to her being in his bed, for she was after all, rounded in all the right places, but it was Tiola he wanted. Tiola he loved. Tiola he could not have.

Suddenly he knew exactly what he was going to do.

"Before I even consider smuggling brandy, I have a mind," he said, his thoughts racing as he wandered over to a chair, sat, "to visit the plantation my half-brother owned until recently. The new owner wishes me to collect some merchandise stored there."

"Your brother's plantation? La Sorenta?" 'Cesca queried. "The place was in a sorry state when last I saw it. Phillipe Mereno abandoned it."

Jesamiah slid his chair backwards, the legs scraping on the tiles as he hurried to his feet. "Say that again?"

"Phillipe Mereno abandoned it."

"No, no, you said La Sorenta."

"*Sí.* One of the last indigo plantations here on Hispaniola —many of the others are growing sugar cane now; it is easier and cheaper to produce." Catching Jesamiah's expression, she added, "The plantation in Virginia, is that not also called Sorenta?"

All manner of memories were again swarming into Jesamiah's mind. The box had been unlocked, its lid flung wide and the contents were rushing out haphazardly in all directions. "We had always been told it was named after my father's ship."

"It was," Escudero confirmed with a single nod of his head. "And the ship was named after the plantation here on Hispaniola. The vessel belonged to a good friend of mine and your father's, Capitán Carlos Mereno." He watched, Jesamiah's astonished expression as the information sunk in. "Your father and Carlos were partners, the vessel *La Sorenta* was a joint venture; Charles was to transport the cargo, Carlos to run the Hispaniola estate."

Jesamiah's head was reeling. All this new information to be taken in—why had Papa never said anything of all this? "So what went wrong? Did they argue or something?"

Gravely señor Escudero shook his head. "Carlos Mereno fell in love..."

Cynically, Jesamiah interrupted; "And they fell out over wanting to bed the same girl, I suppose?"

"Carlos was murdered on his wedding night. He was dragged from the bridal bed, gelded and disembowelled. The woman was screaming, there was nothing she could do to stop it. The man who did the deed then raped her."

A feeling that he really did not want to hear anything more crept into Jesamiah's belly. "My father?" he asked. He had cultivated a deliberate indifference towards the man who had shown little obvious interest in his younger son, but he would never have believed him capable of such barbarism.

"No, not your father, her brother. The bride was raped by her own brother. Your father found her the next morning; he bundled her on to his ship and got her away. Much later, two years, maybe three, we discovered he had purchased a tobacco plantation in Virginia, taken Mereno's name, and for the sake of decency, married Constella del Gardo himself."

Coldness as solid as ice spread through Jesamiah. His heart seemed to stop beating, he felt his guts twist in his stomach. His throat dry, the words sticking to his tongue, he repeated, "Constella del Gardo?"

"Don Damián del Gardo's twin sister, *sí*. Phillipe's mother."

Jesamiah sat down heavily. He felt sick. "I never knew who she was, or where she came from. I don't think Phillipe did either. If he did he never said." He looked up, the shock ashen on his face. "Bloody hell, Don Damián's sister? Was that the cause of the feud?" He shook his head, finding it difficult to think straight. "Of course it was. I had no idea of any of this. None at all."

Linking his fingers, he chewed his thumb, thinking, digesting it all. Did knowing this matter? Not really. The information belonged to the past, and the past was done with. The present, the future, held the importance. Except, the past had a nasty habit of making a damned nuisance of itself by lingering in the shadows and leaping out to trip you up when you least expected it. And the future? Who gave a damn about the future when it stretched away empty and desolate? When it was to be without the woman he loved?

He rubbed his hands along his thighs, decision made. "Is there any indigo stored there?" he asked, trying to outrun the insidious whispering of the resurrected memories that, already, were like burrs irritating against his skin.

"Indigo?" Señor Escudero repeated. He puffed his cheeks, shook his head, "There has been no indigo at La Sorenta for many years."

Frowning, Jesamiah considered the statement. "Oh. It's all sold and shipped for trade then is it? None of it's been kept?" He wondered if it was wise to trust these people. Jennings had talked of rebellion and spies—whose side were these Escuderos on? Del Gardo's or the rebels'? Did it matter? Even if the delightful Francesca passed every detail to her bedmate he would soon be gone from here. It was regrettable if they got into trouble because of his broken parole, for they appeared to be decent folk who were trapped in difficult circumstances. But it really was not his problem. He had enough of his own to be dealing with without shouldering theirs as well.

Reaching a decision he threw caution to the wind. "I was told of a secret cache of indigo. I've been commissioned to collect sixteen barrels and ninety-seven kegs of it."

Francesca had been pouring more coffee, her hand slipped, the cup, saucer, crashed to the tiled floor, coffee spilling everywhere, the sound masking her simultaneous gasped cry.

"Oh!" she said, flustered, "how stupid and clumsy of me."

Jesamiah went to help her pick up the broken pieces of china, although she insisted the servants would do it, but it was an opportunity to smile at her, to brush his hand against hers.

"If you permit me to use your boat, señor Escudero," he said in Spanish as casually as he could, "I will undertake to do what I came here for, and find you some brandy at the same time."

The old man stroked a disfigured finger down his neatly trimmed moustache, pursed his lips. Answered in Spanish, "Ninety-seven kegs you say?"

"And sixteen barrels."

The señor pursed his lips, shook his head. "I am afraid I know nothing of any cache of indigo, but there would be no harm in you taking *Kismet* to La Sorenta I suppose, but as we said, because of your parole, 'Cesca must accompany you. The steward there, a señor Mendez, would be the better man to ask about this indigo." A smile twitched over the Spaniard's lips. "And while you are there, you may as well fetch my brandy. He will know where Wickham stored it."

Narrowing his eyes, tilting his head, Jesamiah smelt a distinct whiff of rat. "And why would he be knowing that?"

'Cesca glanced briefly at her father-in-law, who nodded almost imperceptibly. She laid one hand lightly on Jesamiah's arm. Said, very quietly, "I am afraid I lied to you. We knew James Wickham very well. Señor Frederico Mendez is—was—his grandfather."

CHAPTER SEVEN

SUNDAY AFTERNOON

~ *He is in love with someone else you know.* ~

Tiola heard Rain's soft whisper and stirred in her sleep. The words echoing, meaningless, in her head.

He is in love with someone else...He is in love with someone else... In love... in love... in love...Someone else... Someone else...

~ *I have seen him kiss her.* ~

~ *Who? Who is 'he'?* ~

Somewhere very distant the rain pattered its sing-song chatter as she scurried against the leaves of trees, bright-coloured flowers and green, refreshed plants. As she dabbled and danced into shining puddles.

~ *Unless you stop him, he will make love to her.* ~

~ *You stop him.* ~ Tiola wanted to sleep. She did not want to wake.

~ *Why should I? He is nothing to me.* ~

Tiola smiled drowsily. That, she was aware, was not true. ~ *Do you not love him, then, Rain?* ~

~ *No!* ~ Untrue.

The smell of fresh-washed earth, of wet grass and clean air filled Tiola's senses. Almost, she was awake. Almost.

Again, she repeated, ~ *Who? Who is he, this spirit you do not love?* ~

~ He is no spirit. He is a man. He is Jesamiah. ~
Jesamiah. Jesamiah?

It took a great effort for Tiola to wake, to force her mind to concentrate and to make the silence, that had lulled her in its depth of oblivion, heard. An effort to catch the words she needed and to shout them aloud.

~ Jesamiah? There is but one woman he will ever love. And I am that woman. ~

"Jesamiah?"

"My dear?" Stefan laid the damp linen towel across Tiola's forehead, held her hand as her eyes fluttered and she began to rouse. That slut who called herself a maid was blind drunk somewhere in the hold, her skirts stained with semen. How many of the crew had been at her? All of them by the repulsive look of her!

Stefan had dismissed her on the spot, told her she would receive no wages, that if he saw her anywhere near his wife again he would personally send her over the side. The reason for Tiola's prolonged sleep was plain; Stefan had found the almost empty vial of laudanum. Guilt, compassion; a feeling of fondness, maybe even a slight tinge of love? For whatever reason, he sat with Tiola as she began to wake. He patted her hand, smiled at her as her eyes fluttered open.

He kept the false smile as she again whispered a name.
"Jesamiah?"

Chapter Eight

The brig handled well. Taking a minimum of crew they had set sail in the early afternoon, when the rain had washed itself out and a watery sun had broken through the mist. Reluctantly Jesamiah had agreed for 'Cesca to sail with him —not that he'd had much of a say in the matter, one of his keepers had to accompany him, and it could not be the old gentleman. Part of him wondered why 'Cesca was so eager to join him on a choppy sea in a strong wind, with the possibility of more rain not far away. Another part of him, situated in his breeches, knew exactly why she was here.

Luffing *Kismet* in towards La Sorenta's jetty, he began to experience renewed feelings of doubt about this whole escapade, his suspicions growing stronger as they neared the shore and he realised the estate was not merely dilapidated, but was in an advanced state of decay. It had been so for years, by the look of it. He glanced across the quarterdeck at 'Cesca, saw her chew her lip, her fingers drumming against the rail.

Now why is she so agitated? he wondered. *She's been like a dog with fleas since we slipped our mooring.* He returned his attention to critically assessing the place. There was no tactful way to word it, the estate was a dump. Van Overstratten had been sold a pig in a poke. The thought cheered Jesamiah immensely as *Kismet* bumped against the jetty and two of the crew leapt nimbly ashore, two others tossing them mooring lines.

"I wondered," he said to 'Cesca as the boat was made secure, "why my brother was allowed to keep this estate. I would have expected del Gardo, because of his greed, spite and the old feud, to have confiscated it. I see now why he didn't bother. It's valueless. There's nothing worth claiming, there hasn't been for years has there?"

She made no answer.

The house was three-storied and had many windows, most of which were broken or boarded up with wood and sacking and looked as forlorn as everywhere else. Shutters were hanging off their hinges, the white lime on the walls was faded, cracked and peeling, in several places the bricks beneath were showing through. To the left stretched weed-choked fields. Only one small acre of stubble with a few straggled root vegetables had been cultivated. There had been no indigo grown, harvested and produced here for years. To the right, a straddle of buildings also in desperate need of repair. Stables—empty—workshops, processing huts, storehouses. Over it all, a lingering, unpleasant odour, a mixture of stagnant sewage, damp, mildew and rotting vegetation. No trace of the strong, distinctive, smell that would emanate from the production of indigo dye. A short way along the shoreline half a dozen thin and wretched slaves huddled under the crude shelter of an open-sided thatched hut which did little to stop the prevailing wind. No men, only weary white European and black African women.

As a pirate captain Jesamiah had proven, over and over again, that a man with a free choice worked harder than one with resentment in his heart. His father had often argued that enslavement was a better sentence than the noose, which, now he was a man grown, Jesamiah had to concede was true. Arrested in England for stealing, poaching and other minor offences, convicts were shipped to the colonies as punishment—women and children mostly, the men were drafted to serve in the army and navy. And then there were those here in the Caribbean who were the offspring of the Irish wretches who had suffered under Cromwell's rule—but while many an Englishman quibbled over the squalid treatment of a man or woman with a white skin, very few balked at the cruelties heaped on the Negroes.

Jesamiah disliked all slavery, took no part in the trade. Most pirates avoided the slavers; the ships stank too much for one thing, the cargo was riddled with disease, already dead or close to dying and there was very little else of value aboard. The only attraction was access to the women, and Jesamiah had never been that desperate. Blackbeard attacked slavers, but unlike him, Jesamiah was not insane.

A man was standing in the doorway of the house, shielding his eyes from the bright sun, his grey hair betraying that he was no longer young. He moved to the top of a parade of worn steps, but did not come down to greet them.

Tempted to jump ashore, Jesamiah waited for a plank to be set and offering his arm, escorted 'Cesca to dry land. She knew the man, for she waved and gathering her skirts hurried ahead, running to greet him fondly, kissing his cheek. Jesamiah, following sedately behind, had no doubt that her animated conversation was involving a brief but precise explanation of his presence here.

"Capitán Acorne," 'Cesca said in Spanish, beckoning him up the last few steps, "may I present Señor Frederico Mendez, steward and overseer of La Sorenta."

Removing his hat and bowing respectfully, Jesamiah acknowledged the introduction, also in Spanish. "Señor, at your service. Although forgive me for saying there does not seem to be much here worth stewarding."

Shoulders back, head high, Mendez made no attempt at a greeting, formal or otherwise. All he said, in English, was, "Acorne. I know the name."

"My fame's spread as far as 'ere then, 'as it?" Reverting to English, Jesamiah chuckled as he fiddled with his acorn earring.

The Spaniard met the attempt at humour with stoic indifference. "Not fame señor, infamy. I do not welcome pirates."

"Yet, from what I hear you have no objection to smugglers, and I have no doubt you do not disapprove of the Jolly Roger when it is hoisted from a Spanish masthead?" In the face of hostility, Jesamiah dispensed with formality and went direct to the point. "I do not particularly care whether you approve of me or not, señor. I am here for a reason and the sooner it is sorted the quicker I can be on my way again."

As he spoke he realised how much he meant the words. This situation was ridiculous. He suddenly, desperately, wanted to go home. Not that Nassau was home, but Tiola was there and where she was, was home. Glancing around he very much doubted there was any indigo here. Whoever had told van Overstratten of it had been a liar or... The line of thought hit him like the blow from a poleaxe. Who had told the Dutchman of it? Not Phillipe, that bastard would not have told his own shadow of something worthwhile. So who? Who would have wanted van Overstratten to come here? A wry smile twitched at the side of his mouth as realisation dawned. Someone had told van Overstratten. Someone who knew the Dutchman would promptly commandeer someone else to come and fetch it. If it had ever existed—which Jesamiah was beginning to think was highly unlikely.

Jennings. The cunning bastard. There was something deeper going on here, and it smelt overwhelmingly of rebels and rebellion. Very well, he would play along with the game, see how far he could move the pieces. And see who else was dancing a posy around the maypole. "I have come for the barrels of indigo which, I believe, have been retained in storage for exclusive use by the owner. I would be obliged for you to haul it out and have it stowed aboard my vessel. There is a matter of some brandy as well, so I understand. I am to deliver it to señor Escudero."

He was a captain, he was used to having his orders instantly obeyed, was somewhat disconcerted to find Mendez offering an arm to 'Cesca to escort her within-doors. Over his shoulder the Spaniard remarked; "There is no indigo. The last shipment left here more than ten years ago."

Annoyed that he was being so easily riled by an old man, but equally aware he was losing control of the situation, Jesamiah dropped his hand to his cutlass hilt, the rasp of steel grating on the hanger's lip as he withdrew it slightly. "That was not what the new owner of this estate was told. I come as his representative."

There was no prevarication or hostility as Mendez turned back to face him, just a flat statement as he answered, "Then he was not told the truth."

The cutlass withdrew another inch. "I do not believe you." Jesamiah was over-reacting, but he suddenly resented being ignored and so blatantly made to appear a fool.

"Are you calling me a liar Capitán Acorne?" Mendez indicated the general dilapidated air of the place. "Does it look as if I have anything of value here?"

"Gentlemen, gentlemen!" 'Cesca interrupted, patting the Spaniard's arm and holding the other hand, pleadingly, towards Jesamiah. "There must be a simple explanation, obviously there is a misunderstanding. Señor Mendez, Capitán Acorne is my guest, he has come to Hispaniola to fight on the side of Spain in this idiotic war that we have become embroiled in. He is not here to fight against us, but with us." She gave a light-humoured laugh, "And my father-in-law does indeed want his brandy."

Not wishing to offend, Mendez clicked his heels together, bowed his head towards Jesamiah and apologised with good grace. "My regret, Capitán. I spoke out of turn."

Under no disillusion that this Spaniard, despite his age, would be only too happy to slide a knife between his ribs at first opportunity, Jesamiah accepted the temporary offer of pax. He sheathed his cutlass, removed his hand from its hilt and returned a curt nod.

Indicating the house, Mendez offered, "Shall we discuss matters in a more civilised manner? Over a glass of wine perhaps? My wife is in poor health, but she will welcome company."

Jesamiah felt he would rather discuss things here and now, but it would appear churlish were he to refuse, aside, a glass of wine never went amiss, especially if he could manage to upgrade it to some of the brandy that had been cached away. Inside, he reckoned it was not just the wife who was in poor health, the house looked pretty bad too.

When Carlos Mereno lived here, this must have been a beautiful place, he thought, gazing at the peeling paint and the cracked plaster, his nose wrinkling in disgust at the unpleasant smell of permeating damp and widespread mould. Frowning, he strode across the empty entrance hall to stare at a cobweb-strewn painting hanging on the far wall. He recognised her, Phillipe's mother. He had never known her—she had been dead several years when he was born—but he recognised Phillipe's face in hers. She was standing, pearls dangling from her ears, an exquisite necklace decorating her milk-white throat, drawing the eye to the froth of lace framing the swell of her bosom. Her gown was saffron and blue, a little old fashioned, showing the age of the painting. It had bustle panniers at the hips, not the current inclination of whalebone hoops.

Her lace-gloved hand rested on the shoulder of the man seated beside her. Don Damián del Gardo. Her brother. The old, out of favour curl of the wig, the cut of his coat, the fall of lace on his shirt and the length of his cravat also gave away that this was not a recent portrait. Jesamiah was not interested in their costume, but their faces. They had identical cheekbones, the same angled jaw and sharp chin. Phillipe had boasted the same features. Naturally, del Gardo was younger in the portrait than the man Jesamiah had spoken to yesterday. Good God, was it only yesterday? Surely, last night in that cell had been a lifetime away? This image of del Gardo was not the flab-jawed, paunch-bellied toad he was now.

Feeling renewed anger rising, Jesamiah restrained an urge to draw his cutlass and slash at the thing. Why had his father said nothing of these people or this estate? Why had he kept so many secrets?

Footsteps coming behind! Jesamiah whirled, his hand automatically pulling his pistol from his belt, raising and cocking the hammer back in the one, fluid, movement. His heart was pounding; he hated people coming up behind him!

Frederico Mendez lifted his hands in surprise and surrender. "My pardon Capitán Acorne, I did not intend to startle you." He indicated the painting. "Constella was a beautiful woman."

Exhaling to calm the pounding bloodrush coursing through him, Jesamiah pushed his pistol back through his leather belt.

Not noticing there was anything amiss, Mendez continued talking about the painting. "They were twins. Some said their mother must have lain with different men on the same night, so different were they in character; but you only have to look at their eyes and features to realise they were of the same siring." He tapped various aspects of the painting with his cane, pointing out the areas of likeness. Eyes, nose, mouth; the jaw, the chin.

"I assume you are aware that Phillipe Mereno was my half-brother?"

Mendez bowed his head. "*Sí*, 'Cesca told me, but I knew your father well enough to recognise you."

Jesamiah snorted. "You knew Papa, yet I do not hear you condemning him. He too was a pirate."

"He considered himself a privateer, but it is immaterial, I do not condemn him because your father was my friend. You have yet to prove yourself worthy of him, or my friendship."

His fingers going to where his ribbons should have been, Jesamiah growled and narrowed his eyes. "I have no need to prove myself to anyone, señor."

Mendez shrugged. "Every man must earn respect. It is not an honour lightly given."

"After my father died, did you respect Phillipe when he took this place over?" Jesamiah asked, the animosity slurring his words.

"Phillipe Mereno has never been here. I have not met him."

"And now you won't. He's dead." Jesamiah walked abruptly across the hall, heading to where he could hear 'Cesca talking. "Where is this wine señor? I find I have developed a thirst and grown bored with art."

Mendez's wife was not merely unwell, she was dying. Jesamiah had seen plenty of men on the verge of death to recognise the waxy sheen on her skin and the gaunt, almost skeletal appearance. If she did not have the wasting disease that crept through the body, eating it away as it advanced, then he was a Dutchman. If only Tiola were here! She had once explained the nature of this illness; consumption, a cancer, she had called it. He knew for a fact she had healed some people. Not all though, he felt in his bones it was too late to help this lady. She had been a pretty thing in her younger days, he guessed, for the smile in her eyes, despite her pain, was genuine as he took her hand and kissed it.

"Am I not fortunate," she said with a coughed giggle, "to have such a handsome young man come visiting my sick bed? If I were many years younger, then how fast my heart would be beating!"

"Many years? Nay, señorita, surely you are yet but a girl?" Jesamiah responded.

She laughed, had to pause to cough blood into a linen kerchief, then gain her breath. "How I do love a gallant!"

Like the rest of the plantation, this living room had seen better days. Although it was clean and tidy, the walls were shabby and there were lighter patches where pictures had recently hung—several gaps on shelves and in cabinets. For how long had these two been selling their possessions in order to survive? For as long as there had been no indigo? For more than ten years?

'Cesca sat on a stool beside señora Mendez, chatting quietly of family and women's things, while Mendez served Jesamiah wine. It was passable stuff to drink, but only just.

"This van Overstratten. He is a businessman?" Mendez asked suddenly. "He understands the running of an estate? What is needed?"

"Primarily he is a wine merchant, but he also owns a few sugar plantations. He may know how to regenerate life here, but I doubt it." Thought, *although he'll be a better owner than ever Phillipe was.* "I am surprised my brother did not take more interest. Indigo is a crop worth growing."

The señor shook his head, exhaled a long sigh. "The soil is wrong, the estate has never been profitable, and your father did not require an additional income. He paid us to keep it from becoming a total ruin in the hope that his son would one day be interested in taking responsibility of it." He looked up sharply at Jesamiah, said accusingly, "He never did. Why was that I wonder?"

"I have no idea why Phillipe abandoned you, señor. For my part, until today I had no idea you, or this estate, existed."

"We have received not a shilling for wages or repairs since your father passed away."

Jesamiah shrugged, sipped at the wine, grimaced. It really was poor quality. "Yet you have managed to survive. From the little I know of producing indigo, the Carolinas are becoming dominant in the market. The old days of it being a rare commodity shipped from the East Indies to Europe are now long gone."

Mendez leant forward to refill Jesamiah's glass; "True. Once, only the rich could afford indigo. When the great artists made their portraits of Our Lady they gave her blue to wear because indigo was the highest honour they could grant Her." He smiled, "But now it is grown in the colonies and used to dye cotton cross-weaves like the new *de nim* that is becoming so popular for breeches and jackets."

Jesamiah shook his head, put his hand over the glass; wanted no more of this rank cat's piss that passed for wine. "I am sorry for your situation, señor, but the matter is nothing to do with me. Stefan van Overstratten is the owner now."

Mendez gazed at him steadily, a proud man, unused to begging. "What will become of me and my wife? She is dying and I am too old to serve a new master."

Ashamed of his earlier outburst, Jesamiah felt pity for them both. It was his dead brother he had been annoyed with, the ungrateful wretch, not this couple who had been trying their best to hold together what little there was. But how could he make promises? That was for van Overstratten to do.

Oh bugger him, he thought. *If my father liked these people then they are good enough for me.* "I personally will see to it that the Dutchman attends your needs, and if he does not comply, then I will provide you with a suitable home. That is, if you are prepared to accept the aid of a pirate?"

Lifting his head Frederico Mendez challenged him. "And why would you do so?"

Setting his glass down on the side-table, Jesamiah answered with a lopsided smile. "Because as I said earlier, señor, I have no need to prove myself. Unlike my brother I am not a bastard. I did not love my father as much as I should perhaps, but I respected him and I perceive that he had respect for you."

Señora Mendez had overheard, she was trying to rise, her grateful tears brimming, her frail body trembling. "You are so kind, Capitán Acorne, but we could never repay your generosity."

"All I want is the brandy Wickham left with you for señor Escudero, and those sixteen barrels and ninety-seven kegs of indigo."

Silence held its breath. Outside the window a bird shrilled in a swirl of wings and squawked alarm, a man called something, the words indistinguishable. Jesamiah recognised the voice as that of the *Kismet*'s sailing master.

Raising one eyebrow Mendez exchanged a discreet nod of agreement with his wife and flicked a glance towards 'Cesca who also, imperceptibly, nodded.

"Alas, the brandy is not here. Del Gardo comes, every so often, to poke and pry into the weeds and the ruins. I have never given him opportunity to find anything of worth."

"So where is it?"

"At the convent of Our Lady de Compostela."

An hour's sail away, more than that if the wind was not favourable, and then a trek inland. "I know it. It sits in the hills above the village of Puerto Vaca."

Jesamiah did not add that when he had sailed as a pirate aboard the *Mermaid*, they had frequently put in at Puerta Vaca. They had often slid easily in and out under the cover of darkness and those sheltering cliffs. The jut of a headland had made the village a good, safe, place for smuggling. Or so they had thought. Four years ago they had smuggled in a cargo, ironically, of brandy, spent a couple of days enjoying themselves and when ready to sail, had taken on some new hands. Only they had not realised they were del Gardo's men. When the Guardship came up on them it was obvious they had been waiting to pounce and the bastards had over-powered Malachias's crew. If they had not escaped from that Tower; had boats not been left for them to row to *Mermaid*, anchored, thank the Lord, not too far out into the harbour; had those guards supposedly keeping watch not been dead drunk, then all of *Mermaid*'s crew, himself included, would have died in that dreadful place. Some had. Very badly, some had.

Jesamiah forced the sickening memory aside. "And the indigo?"

Señor Mendez spread his hands, his smile bashful and slightly repentant. "I may have been mistaken about the indigo."

Too bloody right you might, Jesamiah thought. *You were intending to use it for yourself.*

"There is indigo, Capitán Acorne, it is stored with the brandy, but there is not as much as you are expecting."

"How much not as much?"

"I am uncertain. Maybe two dozen kegs?"

Jesamiah rose to his feet. "Sold the rest have you?" he said. He didn't blame Mendez, he would have done the same. More or less what he intended to do—sell it for his own benefit.

'Cesca's eyes were bright with excitement. "Will it take us long to sail there?"

"Us?" Jesamiah queried, his own eyes narrowing into a rutted frown.

Francesca sighed. They had argued this same point already, why was this man so belligerent? "You cannot sail without me. If you do, you will be breaking your parole."

Sod the parole, Jesamiah thought. Said, giving one of his most irritating smiles, "So I will." He turned to Mendez.

"How do I get the cargo? I have a suspicion I ain't going to be able to wander in among all them virgins and just take what I want."

"You will need to speak to the Reverend Mother." Señora Mendez held her hand towards Jesamiah; she was stick thin, he could count every tiny bone that showed through her almost transparent skin. "Please, Capitán, would you take her a message? Would you tell her I am ready for my daughter, Angelita, to come home?"

Jesamiah hesitated; that would mean he would have to bring her here. He just wanted to get on, fetch this illusive cargo, find *Sea Witch* and sail back to Nassau.

"*Por favor*, please. I would go to my God with my heart set at peace."

"You had two daughters then? One is a nun, the other was James Wickham's mother?"

Now why did I ask that? Jesamiah thought to himself. *Stay out of this... Fetch the prize then clear off. Don't get yourself involved.*

Señora Mendez smiled, her dying eyes filled with elusive hope and the expectation of better things to come. "No, Capitán. We have just the one daughter."

"But I thought your daughter had...?"

Closing his mouth, Jesamiah did not finish the sentence. He was already realising he had been fed a pack of lies.

CHAPTER NINE

Don Damián del Gardo did not trust Francesca Ramon Escudero any more than he had trusted her dead husband. She was English, and for all her protestations of loyalty to the Catholic Faith and the Spanish king, del Gardo was certain that if pushed she would suddenly discover her English roots. He threatened to kill the boy often, but the woman was too stupid to realise it was an empty threat, that if he were to do so he would lose the only hold he had over her. Although he was now beginning to wonder if it mattered. She had neither enthusiasm nor talent in pleasuring him, unlike the pretty, almond-eyed, dark-skinned girl he had recently taken to using and who appreciated being promoted to the position of governor's mistress. What slave would not be eager to earn a chance at regaining her freedom?

Add to that, Francesca was losing her looks. Dark circles were often ringed under her red-rimmed eyes; the woman wept too often. And she had told him so very little of interest. Unlike his other spy who had, four years ago, informed him of the rat's nest at Puerto Vaca. A stop had been put to the vermin there, but Acorne's arrival had made del Gardo wonder how many of the nestlings had escaped the noose. At the time he had not been convinced the troublemakers had all been exterminated, despite torturing the Escuderos for information. Killing Francesca's husband had been a mistake, but retribution had been necessary, he had been so very, very angry at the contrived escape of those English pirates. He was certain it had been organised by Louis Escudero, but the old man had not admitted a thing. One of them, though, had supplied best brandy to the night guard and arranged for the doors to be left unlocked; for boats to be made ready. A pair of stubborn, dumb mules those two men. Escudero had still said nothing, even after he had witnessed his son's death. Nor had he said anything since to incriminate himself, not even to disclaim the official explanation that Ramon's death had been an unfortunate accident.

It had galled del Gardo even more when discovering, much later, that one of the pirates imprisoned in the Torre del Homenaje had been the younger son of Charles Mereno. If he had known it then, the bastard would have suffered. He would have strung him up and personally peeled every piece of skin, inch by slow inch, from his living body.

How he had refrained from doing so when Acorne had strutted in as confident as a madam in a brothel, claiming to want to fight for Spain, he would never understand. Except, Don Damián del Gardo knew of several different ways to skin a man, and it was not just Acorne's hide he wanted. He needed the man known as Chesham. Oh, he knew about the English spy who went by the code name Francis Chesham, but who he was he had yet to discover.

There had been several men and women tortured, but they had either not talked or had not known. He had so hoped to find out from Francesca. Again, he wondered whether she had outgrown her usefulness. His spy in the rat's nest at Puerto Vaca had frequently informed him of Wickham's comings and goings, but nothing of Chesham. Del Gardo smiled to himself as he fingered his neatly trimmed, pointed beard. So sad that Wickham had drowned. So unfortunately sad, his ship springing a sudden leak like that, and nobody had suspected a thing. What imbeciles these rebels were!

Was Wickham Chesham? There was that possibility. Del Gardo continued to stroke thoughtfully at his moustache and beard. He was supposed to be listening to the monotonous drone of his chief financier who was mumbling something about no more money to finance them through the next week, let alone a war. If he did not trust Francesca, nor her father-in-law, he trusted Acorne even less. He was convinced the pirate would end up at Puerto Vaca where Wickham had so often come ashore with his smuggled kegs of brandy and barrels of indigo. Had the fool really thought that del Gardo did not know of it? Had he thought that by ensuring the set spy was out of the way on those contraband nights that he would get away with flouting the law? The idiot. Had it never occurred to him that del Gardo was not a fool? That there was more than the one spy at Puerto Vaca?

That was where the answer lay about Chesham, he was sure of it. Wickham had been clever, outwitting his spies, running rings around everyone. Hah, he had not been so clever at the end though, had he?

Abruptly, del Gardo got to his feet and swept the financial adviser aside.

"Stop your whinging, you imbecile. Go steal what we need. If I do not find the leaders supporting this den of rebels we will have no need of financial assets; we will all be dead!"

He swept out, barking for a messenger to be sent to the captain of the guardacostas, and for his own ship, *La Santa Isabella* to be made ready.

CHAPTER TEN

Why he was doing this, Jesamiah had no idea. The only conclusion he had come to was that he had been out in the rain too long and it had rusted his senses.

In Spanish he ordered the man at the tiller to nudge *Kismet* a point closer to the wind, automatically checking the set of the sails on her two soaring masts as he did so, watching for that slight quiver that told him he could push the vessel no harder or he would be dealing with split canvas.

"She is a good little craft," he said to 'Cesca, who was leaning over the larboard rail watching the foam froth away into the white-capped rollers. "Your father-in-law knows a good boat when he sees one."

He thought it was a neutral thing to say; they had exchanged another round of harsh words before leaving La Sorenta, 'Cesca insisting on coming and Jesamiah insisting she was to remain behind. The first half-hour after setting sail he had not spoken a word to her, annoyed because he had lost the argument.

Breathing in the invigorating tang of freedom 'Cesca turned around to lean her back on the rail, to watch Jesamiah. His right hand, she noticed, was often fiddling with his acorn earring or twiddling a curl of his hair. An unconscious, and she had to admit, endearing, habit. "My father-in-law knows many things," she answered enigmatically, her voice a purr. It had been Jesamiah who had argued, not her.

Walking unsteadily across the few yards of the sloping quarterdeck, her red gown with its embroidered pink petticoat and supporting whalebone hoop, was caught by the wind and lifted upward at one side, showing more of what lay underneath than was decent. Scarlet knitted silk stockings with pink-ribbon garters. Long, enticing legs with a glimpse of white flesh at the thigh.

Had the wind not been blowing a force of knots, Jesamiah might have wondered if she had organised it deliberately. The view was certainly having the right effect.

She laughed, pushed the ballooning gown down and joined him beside the tiller. The sails were stretched tight, almost to their limit, the rigging and stays mithering at the intense pressure put upon them. Again Jesamiah asked the helmsman to adjust the tiller, skillfully keeping *Kismet* on the right edge of strain.

"I'd advise you to not wear those hoops while aboard, señora," he said, trying to sound casual and not at all interested in what he had glimpsed. "Fashion is designed for court balls and the drawing room, not for a wet and windy deck. You would be better off below."

"There is nothing to do below."

What do women do to amuse themselves at sea? he suddenly wondered. Apart from Tiola the only females he had known aboard a ship were whores, and they had never been at a loss to know how to amuse themselves. Tiola had been with him on the *Sea Witch* for those few days after she had rescued him from Phillipe, but she had been kept busy patching up his many hurts.

"Can't y'sit and sew, or read?"

"No, I cannot," 'Cesca snapped.

The ship heeled to larboard, spray sluicing over the bow and into the waist producing a shouted grumble from the men. In their mutually combined opinion this temporary captain was pushing the *Kismet* too hard. They had laid wagers on how soon her canvas would rip, or a sail blow out. Several, shaking their dripping hair, had the nerve to glower at Jesamiah. One man partially raised a clenched fist, lowered it as soon as his companion nudged him to caution. Jesamiah pretended he had not seen, merely making a mental note of the man's face. Had they been aboard *Sea Witch* he would have been tipped over the side by now.

There were fifteen on the crew, including a carpenter, galley steward and the sailing master. A landlubberly lot, used to sailing coastal waters in good weather with a kind wind.

"Tell me," Jesamiah said, "I'm curious. I was told Wickham's mother had killed herself. Threw herself off a cliff or something."

"Who told you that? Why would she?"

Jesamiah regarded 'Cesca steadily, eye to eye. "Maybe she was picky about the company she had to keep." By the momentary silence he guessed 'Cesca knew exactly to what he was referring.

She shrugged. "Let us say she took the opportunity to serve a higher authority. And the one she had served, because of his conceited pride, did nothing to quell the false rumours when they began to circulate."

Jesamiah understood her meaning. Where else could a woman go for safe protection from a monster who committed rape? Convents, as he well knew, were not entirely populated by young virgins innocent of carnal matters.

Kismet rolled with the next wave and 'Cesca lost her balance. With a squeak of alarm she stumbled, by good chance, fell into Jesamiah's arm which he, conveniently, stretched out to catch her. As a supposed accident he had not seen it better done. She was good, this woman. But then, she had said she had been an actress, apparently, she had not lost her talent.

One hand fluttering dramatically to her breast, 'Cesca clung to him with the other arm, her body pressing close, not minding the dampness of his coat or the wet dripping off his spray-soaked hair. Her own, she supposed was as damp and straggled. She peered into the mist of low cloud that shrouded the mile-distant coast. "How much further?"

"Not far. An hour maybe? We're having to beat up against this wind, we'd have been quicker if it had been blowing from the opposite direction."

Shifting his balance to compensate for the lifting dip and roll and the extra weight of 'Cesca leaning against him, Jesamiah studied the sails, waited a moment, watching for the foretopsail to quiver... There! "Hands make ready to wear ship!" he yelled. "Señora, I am rather busy at this precise moment. I repeat, you would be more comfortable in the cabin." He said it with a firmness that implied he would not be gainsaid yet again.

Turning to leave, she lowered her lashes to peep at him. "Will you join me later, Capitán? It would be a warmer and dryer place to converse."

"I ain't particularly interested in conversation, but if you could get that slovenly whoreson who has the nerve to call himself a steward to make me coffee, then I will come below as soon as I'm certain these idiots won't sink us."

He smiled as she made her way along the deck and gingerly eased herself, backwards, down the narrow steps of the companionway ladder, her hands gripping the rails as if the whole boat was about to rear upwards. Actress she may be. Sailor she was not.

"Get a bloody move on!" he bellowed, his attention going back to the hands who were idling in the waist. "I said stand by to wear ship, why the fok ain't ye at y'stations?"

That was better, a couple of them actually trotted. Aboard *Sea Witch* they would have run. Patiently, he waited for them to reach for the larboard braces, for their fumbling fingers to loosen off clewlines and buntlines. They were slow, not showing the deftness of his own men. Jesamiah took a breath, swallowed the urge to roar a reprimand. These were not pirates; they had never sailed this boat to save their lives, had never made a fast Chase after a Prize and had never fought their way aboard a fat-bellied East Indiaman ripe for the plucking. These were fair-weather sailors. For all her sleek lines, fresh-painted white hull, gleaming brasswork and spotless varnish, he did not think that *Kismet* had been at sea in a storm since the day she was launched.

"Stand by aft!" He wiped a new burst of wind-blown spray from his face with his sleeve, frowning, studied the set of the sails; watching, listening to every mutter and mither the *Kismet* made. "Let go and haul!" Then, impatience getting the better of him, "Shift yer fokken arses! Look lively there—another hand on the forecourse for fok sake!"

Easing on the one forecourse yard would exert too much pressure on the sails and cordage; all the yards had to swing together, and the course was the hardest to turn.

As the tiller was put over the canvas cracked and billowed high above, and the taut, sodden rigging screeched and complained. The sea churned into white foam under the lee rail as the *Kismet* came round.

"Meet her!" Jesamiah bit back another cursed oath, waited. "Right, that's fine, let her fall off a point *por favor*." Added, "You did well all of you. Well done. I'm impressed." He wasn't, it had been done tardily and without care, but he was a firm believer in dangling carrots, not beating with sticks.

The floggings will cease when morale improves. Jesamiah laughed wryly to himself; a favourite jest of

Malachias Taylor. He had shouted it often when the men had been in a disagreeable mood. It had always raised a smile.

The masts swayed upright and then leaned over as the wind took the sails within its full thrust. Had he decided to tack instead of wear ship they very likely would have missed stays, and then they would have had to start all over again, lose time and maybe damage something. Pirates could not afford the safe effort of wearing ship. Tacking was quicker, though more difficult, for the men had to be sharper. In a fight, fiddling about with sedate manoeuvres could be the difference between win and lose, life and death.

Ah well, never mind; they were not on a chase, these men were not his crew, and this was not his vessel. Thrusting his hands deep into his coat pockets, Jesamiah ordered the sailing master to carry on and slithered down the companionway. He may as well keep 'Cesca company for half an hour or so. He grinned to himself. Unlike her, he could think of many interesting things to amuse them both.

CHAPTER ELEVEN

There was no point in preamble, the woman had been making it quite plain what she wanted from the outset. Investigating the well-stocked wine cabinet, Jesamiah offered her a drink. Pouring her a generous red, he helped himself to a large tot of rum, sat next to her on the locker seats below the stern windows. Only four, *Kismet* was smaller than *Sea Witch*. She was furnished well, everything in mahogany; desk, table, lockers, cabinets, all fitted neatly into her shapely curves like a woman's tight-laced stays and bodice.

"So," he said, savouring the warmth of the dark rum as it slid down his gullet, "What exactly are you going to tell del Gardo about me? You going to mention this indigo to him?"

She had the grace to blush. "I am sure I do not know what you mean."

"No?" He slid his arm around her waist, shifted closer. "I were born almost twenty and five years ago, darlin', not yesterday. I ain't wet behind the ears and I ain't a blind fool. Your father-in-law is my parole keeper on paper only, you are Don Damián del Gardo's mistress and he expects you to dig for worms don't he?"

Again she began to repeat, "I do not know what..."

"What, and when, do you intend t'tell 'im?" Deliberately Jesamiah had slipped into the clipped, uneducated, accent of the base sailor. "For a price, I'll tell ye anythin' y'want t'know; but I ain't guaranteein' it'll be the truth."

He moved his hand to the hem of her skirt, was under and running his fingers up her left stocking. The street doxies never wore much beneath their overgown and petticoat; they had a living to make, time spent with one man meant fewer shillings earned with others. Women of rank and money had layers that even a mole would be hard pressed to tunnel his way through. Jesamiah had long ago discovered that the amount of ribbons, bows, laces and what-nots involved with a woman's gown, shift, petticoat, undershifts and stays meant that instant reward could only be accomplished by going under and up. Fully undressing a well-clad woman for a quick-flung romp was nigh on impossible. He tugged at one of the ribbons to her garter, pulled the silk loose and drifted his fingers higher; found the soft flesh of her inner thigh that he had so tantalisingly glimpsed earlier.

"Captain Acorne, I assure you I have no intention of reporting anything of interest to del Gardo."

Leaning seductively forward, not believing a word of it, Jesamiah carefully placed his mouth over hers in a lingering, intimate and erotic kiss.

'Cesca threaded her arms about his neck, parted her lips wider and wriggled her hip into his groin, moaned as his fingers delved higher and found their destination. Del Gardo had never inflamed her desire like this. With him it was flat on your back, skirt up, a moment of bruising discomfort and it was all over. Her husband had been a lover, he had touched and aroused her—but not like this! This was exquisite! She began to undo the buttons of Jesamiah's breeches, realising suddenly that her assurance of saying nothing was perfectly true. She had no intention of making love with Jesamiah Acorne in order to riddle information out of him. Del Gardo could go suck himself. This was for her!

Sensuously, she eased her fingers inside his open breeches, was surprised and disappointed to find he was not ready for her. Hesitating, she withdrew her hand. Surely she did not have to perform those same degrading acts with this pirate to get him erect as she did for del Gardo?

The sharp knocking on the door made her jump.

"Shit," Jesamiah muttered beneath his breath. "What? What d'ye want?"

From beyond the closed door the steward answered: "Coffee, Capitán. And I am to inform you the headland is in sight."

Bugger, they had sailed faster than Jesamiah had estimated. With a rueful grin of apology he kissed 'Cesca again, lighter, but still on her mouth, and re-buttoned himself. "Sorry, darlin', ye'll 'ave t'interrogate me another day."

He retrieved his hat and cutlass, heaved on his coat and opened the door. Taking his coffee from the man waiting outside, he hurried back on deck where he took a gulp of the hot, black liquid and closed his eyes in relief. What he would have done had the steward not salvaged his potential embarrassment he did not know—or care to think about. Never, ever, had he not had an erection with a woman. Never.

He should not have thought of Tiola; how her legs were smoother, more slender than 'Cesca's. How she would wrap them around his hips and draw him right in... Oh God! He leant his back against the mast, rested his head on its upright solidity acutely aware of his own, opposite, state. He wanted Tiola. He did not want, for all her pretty green eyes, latest fashion, poise and elegance, an English woman who was widow to a Spaniard, mistress to del Gardo and very probably the tale-tattler whom Jennings had hoped he would unearth. He wanted Tiola, damn it! Tiola!

Furious, ashamed at his impotence, he hurled the china cup away throwing it, with an explicit oath, into the sea. Stood where he was, head back, eyes closed. And the rain began to drizzle, dabbing gently at his upturned face.

CHAPTER TWELVE

SUNDAY EVENING

Tiola sat, staring out of the stern windows of Stefan's sloop. This cabin was much smaller, not as grand as Jesamiah's beautiful ship. It was a comfortable cabin, plush velvet, walnut furniture, white-painted walls. Beyond this small room was a dining area, beyond that a cupboard that had the grandiose impertinence to call itself a bedchamber. All of it was tasteful, luxurious and elegant. How she longed for the untidiness and those two gape-mouthed cannons in Jesamiah's muddle of a great cabin!

Stefan sat at his desk writing letters, scratching away with his quill. The noise, *scritch, scritch, scritch*, was driving Tiola insane. She wanted to jump up, scream and shout at him. Wanted to demand to know where they were headed, but she just sat here, staring, staring at the sea, listening to Tethys mocking her.

~ *You are too weak to fight me? Ah, what a pity, I was looking forward to the enjoyment of destroying you. I will get no pleasure from your defeat if you do not try to fight back.* ~

Tiola made no answer.

~ *You are a creature of the Earth, Tiola Oldstagh, you have no authority over me.* ~

That was not quite true. Tiola could not command Tethys, but she could cajole, bargain with, or trick her. At the very least she should be able to protect herself from the mental battering that Tethys was giving. But she just sat, staring at nothing. And listening to the taunts.

She was weak, her ability had been drained to its lowest ebb. She was like a plant left overlong in a pot where the water had run dry. Bloom, leaves and stem drooping, on the verge of curling up and withering to dust. All it needed was fresh water and the plant would regain its life and beauty. Except, in Tiola's case it was not water she needed but land, the solidity of the goodly earth to regenerate the power-giving life force that had sapped away from her.

She gazed out of the sea-salt encrusted glass of the windows, and all she saw was the grey, rain-laden sky and the even greyer sea.

CHAPTER THIRTEEN

On the quarterdeck, squinting upward at the main truck from where señor Escudero's flag streamed and cracked, Jesamiah assessed how long it would be before the fine drizzle turned to heavier rain. The highest point of the island was wreathed in black cloud, a sullen mist blanketing everything above eight hundred feet.

He spoke to the tillerman, a member of the regular crew who knew these waters. "Wind's shifted. Let her fall off a couple of points if you will; we'll weather this headland as close as we can. Hope we can make harbour before the next dousing hits us."

"I am not certain, Capitán..." the man began in hesitant English, then faltered to silence under Jesamiah's formidable stare.

"Not certain of what?"

"*Nada*. Nothing, Capitán."

The tiller creaked over, Jesamiah watched the sails and compass like a hawk, several hands ran to re-trim the yards and braces. At least they were shifting their sorry backsides a bit quicker now.

"Land on the lee bow!" someone called in Spanish, anxiety thick in his voice. Then, "Almost dead ahead, Capitán!"

Although he had not been to the village of Puerto Vaca or plied this coast for several years, Jesamiah knew these waters better than this fragile crew. They had never had to smuggle a cargo of contraband ashore, had never run hard on a tide while clinging like limpets to concealing shadows. The headland, a bluff of mist-shrouded scrub and tree-covered rock, seemed very close, but knowing its apparent nearness was nothing more than a misleading illusion, he was unconcerned. Even so, if this wind veered suddenly they would find it hard to claw away again.

He had been a mere lad the first time he had sailed here aboard the *Mermaid*. As he grew in height and ability, he had progressed to foretopman and after they had escaped from that tower, Malachias had made him quartermaster, second in command. The promotion had hurt at first, knowing he was replacing a good friend whom he had watched die. But as Malachias had said, life moves on, it's no good standing still and letting it sail without you.

She had been a good craft, the *Mermaid*; shallow on the draft and with a turn of speed that, under normal circumstances, no lumbering excisemen or guardships could hope to match. He had been almost as fond of her as he was of the *Sea Witch*. He smiled at the thought of her, his beloved ship. No use thinking of *Sea Witch*; Rue would take care of her, and for all his knowledge of these waters, if he did not concentrate these dolts who liked to think of themselves as sailors would be justified with their growing apprehension about the imminent likelihood of running aground.

"Leadsman to the chains if you please," Jesamiah called. "Begin sounding in five minutes. Take in the foresail."

"May I bring her up a point, Capitán?" asked the man at the tiller, a tremor quivering his anxious words.

"Sí." Peering up at the masthead Jesamiah felt the rain grow heavier. It would soon change to a downpour, not that it mattered, he was wet anyway from the spray; it would be nice to see a bit of sunshine for a change though.

The foresail was flapping and booming up to its yard, the men spread above it fisting and bullying the canvas into place. Forward, the leadsman's arm was rotating slowly, then he released the line and watched it splash down over the bow. A pause. "By the mark, nine!"

The tillerman kept his gaze fixed on the compass. Jesamiah could imagine what he was thinking, that he was waiting for the sound of something scraping along the keel, then the jolt as they hit the shallows or submerged rocks. Few sailors could swim, and there were sharks skulking in these waters.

"And a quarter less nine," the leadsman called after another cast. There was plenty of water below them. Jesamiah had run in closer than this on *Mermaid*, but then, *Kismet* was not a boat he knew intimately. He did not know what he could or could not ask of her, and like all females she had a mind of her own. The land rose up, almost sheer, ahead of the bowsprit.

"By the mark seven... by the mark... *¡mierda, Capitán! ¡Cinco!*—Five!"

Thirty feet of water. "If you cannot restrain your opinions, *mi amigo*, I suggest you give the lead to someone more competent," Jesamiah remarked drily. He lifted his telescope, studied the land. The mist shrouded much of it, but he could make out trees giving way to meadows and wind-driven, white-laced foam running up onto a strip of sanded beach. The wilder spume of water boiling against a straggle of rocks beneath the jutting headland. He lowered the glass. "Bring her up two points."

The braces squealed and the yards groaned as the men, relieved, leapt to do as he bid, and as *Kismet* headed up further to windward and the headland swung backwards, the rain moved into the widening gap between.

"You'd best go below, señora. The moment we round the shelter of this point we shall be drenched," Jesamiah said to

'Cesca, who had appeared on deck, a cloak thrown over her gown, which, he noticed, was now without its support of hoops.

"I do not mind the rain," she answered, tying the laces of her cloak tighter, then gripping the hood with her left hand. "I am enjoying the freedom. Being here is unexpectedly invigorating. I had forgotten what enjoyment is."

"*¡A Dios gracias!* By the mark nine!" the leadsman shouted. Deeper water. The cheering shot upward towards the sky.

"Stand by to wear ship! Stop that fokken noise, you men! Anyone would think we'd been about to drown. What's the matter with you? You think I don't know how t'sail a boat? Hands to braces, look sharp there!"

Topmen scurrying to obey, were of a sudden impressed by Jesamiah's seamanship. He barked orders with the menacing growl of a fighting dog. That too, was beginning to impress them. The tiller went over, and Jesamiah reached out to steady 'Cesca as the boat heeled, the deck tipping at a steep angle. The woman grabbed for a backstay, however, and he moved aside.

Kismet rounded the headland and the full force of wind and rain hit them.

"You really ought to get below!" Jesamiah shouted above the roar of the wind. "It ain't a good idea for you to be out 'ere. You there, that man! Where the fok d'ye think ye be runnin' to? All 'ands on deck means all bloody 'ands, including your pretty white lilies!"

'Cesca did not want to be in the warm and dry. She would be quite content wrapped in this pirate's arms, her head resting against his chest. He had smelt of tar and hemp and rum. Of masculine sweat and desire. His exploring fingers had excited her, made her want him badly, surely had they not been interrupted he would have responded to her?

"I am happy here," she said, lowering her lashes before raising them to meet his eyes. To her fury, he deliberately turned away.

Bowling onward, lifting and swooping over the churn of rain-lashed rollers, *Kismet* steadied and headed, straight for the river mouth that neatly dissected the white sands of the shore. From what he could see, the village had not changed. A sprawl of haphazardly placed timber buildings ranging along the western bank of the river. The church at the top of the street, and sitting a little higher than the village, was of stone, its white-limed walls standing out like a shout in front of the green foliage of the crowding forest which stretched upward into the spread of hills behind.

On the east bank opposite the village, black mangroves heaved with their customary population of birds. Pelicans, herons, oystercatchers and frigates, all eager to grub for the shrimps, shellfish and small fry that made their home among the dangling tangle of roots. There were American crocodiles too, Jesamiah noticed. One on the shore, a couple resembling floating logs, in the still water. A sudden flurry of spray, all the birds took flight, calling and shrieking in alarm. All except one, which fluttered wildly but in vain as, screeching, it was dragged under by a pair of tight-gripping jaws. Within moments the birds resettled to their foraging.

Pretending he had not noticed 'Cesca's disappointed scowl Jesamiah pointed ahead. "You'll soon be ashore in the dry, señora. We timed it well, another half hour and it will be dark." He had a ship to sail, and the woman's presence was becoming most distracting. Best to ignore her; the open deck of her father-in-law's boat was not the place to complete unfinished business.

Bugger, he thought, shoving aside the erotic image and feel of his fingers poking beneath her gown. *It's a bit bloody late to be getting it up now!*

Kismet was a handy, obliging little craft; she luffed neatly up to the jetty, the crew, now they were certain of what was beneath them—mud and sand—working quickly and efficiently. 'Cesca said not another word. As soon as they were made fast Jesamiah sent her ashore with two men to accompany her. Despite the rain and their renewed grumbling, the remaining crew were ordered to make everything tidy. He had never left *Sea Witch* looking like a tattered whore; nor would he leave the *Kismet* so.

When he finally stepped ashore a slave boy, waiting patiently in the rain, handed him a curt note. Written orders to attend the harbour master in his office. Why was he not surprised to receive yet another hostile welcome? What was it with these Spanish? Had he grown horns, fangs and a forked tail or something?

CHAPTER FOURTEEN

"Look, I carry only ballast. Shingle and rock. We're heading down the coast but I didn't fancy continuing in this foul weather, not with the señora aboard. So if I am not importing anything how the hell do you work out I have to pay import tax on top of a mooring fee?" Jesamiah's fingers were twitching towards where his ribbons would be; this oaf before him, the harbour master, was a bald-headed, round-bellied, money-grubbing idiot. He'd not yet met a harbour master who wasn't.

For the third time Jesamiah repeated himself, slowly and clearly in precise Spanish. "I have nothing to unload. My hold is empty."

"But you brought things ashore."

"Sí. My passenger, señora Ramon Escudero, had her clothes' trunk with her. She is a woman, what do you expect? Women always travel with a hold full of luggage."

"Then you have a passenger, so there will be duty to pay." The harbour master held out his hand. "Pay me, mariner, or I will impound your boat and have you thrown in gaol."

Jesamiah gave up the argument and fished into his pocket for a handful of coins. "You'd better bloody keep a close eye on her mate; if I find one scratch on her hull because you've allowed some lubber to moor too close I'll

259

shove these pieces of eight where the sun ain't ever goin' t'shine. Understand?"

Jesamiah slammed them down on to the neat and tidy desk, scrawled his name against that of the *Kismet* in the harbour book and stomped out.

Cramming his hat tight on to his head and tucking in his chin, he ran up the incline of the cobbled road to the Sickle Moon, a tavern slumped beneath an overhang of rocks. Those rocks had probably hung suspended from the hillside for centuries but had always appeared precariously dangerous to Jesamiah's eye. A painted sign of a new moon hung from a bracket fastened to the rock face. Pausing, his hand on the door latch, he took a quick glance up the narrow, steep, street. No one. The place was deserted. Hardly surprising with the rain lashing down like this, anyone with an ounce of sense was tucked safe indoors. He peered the other way, down towards the harbour and caught a glimpse of a shadowed figure hurrying away from the cluster of official buildings. She looked vaguely familiar, much like the woman he had seen in rain-swept Nassau—nay, what was there to go on? The swirl of a grey skirt and the glimpse of wet hair? She could be anyone! He chuckled. So, that was the cause of the harbour master's annoyance. He'd had his private, probably illicit, pleasuring interrupted.

Ducking in below the door lintel, Jesamiah met with the warm fug of steaming woollen coats, male sweat, tobacco, lamp-oil and smoke. A dozen men sat at tables made from old barrels. Two men were playing cards, another two were arguing over something, although not heatedly, more of a spirited discussion with accompanying highly animated arm gestures. The entire room fell stone silent as he strolled in and crossed to the bar where a sallow-faced doxie was propped up by her elbow. Watching him, a slight frown creasing her brow as he approached, she pulled her bodice down slightly to reveal more of her already well-displayed bosoms, and tweaked her skirts, showing a generous glimpse of ankle.

Normally he would have gone straight to lean alongside her, with a rum in one hand and one of her well-endowed breasts in the other. Ah well, business had to come first. And he was not quite sure if the same embarrassing thing would happen here as it had in *Kismet*'s cabin—or more precisely, had not happened. At this moment he was not prepared to risk another disconcerting experience of impotence.

"Hello Mireya," he said, standing a few yards in front of her, hands shoved deep into his pockets. "Remember me?"

She sidled over to him, took hold of his chin and turned it to left and right, studying his face critically. "I see a man where there was once a boy. You are not the fresh-faced youth I bedded last time you were here, Jesamiah Acorne. Are you a man now in other areas as well?" Her hand went towards his crotch but he clamped his fingers around her wrist and backed away a pace or two.

"I'm a respected Captain now, darlin', these lines of maturity on m'face are the marks of responsibility, and I take m'responsibilities seriously. I'm 'ere on business, not pleasure."

"Last time you were here you said nothing was more important than pleasure."

"Well I were right, 'nothing' *is* more important." Glancing around the tavern he saw no other face he recognised. "Where's Emilio? His wife?"

Mireya tossed her head, sniffed and then shrugged one brown-tanned shoulder. "Dead. Been dead these four years. The Sickle Moon's got new owners. He don't treat me as well as Emilio did though."

Jesamiah was sorry to hear the news, Emilio had been a good man, a good smuggler and a good friend. His wife had been good in bed too. He was not going to say that to Mireya, however, for she was one of those tavern whores who liked to keep clients to herself.

"What did they die of?"

"Del Gardo strung them up from that beam over there soon after you were last here. Said they were rebel spies. Said they were too friendly with you English." She sneered the last, disgruntled that he had turned her down.

Involuntarily Jesamiah looked towards the beam she indicated with a toss of her impertinent chin. Double chin, she was beginning to run to fat, was not the pretty thing he remembered from four years ago.

Del Gardo was right about Emilio being friendly with the English, but not about the rest. At least, as far as Jesamiah knew. He had been hoping Emilio would have been able to shed some light on the several conundrums that were bothering him. Damn. He would have to find someone else to ask now. He certainly was not going to solve any puzzles by asking 'Cesca—she was riddle number one!

"A woman came in a short while ago, a señora Francesca Escudero. Where is she?"

Mireya pouted jealously at his question. "If you would rather poke her than me..." She pointed towards a discreet door at the rear.

Jesamiah took her cheeks between his fingers, kissed her on the mouth and with his other hand, pressed a gold coin into her cleavage. Helping himself to a bottle of rum, he unstoppered it and took a long, satisfying mouthful. "I'll get back to you darlin'. Promise." More often than not, Jesamiah never kept a promise.

Distracted, he did not notice one of the men finish his ale, set an ostrich-feathered hat over his thinning grey hair and disappear at a jog trot into the rain.

Sauntering to the rear of the tavern Jesamiah turned and winked at the girl. "Tell the landlord I'll pay later. With the rest of what I'll owe."

Appeased, the girl preened and retrieved the coin.

Pushing the door open he could hear 'Cesca talking. Being naturally curious he paused to listen, taking one or two long swigs of the bottle as he stood there.

"You say a pirate brought you here, señora? Can he be trusted? Do you not think he could bring us trouble?"

"He is not as much trouble as the trouble I will be in if I do not have anything to tell del Gardo when I return."

Swallowing a fourth gulp, Jesamiah felt intense disappointment swell his innards. He liked 'Cesca, had been so hoping she was not what he suspected her to be, but then, who was he fooling? For all her fancy ways, she was del Gardo's whore, and the honesty of a whore was no more dependable than the honesty of a pirate. He pushed the door wide, deliberately let it bang against the wall behind as he swaggered into the kitchen.

'Cesca was sitting beside a lively fire, her bare feet in the hearth, a blanket around her shoulders hiding the fact that she had stripped to her undershift. Her cloak, the scarlet stockings, embroidered pink petticoat and the red gown dripped from a wooden-framed rack suspended from the ceiling. In her hand, a glass of cognac. The other woman, ample in bosom and buttock, and everything in between, was stirring a pot of stew hanging from the iron firehook.

"I take it you know each other?" Jesamiah observed as he joined 'Cesca beside the fire, steam rising from his wet coat, rain dripping from his hat as he removed and shook it.

'Cesca grumbled and moved aside as the wet showered her. She could feel her bad temper rising higher, knew she was being silly, but his rejection of her had hurt. She had so wanted Jesamiah there in *Kismet*'s cabin—had been so ready for him, yet as soon as they had been interrupted he had dropped her as if she were poxed. Why had he not shouted for the steward to go away? Why had he not ignored the wretched man and continued making love to her? Why? Oh, she knew why! Men were all the same, they used women as if they were blocks of wood. No man ever considered that a woman had feelings of her own!

Pouting she snapped, in Spanish, "This is Madelene, the landlady. She does not speak English."

Jesamiah bowed and removed his coat, hung it beside his hat on a peg. So, 'Cesca and Madelene were friends? She seemed to know a lot of people, did 'Cesca Ramon Escudero.

He guessed, from the shrewd way Madelene was looking at him, that he was being assessed for how much he would pay for a tumble with the girl outside. Or herself. If the gossips of fashion were to be believed, it was hips and buttocks that were appealing to men at the moment. Jesamiah did not agree, he was a bosom man. He liked big breasts, and Madelene's were the size of over-ripe melons about to burst their skin, but he'd never had much of a fancy for a woman old enough to be his mother. For all the amount of enticing flesh escaping over the top of a tight-laced bodice. He chuckled to himself. His preference was for large tits, yet the woman he loved, the woman he wanted as his wife, was so slight she barely sported any bust at all.

Sitting on a chair beside the table, he stretched one boot towards the fire and brought the other foot over his knee to inspect a crack in the sole. No wonder his stocking was wet. "You going to arrange transport to this convent then?" he asked in English.

"While you were dallying outside, I have already hired two horses for us."

He grunted. His backside did not much like horses.

Madelene served stew into a bowl, placed it on the table in front of him. It smelt good. Goat stew with a thick gravy, spiced with ginger and herbs. One or two blobs of fat and lumps of gristle floated on the surface, but used to food that was stale, mouldy, bad and riddled with weevils, Jesamiah did not notice. He wolfed it down.

Belly full, he tipped his chair back, balancing by resting the holed boot on the edge of the table. He stretched, realised the lash marks on his back were uncomfortable but were no longer hurting. Tiola had said her various salves would heal them quickly.

Irritably he removed his foot and let the chair drop, square, to the floor. Why had he remembered her again? He would have to learn to stop this. To stop seeing her face, hearing her voice. Stop wanting her. He drank more of the rum, said to 'Cesca, "I assume you've also sorted yourself a bed for the night?"

'Cesca had remained seated by the fire; she made a valiant attempt to be congenial. "There are three rooms upstairs. One belongs to Madelene and her husband, one to that spot-faced slut outside, and one for weary travellers. I have taken that room."

Dare I? Dare I try once more? she thought.

Gathering the blanket tight around her she rose, swayed over to him, emphasising the movement of her hips. Deliberately allowed her covering to slip slightly, exposing a good portion of her breast, and a glimpse of the nipple as she bent forward to whisper into his ear. "You are welcome to share with me."

Jesamiah knew all about the number of rooms upstairs. He gulped a few more mouthfuls of rum. It had been a long day. Last night had been longer. He was tired and had no intention of sleeping with her, just in case of... well, in case he couldn't get it up. He was more than a little drunk after all. What if it was permanent? What if Tiola had put a spell on him to ensure he remained faithful? He dismissed the idea. She had promised she would never use her Craft on him. Maybe it was just one of those things that occasionally happened?

Or maybe not.

There was only one way to ensure he maintained his reputation. He had to decline 'Cesca's offer.

Placing one hand over the revealed breast, he smacked a kiss on her lips. "If y'care to nip upstairs and get the sheets warmed, I'll mebbe fit ye in as soon as I've emptied me bladder, passed this wind and got me shillin's worth from that wench out front."

'Cesca slapped him. He didn't blame her.

The door slammed as she walked with dignity from the kitchen, he heard her run up the stairs though, heard her chamber door slam.

Bugger, he thought, *bugger, bugger, bugger*.

Avoiding Madelene's disapproving glare he drank more of the rum and considered moving to what promised to be a more comfortable chair in the corner, but he ought to check on the *Kismet*, ensure her mooring lines had not come loose. He stood, a little unsteadily, reached for his hat and coat. Said nothing as he sauntered out. There was nothing, really, that he could say.

CHAPTER FIFTEEN

SUNDAY NIGHT

La Sorenta. Stefan van Overstratten had expected more than a ramshackle hotch-potch of mud huts and lean-to shelters most of which were falling down. All he could see of the two enormous storehouses were lighter patches of bleak, grey, evening sky through the gaping holes in the walls. Except for the black silhouette of beams and rafters, neither of them had a roof. The house was a ruin—the fields? Perhaps it was just as well he could not see the fields.

"This is disgraceful," he bawled, swiping at a clump of ragged weeds with his walking cane. "A shambles, a pigsty, a..." He faltered to a stop, lost for suitably expressive words.

There was nothing señor Mendez could say as a counter argument. It was all true, and twice now the plea that this was not of his doing had fallen on deaf ears. The Dutchman, justifiably, was in a rage. Mendez kept silent and took the verbal blows. There was no use in denying what the man could see with his own eyes.

Stefan's rage was made the more potent for the person he ought to be shouting at was a corpse somewhere at the bottom of the Atlantic Ocean. Mereno had cheated him. All this waste ground was of no recent demise, the place had been decrepit for years. His anger was heightened by the fact he knew this to be his own fault. He had told Phillipe he was in the market to buy more land, had already purchased a tobacco plantation from him—that had been a flourishing establishment, but only small, one-hundred acres. La Sorenta was to have been his triumph over his brother-in-law. Now he knew why Phillipe had sold it so cheaply. Now he knew why the bastard had wanted to leave Nassau in such a hurry. And Acorne had killed the cheating whoreson? Stefan never thought he would be grateful to that pirate for something.

Frustrated, defeated, Stefan sank to the top step of the shallow flight that led up to the house and dropped his head into his hands. This estate was a ruin, and so was he.

With a deep, sorry, sigh and lifting his head, Stefan faced his one, last, hope of survival. Asked; "The indigo. Please tell me there are barrels of indigo stored here."

Señor Frederico Mendez spread his hands, lifted his shoulders, let them fall. What could he say? He could only tell the truth.

"I am sorry, señor, there is no indigo here. There has been no indigo here since señor Charles Mereno died, more than ten years ago."

CHAPTER SIXTEEN

They were waiting for him. Three men hit him, hard, one with a fist to the stomach, one with a cudgel on his shoulders and the third, as he sank with a groan to his knees, kicked a boot into his groin.

That's m'excuse sorted for not entertainin' the ladies, Jesamiah thought grimly as he went down. With another blow to the back of his head, fell unconscious.

He awoke, with no idea of how long he had been out cold, to find himself suspended by his wrists from a meat hook attached to an overhead beam. His arms and shoulders were taking the full weight of his dangling body. His first thought was that this was a bloody undignified way to wake up. His second was a bitten off scream of pain.

The bruising had barely faded from the damage Phillipe had done to him, his ribs were still not healed and now it felt as if they were broken again; his right eye was crusted with dried blood and his back hurt like the damnation of the devil. He'd had better days.

Squinting through one eye he discovered he was in a cellar; barrels and kegs were stacked on two sides, wooden chests and tall racks of bottles on the other two. The foetid air was damp and musty, smelt of rat pee, mouldering wine and stale tobacco. Another blow, this one to the small of his back. He felt moisture trickling beneath his cotton shirt. Sweat? He had a feeling one of the lash marks had opened up, it felt more like blood. The floor was only an inch or so beneath his feet but it could have been a mile away for all he could do to reach it and take the strain off his screeching muscles.

He recognised where he was; in the cellars beneath the Sickle Moon. On his last visit down here he had satisfyingly poked Emilio's wife on top of that old chest over there. One of the men had left his hat on it, a black hat with a curled ostrich feather. What was it he had been told about Emilio's wife? Ah yes. She was dead, hanged as a spy.

"So, you are awake. Perhaps you will be good enough to tell us why you are here?" Someone, a man stinking of garlic, said in Spanish.

"Go suck yourself." Perhaps not the wisest of replies, even in fluent Spanish. A fist connected with Jesamiah's stomach.

"I ask again. Why are you here? We do not trust bastard pirates."

"Just as well I ain't no bastard nor a pirate then, ain't it?" Another blow. Jesamiah grunted, what the heck—he had nothing to hide. "I am here with señora Ramon Escudero. We've come to fetch someone's daughter home to her dying mother."

"Have you now? More likely you've come to steal our valuables."

"Got valuables worth stealing 'ave you? I ain't noticed any."

"Or maybe you've come to spy on us, to tattle tales to del Gardo, like you did last time."

So that's what this was all about. Del Gardo. By God he loathed that man! He struggled to loosen the cord chafing at his wrists and protested indignantly, "I ain't no intelligencer spy! Who the fok suggested I was? It's a bloody lie!"

Pirate, bastard, whoreson... most insults he could tolerate for most of them were true. Spy? He was not a spy.

Spies were weasel-gutted, black-hearted ferrets. Apart from 'Cesca. She was a spy, well, she was spying on him.

It occurred to him maybe that was why he had not been able to get aroused when he'd had the chance to have her. Perhaps it was nothing to do with Tiola and woven spells. On the other side of the deck, perhaps it had everything to do with Tiola. That and a guilt of conscience.

One of the men, with a wicked scar slicing across his forehead, withdrew a knife from its sheath, ran the blade over the stubbled whiskers of Jesamiah's cheek. "You need a shave mate. Shall I give you one?" He shifted the knife lower, moved it down Jesamiah's sternum, prodded his stomach and stopped at his genitals where he poked the tip a little harder.

Jesamiah willed his body to relax, tried not to show fear. It wasn't easy.

"I say you are a spy."

"And I say I ain't."

Scarface brought the blade upwards again to Jesamiah's throat and drew a trickle of blood just below his Adam's apple. "I think it strange that not long after you were here last time, Emilio and his wife were strung up. You and the others—who was it now? Ah, sí, Taylor was your capitán. If I remember rightly, he and almost all his crew escaped the Tower and sailed away, unharmed." The knife bit again. "Now how did that happen to be, I wonder? Talk for your freedom did you? Talked to Don Damián del Gardo about Emilio being a rebellious traitor to Spain?"

"Emilio was never a traitor, he was a good friend, none of us would have betrayed him! If you knew me before, then you would know that also!" It occurred to Jesamiah that he did not know this man, had met none of them, yet clearly they knew who and what he was. How was that so? Something here stank as rotten as old fish.

A door creaked open somewhere behind and to his left. A waft of air made the candles flicker, brought in the sound of talking and laughter from the tavern above. Footsteps descending wooden stairs, a bobbing light.

Closing his eyes Jesamiah prayed it was not a fourth person coming to add to the fun. What was it they wanted? He had told no lies here, admittedly neither had he told the whole truth, but they knew nothing of the indigo. If they did, would they not be asking where it was hidden?

"Leave him be, you great oaf!" Madelene.

"I apologise for my idiot of a husband," she said as she set the lamp down on a barrel and indicated Jesamiah was to be released. "My dotard here," she pointed to Scarface, "keeps his brains in his codpiece, and as his pizzle is only this big," she indicated less than an inch, "that is not much brain."

Grinning weakly, Jesamiah tried to shout not to cut him down, but it was too late. Scarface had pulled a keg over, climbed up and slashed through the cords with his knife. Falling heavily to the floor the jolt shuddered through Jesamiah's body. He lay, winded, hurting too much even to groan, his body rigid as the restricted blood rushed into his hands and arms.

"Maybe it was you who betrayed Emilio," he countered to Scarface. Pins and needles were shooting down his arms. "Maybe you wanted the Sickle Moon and found an easy way to get it?"

Scarface lifted his boot to kick out but his wife snapped at him to not be so stupid. To Jesamiah said, "My husband got that scar fighting the soldiers who came to hang Emilio and his wife. Emilio was his brother."

"Ain't always much love lost between brothers," Jesamiah remarked hauling himself to his knees. Thought, *I'd 'ave hung mine with no bother.*

With a huge effort of willpower he managed to get to his feet, massaging his wrists as he did so. He tottered to one of the racks, lifted down a brandy bottle. Finest French. That would do.

Seeing a glass on a shelf, Madelene dusted the cobwebs from it with the hem of her skirt, offered it to him. "'Cesca has told me why Capitán Acorne is here," she said to her husband. "Had you bothered to ask me, you idiot, this unpleasantness would have been avoided."

Refusing the glass, Jesamiah unstoppered the bottle and drank straight from it. Aye. Finest French. He hoped 'Cesca had kept the matter of the indigo—and the brandy—to herself. He did not want its whereabouts broadcast to the entire island.

"The capitán," she added, "is here to fetch home the daughter of señor and señora Mendez."

A laugh almost broke from Jesamiah's face, would have done had his ribs and cheeks not been so sore. Scarface's expression at his wife's announcement was a picture. First surprise, then puzzlement, then doubt. Every feature, every wrinkle, fold and crease was working to understand the implication. His laugh faded as Scarface finally digested the statement and spat it back out like a belch.

"It is a lie. Why would Frederico send a pox-riddled scum-boat of a pirate to fetch her? He would not be trusting the likes of him with a nun."

After another generous swig, Jesamiah gingerly tested whether he could now flex his arms or not. He could, just about. Continuing speaking in Spanish, he snapped, "I am no longer a pirate. I was granted amnesty and I am here to fight for the Spanish with del Gardo's fleet."

The Spaniards laughed belly gusts of mirth. Scarface bent double, his hands resting on his knees. Tears of amusement rolling down his face he lifted his head to point at his wife. "And you call me the oaf? You actually believe this nonsense?"

He moved quickly, rising up, his fist bunching ready to land square in Jesamiah's belly. Only Jesamiah was the quicker. He spun sideways, kicked, catching the Spaniard sharp at the back of the knee. Already off balance he toppled forward and Jesamiah finished the manoeuvre by smashing the bottle down on his head.

Brandy, blood and glass spread in a nasty puddle on the floor. Indifferent, Madelene stepped over her unconscious husband without much care, and selected a second bottle; good brandy but not the same expensive brand. She handed it to Jesamiah who was breathing heavily from the agony of protesting muscles.

"Anyone else?" he asked, holding the bottle by its neck and raising it high. The other two shook their heads, backed away.

Wandering over to the chest where so long ago Emilio's wife had pleasurably serviced him, he tipped off the hat and sat, gulped down the brandy enjoying the warm fire as it slid down his throat. Wondered whether, if he drank the bottle dry, it would deaden the pain where the cat had cut him. Damn it, only a short while ago he'd thought he was on the mend. Bugger these stupid turds!

"My husband made a mistake," Madelene said. "You are our guest. How can we make amends?"

Her face was blurring, her voice ebbing and flowing. Jesamiah had no intention of accepting an apology. He did have every intention of finishing the brandy, however.

Amends? Mistake? By God, when he was able to get to his feet again he would teach these bastards a lesson they would not forget in a hurry! But in a minute, not right now. In a minute, when the brandy was gone.

CHAPTER SEVENTEEN

MONDAY MORNING

Cold water splashing on to his face awoke Jesamiah abruptly. He moaned, pulled the now wet blanket higher over his head and muttered an expletive as would have shocked even his quartermaster, Rue.

Another dousing. "I suggest you wake up and get up. It is ten of the clock. The horses are saddled and I have been waiting for over an hour."

Jesamiah thought of burrowing deeper, but once awake he rarely went back to sleep. He emerged from beneath the covers, ran a hand through his tangled hair. His mouth tasted as if it were filled with sand, his head ached and his eye throbbed. Touching it tentatively he winced. He could do with a shave too, his face was itchy. It would have to wait.

"That should have been tended," 'Cesca said, tossing his clothes at him as she retrieved them from the floor. "I assume you got drunk, picked a fight, then celebrated your victory with her?" Irritably, she pointed at the covered, lightly snoring hump at his side.

Through the hazy fug of his spinning brain, Jesamiah gradually become aware that he was not alone in the bed. He frowned, peered under the blanket, shook his head in bewilderment and instantly regretted the action as the room spun dizzily for several turns.

"Don't remember," he confessed. "I remember three bastards asking me questions in a not very polite manner. And a bottle of brandy. Might 'ave been two bottles. Don't remember 'er though." He looked again. Mireya was naked and on her back, her mouth open.

Finding the second of his boots beneath the bed, 'Cesca stood it with its pair. "I suppose you had no difficulty in accommodating her over-sized charm," she said cuttingly, her expression rigid with disapproval.

"Can't say as I recall what I did. Not often I forget those sort of charms though." Half-hearted he attempted a grin, mimed holding large breasts, but feeling the pull of bruised muscles and clearly remembering receiving the blows that had caused them he swung his legs from the bed instead; stood, stretched. He too was naked.

'Cesca suppressed a gasp, hastily looked away on the pretence of searching for something. His nakedness did not embarrass her, but the scars on his body were terrible. So many of them! The zigzag of white was patterned along his forearm, marks on his chest from bullet wounds; newer scars on his thighs and buttocks and raw lash marks across his back! She blinked away shocked tears. He had been flogged, and only recently—how much he must have endured!

Unaware of her pity, Jesamiah let the room settle its whirling then reached for his cotton shirt that she had tossed to the bed, pulled it on, its length hiding any further need for modesty. Scratching his backside he wandered over to the piss pot. He looked at her, one eyebrow cocked upward. "Do ye watch del Gardo take a piss then?" he drawled.

Blushing scarlet, 'Cesca whirled around, turning her back on him. Directing his stream of water, he said, attempting to appear unperturbed by her presence, "You ever 'eard of Master Samuel Pepys?"

"Naturally. I received an excellent education. He wrote a vibrant description of the Great Fire that swept London during the reign of Charles II."

"That's right. 1666." He finished urinating, yawned, searched for his breeches and pulled them on. "Did y'know he had a balcony built outside his upstairs dining room? He put a pot out there for his guests to use so they wouldn't 'ave t'leave the room and miss any conversation. Mighty civilised idea if y'ask me."

Vaguely he was remembering the rest of last night. He had said something to Madelene about Mireya's amazingly long legs—was that before or after they had offered her as recompense? His coat was strewn over a chair. Unsteadily, he checked the pockets, was relieved to find his money pouch was where it should be. Leaning his shoulder against the wall he closed his eyes while the room continued its mad spinning. He had been drunk many times but had never forgotten the pleasures of fornication before. He took pride in his lovemaking, even with paid whores he was never clumsy or negligent. Last time he was here he had spent an entire afternoon in bed with Mireya, and had still wanted more of her inventive delights. He sighed, she had either lost her touch or he had drunk more of that brandy than he realised.

To cover her embarrassment 'Cesca snapped, "The horses are outside."

Water, Jesamiah discovered, was in the jug on the washing stand. It was dusty and had a distinct brackish tinge as he poured some into the cracked china bowl and splashed his face and neck, then rubbed at his teeth with a finger. "I don't much like horses."

"I have no intention of going to the convent on foot, nor will a carriage take us. We are going into the hills where the tracks are narrow."

"How do we fetch these barrels then?"

"I expect the convent has pack mules we can hire."

Pulling on his stockings and boots, then his waistcoat, he mulled over what to say next. He was aware of the nunnery but he tended to avoid convents and monasteries. The second because celibacy horrified him, the first because being a nun, in his opinion, was a waste of a good woman. He did not want to add to 'Cesca's obvious pique, decided that silence was his best ally.

His hat, cutlass and pistol were heaped on a wooden blanket box in one corner. Buckling the scabbard strap across his chest Jesamiah took another look at the sleeping whore. She was not as pretty as she used to be, but then, no one was pretty compared to Tiola. He sat heavily on the edge of the bed again, his head sinking into his hands, guilt gnawing at his innards. Hell's teeth, poking a whore was not a betrayal! Was it? Taking a doxie was nothing more than a few moments of personal comfort and release. It was not love, it was not passion. It was sex, nothing more. All the same, discounting the aborted attempt with 'Cesca this was his first time with another woman since he had committed himself to Tiola. Tiola was the one he wanted in his bed, Tiola was the one he wanted to make love to.

Then he remembered his dream of seeing her with van Overstratten; the obvious pleasure they were sharing. He knew her Craft, knew she could put thoughts into his head. Was that her way of making it quite plain that she wanted nothing more to do with him? If so, did it matter who he bedded? This whore or 'Cesca? There was no need to stay faithful. Tiola had gone, had sent him away, shut him out of her life. He groaned, tried to tell himself that it was not true, that Tiola would never be parted from him—but if that was so, why had she not spoken to him in their special way? Why did he feel empty and abandoned? He put his hand on his heart. Why was she not in here, with him, where he loved her?

Now he was gathering his senses last night was coming back to him. Mireya had been as drunk as he was. They had stumbled up the stairs together, got as far as undressing and she had more or less passed out. Had he taken her anyway, to prove he could do it? For the life of him he could not remember. He reached out to touch the sleeping girl's shoulder, fingered her hair. He'd best leave her some money, in case he had. Even if that bitch of a landlord's wife had given her for free, he would not take advantage. Whores earned little enough as it was.

'Cesca was standing at the open door. Seeing him touch the girl's hair raised her hurt again. He had rejected her and spent the night with a ragged slut. She was being stupid and childish to mind, but emotion and desire were two very difficult things to control. Jealousy was even harder.

"Did you manage to get it up for her, then?" she remarked spitefully. "Or did she have to work for her shilling? If you are not downstairs in fifteen minutes I will leave without you." The words tumbled out from her mouth harsher than she had intended.

Ignoring the first part, mortified that she had realised his difficulty, Jesamiah answered as tartly. "Go then, that's fine by me!" Then lied, "And since you wanted to know, aye, I filled her belly."

Furious and ashamed at her outburst, 'Cesca slammed the door behind her.

Jesamiah flinched as it banged, held his head tighter. Damn it, could the woman not at least try to be quiet? The girl in the bed turned over on to her side, began snoring again. He swore, crammed his hat on his head and went out, leaving the door wide open.

Scarface was waiting at the bottom of the stairs. He extended one hand, palm uppermost as Jesamiah slowly descended.

"*Diez escudos, por favor.*"

"¿*Qué?*"

Narrowing his eyes, his hand quietly dropping to his cutlass hilt, Jesamiah walked very close to the landlord of the Sickle Moon, and jabbed his shoulder with one finger. In English, said; "Listen bastard, I ain't ever paid ten escudos for a whore, and I ain't goin' t'start now, savvy? Especially as the way I recollect things, we agreed she'd be on the 'ouse on account of that little matter of a mistake you made." He prodded harder. "In my book, you ought t'be paying me the escudos, and a damn sight more of 'em than ten. Not even a fresh virgin would be enough recompense for what I'm sufferin' this mornin'."

As bluff went it was good, but Jesamiah had a knack of knowing when someone was attempting to cheat him. He grinned, a nasty leer, and said in Spanish, "I'll tell you this for free though, mate, she's lost 'er talent an' sailed on past 'er prime. It weren't nothin' memorable."

That should put a stop to any embarrassing gossip should it happen to arise. Jesamiah winced, wished he had not thought of that particular turn of phrase.

Feigning his usual cockiness, he whistled as he stepped out into the sunlight, his hand thrust deep into his pocket to conceal the three-quarter full bottle of rum that he had quickly, and expertly, lifted from the bar as he had sauntered pasty. There had been two bottles. A pity, he only had sufficient room for the one.

CHAPTER EIGHTEEN

Francesca was already mounted on a drab looking flea-bitten grey mare. To avoid eye contact, she was tweaking the lay of her dark blue riding habit arranging the folds of skirt to fall elegantly over her immaculate boots. It did little to conceal the shape of her thigh. The groom was busily picking his nose while holding the second animal, a scrawny bay gelding with a ewe neck and cow hocks.

Jesamiah patted the animal's thin neck, checked the girth cinch was tight—he had no intention of making a fool of himself by trying to mount with a loose saddle. "Hope you packed something to eat señora, m'stomach thinks m'throat's been cut."

"If you had got out of bed earlier you could have breakfasted."

This is going to be delightful, he thought mournfully as he adjusted the stirrup length and settled in the saddle. He produced the bottle from his voluminous coat pocket that already bulged with a variety of acquired items and pulled the cork out with his teeth. "Want some?" he offered, waving it in her general direction.

Tilting her nose upward 'Cesca kicked her horse into a trot, its shod hooves clattering on the cobbles. Taking a mouthful then tapping the cork into the neck and sliding the bottle back where it would be safe, Jesamiah encouraged his nag to amble after her.

On the corner, where the street began to narrow, a pie stall displayed a few sorry-looking, slightly charred specimens in a basket. Reining in, Jesamiah surveyed the limited choice. "*¿Qué es esto?*"

"*Cabra, señor,*" answered the black slave boy half-heartedly brushing flies away with a horsehair swish.

"Got anything that ain't goat?"

Chewing his lip, the lad solemnly shook his head.

"I'll have goat then." Feeling in his pocket Jesamiah flipped the boy a coin. "Make it two."

The track rose up sharp and steep from the village, the going muddy and slippery after the rain, the horses squelching, fetlock deep, through the narrower areas between outcrops of rock. In the shade the mud would stay for several days, but with few clouds in the sky and the heat rising as noon approached, already some areas were drying into crusted ruts.

Taking his coat off, Jesamiah laid it on the horse's withers. The animal was already sweating. So was Jesamiah; 'Cesca looked cool and elegant.

How do women do that? he wondered. Concluded it was because they did not have breeches, waistcoat, an array of weapons to carry and had thinner blood. Followed his musing by contemplating a lady's undergarments. Did stays and such soak the sweat away?

She was an attractive woman, but very different from Tiola. Five inches taller, plumper, especially at the hips and bosom. Tiola had neat little apples. Why was he thinking of Tiola? Why couldn't he set her aside as he did any other woman he encountered? The answer to that was simple. Because he did not love those other women.

Munching on the second pie, swilled down with more rum, he was pleased to discover the headache had almost gone, but within two miles his back was beginning to ache, and his thighs to protest. Riding, he mused was not congenial to a sailor who had not sat astride a horse in more than ten years. He was considering whether to get off and walk, would have done, but he reasoned his boots would rub and 'Cesca would mock him.

Turning left-handed on to another track the view opened up below to show the wide sweep of the sea, the sun sparkling in all the varied shades of blue from sapphire to turquoise and azure. Looking down on the roofs of the village he could see it was spread out in a narrow, s-shaped ribbon, a busier place than he expected. The *Kismet* was safe at her mooring. His keen seaman's eyes picked out a smudge on the horizon. Reining to a halt he hurriedly fished out his pocket telescope, extended it. T'gallants and tops'ls, the rest hull down. Disappointment ripped through him, for a moment he had thought it could have been *Sea Witch*. He couldn't be certain at this distance, but had a nasty feeling it was the guardacostas. The guard ship.

He studied *Kismet*. Men were aboard. As he watched the maincourse spilled from the yard. What the...? Ah, he remembered now, he had mentioned to the sailing master that he was not happy with the state of the canvas; it needed inspecting for worn patches. Good, he was being obeyed at last. He collapsed the telescope, was about to return it to his coat pocket but out of the corner of his eye caught a slight movement. Extending the telescope again, he raised it to his eye and focused on two riders following in their wake along the lower level of the track. One wore an ostrich feather in his hat. Tiola liked ostrich feathers, he'd promised to get her an armful one day. Blue ones he had said, to match his ribbons. Waste of a promise.

"Many people visit this convent?" he asked as he persuaded his nag to move forward.

"I do not believe so. It is a small sanctuary of about thirty nuns. Columbus himself founded it in honour of his wife." 'Cesca was also observing the riders. They were ambling along at a walk, appeared to be dressed in no particular fashion—no sign of uniform or muskets. "I expect they will continue along the main track, not branch off as we have done. Unless you are seeking God or medical aid, there is little to draw people up to the convent."

"There's virgin nuns," Jesamiah retorted with a lascivious grin, baiting her.

'Cesca ignored him. After the loss of her husband she had been tempted to join the nuns, not for any piety, more for the peace and the protection against the parade of men who had very soon taken an eager interest in filling his place. For the money she had been left, not for her. Had she known del Gardo would send for her one night eighteen months into her widowhood, she would have gone to the Sisters. She had refused him, claiming she mourned Ramon. He had appeared to accept her excuse, entertained her at dinner and provided a carriage to take her home. There she had discovered the house ransacked, the stables burnt down, her father-in-law bleeding and beaten, and her son taken. When Don Damián del Gardo next sent for her she did not refuse him again.

And now, here she was these long, weary months later, riding with a handsome young man and wondering how she was going to be able to betray him. She would have to do so, for she needed to stay in del Gardo's good graces, and for her son to survive she would have to tell that fat bastard something relevant about Jesamiah Acorne, and the truth of why he was here.

The track remained steep but had become heavily wooded. Trees swarmed up the hill to their left and marched steeply downward on the right, giving only glimpses of turquoise sea through the rich, green foliage. The air was heavy with the smell of citrus fruit, exotic flowers, damp leaf mould and earth; was alive with the calls and trills of birds. Peering through a gap where several trees had been flattened by a recent hurricane, Jesamiah could no longer see the men below, but ten minutes later when the woods gave way to heavy scrub and barren rock, they re-appeared on the track lower down. They had not gone straight on where the tracks divided then.

"Why do I get the feeling we are being followed?" he asked casually.

'Cesca looked over her shoulder and down through the tangle of shrubs and trees cluttering the hillside. She recognised the familiar bob of an ostrich feather. That man was such a fool. Why del Gardo used him as a spy she had never understood, he was hopeless at concealing himself. Well maybe he was useless at his job, but she was not.

"Maybe they are traders?" she lied as casually. "The convent requires supplies, after all; or maybe they are making a pilgrimage? It is nothing sinister. Do you always see shadows Captain Acorne? Or are you just nervous because you are nursing a surfeit of drink and a tired pizzle?"

Tightening the reins as his horse stumbled, almost pitching him off, Jesamiah could not respond immediately. Once he had shifted his sore backside into the saddle again he turned to her. "I assure you, ma'am, it don't get tired."

She arched an eyebrow at him. "No?"

"No," he snapped back. "It just gets reluctant around governors' sluts sometimes."

He winced as he saw the look of dismay colour her face. What in the world had possessed him to say that? It was unkind and unnecessary. He liked the woman, it was not her fault del Gardo was using her, no more than it was his fault that he was in a bad mood because of missing Tiola.

She kicked her mare into a trot, pushed past and urged it to canter.

"I'm sorry!" he called, genuinely apologetic. "I didn't mean it!" The wind took his words, sent them outward, floating down over the scrub and bushes towards the dazzle of the sea.

Her mare was thin and unfit, the hill rising steeper and she could only canter a short way. Soon, puffing and blowing, 'Cesca had to bring her back to a walk.

Kicking with his heels, Jesamiah bullied his tiring beast into a trot to catch her up.

"I'm sorry," he repeated. "I'm sorry I didn't share your bed last night. I'm sorry I'm a bastard of a lying pirate, and I'm bloody sorry that the woman I love ain't here to prove to you that I'm sorry!" It all came out in a rush. "I had to leave 'er behind," he confessed. "The situation in Nassau made me choose between saving m'ship or being with her. I chose m'ship and I'm bloody regretting it. So I'm sorry I'm takin' me anger out on you, but there ain't anyone else 'ere I can trust to talk to like this. Only you. And I ain't certain I can trust you, neither."

"At least you had the opportunity to make a choice," she answered tartly, "I do not."

Assuming she was referring to del Gardo, Jesamiah forced the bay to trot a few more shambling paces to come up beside the mare. He reached across, took 'Cesca's hand. "You can always make a choice, darlin'. If you make the wrong one, all you have to do is find the strength to put it right."

"Will you put your wrong right?"

She meant his not making love to her last night, and bit her lip when, misunderstanding, he answered: "Don't know if I'll be able to. She's gone back to 'er 'usband and my prick's bein' rubbed to a stub by this saddle, so there ain't much 'ope fer me, is there?" As he had calculated, despite her annoyance, she laughed.

The track narrowed and they had to ride in single file. 'Cesca was grateful for several things had began to occur to her. Those men following, the one with the ostrich feather the rebels had known about for months now, but who was the man with him? Was it the landlord of the Sickle Moon? What had Jesamiah called him? Scarface? Scar Soul would be as appropriate. He was a surly, bad tempered man, nothing like his elder brother. Emilio had been a gentleman. And he had been loyal.

Riding in silence she pondered on Wickham's theories. He had been certain that Scarface was also del Gardo's man, but they had never, yet, found proof of it. And there was a third person, she was convinced of that. She had tried worming the information from del Gardo, but he never made any secret of the fact that he did not trust her. That was why she had to be so careful, that was why she had to ensure she told him just enough information to keep him sweet, to make him believe that she was serving him and not, where and when she could, the rebel cause. She peeped back over her shoulder, smiled at Jesamiah, tried to peer down the hillside but the woods were thickening again. It had just occurred to her; maybe those two were not following Jesamiah, but were watching her.

Del Gardo was planning something, she was sure of it. Once they reached the convent she would let the rebel leaders know of her suspicions, and when they made their move, they would have to be careful. Very careful indeed.

Unaware of her musings, Jesamiah had been making a few of his own.

"Angelita," he said. "That's an unusual name for a nun. Don't they adopt saint's names when they take their vows?" Hastily clarified, "Not that I know much about nuns."

"Usually, but not always."

"I had a governess called Angelita." No answer.

"She lasted about a month. My brother didn't want a governess, he was too stupid to learn anything. He had a habit of making sure they didn't last long by hiding headless rats where they would do most damage. Angelita found hers when she dressed one morning. It was in her undershift. I got the blame, Phillipe always ensured I got the blame. Papa himself whipped me for that one." Bitterly, he added, "Six stripes with a birch to m'backside. It wasn't the beating I minded but the injustice. I'd tried to tell him it wasn't me, but he always favoured Phillipe. He never believed my side of the story, never listened to me. He would say things like, 'be a man' and, 'you will never survive life by whinging, boy.' He knew Phillipe was a bastard, I'm bloody sure he did, but he never did anything to stop it. Six stripes? Oh aye, and the other six Phillipe gave me for trying to tattle to papa!"

'Cesca turned in her saddle to stare at him, appalled. She nearly spoke, but what could she say?

"I liked Angelita, she was young and pretty and a good governess. I thought she liked me. That was the real hurt, seeing her tears as she left the house. 'You betrayed me'," she said. I hadn't, but what could I do to prove it?"

Scarface had said the same last night. "You betrayed Emilio." Jesamiah had never betrayed anyone in his life, but it seemed, yet again, he had been accused of another's deceit. And the beating for it had been as painful. Emilio had not been a spy, but he had been a rebel and he had been a friend.

Jesamiah looked out to sea, the immense stretch of shaded blue, the silver line of the horizon where dark clouds were massing. That ship would be hull up now, if he was to get out the telescope and have a look. Why? It was not the *Sea Witch*. Why would he want to look? He closed his eyes, felt the chill of the wind on his face, smelt the sweet tang of citrus fruit, wet grass and earth, the warm, hay smell of the horse. Heard the wind sighing through the palm trees, the jingle of the bit rings, the occasional clink as the horses' shoes rapped on a stone. The buzz of insects. He did not want this! He wanted to feel the woodwork of the taffrail vibrating beneath his hands, *Sea Witch*'s deck trembling beneath his feet; hear her rudder grinding and mithering, listen to the creak of the stays, the clatter and slap of the halyards and blocks. Wanted her lift and dip and roll, the boom of her sails.

How had they all escaped from that Tower? Few got out of there alive and in one piece. Had Malachias Taylor betrayed Emilio? Taylor, the man who had taught Jesamiah everything he knew about ships, sailing, fighting, getting drunk and bedding a whore. The man he had worshipped as a hero and a friend; who was never, even now he was dead, far from mind. Not one of the crew had questioned that escape. When the door to their cell had been left open they had run, and kept running. It had never occurred to him that maybe Malachias Taylor had made a bargain. Had he told all he knew about the rebellion, betrayed Emilio and his wife in exchange for forgetting to lock a door? It grieved Jesamiah that maybe Malachias Taylor had been a traitor. On the other side of the mast, had they not escaped, he, Jesamiah, would now be dead, put in his grave by unbearable agony. And did telling what you knew about one friend to save your others count? Betrayal carried a hideous price. Someone always had to suffer for its cost. Never betrayed anyone? Huh, had he not? He had betrayed Tiola by choosing *Sea Witch* and running. So who was it now suffering? Tiola? Him?

"Why did you ask about Angelita?" 'Cesca asked, breaking his thought and jolting him back to the present.

"It's the meaning of the name I'm interested in."

The path ahead narrowed to wind around a tumble of rocks that, judging by the growth of grass and shrubs, had come down many years before. On the far side a stream formed a hollowed pool across the track, several yards wide, before continuing in a cascade down the sheer drop. Jesamiah allowed his horse to stop and drink, then kicked it forward, splashing through the almost knee-deep churn. Angelita. The governess had talked to him about the Greek and Roman origin of names. What had he been? Nine? Ten, years old? He could not remember any of those meanings now, except for one. Hers. He had asked if her name had a meaning. Angelita.

"I'm just curious to know," he said as casually as he could to 'Cesca, "Whether señor and señora Mendez know that Angelita means 'messenger'."

Was he still seeing shadows where none existed? Maybe, but he would bet his last shilling that they did know.

CHAPTER NINETEEN

MONDAY AFTERNOON

Looking through the telescope, Rue studied the sail with care. An English trader outward bound from Jamaica. She would be rich laden, and an easy picking. He passed the telescope to Isiah Roberts, who peered through it a moment then solemnly handed it on to Mr Janson, old Jansy.

"Well?" Rue said. "What do you say?"

Although they often called Mr Janson old, he was, probably, only in his early fifties. He actually had no idea of his age. He was a man grown when William and Mary were invited to England as king and queen in 1689. He remembered hearing stories, as a very young nipper, of Henry Morgan's exploits in the Caribbean, although at a tender age the names and places had all sounded exotic and meaningless. He had gone to sea, he reckoned, when he was about ten. Had seen more battles, served aboard more ships under more captains, than the rest of the *Sea Witch*'s crew put together. He handed the telescope to Nathan at his side, chewed thoughtfully on his wedge of tobacco. Spat the residue over the side.

"I don't like it," he finally announced. "The moment we touch an Englishman we might as well put our own 'eads in a noose. I signed an agreement of amnesty, swore on me name as it were. I ain't 'appy with goin' back on m'word."

General mutters of agreement from the rest of the crew. Rue looked at them all, Jimmy Stradler, Old Barnsey, Peter Piper. Joseph, young Jasper. Chippy Harrison. Finch. The rest of them. "So it is a vote of *non*?" he said after a moment.

Some just nodded their heads, a few muttered *aye*. That was the way they did it aboard a pirate ship. Democratically. By the vote. Even though, technically, they were not, now, pirates. Not until they attacked another ship again, although Rue did not want to point out that after what they did to the *Challenger* they were probably now under sentence of death by hanging anyway.

Nathan had been the only one to remain silent.

"And what of you, Nat? What say you?" Isiah asked.

Being quartermaster, Jesamiah's next in command, Rue had taken charge as soon as they were clear of any Spanish guns and had reached open water. Isiah Roberts was the first mate, but since the start of this waste of time disagreeable cruise, Nat had slid into his shoes as Rue's second. Isiah was quite happy with the arrangement, he was a good sailor but not as good as Nathan Crocker.

"If we pass her up," Nat said slowly and carefully, "we could be signing Jesamiah's death warrant. Del Gardo will kill him if we do not show up with a captured Prize. And that beauty over there is a Prize worth taking."

"I'd lay my life down for Cap'n Acorne," Finch announced. "You know I would, but there has to be another way. I ain't too keen on swinging. And he could already be dead."

That was true. Several of them nodded.

"We could be returning to piracy for nowt."

"He ain't dead!" Jansy stated with a firm nod of his head. "You all 'ear me? He ain't dead. We start thinkin' like that we're as likely t'make it true. He is not dead."

Silence as they all studied the trader. She was making good headway, if they did not give chase soon they would lose her, they would never catch her up. *Sea Witch* was fast but she was not sailing her best, even close hauled as she was now, she was sullen. She was whinging as if she were a toothless old lady with severe joint ache. If ships could sulk like a woman wronged, then *Sea Witch* was a wench in one dandy of a petticoat strop.

"And what do we do with our Spaniard?" Jasper asked, his arm in a sling to ease his healing shoulder, his free hand reaching out to take the telescope and pass it to Toby Turner.

The Spaniard. Capitán de Castilla. They had sorted him almost as soon as they had weighed anchor; Finch knew where Jesamiah kept the best brandy and Jansy had access to the laudanum. The two combined had provided an immediate solving of the problem. De Castilla was sound asleep secured in the sail locker.

"I still say we feed him to the sharks," Old Barnsey said.

"And I say that could be a waste of something to bargain with," Rue answered firmly.

"I might only be young," Jasper offered, "but don't del Gordo need all the captains 'e can get if we're at war?"

"Gardo," Nat corrected. "His name is Gardo not Gordo."

Jasper grinned. "I think Gordo suits 'im better, it means fat or pig or something." It was his turn for the telescope. To compensate for having the use of only one arm, being that Jansy was a good deal shorter than himself, he rested it on the older man's shoulder. Squinting, peered through the eyepiece.

"I think we ought t'try an' swap 'im fer the Cap'n. We anchor somewhere, march across land and make our demand. De Castilla for Jesamiah. Fair trade." That was Toby. He had been making the suggestion ever since they left Santo Domingo. No one had listened to his daft idea then; were not doing so now.

"Stop hopping about Jans. You're jiggling me." Frowning, Jasper peered again, re-focused. "I ain't certain," he said slowly as he handed the glass to Rue, "but ain't that a sail coming out from the other side of that headland?"

Rue snatched up the bring it close. Studied where Jasper pointed. Cursed. "*Merde*! It's the guardacostas!"

A moment of flurried panic.

"We're fighting for Spain, we fly Spanish colours," Isiah pointed out.

"You reckon those bastards will take that small fact into account?" Rue snapped. Then he began to issue orders to get under way.

"We'll not outrun her," Nat added, shaking his head. *Sea Witch* was grumbling and muttering to herself, no matter of cajoling or bullying would get her to outrun that guardship. She was fretting, and not one man on board did not know why.

"We could always drop anchor at Puerto Vaca," Jansy offered. "It's only a couple o' miles further. They'll mebbe not bother with us if we don't make an exhibit of ourselves. Got a nice tavern there, they 'ave."

Jasper was staring through the telescope again. "They've not seen us," he announced, excitement and relief in his voice. "They're turning for the trader—look!" He flung out an arm to point.

The guardship was heading straight for the Englishman. This was war, it was not wise for ships, especially when full laden with a rich cargo, to sail into enemy waters.

"Thank the Lord we didn't draw attention to ourselves by chasing 'er!"

Jasper's comment spoke for them all.

CHAPTER TWENTY

The nunnery was perched beneath a high, rocky outcrop; an austere place with blank stone walls and a gateway that was shut and bolted.

To keep us out or them in? Jesamiah wondered with amusement as they waited for the porteress to squinny through the grill at them, then sourly permit entrance. They rode through into a dank courtyard and dismounted. It reminded Jesamiah of a prison.

"Is this a silent order?" he asked warily peering around. "I ain't keen on being in with a habit of nuns at the best of times. If all they're goin' t'do is stare at me, I think I'd rather wait outside." His legs felt like marrow-jelly and his backside, tool and tackle chafed raw; he doubted he could walk a yard without groaning, but outside he would go if necessary.

Looking as fresh as a dawn-kissed daisy, 'Cesca's smile was amused as she saw him surreptitiously ease at the seat of his breeches. "In discomfort?" she asked.

"I ain't fashioned for straddlin' a nag," he growled. The ride, added to last night's beating, a flogging several days ago and not properly healed wounds from his brother's vicious treatment were severely taking their toll. All he wanted to do, despite it being only early afternoon, was go to bed and sleep. Preferably forever, but if that was difficult to arrange, for a few years at least.

A high ranking official swept down a flight of stone steps, her wimple billowing like sails come loose from the yard; hands folded into the drape of her sleeves. She acknowledged 'Cesca with a slight nod of welcome, glowered fiercely at Jesamiah.

Undaunted, he made as polite and graceful a bow as his body would permit, and rounded his speech into that of an educated Spanish gentleman.

"Sister, I give you God's good greeting, and crave your forgiveness for this intrusion into the sanctuary of your peace. We have come with a message for the nun called Angelita."

The sister's eyes darted from him to 'Cesca, back again, then she sniffed haughtily. In her late fifties, Jesamiah reckoned, and if she was innocent of a man, then he was a virgin. Her look of disdain was not merely because he was unshaven, with tangled hair, grimed hands and torn nails. Nor, despite his display of manners, had it anything to do with him being a knave and a scoundrel.

Spurned by a lover? he wondered, or ill-used? Being deliberately provocative he gave her one of his most dazzling and lascivious smiles.

Her look of iron made him lose the smile. "I know of no one here with that name."

Now why had he guessed she was going to say that?

'Cesca had a knack of being able to lower the cadence of her voice, to make it subtle and charming. The actress in her again. She could coax a bird down from the trees, Jesamiah reckoned. "Your Mother Superior, sister, will know of whom we speak. Angelita's mother is dying and wishes to see her."

The nun's antipathy softened somewhat. "Alas she is not here. She will be back tomorrow. You are more than welcome to rest in our guest quarters until then."

Thank God and the angels for that, Jesamiah thought, not relishing the pain of getting back on a horse too soon.

The nun beckoned to one of the novices gathered to one side of the courtyard, pretending not to be interested in the newcomers, and sent her to fetch someone to take care of the animals; ordered someone else to escort their guests to the lodge situated to the rear of the convent. Before they turned a corner Jesamiah glanced over his shoulder, observed the sudden flurry emanating in their wake. A servant was cramming a hat on his head as he ran out of the gate, the sister, her habit lifted almost to her knees, was hurrying up a long flight of steps. The calm tranquillity sent into battle frenzy.

Now what is going on? Jesamiah thought as he followed 'Cesca and the nun, bullying his stiff, aching and protesting muscles to move.

He snorted a muted guffaw of laughter. *It's as if they are clearing for action. They'll probably be running the bloody guns out next.*

CHAPTER TWENTY-ONE

The afternoon dawdled as it trundled by. The sun was hot, there was not much wind, although the heaviness in the air made it a reasonable assumption that the storms were not yet over. Flies buzzed, but not much else moved.

Tiola had refused to return aboard Stefan's sloop. Señora Isabella Mendez was dying; she needed someone with medical knowledge to ease her through the last few days of intense pain, and with an adequate strength to help señor Mendez watch her die. Not that Tiola was certain she possessed that strength, but she could not, would not, abandon these two elderly people.

A lizard scuttled across the cool floor tiles. Tiola wished she had its energy.

"I will not come back for you!" Stefan had shouted.

"I do not want you to come back," Tiola had answered mildly.

"You are ill. How can you help that woman? You can barely stand on your own feet!"

Had Stefan shouted it with even a hint of compassion, Tiola would not have answered as she had. "Then maybe we will die together. That will please you, will it not?"

Unable to disagree, ashamed of his anger and the truth, the Dutchman had whirled on his heel, ordered the mooring ropes cast off and had sailed away an hour after dawn.

Tiola was not a seer, she could not tell, or predict, the future, but she did know she would never see him again. She was sorry for it, for she had once been fond of him and all that had happened had not been entirely his fault. But would she see Jesamiah again? That was what worried her, not the outcome of Stefan's fate.

She had to regain her strength, and gain it quickly. At least here on solid land she had more chance to do so. Hispaniola was so much larger than New Providence Island with its untidy sprawl of Nassau Town. Here there were rivers and fields and hills and mountains. Miles and miles of rock and earth. Here, Tethys could not reach her. Here, she could find herself and properly restore her ability of Craft. And then, once she had regained her strength, there would be nothing that Tethys, Rain, any one or anything could do to stop her speaking into Jesamiah's mind. Except for Jesamiah himself.

The rage that had consumed Stefan van Overstratten was a new experience to him. Yes, he had been angry before—bloody angry—but never in such a fury that his whole body shook and his legs turned to marrow jelly.

He knew, *knew*, that Mendez had lied to him! All his threats, his promises to burn the place to the ground, to throw the pair of them out into the wilderness had come to nothing. The Spaniard had consistently stated there was no indigo. Acorne had been there though, Stefan had discovered that much—a coin tossed to one of those skinny slaves. She had babbled it all; how a boat had tied up to the jetty, how the handsome man with curled black hair and a gold acorn dangling from his ear had swaggered ashore and then sailed away again. To fetch the indigo—van Overstratten was sure of it. Mendez was telling the truth, it was not at La Sorenta. Not now, *neen*. Acorne had it!

The Dutchman's anger turned against Jesamiah. The bastard had taken everything he had. His ship, his wife, his pride, his fortune. Well Acorne would regret it! He strode up and down the deck, peering every so often over the larboard rail. His sailing master had spotted a sail fifteen minutes ago —something large and moving fast, a distance off, but she had three masts, could well be *Sea Witch*.

The fact that she could be any ship at all did not occur to Stefan. He was willing it to be Acorne, praying it was. Nor did it occur to him that Jesamiah would not be with his own ship. There was no reason for him not to be, so why would he have even thought to ask Mendez?

"There she is sir!" One of the hands leant eagerly over the rail, pointing, grinning his triumph. Then his enthusiasm faded into disappointment. "Oh. It's a Spaniard. Probably the guardship after that English trader we saw a while ago."

Van Overstratten grabbed the telescope from his sailing master, with shaking hands steadied it in the direction where the man pointed. It was all blurred. He could only see the sky, then sea, then... he swore. He had been so sure! So certain it was that pirate!

"Spanish," he spat as he shut the telescope with a snap. "You are right, a damned Spaniard!"

"Begging your pardon master van Overstratten," the sailing master said with a certain degree of caution. "It is the English who are at war with the Spanish, not us Dutch. It would be perfectly in order for us to hail him. Would it not be possible that he has seen the ship we seek? Perhaps he would be willing to help? The *Sea Witch* would be a handsome prize for him to capture. And unlike us, he knows these waters."

Van Overstratten nodded. It made sense. Good sense. "Catch her up, flag her down, raise a signal flag—I don't know, do whatever you have to do, just attract her attention. I need to speak with that ship's captain."

CHAPTER TWENTY-TWO

The nuns called their rooms 'cells'. Jesamiah could quite see why. Unpainted stone walls, a small grilled window with no glass, and not much more than ten feet by eight. Two blankets were on the bed; there was a shelf and a table on which stood a jug of water and its accompanying pewter laver. Nothing else. On one of the walls a crucifix was nailed; irreverently he hung his hat on it. His coat went on the hook behind the door and his boots, he tossed with a grunt of pleasure at their removal, to the floor. He chuckled. Not one of the nuns had dared find the courage to look directly at him, although he guessed several of the younger noviciates had been staring through lowered lashes. Wondering what they were missing?

"You're a bad lad, Jesamiah Acorne," he said aloud as he put his pistol and cutlass on the table. "Thinking shameless thoughts about those dedicated virgins. All the same," he added, "I'd not say no to showing a few of them me wicked ways. Not 'avin' done it before they won't know 'owt is wrong if I can't get it up will they?"

He stretched out on the bed, disappointed to find it was hard and unyielding. Soft down would have been nice; fell instantly asleep. Was awoken half an hour later by someone tapping on the door, and not waiting for a response, walking boldly in.

Regarding 'Cesca, through only one eye half opened, Jesamiah drawled; "Do you always make a habit of entering bedchambers unannounced? Or is the privilege reserved for me alone?" With a sudden thought he sat up, regarded her suspiciously. "You're not planning on chucking water over me again are you?" He patted the bed to show it was empty, "I swear I ain't abducted some innocent novice and 'idden 'er under the blanket."

Despite her determination to be prim, 'Cesca found herself laughing. He was so absurd! She amended her resolve, it had been a ridiculous one anyway. *If I am falling in love with him, God help me*, she thought.

Sitting on the edge of the bed she folded her hands in her lap, took a few moments to gather herself. Jesamiah lay back, re-closed his eyes. She would spit out whatever was stuck on her tongue as soon as she was ready.

"I have not been entirely honest with you," she finally admitted.

"I know."

'Cesca glanced sideways at him. "This is not easy to say, Jesamiah, please do not make it harder for me."

He grunted, threaded his fingers together over his stomach and waited.

"Can I trust you?"

Without opening his eyes he shook his head slowly. "I'm a pirate darlin'. The only thing you can trust about me is that you can't trust me."

She smiled. A good enough answer. "There are things you ought to know."

"I've already guessed half of them."

She looked up sharply, her breath catching; he could not possibly have guessed!

"One thing's for certain," he said, sitting up and swinging his legs to the floor, "I'm laying a wager that Reverend Mother will be here long before she was expected." He went over to his coat, fumbled in the pocket, brought out what was left of the rum. Holding the bottle up he offered her a drink first, she refused. There was less than a quarter of it left. He drank most of it straight down.

"Ah, that's better." He wiped the residue off his moustache. "The only thing I ain't figured is what the code words are for. I assume they're just triggers."

Her brows furrowed, puzzled. "Code words?"

"Sixteen and ninety-seven. Nobody twitched until I said those numbers. It's a date ain't it?" He was walking about now, up and down the narrow cell, waving the empty bottle. "You all fair 'opped a jig after I mentioned it. Even señora Mendez." He stopped before 'Cesca, peered close into her face. "I'd lay a wager that sixteen ninety seven was the year del Gardo became governor. Am I right?"

He waited for her to answer. She said nothing. He continued walking. "Angelita then. No such nun? I saw how that old biddy's eyes flickered. The name means messenger, an' that's what I am ain't it? A messenger boy." He stopped in front of her, took hold of the hair at the nape of her neck and putting a finger under her chin, tilted her face upward. "Jennings was wetting his breeches to get me here. The cunning old bugger managed to contrive it, didn't he?"

'Cesca closed her eyes, visibly sagged. It was futile to deny everything. "The code has been in place for months. Wickham set it in case anything happened to him. As it unfortunately did. And you are right about the date and del Gardo. When someone came from Nassau and mentioned 1697, in whatever disguised form, we were to take him to Mendez."

"Who was primed with a second code word. His daughter's name. Very clever. It was lucky I came across you right from the start then, eh?"

She shook her head. "Luck had nothing to do with it. Diego—James—knew that anyone Jennings sent would be picked up somewhere and eventually brought to me or Mendez."

"So you're not spying for del Gardo then? You're bluffing him?"

She half shrugged. "I do what I have to do. We have supporters in all villages. Several at del Gardo's court." She smiled up at Jesamiah apologetically. "We were expecting someone to come. It took us a while to be certain you were the right person; we had our doubts that you would be released so easily into our care."

Jesamiah brushed his finger slowly down her cheek. His lips were very close to hers as he said, "Don't you dare tell me I was beaten up last night as a way of making sure."

She gasped. "That was nothing to do with me!"

He noted she had not denied it, though. "That man with the ostrich feather hat. He was one of the bastards. He has been following us today. Is he del Gardo's man?"

Very steadily she looked at him. "I do not know. He could be. Diego Wickham always suspected Mireya."

He kissed her on the lips. "And the indigo? Please don't tell me there ain't no indigo."

She gave him an apologetic smile. "My father-in-law's brandy is here. Diego brought everything to the convent for safe keeping, disguised as provisions for the nuns: flour, grain, and such. It is the one place del Gardo would not dare search."

Not quite the reassuring answer he wanted. He kissed her firmer, more insistent; moved his hand to inch up the folds of her skirt. "And what are you going to tell del Gardo about me?" he murmured.

Tempted to putting her arms around him she pulled away. "The day I keep quiet, is the day my son dies. I have to tell him things. I try to keep it trivial but convincing."

He nodded. "You told him about Emilio."

Emphatically she shook her head. "No. He already knew. I did go to don Damián to plead for my husband, though. Do you blame me? I was trying to save Ramon and his father from torture." She looked at him steadily, tears pricking her eyes. "They were arrested after helping their friend, Malachias Taylor and Mereno's son—you—to escape."

Puffing his cheeks Jesamiah sat on the bed next to her, his hands rubbing his thighs. Relieved. It was not Malachias who had betrayed Emilio then, thank God for that. He did not want to think of Malachias as a betrayer.

"That information don't exactly make me feel any better. Because of me, Emilio and his wife were hanged—your husband killed and señor Escudero tortured."

The tears were beginning to trickle down her cheeks. She shook her head, took his hand. "No, not because of you. Because of whoever betrayed Emilio." The tears were falling freely. "Del Gardo told me there was only one way to free my husband, and that was for me to sleep with him. I prostituted myself to get Ramon back. Only I didn't know he was already dead." She stared into Jesamiah's eyes, hoping he would not despise her. "Months later, when he sent for me to become his mistress, I told myself it did not matter what I did, for I was already soiled and filthy from his foulness."

Very, very gently Jesamiah kissed her again, only this time he did not touch her. "You are not soiled or filthy, 'Cesca. You are very beautiful. And if I were your husband I would be proud of you."

She rested her head into his chest and wept a little. Through her tears, sniffed, "Even though I must tell del Gardo something about you?"

Jesamiah stroked her hair, lowered his hand to her back. "I'm sure we can think of something plausible to keep him happy." He shrugged; "I think I already suggested it once, why not tell him you have discovered who Chesham is—was?

Even Henry Jennings didn't know it, so I suspect del Gardo would bust a gut to have the information."

She frowned. "Chesham?"

"Aye, you remember, Chesham. The poor sod who died. I was told he spied for England, that his identity was a well-kept secret. Tell del Gardo I came here specifically to find him for Jennings; that I am bloody mad I found him to be very dead."

She smiled, wiped at her tears. "I suppose it might be useful to tell him that."

Jesamiah stretched out on the bed, he was very tired, did, desperately, want to sleep.

Turning slowly around, 'Cesca laid her hand on his chest. "I was being silly last night and this morning. I'm sorry. I am scared for my son, and I so want to find a way to take him from del Gardo, so want to be free of that evil monster. But I am starting to love you Jesamiah Acorne."

She sighed, picked up his boots and took them with her. They needed new soles and heels. A good clean. The nuns' cobbler would make a good job of all three.

Jesamiah was snoring gently. It seemed that making love with this pirate was never going to happen.

CHAPTER TWENTY-THREE

MONDAY NIGHT

The persistent knocking on Jesamiah's door woke him from several hours' worth of a deep sleep.

"Fokken hell, where does a man have to go to get a decent rest around here?" He rolled off the bed, found his legs gave way as he tried to stand, a combination of rough treatment from various boots and fists and whips, and a horse's unyielding backbone. He grabbed hold of the wooden bed-head, massaged some life into his inner thighs, bent and straightened his knees, grunting and wheezing as he did so.

The knocking grew louder. "*¿Señor? ¿Capitán Acorne?*"

"*¡Yo voy!* I'm coming." He opened the door, rubbing at his groin. Found a nun he had not seen before standing outside. Hastily he shoved the rubbing hand behind his back and grasped the top of his partially unbuttoned breeches with the other.

In her early forties, she had curves in all the right places, was a few inches shorter than himself and extremely pretty. *What a waste*, he thought.

"I would be obliged if you would get yourself dressed and to the courtyard. We must leave immediately," she said.

"Whoa, whoa, heave to there Sister! Why?" Jesamiah raised his hands, remembered his loose breeches and made a grab for them. "And who exactly do you mean by *we*?"

She handed him his boots. "They have been repaired for you. I am Juliana Maria, the Reverend Mother of this convent." She smiled at him, not a shy, tentative little whisper, but a full broadside of confidence. "You would know me as Angelita Wickham."

"So you do exist. Your mother was asking for you."

"Her exact words were, I believe, '*I am ready for my daughter, Angelita, to come home.*' Is that not correct? I have already spoken at length to 'Cesca."

Code. He had been right then.

"I'd be happier if I knew what was going on. This is like sailing into unknown waters without a chart on a cloudy night. I ain't sure about hitting the rocks."

"God will guide you, Capitán Acorne."

He was not certain about that either, but kept his doubts to himself. The Reverend Mother drew breath, "I have no time to explain, please, just do as I say." She handed him an ebony casket, about five inches long, three deep and four wide. The carving on the lid was exquisite, if somewhat macabre; a face of a man with scimitar fangs that appeared to be inlaid with a shimmering type of silver ivory. Delicate, thin-cut slivers of what could only be sapphires formed the eyes. No whites, just the blue jewels. For his shoulder-length hair the wood was polished to a high shine. On the side were howling wolves and coiled snakes. For all that he was obviously meant to be the devil, the creature was most wondrously beautiful.

"What's this?" Jesamiah asked.

"It is for Captain Jennings, a thank you gift. I would ask you to deliver it to him."

Jesamiah shrugged, tossed the casket to the bed. "Can't promise it." He had no intention of going anywhere near the man ever again.

"He would not have sent you if he did not trust you."

Oh great, Jesamiah thought. "I'll try. Will that do?"

"I too have faith in you. Now, I am concerned about those men who were following you, we must be gone from here. We may need your pistol; ensure it is primed. Naturally, I do not possess a firearm."

"Naturally."

She whirled to leave, her habit and veil flying out like spread wings.

"May I ask..."

"No Capitán, you may not. We have work to do."

Suddenly feeling as if he were steering with a shattered rudder, Jesamiah protested: "But the indigo? I ain't leaving without my barrels!"

Hands on hips, head cocked to one side she turned to him. "The barrels and kegs we have are already secured on to pack mules. We are to take them to Puerto Vaca and load them aboard the *Kismet*. Please, get your boots on and," she looked pointedly at his crotch, "button your breeches. We are waiting for you."

Despite himself he was aroused. She was beautiful in an elegant, mature way. Her skin was flawless, her cheek bones perfectly angled. Wide, dark eyes. It did not seem fair or right, to Jesamiah, for a nun to be this alluring.

He grinned, content that his personal bits seemed to be in a satisfactory working order again; found his boots; arrayed his weapons as he liked them—pistol through his belt, with the canvas cartridge bag and powder flask in the hollow of his back. Cutlass nestling, like a lover's familiar hand, into his hip. Everything handy and comfortable. He slipped on his coat, picked up the casket. It was definitely ebony because it was black, but it was an ebony he had never seen before. He stared at the face, drawn to it, almost mesmerised, then curiosity got the better of him. He flipped the gold catch, opened the lid. Purple velvet lined the box, snugly fastened inside was a plain, gold, crucifix almost the same width and length as the padded interior. The gold would be worth a bit, but as a gift it was nothing spectacular. Shutting the lid he shoved the casket into his voluminous pocket. Put on his hat. Nothing he liked better than the prospect of a fight. Not that he had ever fought alongside nuns before, but he had discovered in the past that some first time experiences turned out to be quite enjoyable.

The courtyard was full of mules and about thirty men, some on horseback, others on foot. Hard, tough men; fighters bristling with weapons. Jesamiah touched his hat at the one with a trailing moustache who was watching everything with the eyes of a hawk. Their leader. He had to be. Gruffly, the Spaniard acknowledged Jesamiah's respectful salute.

Not at all like a demure nun, the Reverend Mother was swinging herself up into the saddle. A servant held a horse for Jesamiah, not the scrawny, knock-kneed nag he had arrived on but a chestnut with clean lines and spirit. 'Cesca was already mounted on another new, good horse.

"Don't often see their sort in a convent," Jesamiah remarked about the men, as flicking aside his coat and gritting his teeth, he set his foot in the stirrup and mounted. Lowered himself gingerly into the saddle, was pleased to find the ache of his muscles and backside was not too bad.

"That is because a convent does not often get the call to raise a rebellion," 'Cesca answered with a smile.

"So that's what we're doing is it?"

'Cesca laughed, pointed behind her to where the hills rose black against the night sky, that, although cloudy, was clear of mist. "Look," she said, "we have been busy while you have been snoring."

Against the blackness a flare of light, flickering and burning, bright and fierce. A signal beacon. There would be another in the chain, and another beyond that, Jesamiah guessed. "Just as well the rain's backed off," he remarked.

"We kept the beacons dry and they are saturated with tar, they would burn in any weather."

Jesamiah had actually meant visibility could have been impaired but these people did not need him stating the obvious. They probably had an alternative method of communication. If they did not, well that was their problem, not his.

"And they indicate?" he asked, but his words were drowned by the noise of the pack mules being urged forward, each one led by a mounted man. The courtyard echoed with the clatter of hooves, braying mules, the shouts and a wild, spontaneous cheer as the leader kicked his horse into a trot and ducked out through the gate, the Reverend Mother also laughing, close behind.

Not exactly a silent order, Jesamiah mused wryly.

Rubbing at his beard, the extra growth beginning to irritate, Jesamiah was counting the mules as they were led through the gate. "I see twenty beasts," he remarked. Did another quick tally in his head. "Eight carried one barrel, the rest two kegs apiece. By my reckoning, I make that thirty-two. Not exactly sixteen and ninety-seven is it?"

No one answered him.

'Cesca had kicked her horse into a trot.

"Will someone tell me what we are bloody doing!" he shouted at her back, then cursed vehemently as his horse skittered sideways to avoid the kick of a belligerent mule.

"*¡Comencemos la rebelión!*" she called over her shoulder. "We go to start the end of that pig, Don Damián del Gardo!"

"I don't want to bloody get involved!" he protested. "I only want my indigo!" Guessing as he said it, that if there was indigo in those barrels, then 'Cesca was as chaste a nun as he was a celibate monk.

CHAPTER TWENTY-FOUR

Stefan was pleased with himself, it could not have gone better had he planned it. The Spaniard had turned out to be *La Santa Isabella*, Don Damián del Gardo's flagship, with the governor himself aboard. And he had been most interested in what the Dutchman had to tell him about Jesamiah Acorne. Interested enough to invite him aboard.

Sitting in the pleasant surroundings of the governor's dining room aboard the ship, the table scattered with the debris of a most excellent meal, Stefan felt a warmth of contentment wash through him. It could have been the company. He was surprised, for he had always assumed Spaniards to be harsh and arrogant men, yet these were most congenial. Or it could have been the after taste of the roast pork, or the brandy, or the fine cheroot he held between his fingers, but it was more likely to be the pleasing fact that, according to Don Damián del Gardo, Jesamiah Acorne was not going to see the coming of another dawn.

Stefan inhaled deeply, then watched the smoke plume from his lips. He had to make conversation through the first officer, the only one who spoke a mutual language of French; Stefan knew no Spanish, the others very little English, and no Dutch.

"Forgive my questioning, but can you be certain Acorne will be at this village we are making for, Puerto Vaca, you say? He is not always a predictable man."

The first officer translated and Don Damián leant back in his chair, belched, then patted the bulk of his stomach. "I think I can safely predict he will be there. I have signal stations along my coast. His movements have been closely watched, one way or another. I merely wait to spring the trap that he and others of this silly little rebellion have so casually walked into."

His grin was self-satisfied. The men around the table laughed, one even applauded.

"These rebels think they are so very clever," Don Damián added, gloating. "Yet they have no idea of the woman who has so consistently betrayed them. When they find the courage to creep out from their sordid little hovels and try to march on Santo Domingo, they will be cut down like weeds with a scythe. I have no fear or worry of them."

About to translate, the first officer was interrupted by a discreet knock at the door. The officer of the watch. A brief exchange, a few flurried words and Don Damián ordered the brandy to be sent around the table again.

"What is it?" Stefan asked, leaning sideways to talk discreetly to his willing translator. "What has happened?"

The first officer turned his head to speak into Stefan's ear above the sudden roar of the governor's guffaw of amusement.

"It seems we may catch the two birds with the one stone. Is that not the English expression?"

Stefan spread his hands, looked blank.

"We have come up with our guardship. She has taken us a fine English prize it seems, but that is incidental. We have the *Sea Witch* cornered. She is anchored at Puerto Vaca."

Stefan did not quite understand Del Gardo's meaning. He thought they had said that Acorne was already wherever it was they were heading to. He shook his head, but he was pleased. If *Sea Witch* was there, then maybe so was his precious indigo. He did begin to wonder how he was going to be able to get at it, as his sloop was now sailing in consort and was under the constant eye of the Spanish. Would they be wanting to confiscate it? Ah, he would worry about that later. He had to find that damned thieving scum of a pirate first!

He also wondered why these men had been talking of another vessel called the *Kismet*. Of what relevance was she? Another pirate ship, perhaps? But with Acorne penned like a monkey in a cage, what, at the moment, did any of the rest of it matter?

Chapter Twenty-Five

The acrid smoke from tarred torches filled the night air, and the partially covered lanterns bobbed, making wildly swinging shadows and eerie pools of light ahead and behind. The laughter and excited chatter had died away after the first mile, most of the men were riding or walking in silence; only the murmur of low conversation and the occasional muttered curse broke the natural sound of the night noises.

Juliana Maria, the Reverend Mother, was riding at the head of the column behind the gruff Spaniard who took the lead. Somewhere ahead of them a man was riding point. So many things had become clear to Jesamiah; as many remained to be answered. His main thought was that he did not much like being used. And used he had been.

"Jennings manipulated me coming here right from the start, the bastard. He'll owe me for this," he grumbled.

"Diego spoke often of Captain Jennings," 'Cesca said, her horse's head level with his left leg. "Is he a friend?"

"Not any more he ain't."

The track narrowed again and she had to drop behind; not for another ten minutes was she able to resume a conversation. "When del Gardo forced me into his bed and first violated me, I joined the rebellion. Until then I had no interest in the things men pursued, but I did care for my husband and my son. And I began to care deeply about that monster being deposed. I cannot believe that it is at last about to happen."

Jesamiah made no comment. Some of these men here seemed to know what they were doing, the Reverend Mother certainly did—but most of them were farmers and servants, probably one or two were slaves. Their weapons were old, some, he had noticed, were rusty and bent. They were nothing more than a hotch-potch rabble. If the others being summoned to the rendezvous, a few miles from Santo Domingo, were of the same uninspiring quality, then this rebellion would be over before it started.

How many, he wondered, will turn tail and run at the first sound of gunfire? Few of them would stand and fight against a trained soldier. He shrugged, it was none of his business. All he wanted was his cargo, although he had extreme doubts about the existence of any indigo. These mules were carting something though. Gold with any luck. Whatever it was, he was going to have it.

The moon sailed out from behind a ragged patch of cloud to peep briefly at them before hiding her face again, and a breeze ruffled the trees. The quick glimpse of light had illuminated the dark, night-shadowed sea spread way, way below, creating a silvered path that looked solid enough to walk on. Not a sail in sight, not that it would be easy to spot a ship that was being sensible and not sailing with her topgallants spread.

Already he was missing the sea, craving its motion, its smell. He wanted a deck beneath him, not an uncomfortable horse. Wanted to be on board a ship, not riding down a steep hillside in the dark with a bunch of rebels who would probably get themselves killed in their first skirmish.

"Did Juliana Maria give you the gift for Captain Jennings?"

Jesamiah patted his pocket, nodded. "She did."

316

Some of the mules, always contrary creatures, were nervous of the dark and the moving shadows. Maybe they were catching a little of the apprehension that was there in a few of the men. The sound of a waterfall tumbling down the hillside and of animals splashing through the hollowed pool, which Jesamiah remembered from the trek upward, disturbed the night. Then the sound of cursing and men starting to shout, the column shambling to a standstill. The anxious bray of a frightened mule, more splashing and vigorous shouting. It appeared the animal was refusing to step into the deep blackness of the water.

"Cut its throat if it won't damned move!" someone roared, his voice louder than the rising stir of activity. Their illustrious leader, Jesamiah assumed. He had meant to ask 'Cesca his name, but had decided he did not need or want to know. After this was over, except for 'Cesca, he had no intention of meeting a single one of these people again. Half of them would probably be dead soon, anyway.

The man on the horse behind 'Cesca dismounted and marched purposefully forward. Jesamiah had already judged him to be one of those men who claimed loudly to know everything and promptly showed their appalling ignorance.

"I'll get the son of a knock-kneed nag to move!" he proclaimed, as raising his riding whip, he began to help the mule's handler to beat the animal in an attempt to make it go through the water. Inevitably, the creature became more terrified and kicked out. The crunch of shattering bone was loudly audible as its handler's leg was broken. The beating from the other man became twice as savage.

"Fok this," Jesamiah muttered as he dismounted and handed the reins of his horse to 'Cesca.

Stretching his aching shoulders and back, realising now that he was on the move again the pull of the lashes had not been bothering him quite so much, he sidled past the several agitated horses and mules ahead and stopped at the edge of the pool. It looked for the world as if it was a gaping pit with no bottom. On the other side, those who had already crossed were shouting impatient advice, on this side, the man with the broken leg was on the ground screaming his pain. No one seemed particularly concerned about him.

"Listen, friend," Jesamiah said to the brute with the whip, "stop hitting the animal. Can't you damned see it's frightened? You're making things worse."

He was tossed a particularly foul obscenity for his effort.

As the Spaniard raised his leg to boot the animal in the belly, Jesamiah moved in fast, punching his fist hard into the man's back, then again, catching his jaw. The Spaniard dropped like a stone, unconscious.

"I don't go much on cruelty to children, women, animals and pirates," Jesamiah stated, wiping his knuckles on his coat. "Not when they ain't able to fight back." He took up the trembling animal's lead rope and rubbed its sweating face with his hand, crooning to it; talking nonsense. Slipping off his coat he handed it to the nearest person, then pulling a handful of grass from the wayside, waded into the pool. It came up almost to the top of his boots, even through the thick leather, was ice cold. With a grunt of satisfaction he realised the cracked sole had been mended well.

"Come on then you daft mule-brain, if I can stand in here so can you." Holding out the grass he tempted the animal forward a step; one leg plunged into the water. "That's it you lump of brainless bone. Another step. Yes. Good boy." He let the mule eat the grass, then rubbing its face again, calmly led it across to the other side.

There was movement along the line in front and behind, a ripple of laughter, but the leader, dismounting and pushing past his men, was not so amused. On foot he was several inches shorter than Jesamiah, stockier, running to fat and full of his own self–importance. His fist was raised.

"You no hit my men! You bloody bastard!" he snarled in broken English. He made to draw his sword but Jesamiah had his cutlass out even quicker, and was pressing its tip beneath the man's double chin.

"You got something to say to me, mate? If so, I suggest you say it with a touch more politeness. Savvy?"

The leader's hand went to one of several pistols thrust through a bandoleer across his chest. With speed, Jesamiah slashed with his cutlass, spinning the gun away, sending it clattering down the cliff face.

"You make another move and it'll be your hand I send over the edge. Now, shall we proceed or do you want to really annoy me?"

Glowering, the Spaniard walked away, tossing over his shoulder, "I will not forget this insult, English."

"Viva the rebellion," Jesamiah quipped as the line of mules began to move and 'Cesca approached with his horse. He noted as he mounted that she had his coat over her mount's withers. He grinned into the darkness as he encouraged his rescued mule to walk nicely beside his horse. Whatever was in these kegs, at least he now had hold of two of them.

"I have a talent to make friends," he said. "It's keeping them I find difficult."

'Cesca laughed.

CHAPTER TWENTY-SIX

They had reached the woodland, the track winding dark and ominous through its overhang of gloomy shadow. Even the moon had deserted them, for the cloud cover had gathered in. One of the men ahead, apparently on foot for he had no horse, had pulled aside and was urinating against a tree. As Jesamiah rode past, the light from a lantern caught his face and hat. The distinctive ostrich feather.

"Hey, you're not with us," Jesamiah said, partially looking back over his shoulder, then realising he had to duck under a low branch; cursed as another whipped back from the rider ahead and caught his horse's face. Simultaneously, two bright flashes and loud bangs. The smell of smoke and gunpowder. Firearms! The animal tossed its head high, almost hitting Jesamiah's nose, then, squealing, it shied violently sideways and the mule, bucking wildly, plunged forward. Jesamiah was thrown as the horse stumbled a few paces, tried to regain its balance then pitched onto its nose, quite dead.

In a straggle of arms and legs Jesamiah tumbled down the steep hillside. He grabbed at a branch, which snapped, and grasped another which stopped his fall. Looked up in time to see the mule, still bucking violently, blood cascading from its flank, slip and fall downward crashing through the trees. The night sky lit up in a flare of light and a booming blast. Instinctively, Jesamiah ducked his head and threw his

320

arm across his face as the woodland below him burst into flame. Gunpowder! The kegs contained gunpowder!

Pistol and musket shots were *pop-popping*, the flash of sparks in the pans; the puff and acrid stink of smoke. Men shouting and cursing, horses neighing, mules panicking. Militia; Spanish soldiers; del Gardo's men! Ambush!

On his feet again, Jesamiah automatically had his pistol drawn. He took aim, sighted a man above him on the partially burning hillside; fired, did not wait to observe the resulting spatter of blood, bone and brain. Had other, more important things to think about. Scrambling upward, moving more by necessity than agility, his eyes were riveted on 'Cesca and her horse which was rearing almost vertical. He shouted as she fell backwards, noting incongruously that she was clinging to his coat, her mouth open in a scream he could not hear above the shooting of pistols, muskets and the shouting. Riderless, the horse bolted, reins and stirrups flying, several equally as terrified mules galloping in its wake. Jesamiah bellowed her name, scrabbled that last yard upward and ran, arms pumping, feet scrambling for a foothold on the track that was already churning with spilt blood.

A face, distorted by the killing-frenzy, loomed in front of him; reversing his pistol, he hammered the butt between the eyes and then stamped on the fallen man's knee. Elbowed someone else aside—Spanish militia or rebel mercenary he never noticed. No time to reload, it was to be blade against blade at close quarters now.

Men were using fired muskets like clubs. The noises were macabre: the scream of a dying horse and the bray of wounded mules. Grunts of effort and sharp intakes of breath; the occasional curse, and the clash of steel on steel. Men had no breath left for shouting. Every desperate effort was being put into staying alive.

Jesamiah shoved his useless pistol through his belt and drew his cutlass; used it like an axe, holding the hilt two handed, swinging the heavy blade from side to side as he drove forward to where he had last seen 'Cesca. Strike. Strike again, wrench the blade out from bone, guts and flesh. Ignore the sweet smell and sticky warmth of fresh blood; the sickening squelch as the blade sucked free.

He killed a militiaman by slicing his bloodied cutlass blade through the throat. Where the bugger were they coming from? How had they known to be waiting here? Briefly he thought of the ostrich feather, the two men following them. How had they known they would be coming back down this track? Another enormous bang and whoosh of exploding air, and more of the dark woodland burst into bright-lit clarity, trees were on fire, the flames spreading westward, fanned by the wind. The few mules left fled onward down the track. Incongruously, Jesamiah had time to reflect that at least they were heading for Puerto Vaca.

He slashed to the left, taking the cutlass through a man's eyes, deep enough to sever into the skull and brain; whirled around, the momentum carrying the cutlass through its own weight to slice through another's chest. The cutlass, a killer's weapon, and Jesamiah, for all his congeniality, for all his charm, daring and humorous jesting, was a man who knew how to kill. Especially when he was angry. And he was. Very, very angry.

He had no idea whether a single one of those barrels and kegs had any indigo or brandy in them, or whether they were all gunpowder. While the black powder was useful it was not exactly valuable. The smoke from fired guns was thick and choking although the *bang, bang, bang*, had almost ceased as the last bullets were fired. A few of the dying men were moaning for help; two injured horses were struggling to get up, but nothing, no one, was in Jesamiah's mind except the need to reach 'Cesca.

The glint of a sword in front of him. He parried with his cutlass, the fighting madness devouring him, making him kill by instinct and reaction. A sweating brow; a black moustache. A leering grin a grimace of fear—glimpses only of men appearing briefly before him. Another silver blade lunging, hot fire along his arm, blood trickling down to his hand. He swept the blade aside, struck again, and again, and again with precision and strength, speed and ability. But his injured arm was growing heavy, his muscles weary. He would not be able to fight like this for much longer.

Without pity; strike with your blade, kick with your feet. Do not think—do! Fight! It's you or him Jesamiah! Fight! Malachias Taylor's voice in his mind. Malachias, who had taught him how to stay alive.

A pistol exploded beside his head, he jerked aside tripped over something, a root, a severed arm? Almost fell, recovered. Slashed at a shape beside him, felt an impact, wrenched the cutlass free, and plunged on. 'Cesca was screaming, he could hear her above all the other sounds. Could see her—two men were dragging her, one by the arm the other by her hair. One of them had a lantern, its crazed whirling creating a moving pool of light around them as they plunged downward through the trees, away from where the fires raged. Blood was on 'Cesca's face, she still had his coat, was clutching it to her as if it were a shield.

Something ricocheted off Jesamiah's blade, a numbing shock shot up his arm, a pistol bullet most likely. He ignored the pain, glared into a pair of white, staring, eyes heard the hiss of a sword sweeping inward, but he jumped backwards and it glanced off his belt buckle. Instantly he stepped forward, slammed the hilt of his own cutlass into the wielder's jaw with such force that it snapped the bone. He wanted to cry out to 'Cesca, shout he was coming, but had no breath or energy. Someone else was blocking his path—how many were there for God's sake? Their blades grated with a shower of sparks as the steel ground together, blood-red blade sliding along blood-red blade until the hilts locked and each man held ground. Face to face leering at each other, breath hot, bodies exhausted.

The taverner. The scar on his face unmistakable.

"I'm on your fokken bloody side!" Jesamiah panted, heaving against the man's superior, solid weight, trying to push him off.

For answer, a snarl and an elbow jabbing into ribs that were already cracked and bruised, and Jesamiah realised that Scarface was the one who was not on the right side. His cutlass felt like a lead bar, his arm so heavy, so very heavy. All the other wounds and abuses were betraying him, screaming their protest, the agony coursing with quivering tension across his shoulder muscles and rippling down his forearm. He would have to submit—would have to... Scarface thrust harder at Jesamiah, pushing him off balance. He staggered, stumbled, and fell backwards. Looked up to see his opponent's blade, coming forward and down. Knew this was the end. Hoped it would not hurt too much. He shut his eyes, thought of Tiola. Her dear, sweet face. Her eyes that shone with laughter, the taste of her mouth, the feel of her body against his as he made love to her. Opened his eyes as he heard a shattering bang at close range and a startled grunt.

Angelita, Juliana—whatever her damned name was—lowered the pistol in her hand and gave him a quick smile, began reloading it, the light of the burning trees more than enough to see by. Apart from the crackling and roar of flames, the moans of the wounded and the sound of the rising wind in the trees, the clearing had fallen quiet. The others would be making no more sounds.

"I thought you said nuns did not possess guns," he panted from where he was sprawled in the blood and mud.

"We do not. This is not mine, it is his." She nodded at another dead man nearby. The short, fat, Spaniard, the arrogant leader.

Aye, short friendships. "I think you'll find this bastard here, was your tongue-tattler," Jesamiah said, nodding towards Scarface and pushing himself, grimacing, upright.

The Reverend Mother, as bloodstained and gore-grimed as himself, nodded. "One of them. That is why I shot him, too many of our people have suffered because of the likes of him. As they say, dead men can tell no tales. But he was not alone, there is at least one other, a woman we think." But she was speaking to herself. A shrill scream had sheared up from where the trees dropped away. 'Cesca!

Jesamiah sheathed his cutlass and hurtled down the hillside, her hysterical screams guiding him through the darkness as efficiently as any beacon. He slithered a fair way, ducked beneath trees, slipped, fell and rolled. His face and hands were caught by clawing branches. He slithered some more, but was up on his feet and running. Shoving branches aside by instinct more than sight. The light dim, but because of the fires, enough to see by. He tripped over a fallen trunk, was up again. Clinging to a supple branch he jumped down an expanse of bare rock, stood, breathing hard, heart hammering, in an open clearing.

Behind him, and way over to the left, the night sky was lit by the burning fires of the two gunpowder explosions. Nearer, a dim light bobbed through the darkness of the trees, coming towards him, coming closer. He moved quietly behind a rocky outcrop. Barely taking his eyes from the lantern, reloaded his pistol. He had done it so often he did not have to think about it, barely needed to look at what he was doing. Bending slightly, he rested his left arm on one of the rocks and steadied the end of the barrel on his wrist, only now, in the orange glow, noticing the gash that had sliced through his shirt and arm. It had already stopped bleeding. He'd had worse; it would heal.

'Cesca had also stopped screaming. As the three entered the clearing she was no longer struggling, and only one of the men had his hand gripped on her arm. Jesamiah took several breaths to lessen his laboured breathing and narrowed his eyes; took aim.

It was a good shot. Right between the eyes, the man with the lantern never knew what had hit him. One second he was alive, the next, dead, the lantern falling to the ground where it rolled down the slope, flickered and went out.

CHAPTER TWENTY-SEVEN

For one whole minute the second man was transfixed, standing bolt upright, eyes staring like a startled rabbit; and then he grabbed the coat from 'Cesca's arms and fled.

Jesamiah scurried for the dead man's pistol, yanked it from his belt and taking a chance that it had been loaded correctly and would not go off half-cock, he thumped the hammer back with the side of his palm, aimed and pulled the trigger. A satisfying flash as the pan ignited, a billow of smoke, a bang and a second flash. The running man cried out, dropped the coat, staggered a few paces, his arms whirling like windmills and fell, face down.

Closing his eyes in sheer exhaustion, Jesamiah leant one shoulder against a tree. He ought to check the man was dead. Ought to reload his weapon. Ought to go to 'Cesca, but at that moment all he cared about was staying upright. And suddenly he did not even care about that. He sank to his knees, knelt there, head drooping against the tree, wondering if it would feel a lot better to just die and have done with it. Did not even feel the first few drops of rain.

He could hear 'Cesca weeping. Opening his eyes he looked across the clearing at her. There was enough diffused light to see, and the temporary blindness from the pistol flash had worn off. Like many sailors Jesamiah had good night vision. They needed it aboard ship, for apart from the lamp to illuminate the compass, and occasionally a stern lantern if in harbour or near other vessels, they did not use lights on deck when at sea. Holding on to the trunk he hauled himself upright, wandered the short way down the hill and after toeing at the man—he seemed dead enough—he retrieved the man's hat and his own coat.

"Are those real tears or are you putting them on for my benefit?" he said as he returned to 'Cesca and stood about a yard from her. "You have been playing me for the fool right from the start, haven't you?" He had dropped his own pretence at the common sailor's uncultivated accent that he had used since sailing into Santo Domingo harbour. Jesamiah was an educated man, he could talk with perfect correctness when he needed to.

"No," she whispered, shook her head, "but what is the point of denying it? You will not believe me."

"Too bloody right I won't!" He tossed the hat at her. "Oh you made plenty of noise when you thought we could still hear, but you got friendly with Ostrich Feather pretty quick, didn't you? Did you suddenly decide to change sides, or did you know the bastard anyway? Are you his whore as well? Or maybe he's your pimp? Oh, no, forgive me. My mistake, your pimp was Scarface. He's dead. Don't waste your tears on him."

The tears, however, were streaming down her face. "Please Jesamiah, you must believe I intended you no harm."

"You set them on me at the tavern. You had them beat me up. You knew we would be returning down this track with a load of sodding gunpowder, and you told them where to set an effective ambush. You have been making sure this rebellion does not get to fire even one shot right from the start, haven't you?" He was shouting.

"No! No," she screamed, utterly distraught. "You do not understand!"

"Understand? Understand! Oh, I bloody understand. I understand that you are a liar and a traitor. That all those pathetic little tales of how bad del Gardo treats you were to make me feel sorry for you. Well I do feel sorry, I pity you; want to know why? Because you are worthless. You're of less value than that strumpet I bedded last night!"

"No!" she screamed again at him as she got unsteadily to her feet. "I am not a traitor! It was not me who betrayed you, it was her—that strumpet! I have just found out all about her! Him over there," she tossed a contemptuous look in the direction of the dead man, Ostrich Feather. "He always was a fool and he surpassed himself tonight! He babbled everything!"

She took a breath, ranted on, "Del Gardo pays her—I don't know why we didn't realise it, Feather Hat, or whatever you call him, is her brother after all." Her voice was rising shrill, almost hysterical. "He has just told me that Scarface tattled on Emilio to get the Sickle Moon, that was a fact he kept damned quiet from everyone, even his wife. My sin is that I suspected they were planning something for tonight but I said nothing of it to Juliana Maria, so all that up there is my fault! I should have told them del Gardo was watching the convent, but I bloody didn't!"

"Of course you didn't! You wouldn't tell because you wanted to get this didn't you?" As he was yelling, Jesamiah reached angrily into his coat pocket. He pulled out the casket and waved it under her nose, dropping the coat. "You knew this was at the convent but you couldn't get your grubby little hands on it could you? You had to wait for the code word for it to be released from safety. Wickham was wise to you wasn't he? He knew you were the bitch who led those traitors. He knew all you wanted was this!"

He opened the lid and tipped out the contents, expecting only the solid gold crucifix to fall at his feet. Was not expecting the cascade of sparkling, exquisite, rare, Russian diamonds to tumble from beneath the velvet.

He saw 'Cesca's face, the dismay. Saw her look beyond him, heard her gasp, felt her hand reach to his chest and fiercely push him aside; then the sharp, deep, jolt on the side of his head. Thought, as he crumpled to the ground that he should have ensured her colleague was dead.

Chapter Twenty-Eight

Señora Isabella Mendez passed to her God as the moonlight faded behind a bank of cloud. She felt no pain as she held Tiola's hand, but smiled into the young woman's eyes, knowing only peace awaited her.

Strength was returning into Tiola, swelling within her as she sought for, and used, her great skills of healing. Not to save the woman, the disease was beyond curing, but to ease the pain and send her on to her next journey surrounded by the comfort of love.

The moment Tiola had set foot ashore she had been released from the quagmire that had been drawing her downward, almost drowning her. Tethys had no power on the solidity of land, her limit was the sand of the shore, the sea strand, and the rocks and cliffs that she battered with her relentless force.

~ *I am not one of you,* ~ Isabella Mendez had said to Tiola, her thoughts frail. ~ *But I know of what you are, for I have a little of your kind within me.* ~

Tiola had brushed Isabella's hair from her closed eyes, and straightened her shawl. Señor Mendez, on the other side of the bed, did not attempt to stem the tears that coursed down the tired crags of his old face. He had not heard the words, for they were spoken in the special ways of those who had the Craft. To him, his wife stepped from the sleep of life to the sleep of eternity, and he mourned.

~ I was unable to help my daughter when she suffered, nor could I help my grandson when he drowned, but I can help you as I leave; I can give you what little of the Craft that I have. ~

Tiola was grateful, those small ounces of strength were all she needed to climb out of the abyss of weakness and regain her power in its entirety.

The duty of the midwife; to safely bring into the world the new, young hope of life with its infant faith and its infinite dreams, and to send from the world the tired ebb of a soul ready to rest in the arms of Peace and to dream no more. With gentleness Tiola slipped her hand from Isabella's and touched where a weary heart had beat its last.

She went to señor Mendez, the living taking precedence over the dead, and kneeling beside him, with her gift, comforted his grieving. "She is gone from us, señor, but gone to a better place where she is young and strong again. She no longer suffers the indignities that her old body had forced upon her. And she waits for you. She will be there to take your hand when it is time for you to follow."

Although his heart was broken for the wanting of the woman he had loved since the first flush of youth, Tiola's kindness meant much to him. "Will it be long before I join her?" he asked.

Tiola smiled, touched his heart with her fingertips. It was not an answer she should have made, but she did not have the ability, or the desire, to lie. "No, señor," she said very softly, "No, it will not be long." She was not a seer, she could not read what was to be, what was to come, but she was a healer and she could hear the catch in his shortened breath, and she felt the uneven blood-pulse missing every third, hesitant beat. Before the coming of spring he would no longer be alone.

Leaving him to make his private farewells, Tiola stepped outside and walked down to where the sea lapped at the wooden, weed-slimed pillars of the jetty. The clouds were building thicker, and away to the west thunder moaned and the night sky flickered with distant lightning.

She knelt, dipped her fingers into the green swell of the restless sea.

~ *You cannot permanently harm me, Tethys. I am stronger than you. You cannot destroy me Sea Woman, as you will not destroy the man I love.* ~

The sea slapped against the wooden pillars, sending a cascade of spray brushing against Tiola's face. She wiped the moisture aside and smiled as a patient mother calmly overrides a stamping tantrum of her child. ~ *I respect you Tethys, for you have the ability to be gentle, wise and benevolent, to be serene and beautiful; but sadness fills my heart because you only show the hatred that has spread within and consumed you.* ~

She stood, turned her back on the sea and walked into the hills behind La Sorenta, to where she would become one with the night-shawled, shadowed land. There she waited for her grandmothers to bring her their love and protection, their presence re-awakened by the gratitude of an elderly lady who had been unaware, until her soul took wing, of the small ability she had possessed.

Tiola lay beneath the shelter of the palm trees, and slept. A restful, peaceful, sleep untroubled by dreams. Untroubled by the spatter of rain that wetted her face, and stung upon her hands. When she awoke, she would be whole again. And then, then, she would be reunited with the one she loved beyond all being. Jesamiah.

CHAPTER TWENTY-NINE

TUESDAY MORNING

Groaning, his hand going to the almighty throb of pain stabbing through his head, Jesamiah decided it would be wiser to lie here and die rather than think about trying to open his eyes. Rain was touching at his face, trickling down his nose and chin; a light, gentle rain. A kerchief was being dabbed, not so tenderly, at the blood congealing at the back of his head, a woman was leaning over him. In his mind he saw her as silver-haired, the hood of her grey cloak pulled forward to hide her features. Dangling from her neck, a raindrop diamond. He opened his eyes the vision fled. The woman turned out to be 'Cesca.

"I thought you'd be long gone," he said, wincing as he pushed her administering hand aside and sat up.

"And leave you in this state? Why would I do that?" 'Cesca persisted with her dabbing. She had found the lantern, had rummaged in Jesamiah's belt pouch for his tinderbox, had lit it. The candle inside was growing low, but it's light was sufficient for what she needed.

"Why? Because of something I said, or because of him?" He nodded in a vague direction downhill. Regretting the movement, took the kerchief from her and pressed it tight to the head wound. "I assume he's gone?"

"Yes. With the casket, the crucifix and some of the diamonds."

Jesamiah grunted.

"You have misjudged me, Jesamiah, I swear. Yes, I knew of the diamonds. They were for Henry Jennings and Woodes Rogers. They are—were—the payment we owed for the muskets and pistols they provided; for the shot and the gunpowder. Diego Wickham was supposed to come and collect them, but he had a feeling that something would happen. We used to say that he had a hint of the fairy folk in him, as his premonitions were often right."

She took a shuddering breath. "Diego was my friend, I sometimes felt as though he was my only friend. Between us we decided what information I could pass to del Gardo. On the nights when Diego had a run, we made sure your little whore and her brother—yes, the Feathered Hat was her brother—were otherwise occupied. But I would never have betrayed Diego. Never."

Jesamiah grunted again. He wished he had that bottle of rum. He could do with a tot or two. Or three. "For a moment there, I almost believed you."

'Cesca sat back on her heels, ignoring the rain that was falling heavier. "Yes, I wanted the diamonds," she said suddenly, viciously. "I only decided I wanted them when I was being dragged away by those two sons of bitches. It's all right for you, you are a man. I am a woman, a woman used and abused by del Gardo. Other bastards tend to think that makes me fair game for any of their depraved ideas. Well I decided I was not going to be raped yet again. I decided to bargain with them instead. They knew nothing of the casket or what was in it—but they were pretty damned interested when I told them! Interested enough to leave me alone and agree to split the contents three ways!" She ranted on; "And then I decided being the imbeciles they are, they would have no idea of the immense value of the casket, but del Gardo would. He is a vile pig, but greedy men know by instinct what is priceless."

Jesamiah could not argue with that. He had been aware the casket itself was worth more than a mere gold coin or two.

"And I ran because I realised that if I made del Gardo finally trust me then maybe I could buy my son's freedom." She flung her hand towards the upward slope of the hill, towards where the fires were dying down, put out by the rain. "It's over isn't it? The whole stupid, pathetic idea of raising a rebellion. You saw those useless men. How are they going to fight? Del Gardo's beaten us before we even started. As those bastards were making me run I realised I can't face doing what del Gardo makes me do any more. I can't! If I presented him with that casket then maybe, just maybe, he would let me and my son go!"

Shaking his head, Jesamiah answered her with the truth. "I doubt it darlin'. He's not the sort of man to give up what he enjoys, no matter what the bribe."

'Cesca wiped at her tears. "That casket is made from the Devil's bones." She laughed, unamused. "I thought it fitting for del Gardo to have it."

For a while they sat there, listening to the sound of the rain. The candle within the lantern sputtered and went out.

"What happens now?" Jesamiah asked.

"The rebels will be marching on Santo Domingo, but they will have very little powder. What we had was in those barrels. I don't know how much of it is left. We were to put it aboard the *Kismet* and take it to a rendezvous point a few miles up the Ozama River." She sniffed back tears. "So I doubt anything will happen now. Our men will just turn round and go home."

"There never was any brandy was there?"

"Yes there is brandy, Diego was a very good smuggler. but it is still at the convent."

"And the indigo?"

"I know nothing of any indigo. I suspect your Henry Jennings invented its existence as a method of hiding the code date. It was very clever of him."

"It was the diamonds he wanted?"

"As the payment he was owed. Yes."

Jesamiah snorted. He had to admire Jennings' gall. "The other thing he wanted was for me to find Francis Chesham. Jennings was busting his breeches to know who he was, how to find him. He'll be disappointed to discover that was a waste of time too. The poor sod's dead. I assume Chesham knew about the diamonds?"

"Yes. Chesham did." Another silence.

"You knew him then?"

"I know her. Yes."

A longer silence.

"Her?"

"I am Chesham. Frances Chesham. It was my mother's maiden name. I changed Frances to Francesca long before I married Ramon."

"Oh." It seemed an inadequate answer, but Jesamiah could not think of anything more appropriate to say.

"No one except Diego knew me as Frances Chesham, not even my father-in-law knows. And now it is only you. I would ask for you to keep it so."

Jesamiah nodded. "But that man when he died, he told me his name was Francis Chesham." He reconsidered. "No, maybe he didn't, I just assumed he did. He said 'Ches...' he was trying to say Francesca—*Chesca*—wasn't he?"

Her turn to nod. "He was one of our co-ordinators. He gave nothing of the rebellion away, not even after what they did to him, and it has all been for nothing."

They sat beneath the trees, listening to the rain rattling on the leaves and dripping to the ground.

"I suppose we ought to climb back up this hill. See who and what is left." Francesca said.

"I suppose."

They remained where they were, not moving, not talking, and after a while, no longer noticing the rain. Nor did Jesamiah see the faint outline of a woman in grey watching them from the far side of the clearing, for he had slid his arm around 'Cesca's waist and had kissed her.

Had no problem with functioning as he should this time.

~ *The Witch Woman said I was beautiful.* ~

~ *You are not beautiful, Mother, you are ugly. Ugly because you are always angry.* ~

Tethys did not answer that the Witch Woman had said that to her as well.

~ *You were as angry as me. I heard you.* ~

~ *I was not!* ~

But Tethys was right, Rain was angry. She did not like the pretty red-haired woman. She had tried to stop him liking her, but had failed. She had tried to wake the Witch Woman but had failed in that too. And now her mother was mocking her. Her mother had always mocked and goaded her. She did not like being mocked or thought of as worthless.

Out over the sea, thunder grumbled and began building into black, ominous, angry, storm clouds.

CHAPTER THIRTY

As the light began to strengthen, they found many diamonds beneath his coat. Feather Man had hastily grabbed a few, but most were beneath the leaves or hidden in the grass, some had rolled away. Some lucky person, some day, might find what was left of them. Jesamiah gave half of what they scavenged to 'Cesca, kept the rest for himself.

Scrabbling up the hill proved to be harder than the descent had been. Going down, Jesamiah had let gravity and his own momentum take him. Going up, he felt every ache, bruise, bump and cut. He felt like a tired old man as he grasped at branches and forced his body to take another and another step. At the top, in the pale light of a cloud-covered dawn, the destruction was depressing. Dead mules, dead horses, some with their throats cut to alleviate their suffering. Dead men; the wounded lying, sitting, slumped under the shelter of the trees. Juliana Maria, her habit torn, face and hands smeared with blood, was tending them, a few of the surviving men fetching water, doing what they could to help. Six mules had been caught and were tethered, still harnessed, still with their loads. The gunpowder kegs that had remained intact had been removed from the dead animals and stacked to one side. Parts of the woodland, the scrub, the trees, were charred and burnt; smelt of wet, acrid smoke and soot.

Tipping his hat to the back of his head Jesamiah counted how many men he could use. Eight. The extra kegs would be heavy for the mules, but there was not much further to go. He waited for the Reverend Mother to finish a prayer over a man who was near death, then taking her by the arm, steered her to one side.

"You look tired, Lady. Have you sent someone up to the convent to fetch help?"

She nodded, she had.

Compassionately, Jesamiah brushed his fingers against her cheek. "It's not the end Angelita, this is only a beginning. So your little band has not managed all it was supposed to do, but you still have gunpowder, you still have me, and you still have the *Kismet* down in Puerto Vaca harbour."

She looked up at him a vague light beginning to glow in her eyes again. "You are willing to help us?"

He chuckled. "Not much else I can do, is there? Until I can find my ship, I'm stuck on this island. And I hate del Gardo as much as you do. Although I suppose, hate is not an emotion a nun should be entertaining?"

She smiled. "I am the servant of the Lord and I do his bidding." With her finger she drew the pattern of the cross on Jesamiah's chest. "And He works in mysterious ways. He has sent me you."

"Well actually it was Henry Jennings, but I won't quibble."

She laughed. "What are you going to do?"

"I am going to take this gunpowder and I am going to load it aboard *Kismet*. Then I am going to sail up the Ozama River and find your rebels."

"You are a good man, Jesamiah Acorne."

"Nope. I'm an idiot, but that fact has never stopped me before."

Twenty minutes later all the kegs were strapped to the remaining mules and Jesamiah was ready to move off with the eight men who were willing to continue and do what they could. At least they had bested del Gardo's ambush but at what cost? The rebellion, for this side of the Island, anyway, was almost dead in its tracks.

When 'Cesca came up to him he was not surprised as she said, "I am returning to the convent, I can help with the wounded and," she sighed, the tiredness and despair quivering in her breath. How could she say, 'And I cannot come with you'? He would not have her, he would not take her aboard his ship, love her as he obviously loved this other woman he had spoken of. She took another breath, started again, "I cannot return to del Gardo. I cannot." Tears were brimming, one trickled down her cheek. After she had known Jesamiah? How could she?

"Del Gardo will leave señor Escudero alone, he is an old man who can tell him nothing, and as fond as I am of him, that bastard knows, for all my sins, I would not die for my-father-in-law. But," another tear followed her first, and another, "but I can only pray that he leaves my son alone, for him I would willingly give my life."

Jesamiah brushed the tears away with his thumb. "Well, so there you have it, señora. If he believes you dead, 'Cesca, Don Damián will have no reason to hurt the boy, will he? The Reverend Mother over there successfully killed her persona of Angelita so her son could live. You could do the same. Go back to being Frances, only, don't stay in the convent too long. You're not a nun. You never will be." He gave her a kiss, chaste, on the cheek, turned to go, waving to the man at the head of the depleted column to move out.

'Cesca caught his arm, stopped him from walking away. "Jesamiah there is something you ought to know. Something señor Escudero told me about your father."

"What about him?"

'Cesca told him. Quickly, the plain facts without embellishment.

He said nothing. Merely nodded once, turned and strode away down the hill, shouting impatiently at the men to get the mules moving faster, that this was not a family picnic. His fingers, as he reached the head of the column, went to where his blue ribbons would have been tied into his hair. He dropped his hand to grip the hilt of his cutlass instead. Felt the nausea churning in his stomach and rising into his gullet. Told himself it was the carnage behind him that had stirred this bitter taste in his mouth. He wanted to scream; wanted to rage and shout, to draw his cutlass and kill someone. Anyone, he didn't care who!

~ *Jesamiah*? ~ Tiola's soft voice eased into his sobbing, confused, angry, mind.

Distraught, he did not hear her.

CHAPTER THIRTY-ONE

Only the sight of the sea brought Jesamiah out of his dark and brooding mood. It was grey, white capped where the wind was tossing the surface into leaping, mane-flying seahorses. Grey to match the sullen post-dawn sky that drizzled its persistent fall of rain, and his emotional turmoil.

The sight of the sea and the two ships, one moored, the other at anchor in the harbour roused him. *Kismet* was where he had left her, and the other... the other he would know anywhere! *Sea Witch*. His beloved *Sea Witch*! Her presence filled his senses, joy and relief pouring through him almost as if he were drunk. He quickened his pace, ran. Everything would be all right now. All he had to do was reach his ship. Once he was aboard, once they were sailing all this would not matter any more! Oh, *Sea Witch* was there, waiting for him! *Sea Witch*!

And then Tiola was with him. Tiola! Tiola!

~ Jesamiah? My dear? What is wrong? ~

He stopped short, jerking to a halt, clung to a young tree for support.

~ Sweetheart, oh darlin'! Where've you been? Why weren't you with me? ~

~ I could not be with you, I'm sorry. ~

~ No! You were with him weren't you? You decided you'd rather have your husband than me? Well bloody stay

343

with him! I don't need you! ~ Stupid, irrational anger possessed him. He needed to strike out and Tiola was the one he punched.

~ *Jesamiah, I do not want him. I want you. I love you. Please, what is wrong? What is troubling you?* ~

~ *Nothing's wrong.* ~

~ *Let me help you.* ~

He snapped a belligerent answer. ~ *You can't help me. No one can.* ~

~ *I can try.* ~

~ *Leave me alone! Go back to your husband.* ~

Tears began to course down Jesamiah's face, masked by the falling rain. ~ *I thought you had left me. I needed you and you weren't there.* ~

All the compassion, the love, all her devotion to him flooded her answer. ~ *I will never willingly leave you, Jesamiah! Never willingly! I will always, always, be with you, unless I am kept from you by a force stronger than mine own.* ~ Tiola wanted to be there with him, to hold him and caress him, to help him through whatever was so grievously tearing him apart, she was at La Sorenta, and he was in the hills above Puerto Vaca—but distance had never hindered her before. It did not hinder her now.

He felt a warmth seep through him, the feel of arms going about him, her breath on his cheek. Her smell was in his nostrils, her voice in his ear and mind. He was aware of every fibre of his being quivering as her soul blended into his. The ache in his bones eased, the soreness of the cut on his arm, the lashes on his back, all of it disappeared as she entwined her life-force with his, doing all she could to remove his mental and physical pain. But she could not reach where the stab had plunged and was twisting and twisting and tearing his heart into broken pieces. All she could do was mingle her tears with his and love him.

~ *Tell me,* ~ she said. ~ *Why can you not tell me?* ~

He tried. ~ *My father. My father he isn't, wasn't...*~ The words choked, his despair was too great for him to say those words that were driving him almost beyond sanity.

He walked on down the hill, at every opportunity checking to see that *Sea Witch* was still there, at anchor in the harbour. What if they were about to sail? What if at the next glimpse of her through the trees he was to see canvas tumbling from her spars? What would he do if he were to see that anchor cable being weighed?

Oh God, oh God, don't sail. Rue, don't sail! He ran a few paces to the next opening. *By the Lady of the Sea, by the Queen of the Ocean do not sail!*

Tiola tried again. ~ *How can I help?* ~

Again he repeated, abrupt and curt, ~ *You can't.* ~ And he shut her out, slammed the door. The rage, the hatred, the pain, had totally consumed him, and only one thing, now, drove him. To reach *Sea Witch* and finish this.

"Get a move on," he yelled at the men, "Can't these bloody beasts go any faster than a crawl?"

The track turned and the harbour was hidden from view again. Another two miles, that was all they need go and they would be there on the jetty; another half-hour, less, if they hurried. And then again the track twisted and he saw the mouth of the river and two other ships. Two Spaniards. One was the coast guard, the other, the larger one, he recognised as *La Santa Isabella*. Don Damián del Gardo's ship.

He fumbled for the telescope in his pocket brought it out, focused on the colours flying from her masthead. The flag of Hispaniola, and the personal pennant of its governor. Del Gardo was aboard, here, not at Santo Domingo where the rebels were massing. He was here, and he was manoeuvring into position to blockade the harbour and blast Jesamiah's beloved *Sea Witch* into firewood. He screamed at the men to hurry, to run, to shift their sorry arses. He could not wait for them; shouted at them to come as quickly as they could to the jetty, and abandoning the track, plunged down through the scrub and undergrowth, slithered over scree and rocks; went straight down the hillside, his gaze fixed on the roofs of Puerto Vaca and the masts of his ship, the *Sea Witch*.

When the door of the Sickle Moon burst open, thumping against the wall behind, the men inside paused and turned, almost as one, to stare at the figure who was striding in. He was bloodstained and grubby, his breeches were torn, a few leaves were caught in his hair. His face and hands were scratched. He stood there, just inside the door the rain-laden daylight streaming in behind him, casting his outline into silhouette. But they knew who he was, and the men rose to their feet and shouted and cheered. They surged forward to embrace him, pump his arm.

"Jesamiah, Jesamiah! *Mon ami, mon brave, mon frère!*" Rue did not know what more to say as joyfully he clasped Jesamiah's hand then abandoned pride and hugged him close, kissed both cheeks. "You are returned, you 'ave escaped? *Ah oui, très, très bien!*"

"You think so?" Jesamiah retorted, as he extricated his wounded arm and firmly persuaded his quartermaster to release him. He glared at the crew's eager faces; young Jasper, Jansy, Toby, Isiah, Nat. Nearly all of them were here, some with tankards of ale, others with tots of rum, most with empty platters on the tables in front of them with the remains of bread and cheese and ham.

"Who is guarding *Sea Witch*?" he asked gruffly. "I went to the jetty. There's no one bloody there. So while you are in here, filling your bellies and waiting to take your turn in that bed I can hear creaking away upstairs, who is watching my ship? Who is watching your back and the harbour entrance?" His anger was intense.

The euphoria died away. Men exchanged glances, then looked towards Rue.

"We 'ave a watch, *mon Capitaine*. Men 'ave remained aboard."

"And how many women are with them? If they are there they ain't watching, Rue. *La Santa Isabella* is a few bloody miles away! We're under blockade, we can't fokken get out, and at any moment it's quite likely they'll blow my ship from the water!"

CHAPTER THIRTY-TWO

Always a stickler for discipline, not one of Jesamiah's crew dawdled or dallied when he said jump. Within a flicker of an eye they were hurrying for the boats and pulling for the *Sea Witch. Kismet*'s crew had also been ensconced in the Sickle Moon, Jesamiah sent them running to load the gunpowder that should soon arrive at the jetty. Before joining them, he had his own small task to complete.

Taking the wooden stairs two at a time, he stamped along the corridor and kicked Mireya's door open. She was naked, sitting astride a man, her head back, circling in time with her hips as she worked him to climax, her large breasts bouncing grotesquely against her stomach. Jesamiah grasped her loose hair and yanked her backwards. Her screech sounding like a scalded cat. The man's roar of protest was abruptly silenced as Jesamiah's cutlass rasped across the flesh at his throat.

"You got an objection, Travis, you can make it to me later in my cabin. Not 'ere, not now. Fetch up y'breeches put y'tackle away and fok off. I want a private word with the lady."

She was hurling abuse at Jesamiah, trying to kick out with her feet, scratch with her nails; hissing and spitting. Jesamiah had dealt with furious whores before, knew how to keep one at arm's length. He pointed the cutlass at her belly, forced her to back away, shouted at her to shut up.

"Shut it I said! Stow it!" He raised his fist, making it seem as if he had every intention to hit her. She screeched again, fled into the corner of the room, grabbing up her gown from a chair as she ran; clutched it to herself to protect her nakedness.

"Now, I ain't goin' t'repeat this," Jesamiah said. "Your pimp, or whoever he is, has buggered off with a fortune in gold and diamonds. He's probably half way across Hispaniola by now. I very much doubt he'll be obeying orders and taking the casket he stole from me to Del Gardo. He'll be finding a ship and telling himself how fortunate he is to be rid of the fat slut he's left behind."

Mireya hurled another string of abuse, cut short by Jesamiah's cutlass pricking into her throat. "I'm doin' the talkin', not you."

He lowered the weapon, wandered over to a small table that held combs, brushes, hairpins, pots and jars. He sorted through the clutter, grunted when he could not find what he wanted, went instead to the clothes press at the foot of the bed. Throwing the lid open, he tossed out, one by one, the few badly folded garments. A none too clean lace-edged petticoat made him smile. He put down his cutlass, produced a dagger from where it nestled within his boot, began to cut away at the lace.

"You leave that alone, you English pig bastard!"

"I can easily make you keep quiet," he drawled as he pointed the dagger at her. He ripped the last bit of lace and unthreaded the strand of blue ribbon that was woven through it. Cut it into two suitable lengths and, rapidly braiding a few strands of his hair, threaded the ribbons through it.

"Now then," he said, sheathing the cutlass but not the dagger, "I strongly suggest you pack what possessions you have, plunder your store of coin and find someone who has a little boat who can take you far away. Very far away. I wouldn't advise you t'stay 'ere, because they know about you, y'see. They know what you are an' 'ow easily that tongue of yours clacks in the wrong people's ears. I'm leaving 'ere, so I don't give a shit about you. But there might be one or two on this island who aren't as gentlemanly as me. Who wouldn't stand 'ere givin' you a polite warnin' but would merely remove your tongue an' 'ave 'done with it. Savvy?"

He left the room, closing the door quietly behind him. Was not surprised to hear what sounded like the chamber pot and the chair crash against it, accompanied by the resumption of a torrent of foul language.

The landlady, Madelene, was at the foot of the stairs, anxiously peering upward.

"Reckon it's 'er wrong time of the month," Jesamiah quipped as he pushed past her. "Yours too, you traitorous bitch. You were made a widow a couple of hours ago."

~You said you were going to help me. ~

~ No, Mother, I said I would think about it. ~

Tethys whined as if she were a petulant child. ~You promised me. ~

Rain made no answer, instead, she played with sending a spray of rain over a palm grove, and watched the leaves sway and bounce as she passed by. She paused above a mountain lake and studied her reflection in its perfect stillness. Was she pretty? No one had ever said she was. No one, not one person, had ever called her beautiful.

She asked her mother. ~ Am I beautiful? ~

Tethys was annoyed with her daughter. She slapped high waves up against a rocky shore and drove a tide inward into a river, washing away the banks and felling trees as she passed.

~ You? You are grey and black and you turn the land to mud. And when you lose interest you leave everything to *dry and rot into dust. You? Beautiful? You are naught but an ungrateful wretch! ~*

Hurt, Rain ran away, not caring what destruction she left in her wake.

She would ask the Witch Woman, she thought, but she could not find her. She searched, but still could not find her. Instead she saw the man again, he was striding up and down a wooden jetty, waving his arms at his men who were hauling barrels on to a boat.

He looked magnificent as he walked, his black hair tossing, his blue ribbons flying behind him. She liked blue, it was a nicer, happier colour than grey. She wished she could be dressed in blue. Wished the man could be hers, for unlike her, he and his blue ribbons were beautiful.

And then they had finished with the barrels and he was stepping aboard the boat, and the boat, she knew, was going to sail upon the sea.

He was going back to her mother!

CHAPTER THIRTY-THREE

Thunder was rolling in from the open sea; storm-black clouds were streaming overhead, building thicker and denser by the minute. If the storms they had already experienced had been bad, this one promised to be worse. The sea was churning into a rising swell that slapped and ground at the keels of the two Spanish ships lurking beyond the river mouth. That was one hope in Jesamiah's favour, the wind was wrong for them. All Don Damián could do was ride the swell—and he would have to keep relatively clear, for too easily he could be blown on to the rocky shore on the western side, or into the mangrove swamp, where the water ran too shallow for his keel.

In harbour, *Kismet* was tugging at her moorings. *Sea Witch* anchored in the river, was lifting and dipping with each incoming wave that swept below her, to wash with a boom and toss of spray against the jetty and the shore. Jesamiah had secured his belt on the outside of his coat to stop it flapping and getting in his way. He tightened the buckle one notch. His cutlass, his pistol, bullet pouch and powder flask, had all gone across with most of the men to *Sea Witch*. He would not be needing them aboard *Kismet*.

Ensuring the last keg of gunpowder was roped into place in the forward hold, he nodded at the landsman to cast her off, yelled for the topmen to loose sail and meet her as she rapidly swung away with the wind the moment she was set free. Rue was wrestling with the tiller to keep control. They needed as much sail as she could carry. It did not matter if it was too much; they did not have far to go, as long as she held for as long as it took to reach *La Santa Isabella*. Glancing across at *Sea Witch*, Jesamiah was relieved to see her, in the capable hands of Nat and Isiah, weighing her anchor, the men trundling around and around the capstan, hauling in the heavy cable. She was to follow behind, but ease over to near the swamp and heave to in the lee of the wind. Shallow on the draught she could sit over there quite comfortably until she was needed to play her part. It would be a tricky manoeuvre, but *Sea Witch* was capable of doing it, even in this worsening weather.

Kismet's fore tops'l was set; main tops'l set. Jesamiah cupped his hands around his mouth and yelled angrily at the men aloft, asking what the fok did they think they were doing. "Who said to reef? I never gave no orders for no reefs! Shake it out! Loose all sail, there!"

The orders went contrary to normal storm routine, but this was not normal. It was definitely not normal for a vessel to be making way as the sky turned black, with lightning splitting it almost in two. Nor was it normal for such a vessel to be heading bow-straight towards an enemy, but that was what the *Kismet* was doing.

"Is the gig away?" Jesamiah asked Rue.

The Frenchman nodded, "*Oui*, trailing right behind us as if she is a puppy-dog's tail, Capitaine."

Good. The risk was that *La Santa Isabella*, the guardship, or both, would open their ports and start firing, but the sea was so rough would they be fool enough to do so? They would be awash in minutes.

Without warning the wind hauled round three points and *Kismet* lurched to larboard, her canvas cracking like shot muskets before she paid off again. They were nearing where the river widened and spilt into the sea, the waves had grown higher and lumpier, causing her to plunge and buck. She had too much sail; the masts and stays were creaking and straining. The crew were white faced, anxious. Several crossed themselves.

Sea Witch, approaching her station, had been caught nearly aback, but Nat knew what he was doing. Jesamiah paid them no more heed. He had to concentrate on what he was doing here, else this whole stupid idea would be a waste of effort. The wind was shrieking as if it were an Irish Banshee and the rain tipped down as a solid sheet. *Kismet* dipped to below her forward rails as the open sea rose to meet her, came up again with water streaming from the forward scuppers. Already there were several inches sloshing around below deck. Jesamiah grimaced; if the powder or fuses should get wet...

Any minute now *La Santa Isabella* could fire at them, but so far she was too busy merely staying upright as the wind and sea tore at her. They were in trouble out there. The men aboard her were frantically trying to bring her round into the wind, but Jesamiah could see they had left it too late —they missed stays and she lumbered to a halt. All Jesamiah needed were a few more minutes, but at sea, with a ship at the mercy of the elements, a minute was a long time. Anything could happen in those long, sixty seconds.

Another squall whooshed across the river mouth and caught the guardship. Further out than *La Santa Isabella*, not so well built, she was wallowing like a fat old hog. As the wind hit her, and the rain almost blurred all visibility, she suddenly laid right over.

Hanging on to the mizzen rigging Jesamiah almost lost his footing as *Kismet* also rolled, but lighter, better handled, she steadied, plunged on. The wind was howling around them and through the rigging, the sea yawned ahead, almost engulfing her bow as she dipped, the ship clawing her way out from the clinging grasp of Tethys's lust and greed, as she struggled upward again.

Rue yelled something. Instinctively Jesamiah looked back at his beloved *Sea Witch* but she was in position and in no relative harm.

"*Non, non*! There, there!" Rue was pointing ahead, to where the guardship had been.

"My God, she's gone down!" Jesamiah said, and cursed. Why could it not have been *La Santa Isabella*? But then that would have ruined everything. He did not want the sea to finish del Gardo, he wanted to do it himself.

This was it. They were near enough. The point of no return. Jesamiah hurried forward, slipping and sliding on the wet decks, ducking his face against each sweep of spray as it surged over the rails. He let himself down the forward scuttle, was relieved to find the lantern he had left there was still burning. Was satisfied that it was dry enough down here for what he wanted to do. He took up a slow-match, lit it, blew it to life. Held it to the hastily arrayed trail of fuses and waited those few precious seconds to ensure they were fizzing and sputtering towards the stacked barrels of gunpowder. Would they be sufficient, he wondered? Fawkes had reckoned he needed about thirty barrels or so to blow up Parliament. These few should be ample.

Whirling, he turned, ran back on deck, hurried aft. They had not seemed to make much headway, but with the hail and the wind and almost consuming storm-darkness it was difficult to see anything anyway. Anything except the big Spaniard looming ahead.

"Abandon ship you men!" Jesamiah called as he reached to take the tiller from Rue. "Get your arses off here."

They did not need a second telling. Clinging to the cable rigged from the rails to the gig, they were out, over the side, coughing and spluttering as the sea tried all she could to wash them away. In case they fell, Jesamiah had chosen these men especially for their ability to swim, though he guessed, with those fuses burning any man would have learnt pretty damned quickly.

Rue grabbed at him. "Come on, Jesamiah. Tie off the tiller, let us jump together."

"I'll hold her a little longer, go on, you go. Cut the gig free and row for the *Sea Witch*."

"You are coming, *mon brave*?" Standing up on the rail, Rue hesitated, was suddenly sceptical and worried, his captain had been in a most peculiar mood this past hour.

"Course I am. Get going."

Rue jumped.

"God be with you my friend." Jesamiah had no intention of following him. His plan was simple. Sail straight for *La Santa Isabella*, plough into her, and blow her up.

In a maniacal way, Jesamiah found it exhilarating to stand on the shallow quarterdeck with the wind screaming its raging fury around him, matching his inner madness. The heavy roll and lift, sway and dip as *Kismet* lurched and tossed verging on near loss of control, as if she were a horse rearing then bucking, close to throwing her rider and bolting away headlong. He found the sheer effort of having to keep her steady as the sails cracked and billowed exciting, almost to the point of arousal. If he was to die, as he must, this was how he wanted it to be, pitching himself against the sea and the storm. And ridding the world of an evil bastard who raped women and murdered children. Why he was doing this he did not know. He was too angry, too hurt, to understand his motives. All he knew was that he wanted Don Damián del Gardo dead, and if he was to also die in the process, well, a quick end was preferable to the pain that was ripping his insides apart.

Every stay and shroud was vibrating and humming almost to screaming point. No captain in his right mind would be driving a ship so hard in such conditions, but

Jesamiah was not in his right mind, and what did it matter if *Kismet* was tearing herself to pieces? In less than a minute she would be nothing but smoke and flame anyway. Another tearing cry of thunder shattering overhead, the rain fell hard, beating at him as if it were a woman pounding him with her fists. An explosion roared—Jesamiah started, fearing he had set the fuses too short, but it was the maintops'l ripping into a mass of flapping and twisting streamers. The *Kismet* slewed to starboard, he lost control.

The thunder was cracking so relentlessly that he was not noticing it any more. Lightning was flickering and streaking over and around and through the black clouds. A broken stay fell from aloft and was writhing about on its shackling halyards like a demented sea serpent. More would soon be following.

On *La Santa Isabella*, no one had appeared to notice him—they were too busy gawping at where the guardship had been. Then someone saw the *Kismet*. Too late, for although she was yawing away from Jesamiah and he had totally lost steerage, her bowsprit was only feet from ploughing into the Spaniard's bow—with a great rip of splintering wood her momentum carried her on and forward. Railings, timber, spars, everything was shattering, tearing and splintering and screaming her death knell.

Men were running about in panic aboard the Spaniard, shouting, pointing at the *Kismet*, waving their arms as if that would magically remove her from their own bowsprit. Was that del Gardo himself among them? Jesamiah could not be certain, for he was looking up into another face, one that was staring back at him in open mouthed horror and hatred. How van Overstratten had got to be standing there Jesamiah did not know. Did not have time to think or worry about it, for the fuses blew and what was left of the *Kismet* erupted into savage hell, taking the forward half of *La Santa Isabella* with her.

Tethys rose up in a wall of green water. The sea had claimed one vessel and the lives of every man aboard, but she wanted more, she wanted him! And at last, at last, as the remains of the *Kismet* burnt and sank, she had him!

The water filled Tiola's mouth, the roaring in her ears shattering through her, deafening her as she sank with Jesamiah beneath the churning foam of water that was littered by burning debris and dead and dying men. She was with Jesamiah, as one with him, felt every sense, heard every sound; took that last, instinctive, gasping breath with him, trying to keep air in his lungs as Tethys sucked him down.

~ *Why Jesamiah? Why?* ~ Tiola did not understand. She could not comprehend the deliberate wasting of his own life. ~ *Why? Why!* ~

He made no answer to her pleading cries. Perhaps he did not hear, perhaps he did not choose to hear. Perhaps, it was already too late for him to hear. She would not give him up without a fight! All she had to do was keep him breathing and get him to the surface.

Tiola rarely panicked, but on this occasion she did. She screamed and screamed as Tethys wove her embrace around him, screamed her agony and despair as Jesamiah drowned.

CHAPTER THIRTY-FOUR

Rue clung to the bouncing and rocking gig that somehow, against all odds, had managed to stay afloat, despite the huge mountain of water that had seemed to boil upward from the destruction of the two vessels. The green face of the wave had built and built and then curled over, white foaming at its crest, to hurtle up the river, destroying everything along the banks as it passed. Bringing down trees and buildings, rocks and rubble. Sweeping live creatures into its gape, and tearing vegetation out by the roots. One of his strong hands was clasped around the gig's rigging, the other was twisted into Jesamiah's collar.

By chance, as the torrential rain had momentarily cleared, Rue had seen him thrown into the sea by the force of the blast as *Kismet* had exploded. He had cried out to the men to pull for their very lives, staring and staring at the spot where he had seen Jesamiah go in. And he was there, floating face down! His black hair waving, his blue ribbons so distinctive! Rue grabbed, held on, and the rain, mercifully, eased. Using all his strength, his muscles straining, Rue heaved, struggling to bring Jesamiah's inert body aboard. It was almost as if unseen hands were holding his captain back, clasping him in a vice-like grip determined to keep him there in the sea. But Rue won the battle, and he rolled Jesamiah over the rail, flopped with him to the bottom of the boat to lie there gasping like a landed fish.

Jesamiah opened his eyes, twisted to his side and spewed water from his lungs. After a while, he struggled to his knees. "It'll come back," he puffed. "The wave will have a pull-back. It'll go in hard but unable to spend itself, will pull back and spill where it can." Ashen faced, trembling, he looked at Rue and smiled. "Thank you my friend. Thank you for saving me."

Rue merely stated, "You are a fool."

The surge wave, having reached its height and limit of forward momentum was slithering backwards, returning from whence it came, as Jesamiah said it would. The sucking, squealing noise as it retreated to its own domain of the ocean was horrible to hear as it scooped up everything it could in its grasp as plunder. Trees, lumps of masonry and timber. Small, wrecked fishing boats. Lobster pots, barrels, crates. The carcasses of the drowned. Animal and human. For ages it seemed to slide back and back, and Jesamiah and Rue and the men clung to the sides of the tossing gig until their fingernails bled. The sea was angry and it swirled and lashed at everything it could, boiling with its torrents of green, icy death. But the storm, too, was not finished. In the wake of an ear-splitting crash of thunder another squall came racing down from the hills. Rain scythed across the flooded village of Puerto Vaca and beat down upon the surface of the heaving sea. It stung the men's flesh, drummed against the planking of the gig and hissed into the several inches of water slopping in the bottom. The sea was churning with its own wrath, fighting back, a great battle between the water of the oceans and its daughter, the rain of the skies. A battle for domination, a force of wills. Two elementals pitched in brutal savagery one against the other.

Rain had always hated her mother, and the Witch Woman had been kind to her.

~ *Save Jesamiah. Please Rain, save the man I love. Do not give him to your mother. She will take him down into the darkness of her world, and he is so frightened of being shut away in the dark. ~*

Rain knew that. She had seen his fear when he had been in that tower. And she had seen his smile and his beautiful eyes. He had smiled at her when he had seen her in her form of the Grey Lady. Smiled and saluted her.

~ No, I will not help you, Witch Woman, I think it is best for you to fight your own battles with my mother. But I will help him. For so few see me and smile. ~

The rain battered at the sea with such force that it stirred the surface into a froth of yeasty foam. She drove upon the ocean relentlessly and unremorsefully, without pity or mercy, beating, bullying her mother down. Driving horizontally she forced Tethys to subside, pounding at the high, crested waves until they were flattened into submission.

And then the rain stopped as suddenly as it had started. The storm was gone, and the sea was flat and calm.

CHAPTER THIRTY-FIVE

Jesamiah and Rue lay in the bottom of the gig, sodden, breathless and battered. The men rested on the oars, their energy spent. The sickening bobbing was easing, and the sky overhead was paling brighter into a fresh blue. The black clouds were rolling away into the distance as quickly as they had come.

"I hope that's the end of the rain," Jesamiah remarked. "As much as I don't mind a dousing, I'm sure I'm getting webbed, bloody feet."

Rue could only nod, too exhausted to answer.

Raising his head, Jesamiah searched for the *Sea Witch*, found her hove to where she was meant to be, over by what was left of the mangrove swamp. The mangroves would survive, so would the palm trees, and the vegetation would re-grow. The village, when Jesamiah turned to look was battered and damaged, but much of it had survived. Although the Sickle Moon had gone. The overhang of rocks had tumbled down and engulfed it. Jesamiah was not sorry to see its demise.

Every bone in his body was broken, or so it felt. He would not be surprised to find, when he stripped his clothes, that he was bruised blue and black from head to foot. Giving encouragement, he chivvied the men into pulling for his beloved ship. It was over. Finished. What the islanders did with their rebellion was up to them, but del Gardo was dead, and very likely, because of it, so was the rebellion. What was there to fight against now that the prime object of their hatred was removed?

He wondered if he would see 'Cesca again. Doubted it. Was partially sorry, but then, he did not need her, for he had his Tiola back.

~ *Jesamiah?* ~

~ *Yes sweetheart?* ~

~ *Are you all right?* ~

~ *Not really.* ~

~ *Will you come and get me? I am waiting for you at La Sorenta.* ~

~ *Do you doubt that I would not?* ~

She sent him the feeling of a loving embrace and her lips touching his. No, she did not doubt it.

There were many dead floating in the water. Two Spanish ships had gone down; men had drowned, men had been blown to pieces by an explosion of gunpowder. Some of the bodies were not whole, some had horrendous burns. Gunpowder was not a kindly stuff. Jesamiah vaguely searched the dead, hoping to find what remained of del Gardo. A movement caught his eye. He frowned, peered over the side, saw a man feebly trying to swim. Recognised the bastard's arrogant face; watched him struggling, watched him trying to reach for a piece of wood to use as a float. Why did the fool not give up and die? Jesamiah looked away, pretended he had not seen.

Tiola would ask. She would want to know what had happened to Stefan. He would tell her he had seen the bastard's dead body and then all this would be over. No, he could not do that, Tiola always knew when he lied. How could he be honest about it? *He is dead, sweetheart, I watched him drown.*

Jesamiah swore and ordered the men to alter course. He leant over the side and made a grab for van Overstratten's hand.

"Stefan, take hold! Come on man, you are alive, we have survived. Make an effort!"

Close to complete exhaustion, the Dutchman looked up and saw Jesamiah Acorne.

"*Donder der op naar de hell!*"

Jesamiah did not understand what the Dutch meant, but he could roughly guess.

"There was no indigo," Jesamiah said. "Jennings used both of us. We have both been played for fools." He leant further out, made a grab for Stefan's coat. Missed. A little bit more... a little more.

Was that movement in the mud-churned water behind Stefan? Debris floated everywhere, several uprooted trees, trunks had already bumped against the gig's hull. A log was floating towards Stefan. Perhaps the man would be better to grab at that?

Jesamiah shouted, urgently reached out as far as he could. "Come to me! Kick hard man! Come on! Come on!"

That was no log! It had eyes and teeth and jaws, and its home among the salty mangrove swamps had been destroyed, making it angry. Jesamiah touched Stefan's fingers, strained forward, caught his wrist, clung on. Gasping with relief he hauled, Stefan's grip curling into his own. Rue was beside him, also leaning down, reaching out.

"I have you!" Jesamiah cried, "I have you!"

And then Stefan shook his head and stared up into Jesamiah's eyes. "*Jij wint piraat. Zorg goed voor haar,*" he said, repeating it in English as, deliberately, he let go.

The muddied water churned into a sudden, brief, flurry of white foam and red blood as the swamp crocodile closed its jaws around Stefan and took him under.

The words, *You win pirate. Take care of her,* echoed in Jesamiah's head. Stupidly, incongruously, he sat there in the water at the bottom of the gig, and wept.

As the storm abated and the sea calmed, Tiola spoke to Tethys.

~ Why do you pursue Jesamiah? Why do you try to take him from me? ~

~ Because I have only daughters and I want a son! Because he is mine! He was born in the sea and I want him to stay with me, to be mine! ~

Tiola threw back her head and laughed, not unkindly, but amused. ~ But he has always been yours, Tethys! You do not have to take him to where he will become nothing more than bones and rotting flesh to keep him. Always, it will be his ship and the sea that are important to Jesamiah. Always, he will answer and come to you when you call, not to me. He loves me, but he belongs to you. He is of the sea. He always will be. But if you take him now, he will die and the light and the life that is his will be gone forever. ~

Tethys was silent as she listened and mulled the words in the shifting tides of her mind.

~ Do you want him as a corpse, my Lady of the Sea? Or do you want his laughter and his joy, his strength and his beauty? Where the sea is trapped upon the shore, there is no movement. There is no tide, there is no surf, there are no waves. Just old, stagnant water that dries to nothing more than salt. Do you prefer that pool as your realm, or do you prefer the wide freedom of the glorious ocean? Would you prefer the dead bones of a man or the vibrancy of his life? ~

Tethys was crooning, almost crying, a sound of waves upon the shore. ~ Jessh...a...miah. Jessh...a...miah. ~

~ I say again Tethys, he always has been yours. He always will be. He loves the sea. He cannot exist without being on or near you, the sea. ~

Tiola waited for an answer. It was a long time in coming.

At last, Tethys subsided into the depth of her realm to think about the witch-woman's words. Was he, indeed, hers? As he always had been. Always would be?

At least, for now.

CHAPTER THIRTY-SIX

THURSDAY EVENING

Jesamiah slept for almost two days. He awoke once and cried out in misery, but Tiola was there, beside him, her arms around him, her voice crooning and comforting, hushing him back to sleep. Over and over she repeated that it was all right, that everything was all right. He buried his head in her lap and wept, and murmured that it was not.

"'Cesca told me the truth," he admitted through his tears. "All those years when I was a child I endured the humiliations, and the pain and the fear. I need not have done. I should not have done."

Tiola, kissed him, held him tight and close, said nothing, let him talk. Let him release the hurt that was eating into him.

Jesamiah looked up at her, tiredness etched into his bereaved face. "My father," he said, "had only one son. He gave the other his name out of honour for the woman, but the child was not his son. He had no right to the name Mereno. Had no right to be there in Virginia. Had no right to anything."

"Oh Jesamiah, Jesamiah!" Tiola's heart was breaking along with his.

"I suffered all that for nothing. Phillipe was not my brother." His breath shuddered as he finally acknowledged the truth and confessed it to the woman he adored. "Del Gardo fathered him through an act of rape. My father gave his mother refuge, a home and a name, but he was *my* father. Not Phillipe's. My father gave him everything that should have been mine. Even his love. Why? Why?" Jesamiah's distress was consuming him, all those years of pain and fear running in a blind panic of returning memories.

"Father knew how Phillipe treated me, he knew of the cuts and the bruises and the fear, but he did nothing. He knew all that, and knew he was not my bloody brother! Knew he had no right to be there! He was my father, yet he abandoned me to the sadistic evils of that fucking bastard!"

His voice cracked as he spewed the next words. "The times Phillipe called me a bastard, the times he made me call my mother a whore! And it wasn't me! It wasn't me who was the bastard, nor my mother the whore!"

All Tiola could do was hold him and hush him to sleep, and hope the pain of knowing the truth had not stabbed too deep, that eventually he would come to understand why his father, why Charles Mereno, had acted as he did.

One day, perhaps, she would be able to show him why. One day, but not yet.

CHAPTER THIRTY-SEVEN

SUNDAY AFTERNOON

Exasperated, Jesamiah swept the charts scattered over his mahogany table to the floor, strode across his cabin and taking the rum from the cabinet poured himself a more than generous measure.

"That will not solve your problems," Tiola observed, not looking up from the book she was reading. It was one of the things she loved about Jesamiah, his ability to take a breath and carry on, regardless of what cruelties life hurled at him.

"No, but it makes me feel better."

With a sigh, Tiola uncurled her legs and leaving the book on the window seat went to him. She threaded her arms around his waist and tucked her head into his shoulder. "Can I help?" she offered.

"Aye, you can conjure up a wind that will take us far away to where there are islands with plenty of fresh water and meat. Where there are no storms, no waiting gallows, and no bloody Royal Navy frigates under command of a certain Commodore Edward Vernon about to appear over the horizon, ready to blow us to Kingdom Come."

Finch bustled in, grumbled about the mess. "Can't you keep this bloody place tidy fer one bloody minute? What'm I supposed to do fer yer dinner then? I got a nice bit of ox tongue."

"That'll be fine Finch, thank you," Jesamiah answered.

"An what'll I do with that Spaniard, de Castilla? Do I let 'im out now or keep 'im locked away?"

"Let him out if you wish."

"'E keeps as sayin' 'ow he wants to join us."

"Whatever for?" Tiola asked, astonished. "I thought he hated us, hated Jesamiah?"

Finch was picking up the charts and sliding them back into their drawer beneath Jesamiah's desk. "'E do. Apparently 'e 'as a wife 'e 'ates even more."

Jesamiah laughed. "Half the men aboard *Sea Witch* are here for the same reason." He tapped his finger on to the tip of Tiola's nose. "Start worrying, lass, when I talk about transferring to a different ship."

"You want coffee then?"

"Yes please, Finch."

Sniffing loudly Finch laid the last chart on the table. He stabbed a tobacco and tar-stained finger in the middle of it. "It's this one yer want. The Bahamas. New Providence Island."

"Thank you Finch. You may go."

Alone again, Jesamiah rested his chin on Tiola's head. "I don't know why I put up with him."

"For a similar reason as to why I put up with you?"

"What? Because he's handsome, charming, fun to be with and good in bed? I don't think so!"

Tiola laughed, which made Jesamiah laugh.

He needed to make peace with himself, and his past, but he also had to make peace with the present, for Commodore Vernon would be seeking him out and there were things he had to say to Henry Jennings. Several bones to pick over. And a few diamonds to be delivered?

Jesamiah had thought to keep the large handfuls that he had in his pocket, but then he had figured that perhaps were he to get them to Jennings he could bargain some form of pardon for the crew.

"Finch is right, you should return to Nassau."

Jesamiah snorted and walked away from Tiola, went to the rum for a refill. Maybe, but not just yet. He had to gather the courage to sail into a lion's den first.

"Jennings sent you to Hispaniola, my luvver. You did what he asked of you. He can sort things out."

"Oh aye, sort things as far as the noose!"

"Your coffee." Finch trundled in with a tray of coffee pot, sugar bowl and cups. He liked to do things properly when Tiola was aboard. Beside the pot rested a black leather tobacco pouch.

"You'll be needin' this an' all I reckon. I assume you've been lookin' all over fer it? Bloody fine captain you are, loosin' things so bleedin' important. Get us all 'anged one day, the way you bloody carry on." He stomped to the door, said as he went out. "Dinner in 'alf an 'our."

Tiola was at a loss. "Why would you be wanting to look for a tobacco pouch? You do not smoke."

Frowning, Jesamiah set his rum glass down and slowly picked the pouch up. "It belongs to Henry Jennings. He dropped it that night twelve days ago when I had to run from Nassau."

My God, he thought, *was it only twelve days? It feels more like a lifetime.* "At the time I wondered..." He paused, said slower, "At the time I half wondered if he had deliberately dropped it."

His fingers flew to open the pouch, excitement lighting his face. "The wily old dog!" he laughed. "The cunning old bastard!" He pulled out the folded paper inside, opened it, laughed again and twirled Tiola around his cabin.

"Finch!" he yelled, "Finch, I love you, you miserable, ugly, wonderful old git."

From the galley a rattle of pots and pans and a scathing, extremely rude, retort.

Tiola was reading what was on the letter. It was signed by Henry Jennings and bore Woodes Rogers' official seal.

"It's a Letter of Marque, sweetheart," Jesamiah explained. "It states that in the interest of declared war with Spain, whatever action I followed I was doing with the express approval of the King's representative of the Bahamas Colony of Nassau, New Providence Island. We've been legal all the time! We can go home with flags flying and heads high —and not have a single word spoken against us!"

He laughed again, grinned like the rogue he was. "And thinking it over, I might just as well be keeping those diamonds for m'self, eh?"

Rain was happy as she danced off across the land, for the black-haired Witch Woman had said that there was nothing more beautiful than a clear, rain-washed, sapphire-blue sky, and the glorious triple arc of a perfectly formed rainbow.

THE END

DROP ANCHOR

AUTHOR'S NOTE

The first Voyage in this series, *Sea Witch*, had at least a skeleton framework of historical fact as a basic plot, for *Pirate Code* I had to invent a story from beginning to end. Sad to say, none of it actually happened.

Woodes Rogers was a real person, he was Governor of Nassau on New Providence Island in the Bahamas. He did have financial difficulties because the men who had sponsored his circumnavigation of the world procrastinated about paying his share of the spoils, and he financed much of the refortification of Nassau out of his own pocket. Some years later than this adventure is set, he ended up heavily in debt. Henry Jennings existed and so did Captain Edward Vernon—although I have no idea if they were in the Bahamas in 1718.

There *was* a rebellion on Hispaniola (now known as the Dominican Republic) but not at this time—although who knows, maybe an earlier uprising just never got off the ground and was not recorded.

The one fact that is true; there was a brief war with Spain around 1718 and Woodes Rogers did rescind the agreement of amnesty for the Caribbean pirate community. The pirates were expected to set sail and fight for England. Pirates being pirates, most of them decided that the British Government was not worth fighting for and went to fight on the side of Spain instead. I like to think the idea was initiated by my Jesamiah.

There is one other small reference to a real person, Edward Teach. The notorious pirate, Blackbeard. He will take a major role in the next voyage, *Bring It Close*. And you may be wondering what happened to that ebony casket? You will find out in Voyage Five—*On the Account*.

Helen Hollick
2019

Plan of the sails and masts of a square-rigged ship

Sails

1	Flying Jib	8	Main Topgallant Royal
2	Jib	9	Main Topgallant
3	Fore Staysail	10	Main Topsail
4	Fore Topgallant Royal	11	Mainsail or Main Course
5	Fore Topgallant Sail (pronounced *t'gan's'l*)	12	Mizzen Topsail
6	Fore Topsail (pronounced *tops'l*)	13	Mizzen Sail
7	Foresail or Fore Course		

Masts

A	Bowsprit/Jib-boom	F	Main Topmast
B	Foremast	G	Main Topgallant Mast
C	Fore Topmast	H	Mizzenmast
D	Fore Topgallant Mast	I	Mizzen Topmast
E	Main Mast	J	Ensign and Ensign Staff

Glossary

Various sailing terms used throughout the *Sea Witch* Voyages

Aback—a sail when its forward surface is pressed upon by the wind. Used to 'stop' a ship.

A-cockbill—having the tapered ends turned upward. Said of the anchor when it is hanging ready from the cathead.

Aloft—up in the tops, at the masthead or anywhere about the yards or the rigging.

Articles—Each man when coming aboard 'agreed the Articles'. Some pirate ships were run on very democratic lines. The crew elected their captain, agreed where to sail, divided the 'spoils' fairly etc. Most rules were sensible things like no naked flame below deck, each man to keep his weapon clean and ready for use; and no fighting aboard ship.

Bar—a shoal running across the mouth of a harbour or a river.

Bare poles—having no sail up, the bare mast.

Belay—to make fast or secure. Also: 'Stop that', 'Belay that talk!' would mean 'Shut up!'.

Belaying pin—a short wooden rod to which a ship's rigging is secured. A common improvised weapon aboard a sailing ship because they are everywhere, are easily picked up, and are the right size and weight to be used as a club.

Bell — (ship's bell)—used as a clock, essential for navigation as the measurement of the angle of the sun had to be made at noon. The bell was struck each time the half-hour glass was turned.

Best bower—the larboard (or port) side anchor. There are usually two identical anchors on the bows of a vessel, the second one is the small-bower.

Bilge—the lowest part of the ship inside the hull along the keel. They fill with stinking bilge water or 'bilge'. Can also mean nonsense or foolish talk.

Binnacle—the frame or box that houses the compass.

Bosun—short for boatswain, usually a competent sailor who is in charge of all deck duties.

Bosun's chair—a platform on ropes made to form a chair-like structure, and hauled aboard.

Bow—the front or 'pointed' end of the ship.

Bowsprit—the heavy slanted spar pointing forward from the ship's bow.

Brace—rope used to control the horizontal movement of a square-rigged yard.

Brig—a two-masted vessel square-rigged on both masts.

Brimstone—formerly the common name for sulphur.

Broadside—the simultaneous firing of all guns on one side of a ship.

Bulkheads—vertical partitions in a ship.

Bulwark—the raised wooden 'walls' running along the sides of a ship above the level of the deck.

Cable—1) a long, thick and heavy rope by which a ship is secured to the anchor. 2) A measurement of length = 120 fathoms or 240 yards.

Capstan—a drum-like winch turned by the crew to raise or lower the anchors or other heavy gear.

Careen—the process of beaching a ship, heeling her over to her side and cleaning the underside of weed, barnacles and worm; making essential repairs to the part of a ship which is usually below the waterline. A careened ship will go faster and last longer than one that is not.

Cathead—vertical beam of timber protruding near the bow, used for hoisting the anchor.

Cat o'nine tails, or 'cat'—a whip with many lashes, used for flogging.

Caulk—to seal the gaps between planks of wood with caulking (see Oakum).

Chain shot—two balls of iron joined together by a length of chain, chiefly used to destroy masts, rigging and sails.

Chandler—a merchant selling the various things a ship needs for supplies and repairs.

Chanty/shanty—a sailor's work song. Often lewd and derogatory about the officers.

Chase—or Prize. The ship being pursued.

Cleat—wooden or metal fastening to which ropes can be secured. Can also be used as a ladder.

Clew—the lower corners of a sail, therefore 'Clew up'—to haul a square sail up to a yard.

Close-hauled—sailing as close to the direction of the wind as possible with the sails turned almost ninety degrees.

Cordage—rope is called cordage on board a ship.

Colours—the vessel's identification flag, also called an ensign. For a pirate, the Jolly Roger!

Courses—lowest sails on the mast.

Crosstrees—horizontal cross-timbers partway up a mast to keep the shrouds spread apart.

Deadeyes—a round, flat, wooden block with three holes through which a lanyard, or rope, can be thread to tighten the shrouds.

Dolphin striker—a short perpendicular gaff spar under the cap of the bowsprit for guying down the jib-boom. Also called a martingale.

Doubloon—a Spanish gold coin.

Drang—a narrow passageway between buildings.

Drashed—Devonshire word for thrashed, a beating.

Fathom—a depth of six feet of water.

Flukes—the broad parts, or palms, of the anchor.

Fore or for'ard—toward the front end of the ship, the bow.

Forecastle—pronounced 'fo'c'sle'; raised deck at the front of a ship.

Fore-and-aft—the length of a ship.

Forestay—the rope leading from the mast to the bow.

Fother—to seal a leak by lowering a sail over the side of the ship and positioning it so that it seals the hole by the weight of the sea.

Futtocks—'foot hooks'.

Futtock shroud—short pieces of rope which secure lower deadeyes and futtock plates to the top mast rigging.

Galleon—a large three-masted square-rigged ship used chiefly by the Spanish.

Galley—ship's kitchen.

Gaol / gaoler—pronounced 'jail' and 'jailer'.

Gasket—a piece of rope to fasten the sails to the yards.

Grenados—early form of hand grenade.

Grapeshot—or grape, small cast iron balls bound together in a canvas bag that scatter like shotgun pellets when fired.

Gunwale—pronounced 'gun'l'; upper planking along the sides of a vessel. 'Up to the gunwales'—full up or overloaded.

Halliard or halyard—pronounced 'haly'd'. The rope used to hoist a sail.

Hard tack—ship's biscuit. Opposite is soft tack—bread.

Hatch—an opening in the deck for entering below.

Hawser—cable.

Heave to—to check the forward motion of a vessel and bring her to a standstill by heading her into the wind and backing some of her sails.

Heel—to lean over due to action of the wind, waves or greater weight on one side. The angle at which the vessel tips when sailing.

Helm—the tiller (a long steering arm) or a wheel which controls the rudder and enables the vessel to be steered.

Hold—the lower space below the decks for cargo.

Hull—the sides of a ship which sit in and above the water.

Hull cleats—the 'ladder' or steps attached to the hull via which entry is gained to the entry port.

Hull down—a vessel when it is so far away from the observer the hull is invisible owing to the shape of the earth's surface. Opposite to hull up.

Jack Ketch—the hangman. To dance with Jack Ketch is to hang.

Jolly boat—a small boat, a dinghy.

Jolly Roger—the pirates' flag, called the jolie rouge, although its original meaning is unknown. The hoisted flag was an invitation to surrender, with the implication that those who did so would be treated well and no quarter given to those who did not.

Jury-rigged—makeshift repairs.

Kedge—a small anchor used for mooring to keep the vessel secure and clear of her mooring ropes while she rides in a tidal harbour or river. Also used to warp (haul) a ship from one part of the harbour to another by dropping the kedge anchor, securing a hawser to its wooden or iron stock and hauling the line in.

Keel—the lowest part of the hull below the water.

Keelhaul—an unpleasant punishment: the victim is dragged through the water passing under the keel, either from side to side or bow to stern.

Knot—one nautical mile per hour.

Landlubber—(or lubber) a non-sailor.

Langrage—jagged pieces of sharp metal used as shot. Especially useful for damaging rigging and killing men.

Larboard—pronounced 'larb'd'; the left side of a ship when facing the bow (front). Changed in the nineteenth century to 'port'.

Lead line—(pronounced 'led') a length of rope used to determine the depth of water.

Lee—the side or direction away from the wind i.e downwind.

Lee shore—the shore on to which the wind is blowing, a hazardous shore for a sailing vessel particularly in strong winds.

Leeches—the vertical edges of a square sail.

Letter of Marque—Papers issued by a government during wartime entitling a privately owned ship to raid enemy commerce or attack enemy ships.

Lubberly—in an amateur way, as a landlubber would do.

Luff—the order to the helmsman to put the tiller towards the lee side of the ship in order to make it sail nearer to the direction of the wind.

Marlinspike—a pointed iron tool used to part strands of rope so that they can be spliced.

Maroon—a punishment for breaking a pirate ship's Articles or rules. The victim was left on a deserted coast (or an island) with little in the way of supplies. Therefore, no one could say the unlucky pirate had been killed by his former brethren.

Mast—vertical spar supporting the sails.

Molly boy—a homosexual prostitute.

Oakum—a material used to waterproof seams between planks on deck etc. Made of strong, pliable, tarred fibres obtained from scrap rope or rags which swell when wet.

On the Account—or the 'sweet trade'; a man who went 'on the account' was turning pirate.

Ope—an opening or passageway between buildings.

Painter—a rope attached to a boat's bow for securing or towing.

Piece of Eight—a Spanish silver coin worth one peso or eight reales. It was sometimes literally cut into eight pieces, each worth one real. In the 1700s a piece of eight was worth a little under a modern five shillings sterling, or 25p—this would be about £15 - £20 today. One side usually had the Spanish coat of arms, the other two lines symbolising the limits of the old world at the Straits of Gibraltar, the exit into the Atlantic Ocean from the Mediterranean. In later designs two hemispheres were added between the lines representing the Old and New Worlds. Pieces of eight were so widely used that eventually this sign was turned into the dollar sign—$.

Privateer—an armed vessel bearing letters of marque, or one of her crew, or her captain. A 'privateer' is theoretically a law-abiding combatant.

Quarterdeck—a deck at the rear of a ship where the officers stood and where the helm is usually situated.

Quartermaster—usually the second in command aboard a pirate ship. In the Royal Navy, the man in charge of the provisions.

Rail—timber plank along the top of the gunwale above the sides of the vessel.

Rake—when a ship strakes another with a broadside of cannon.

Ratlines—pronounced 'ratlins'; horizontal lines tied across the shrouds to form a rope ladder for climbing aloft.

Reef—1) an underwater obstruction of rock or coral. 2) to reduce the size of the sails by tying them partially up, either to slow the ship or to keep a strong wind from putting too much strain on the masts.

Rigging—the ropes which support the spars (standing rigging) and allow the sails to be controlled (running rigging).

Round shot—iron cannon balls.

Rudder—blade at the stern which is angled to steer the vessel.

Run—to sail directly away from the wind.

Sails—in general each mast had three sails. (See diagram)

Sail ho!—'I see a ship!' The sail is the first part visible over the horizon.

Scuppers—openings along the edges of a ship's deck to allow water to drain back to the sea rather than collecting in the bilges.

Scuttle—1) a porthole or small hatch in the deck for lighting and ventilation, covered by the 'scuttle hatch'. Can be used as a narrow entrance to the deck below. 2) to deliberately sink or wreck a ship.

Shank-painter—the stopper (a short rope) that secures the shank and fluke of the anchor to the cathead.

Sheet—a rope made fast to the lower corners of a sail to control its position.

Sheet home—to haul on a sheet until the foot of the sail is as straight and taut as possible.

Ship of the Line—a Royal Navy ship carrying at least fifty guns.

Ship's biscuit—hard bread. Very dry, can be eaten a year after baked. Also called hard tack.

Shrouds—ropes forming part of the standing rigging and supporting the mast or topmast.

Sloop—a small, single-masted vessel, ideal for shallow water.

Spar—a stout wooden pole used as a mast or yard of a sailing vessel.

Spritsail—pronounced 'sprit'sl'; a sail attached to a yard which hangs under the bowsprit.

Square-rigged—the principal sails set at right angles to the length of a ship and extended by horizontal yards slung to the mast.

Starboard—originally 'steerboard', pronounced 'starb'd'. The right side of a vessel when you are facing toward the bow.

Stay—strong, very thick ropes supporting the masts.

Stem—timber at the very front of the bow.

Stern—the back end of a ship.

Swab—a disrespectful term for a seaman, or to clean the decks.

Sweeps—long oars used by large vessels, especially galleys.

Tack/tacking—to change the direction of a vessel's course by turning her bows into the wind until the wind blows on her other side. When a ship is sailing into an oncoming wind she will have to tack, make a zigzag line, in order to make progress forward against the oncoming wind.

Tackle—pronounced 'taykle'. An arrangement of one or more ropes and pulley blocks used to increase the power for raising or lowering heavy objects.

Taffrail—upper rail along the ship's stern.

Tompions—muzzle-plugs to protect the bore of cannons from salt corrosion etc.

Transom—planking forming the stern.

Trim—a term used for adjusting the sails as the wind changes.

Waist—the middle part of the ship.

Wake—the line of passage directly behind as marked by a track of white foam.

Warp—to move a ship by hauling or pulling her along on warps (ropes); also the name of the ropes which secure a ship when moored (tied up) to a jetty or dock.

Weigh anchor—to haul the anchor up; more generally, to leave port.

Widowmaker—term for the bowsprit.

Windward—the side towards the wind as opposed to leeward.

Yard—a long spar suspended from the mast of a vessel to extend the sails.

Yardarm—either end of the yard.

About The Author

Helen Hollick

After an exciting Lottery win on the opening night of the 2012 London Olympic Games, Helen Hollick moved from a North-East London suburb to an eighteenth-century farmhouse in North Devon, where she lives with her husband, daughter and son-in-law, and a variety of pets and animals, which include several moorland-bred Exmoor ponies. Her study overlooks part of the Taw Valley, where the main road runs from Exeter to Barnstaple, where back in the 1600s troops of the English Civil Wars marched to and from battle. There are several friendly ghosts sharing the house and farm, and Helen regards herself as merely a temporary custodian of the lovely old house, not its owner.

First published in 1994, her pirate character, Captain Jesamiah Acorne of the nautical adventure series, *The Sea Witch Voyages*, have been snapped up by the US-based, independent publisher, Penmore Press.

Helen became a USA Today Bestseller with her historical novel, *The Forever Queen* (titled *A Hollow Crown* in the UK) the story of the Saxon Queen, Emma of Normandy. Her novel *Harold the King* (titled *I Am The Chosen King* in the US) explores the events that led to the 1066 Battle of Hastings, while her *Pendragon's Banner Trilogy*, set in the fifth century, is widely acclaimed as a more historical version of the Arthurian legend, with no magic, no Lancelot, Merlin or Holy Grail, but instead, the 'what might have happened' story of the boy who became a man, who became a king, who became a legend...

Helen's books are published in various languages, including German, Turkish and Italian.

She has written the non-fiction books *Pirates: Truth and Tales* and *Life of A Smuggler in Fact and Fiction.* As an avid supporter of indie writers, she co-wrote a short advice guide for new writers, *Discovering the Diamond.* Recognised by her stylish hats, Helen attends conferences and book-related events when she can, as a chance to meet her readers and social-media followers, although her 'wonky eyesight' as she describes her condition of glaucoma, is becoming a little prohibitive for travel.

She founded and runs the *Discovering Diamonds* review blog for historical fiction and is a regular blogger, Facebooker and Tweeter.

She occasionally gets time to write!

Website: www.helenhollick.net
Blog: www.ofhistoryandkings.blogspot.com
Facebook: www.facebook.com/HelenHollickAuthor
Twitter: @HelenHollick

Email **author@helenhollick.net**
Newsletter: http://tinyletter.com/HelenHollick

Also by Helen Hollick

The Pendragon's Banner Trilogy

The Kingmaking:
Book One of the Pendragon's Banner Trilogy

Pendragon's Banner:
Book Two of the Pendragon's Banner Trilogy

Shadow of the King:
Book Three of the Pendragon's Banner Trilogy

The Saxon 1066 Series

A Hollow Crown (UK edition title)
The Forever Queen (US edition title. *USA Today* bestseller)

Harold The King (UK edition title)
I Am The Chosen King (US edition title)

1066 Turned Upside Down
(a collection of alternative stories by a variety of authors)

Non-fiction
Pirates: Truth And Tales
Life Of A Smuggler: In Fact And Fiction
Discovering The Diamond
(with Jo Field)

THE *Sea Witch* VOYAGES

SEA WITCH
The First Voyage of Pirate Captain Jesamiah Acorne

PIRATE CODE
The Second Voyage of Captain Jesamiah Acorne

BRING IT CLOSE
The Third Voyage of Captain Jesamiah Acorne

RIPPLES IN THE SAND
The Fourth Voyage of Jesamiah Acorne

ON THE ACCOUNT
The Fifth Voyage of Captain Jesamiah Acorne

WHEN THE MERMAID SINGS
a novella prequel, how the young Jesamiah Acorne
became a pirate.

To follow

GALLOWS WAKE
The sixth voyage of Captain Jesamiah Acorne

JAMAICA GOLD
The seventh voyage of Captain Jesamiah Acorne

If You Enjoyed This Book Visit

PENMORE PRESS
www.penmorepress.com

BELLERAPHON'S
CHAMPION
BY
JOHN DANIELSKI

Deep within each man, lies the secret knowledge of whether he is a stalwart or a coward. Three years an un-blooded Royal Marine, 1st Lieutenant Thomas Pennywhistle will finally "meet the lion," protecting HMS Bellerophon at the Battle of Trafalgar.

Not only will Pennywhistle be responsible for the lives of 72 marines aboard Bellerophon but their direction will fall entirely on his shoulders since his fellow Marine officers consist of a boy, a card shark, and a dying consumptive. If he has what it takes to command, it will take everything he's got.

In the course of battle, he will encounter marvels and terrors; from valiant foes to women performing miracles, from the skill of acrobats to the luck of the ship's cat, from a dead man still full of fight to a coward who has none. He and his marines will meet enemy élan will with trained volleys and disciplined bayonets. Most of all, he will meet himself; discovering just how dark his true nature really is.

Europe will be changed forever by Trafalgar, and so will Pennywhistle.

PENMORE PRESS
www.penmorepress.com

The California Run

by

Mark A. Rimmer

New York, 1850. Two clipper ships depart on a race around Cape Horn to the boomtown of San Francisco, where the first to arrive will gain the largest profits and also win a $50,000 wager for her owner.

Sapphire is a veteran ship with an experienced crew. Achilles is a new-build with a crimped, mostly unwilling crew. Inside Achilles' forecastle space reside an unruly gang of British sailors whose only goal is to reach the gold fields, a group of contrarily reluctant Swedish immigrants whose only desire is to return to New York and the luckless Englishman, Harry Jenkins, who has somehow managed to get himself crimped by the equally as deceitful Sarah Doyle, and must now spend the entire voyage working as a common sailor down in Achilles' forecastle while Sarah enjoys all the rich comforts of the aft passenger saloon.

Despite having such a clear advantage, Sapphire's owner has also placed a saboteur, Gideon, aboard Achilles with instructions to impede her in any way possible. Gideon sets to with enthusiasm and before she even reaches Cape Horn Achilles' chief mate and captain have both been murdered. Her inexperienced 2nd Mate, Nate Cooper, suddenly finds himself in command of Achilles and, with the help of the late captain's niece, Emma, who herself is the only experienced navigator remaining on board, they must somehow regain control over this diverse crew of misfits and encourage them onwards and around the Horn.

PENMORE PRESS
www.penmorepress.com

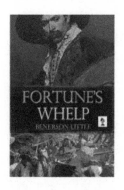

Fortune's Whelp
by
Benerson Little

Privateer, Swordsman, and Rake:

Set in the 17th century during the heyday of privateering and the
decline of buccaneering, *Fortune's Whelp* is a brash, swords-out
sea-going adventure. Scotsman Edward MacNaughton, a former
privateer captain, twice accused and acquitted of piracy and
currently seeking a commission, is ensnared in the intrigue
associated with the attempt to assassinate King William III in
1696. Who plots to kill the king, who will rise in rebellion—and
which of three women in his life, the dangerous smuggler, the
wealthy widow with a dark past, or the former lover seeking
independence—might kill to further political ends? Variously
wooing and defying Fortune, Captain MacNaughton approaches
life in the same way he wields a sword or commands a fighting
ship: with the heart of a lion and the craft of a fox.

PENMORE PRESS
www.penmorepress.com

The Dragon's Breath

by

James Boschert

Talon stared wide-eyed at the devices, awed that they could make such an overwhelming, head-splitting noise. His ears rang and his eyes were burning from the drifting smoke that carried with it an evil stink. "That will show the bastards," Hsü told him with one of his rare smiles. "The General calls his weapons 'the Dragon's breath.' They certainly stink like it."

Talon, an assassin turned knight turned merchant, is restless. Enticed by tales of lucrative trade, he sets sail for the coasts of Africa and India. Traveling with him are his wife and son, eager to share in this new adventure, as well as Reza, his trusted comrade in arms. Treasures beckon at the ports, but Talon and Reza quickly learn that dangers attend every opportunity, and the chance rescue of a Chinese lord named Hsü changes their destination—and their fates.

Hsü introduces Talon to the intricacies of trading in China and the sophisticated wonders of Guangzhou, China's richest city. Here the companions discover wealth beyond their imagining. But Hsü is drawn into a political competition for the position of governor, and his opponents target everyone associated with him, including the foreign merchants he has welcomed into his home. When Hsü is sent on a dangerous mission to deliver the annual Tribute to the Mongols, no one is safe, not even the women and children of the household. As Talon and Reza are drawn into supporting Hsü's bid for power, their fighting skills are put to the test against new weapons and unfamiliar fighting styles. It will take their combined skills to navigate the treacherous waters of intrigue and violence if they hope to return to home.

PENMORE PRESS
www.penmorepress.com

Historical fiction and nonfiction
Paperback available for order on line
and as Ebook with all major distributers

Penmore Press
Challenging, Intriguing, Adventurous, Historical and Imaginative

www.penmorepress.com

Lightning Source UK Ltd.
Milton Keynes UK
UKHW040738020123
414708UK00001B/8